By the same author

Assumption of Risk

KILL ZONE

by

Jim Silver

SIMON & SCHUSTER

SIMON & SCHUSTER
Rockefeller Center
1230 Avenue of the Americas
New York, NY 10020

SIMON & SCHUSTER and colophon are
registered trademarks of Simon & Schuster Inc.

Designed by Leslie Phillips
Manufactured in the United States of America

1   3   5   7   9   10   8   6   4   2

LIBRARY OF CONGRESS CATALOGING-IN-PUBLICATION DATA
Silver, Jim.
Kill zone / by Jim Silver.
p. cm.
1. Vietnamese Conflict, 1961–1975—Fiction.   I. Title.
PS3569.I466K55   1999
813'.54—dc21   98-24428   CIP
ISBN 0-684-84289-0

Acknowledgments

The art of sniping has succumbed to the politically correct nineties, notably with the root word itself. Sniper is almost universally termed sharpshooter, more so in law enforcement usage than in the military.

The fact remains that the men who do this type of shooting remain a special breed. In portraying these unique men I had help from several excellent sources:

First are two books by Peter R. Senich, *The Long Range War/Sniping in Vietnam,* and *The Complete Book of U.S. Sniping,* both published by Paladin Press. The latter reference is a great source on the history of sniping in the U.S. military, while the former reminded me of what being in-country used to be like.

Next is Major John L. Plaster's quintessential bible on the subject, *The Ultimate Sniper,* also published by Paladin Press, and his *SOG/The Secret Wars of America's Commandos in Vietnam,* published by Simon & Schuster. Major Plaster is one of those who did it all for real, and doesn't let that experience alter his mastery of the word. My thanks to him and Mr. Senich.

Over the years I have collected much of the detail used here from other individuals much more knowledgeable. Some of them continue to hold sensitive positions, and cannot be publicly acknowledged here, unfortunately. On their behalf I want to express my gratitude in any event for sharing their expertise, suggestions, and support with me.

Some of those who can be mentioned include Dr. Martin Fackler, Dick Egolf of SIGARMS, Walter Berger of Berger Bullets, Ltd., Corporal Kenneth Cope and Sergeant Jim Diamond, both of the City of Tampa, FL, PD. I met these two gentlemen courtesy of Kevin Parsons, President of ASP, and spent a delightful evening with them. They have allowed this unworthy civilian, many years removed from being a once-dangerous young man, to enter their exclusive circle. I thank you both, for your time, unique humor, and for your friendship.

Kevin Parsons is next. You allowed me to "use" you again, Kev, and I thank you once more for that privilege. In a very real sense Kevin and his company are out there every day, around the world, making things just a little bit safer for us all. My debt to you will never be paid in full, and that's just fine with me. Thank you for your interest as always, your enthusiasm, and for your freely given time.

A word is necessary concerning the Fourth Division. Although fragging episodes did take place in Vietnam, these were anomalies, to the best of my personal knowledge. Further, I am not aware of any such documented incident that involved an entire rifle squad as illustrated here.

The Fourth held their own in the Central Highlands, and came home proud. It was my privilege to have conducted several joint missions, including the last combat operation run by the Fourth during my tour as a military advisor in MACV/Military Assistance Command, Vietnam.

It certainly is not my intent to disgrace the memory of the men in this division in any way. It is simply their misfortune to have been in my area of operations, and thus tagged in the role of "bad guy" for the sake of this story. My sincere apologies if any slight is perceived.

As to the inaccuracies that will certainly be discovered within, I alone take the credit, and the blame. None of the previously mentioned contributed to these mistakes in any fashion.

To the sharpshooters,
the long gunners, and the snipers.
They train to do it right, every time, because they can.
And quietly pray they never have to,
because they must.

1970

Fourth Division A/O, II Corps, Republic of South Vietnam

It was called VC Valley by the American troops that worked it, the area south and east of Pleiku. It ran for twenty or so clicks north from Phu Nhon to QL 14, the eastbound highway connecting Pleiku with Qui Nhon on the coast. The valley was maybe half that distance wide, beginning a few clicks east of QL 19 and running south to Ban Me Thuot. It was a roughly rectangular strip of rugged deep ravines and valleys that blanketed the Central Highlands. It was also an enclave offering a haven for many of the indigenous Viet Cong guerrillas in the province, who staged individual sorties from its protection.

No one liked going in there. The only reason for going was for a fight. There was no other purpose. No one really wanted the ground there, least of all the Vietnamese who lived close to the two bordering highways. It was Montagnard country by tradition, and most of the VC operating in the valley were tribesmen.

When MACV-Saigon wanted a body count, word went down the line to the Fourth Division's headquarters at Dragon Mountain, south of Pleiku, through the division's brigades and battalions, and eventually ended up as an operations order sending the next lucky company in. And they would get the body count. That was assured. VC Valley offered only that, for both sides.

It explained why any sane man would dread going in, especially if he had been there at least one time. Once was all it took to introduce the line troop, the grunt, to what the war in Southeast Asia was all about. No politics, no flag-waving, no mom and apple pie. This was the brutal, hand-to-hand killing.

If you had gone in more than once, the term sane could no longer be applied to you, either. What happened in the triple-canopy jungles either cranked a man up enough to addict him to the savagery of it or scared him enough to do anything, *anything,* to avoid going in again. The oddity was that most of the dog soldiers, the line troops, snuffies, and grunts, still went when ordered to. Combat did that to most men, elevating the duty of doing the job above everything else.

There were others who had a different outlook. They just didn't want to fight anymore. Their solution: kill the ones sending them into the valley.

There was a term for it, popularized by the press, a unique description that came from the simplest approach to the problem. Just roll a grenade into the hooch or bunker of the officer or NCO you wanted to kill. They called it fragging.

* * *

Privates Aceto and Burris were the gun team. Hector Aceto was nineteen, the more senior of the two by a year. He checked the belt going into the M-60 for the fifth time, nervously opening and closing the feed cover again.

"Stop doing that," Burris whispered hoarsely, lying beside him. Sweat rolled down his freckled face. John Burris was Wisconsin Swede, and all of eighteen years old. It was his job to make sure the belt fed smoothly, and to reload it when they ran out. The two of them had been paired up for the past six months and operated like the experienced team they were. Burris glanced at the assault bag holding the two-hundred-round belt clipped to the side of the M-60's breach. The row of linked cartridges fed up and over the C-Rat can attached below the feed chute to make sure the belt fed smoothly. It was a field modification that worked, a trooper's trick to add an edge for that all-important goal: survival.

The usual machine-gun load was a belt of ball and tracer cartridges, mixed four of the former followed by one of the latter. This one was different. It was specially loaded with two hundred black-tipped armor-piercing rounds. Private Burris had seen to it himself. There was another bag right next to it, ready to go. The hardened 7.62 mm bullets would penetrate light metal, like the sides of a Jeep, or the front of an engine block. That was their target.

"Look, I'm OK," Aceto shot back, keeping his voice low. His dark eyes gazed from under the rim of his camo-cloth-covered steel helmet, staring down the opening in the brush hiding them, noting the gun's placement, aimed right down the road where it straightened out from the ninety-degree turn 130 meters away.

"I didn't say you weren't," Burris said back, meaning that of course, he did.

"Shut up, man," Aceto growled.

"Knock it off, the two of ya," Linet said. He was off a few paces to their right lying prone underneath the heavy ground cover, the captured AK-47 flat on the hard red dirt before him. He was the senior man, both in age and in rank, and squad leader for the eight of them. Linet was from Georgia, and his gray eyes were hard and depthless, and befitted a man twice his age. Jack Linet was barely twenty-one. Time there had aged him, as it had the others. Linet had extended the basic thirteen-month tour for the early out, discharged and free upon arrival back in the world at Oakland. Now he wasn't sure that had been such a great idea. He might not make it. He had the edge, the will, and the way. He knew the Nam better than most, and the rest of the squad knew it.

It was Linet's decision that started the discussions, but they all shared the same attitude. They were sick and tired of being fed into the meat grinder, watching their buds getting waxed, wondering who would be next to go. Nixon had announced the start of America's withdrawal from the war. The Fourth Division was slated to go home in July, only a few months away in the troops' opinion. They shouldn't be running any more operations. The war was winding down, and there was absolutely no good reason to go out there and get killed. Let the goddamn ARVNs run their own goddamn war. It was their job now.

But someone didn't care, someone didn't listen, someone still wanted the numbers, the body count for the five o'clock follies in Saigon. Someone still wanted to send their battalion home with the big kill ratio record. Major Ralph-Almighty-Longbaugh, the battalion's S-3 operations officer. He was the planner. The one who issued the field orders. He was the one they needed to stop. And today was the day.

"Just keep the gun ready," Linet said, reminding them. "You guys initiate the ambush. You gotta take out the Jeep in the first burst. You have to stop him in the kill zone."

Aceto nodded. They'd talked about it for hours, each of them committing himself to the deed. It was past time for reconsideration. "Piece of cake, man," he said, and settled down, sighting down the barrel, left hand over the top of the feed cover, right hand lightly on the black pistol grip.

"Piece of cake my ass," Roselli cracked, off to the left. Roselli was from New York, a real wiseguy with black curly hair and a Fu Manchu mustache. Much as he played the role of the hoodlum, he was from Long Island, not the City, and didn't have the connections. He wanted people to think he did, though. Paul Roselli was twenty, with eight months in-country. He'd made rank once, all the way to E-5, then had been busted down for popping an SFC. Now he was back to PFC, with the single thin black stripe on his collar where three used to be. Being busted had given him a real bad attitude. He thought he had found a way to pay some of it back, though, just a little.

"Yeah, I got your piece a' cake right here," Landau added with a smirk. William Landau, Princeton, class of '68, who had found out just how quickly the draft board acted when your college deferment ran out. He was educated, and smug about it. It made him feel a few steps above his squad mates.

Like Linet, he carried a captured VC weapon, an SKS carbine. It was important that they leave some shell casings behind indicating the ambush of the major's Jeep was done by the Viet Cong. It was 1970, and by now, many of the indigenous VC used captured American M-16s and M-60 machine guns, in addition to their own Soviet and Chinese gear. So it wouldn't be unusual for anyone coming after the fact to find such mixed evidence.

Two others carried AKs too: Max Perriman and Mike Madison, a couple of brown-haired, blue-eyed clones from middle America, sons of Illinois and Indiana, neighbors of sorts, mutual draftees spending their final teenage year humping a sixty-pound ruck in the heat and rain of the Central Highlands instead of running fast Chevys along two-lane blacktops back home.

Louis Archer, the squad's black RTO, shepherding the twenty-five-pound PRC-25, kept his M-16. It made for a good mix. He was another New Yorker, from the City this time, the Bronx actually, and damn proud of it, too. Black pride meant something to him. Tall, broad-shouldered, heavily muscled, eleven months in-country, Archer was counting the days left before he would join his brothers in the streets, taking them back from the Man. Now he had the skills, a natural-born killer, all paid for by whitey.

And there was Carlos Madrid, a thin, lithe eighteen-year-old Puerto Rican from Miami, wisecracking in words of four letters or less, accent thick enough to cut with a knife, which incidentally was his favorite combat tool. He carried a long one, the eight-inch Gerber with its elongated Coke-bottle-shaped blade, "Just like a woman's leg," Madrid often said. He had learned about knives on the streets of south Miami. The blades came with pushing grass and smack, the latter beginning to look like the coming thing in Florida.

But he liked his product too much, and he'd taken his habit with him into the service, and across the Pacific to Vietnam. There he'd found shit he hadn't dreamed of in Miami. He was already working on life after the war, planning to set up a line of distributors.

They looked like any regular line squad, with their heavy rucksacks stacked behind them in the bush. Their suspension harnesses were laden with extra ammo pouches, water, smoke and fragmentation grenades, and such. Late-afternoon sweat trickled out from underneath faded, graffitied, camouflaged-covered steel helmets.

Their jungle fatigues matched their attitudes, faded to pale green, old sweat stains ringed in white, newer ones dark green. They were weary and worn down from months of hard use. Some wore field-issue shower towels around their necks and shoulders to catch the sweat and ease the weight of the rucks. Those with the Soviet guns had their issue M-16s or M-79s lying across their packs. They'd get rid of the enemy guns later, bury them where no one would find them again.

Besides the mixed collection of weapons, their feet showed they'd given the matter some thought. Each of them wore a pair of Ho Chi Minh sandals, the simple cut-from-a-tire shoes of the local VC. Their boots and socks were jammed into their rucks. The scene they would leave behind would prove to any moron that Chuck had done in the major. Ol' Victor Charlie had finally punched Longbaugh's ticket home. They had considered everything.

Perriman and Madrid were on point at the moment, up around the bend, watching for the Jeep. The major routinely drove down this stretch of the highway, just before 5:00 P.M., when he was up in Papa-Kilo, or Pleiku, the provincial capital. He did it without a shotgun rider, and always at five o'clock in the afternoon, prime ambush time. It was a cocky, gung-ho thing, as if he were untouchable, flaunting his invulnerability before the VC. The practice, now more of a habit, was clearly against posted regulations. But Longbaugh didn't give a fuck about that, nor about the Viet Cong. It said a lot about his character, this death wish. He never thought about the other threat, the real one on this day. He should have considered it.

It was Perriman's job to radio back the approach of the vehicle. Then he and Madrid would catch the major in a crossfire, adding their AKs to the firing from the rest of the squad. He had argued for using a couple of Claymore mines, command detonated, but had been talked down.

"Where the fuck is Charlie supposed to get a couple of Claymores?" Roselli had said.

"The same place they get our 16s and 79s," Archer had said, backing Private Perriman.

"Forget about it," Linet had said, deciding it. "It has to look like a legitimate ambush. The guns will be enough."

"Why don't we rig up a booby trap, like Chuck would do?" Madison had offered. He subscribed to Perriman's big bang theory. "Y'know, command detonate a couple of 81s, maybe a Four-Deuce."

"What, and you're goin' to hump those mothers out into the

bush like that?" Roselli countered, unimpressed by his squad mate's suggestion.

"Too complicated," Linet replied, interrupting them both. "We need to set this up quick, do it, and boogie. Remember, we're supposed to be running a sweep some two clicks away. Somebody hears about the ambush, or finds the major too soon, and they might send a chopper out to bring us and the other squads back. We'd damn sure better be back where our last sitrep says we are. Unless you guys like the idea of LBJ, or Leavenworth."

The mention of LBJ, Long Binh Jail, sobered them.

"Why don' we just cut the motherfucker's throat, man," Madrid said, his voice soft but shaky. He'd been into the stuff a little too much lately, and they all could see it. He was wired, his eyes a bit too bright. He didn't look good, and the others wondered about him down the long haul. Some of them were partaking of the same stuff, but liked to think they had it under control.

Perriman caught their looks. "Stick with the guns," he had said, ending that discussion.

They waited in the heat and quiet, each of them attending to his own thoughts. Killing in combat was one thing, and they had all done that to some extent by now. But this was not the same. This was murder, plain and simple, and they all recognized the difference. They could all hang for what they were planning to do. But they were going ahead with it anyway.

The radio handset, hung off Archer's helmet next to his ear, clicked twice. Perriman had keyed his handset in the prearranged signal: Major Longbaugh's vehicle was entering the curve before the kill zone. The two-click message meant nothing to anyone listening in. It was used far too frequently on the net, and could mean anything. Besides, they had chosen a little-used frequency, completely different from any of the command pushes. But the NSA monitored all broadcasts in Vietnam, so they were told. They continued to take no chances.

"On the way," Archer said casually, and shouldered his M-16.

Linet glanced right and left, getting all of their attention, and waved once, then motioned straight ahead, down the length of the bare dirt roadway before them. They all hunkered down in the brush, thumbs rotating safeties on the M-16s off safe and around to full automatic. Those with the Russian weapons snicked off their safeties, the AKs making their characteristic loud double click in the sudden silence.

As one they sighted down their weapons and heard the whining approach of the Jeep first, even before it cleared the bend in the road. The engine note changed as the major shifted gears, accelerating up to fifty miles per hour. On this stretch of road it behooved anyone traveling it to go as fast as he could. They listened to the transmission climbing the scale as it came at them.

Linet tapped Aceto on the right shoulder, then held his palm there, a silent signal. The Jeep came at them, a dark black-green square with the faded tan of the canvas top highlighting it, a red-brown cloud of dust billowing up behind it.

Aceto steadied the machine gun on the perforated steel legs of the bipod, centering the front sight blade on the flat grill, his finger resting on the trigger. The Jeep closed to one hundred meters, then seventy, then . . .

"Now!" Linet said quietly, and squeezed Aceto's arm. The M-60 went off, hammering out a long burst at 650 rpm. The effect was as expected.

The armor-piercing bullets struck the front of the Jeep, ripping through the thin uprights of the stamped steel, puncturing the grill and radiator, ricocheting off the heavier metal of the block. Steam exploded out of it in a gush, and the major, startled by the impact, jerked the wheel to the left.

Even before his reaction, Linet fired quickly, in fast, two-round bursts, his second burst lost in the sound of the rest of the squad as they all opened up.

The entire front of the Jeep dissolved in a shower of broken glass, shredded metal, and ripped flesh as their fire merged into the space behind the flat windshield where the driver sat. Fully a third of their shots, almost all delivered on automatic, missed the Jeep entirely. Something in excess of 180 rounds did find their intended target, though, and thudded into flesh and steel, killing the machine, and the man driving it.

The Jeep continued in its leftward curve, still going at speed, nosed down suddenly into the deep culvert ditch, and rammed against the off-side embankment with a loud bang, bouncing up in the air in a shower of red dirt, then jounced back down on its wheels, the two front tires flattened by multiple hits. It took just six and one half seconds to accomplish: the reality of a fire fight. Or a successful ambush.

"Madre de Dios," Aceto said, looking at the smoldering hulk of the shot-up Jeep only a few meters away.

"Fuckin'-A," Landau said. He was grinning as he reloaded the SKS.

Burris said nothing, listening to the ticking and metal groaning coming from the Jeep. He looked at Aceto and back at the Jeep.

No one moved. Then, as if on cue, they all rose and advanced carefully toward the wreck, stepping out of cover into the open space of the road.

They stopped a few paces away from the Jeep, all of them taking in the damage, automatically critiquing their individual performance. It was done reflexively, a trait of combat. Then they looked at the body.

The impact with the embankment had bounced the major out of the driver's seat, against the steering wheel, where he fell back to lie awkwardly between the seats. One booted pants leg stuck out through the shattered glass of the windshield, while the left arm was jammed in an odd angle between the gear shift lever and the passenger seat tubular metal frame. His head and face were behind the same seat.

Roselli and Archer leaned in, checking. The amount of blood and ruined clothing attested to the accuracy, and finality, of the ambush. Roselli said it for them all.

"KIA," he said.

"Groovy," Madison said, staring at the body with a strange light behind his eyes.

Madrid shouldered his way closer, his eyes taking in the spray of blood and gore across the back canvas, and splattered on the dash and seats. They'd really done it, he thought. He leaned closer, looking at the body's awkward position. "We killed you, man," he said tightly, but his face was animated. His had been the last burst, a full mag of thirty rounds. His face reflected the look of the others. They were pumped.

Archer bent over the passenger's side, then reached down to

turn the dead man's head around. His fingers slipped on the blood, and Archer grabbed the slack chin instead. Sightless eyes stared unevenly back up at him from the ruin that was his face. The body showed the impact of over two dozen hits to the torso and face. A couple of rounds had hit high on his forehead, blowing the top of the major's skull off. Bare bone shone white from the mess that used to be his right shoulder. Archer held the head for a few moments, looking back. Then he let go, and the head dropped back limply. "There's your fuckin' body count," he said contemptuously.

Linet came up beside him, looking in. "Get his weapon," he said.

Archer wiped his hand down a pant leg, then reached over and picked up the blood-spattered CAR-15 off the floorboard, then the bandoleer of extra magazines nearby.

"That's it," Perriman said, and looked around quickly. "We ought to get off the road, man," he added.

"That's a Rog'," Linet said. "All right, get your rucks and let's Di-Di. We'll bury the Ho Chi Minhs and the weapons later, per the plan."

They all hesitated a few seconds, still staring at the ruined body of the major, reluctant in the reality of their deed to leave it.

"*Now*, people," Linet said again, letting the command carry through in his tone.

One by one they turned then, and walked back into the jungle. None of them looked back. Linet remained behind, taking in the scene. He was satisfied with their work. They'd done it. Now maybe things would slow down for them. The killing was necessary. They had done it for all of them, hadn't they? The company, and the battalion. They had stopped the insanity, right?

"Damn straight," Linet said aloud, answering himself, voicing his confirmation for them all. He turned, and followed after the squad, ignoring the cold feeling in the pit of his stomach.

* * *

Their nervous euphoria lasted five days. It came down to a handful of glassine bags, in the end, and that peculiar love of the blade.

Three days after the ambush Carlos Madrid had gone back

down the convoluted alleys of the southeast corner of Pleiku, the provincial capital, visiting one of his half-dozen distributors. It had been late afternoon and Madrid had a couple of soldiers with him, new in-country, FNGs, the old hats called them, fuckin'-new-guys. They were looking to score something to take away the heebie-jeebies caused by the anticipation of things to come. Madrid was Mister Connection. He had the rep, the moves, and the network. He was flying on all of that, and of course, a little of the good stuff to keep the edge on. Which was why he hadn't been as thorough in checking the new guys as he should have been.

One of them wasn't so new. In fact, he had been in-country for eighteen months, was actually twenty-two years old, although he looked eighteen, and had worked at busting little dealers like Madrid since he'd been assigned. His real name was John York, and he was a staff sergeant in the Criminal Investigation Division of the Army, the CID. York had ten men waiting to take Madrid and his connections down, under the command of their CO, Captain James Manos.

But things had started to get hinky during the discussions. Greenberg, the other new guy, was a bit too nervous, a bit too quick to answer, and Madrid's radar had gone off. It didn't matter that the kid really was nervous, unsure, wondering what the hell he was doing in this rotten part of the city. Greenberg had guessed that this little spic bastard was ripping him off, and he was big enough to tear his head off if wanted to. And right now he was ready.

Words were said in rapidly escalating tones, and a stupid move by the new kid started the ball rolling. There were no guns, Madrid had always been adamant about that. They were stacked outside the door, with one of his suppliers watching over them. But he had the Gerber in his boot, and it came out in a flash.

The blade punctured the new kid's throat, just a tick under his left ear, pushing its elegant tip up into the base of his brain, and Madrid never heard York's warning shout. The CID team literally kicked the door down, barreling in with CAR-15s locked and loaded. The next thing he knew Madrid found himself face-down on the floor of the corrugated tin shanty. And then his whole world went black.

* * *

Linet took the news in stride. He'd been expecting something like this about Madrid. The idiot had been all but advertising his dealing. "Where'd they take him?" he asked Landau.

"Last I heard was straight down to Long Binh," Landau said. He was plainly worried about Madrid's bust. Word had spread around the base camp at Dragon Mountain quickly. For the eight members in the squad, the news carried a special threat. "You don't think Carlos'd cut a deal, do you?"

Linet's look answered the naiveté of the question.

Aceto voiced what all of them were thinking, coming off his bottom bunk in the big platoon-sized tent back in their company area. The eight of them were the only ones there. Heat shimmers danced down the oil-soaked streets outside the open screen sides of the high-ceilinged tent. "He was there, man. What d'you think he'd do?"

Landau knew better than to challenge the statement. Madrid had been getting flakier, all right. They all knew the stuff was eating away his brain. Now he could hang them all to save himself. "So what do we do?" he asked them all, but meant it for Linet. He was the leader.

"Move the guns," Linet said. "Right now. We go back out there, dig 'em up, and bury 'em someplace else. Just in case."

"What about our own 16s and the M-60?" Roselli threw in. "If Carlos rats out, and they pull rounds out of that Jeep, they can check ballistics . . ."

"Ah shit, man," Archer said. "This ain't TV. They don't do that shit in the Nam."

Linet sent him a withering look. "What's wrong with you, Louis?" he said. "Don't none of you boys know this ain't no goddamn game? We lit Longbaugh up, troops. That's what us good ol' boys in Georgia call a hom-ee-cide." He pronounced each syllable separately, turning his head to take them all in. "Word gets out, and you can bet your sweet asses they'll do everything they can to pin it on us." His gaze came back to Archer. "Yeah, man, they'd check the ballistics, too. And they'd damn sure match up them rounds to our weapons."

"We have ta get rid of the guns, then," Roselli said, making the obvious point.

"Already done," Linet said, smiling for the first time. "That little rocket attack last night took care of that, remember?" They all paused at that, as each immediately knew what he was talking about.

The Viet Cong had sent the Fourth one of several going-away gifts the night before. Just after midnight eight 122-millimeter rockets had slammed into Dragon Mountain, totally at random. One of them had hit in the squad's company area, taking out a part of the tactical operations center, the TOC bunker system. It had also killed the three-man radio team on watch there. A second rocket had exploded amongst the platoon tents. A third had hit the company's S-4 supply tent, destroying several racks of weapons. They had all been down in the bunkers by then, though.

"Combat loss the gear," Madison said, his face showing relief.

"You got it," Linet acknowledged. "I haven't turned in our damage list yet. It looks like a few of our weapons were destroyed when that 122 took out the TOC and that tent." He pointed at Madison and Burris. "You two collect up the guns. Take them out into the country, wrap a couple pounds of C4 around 'em, and blow 'em in place. Bring the bits back here. S-4 will issue new ones, and what's left of the pieces won't identify us to jack shit. The rest of us will move the VC gear. Clear?"

"Yes, sir," Madison said. "Let's go, John."

"What about Madrid?" Roselli said, bringing up their other problem.

"Leave that to me," Linet said. "I know some guys at LBJ."

"Oh wow, man," Aceto said. "You goin' to ice the boy?"

"You know another way?" Linet fired back. "I don't know about the rest of you, but I ain't goin' down for no pillhead. You got that?"

Linet glanced around quickly, then motioned the men closer. "It's like we talked about before, people," he said. "We're all in this together, all the way down the line. All I want to do is walk onto the plane and get back to the World. We did some serious shit to Longbaugh. Now we got to get past it, you know? Either we all do it, or anyone who decides no, well . . ." He left it easy for them to complete the sentence. Then he drove the point home anyway. "And if that means taking out Madrid, then that's what it takes. His brain's all fucked up on that stuff he's been taking. He's likely to tell 'em anything to save his sorry ass." He held them with his eyes for a long count, making sure they understood. "Questions?"

There were none. He hadn't expected there would be. "Just be cool, people," he said. "Be cool, and we'll get through this." He gave them a wink. "We're almost home. Let's get there in one piece."

"Amen to that," Roselli said.

"Yeah, man," Archer chimed in, beginning to strut away. "Get down wit'cha bad self, brotha."

"That's the way, boys," Linet said, soothing them, letting his voice carry the idea home. He was their leader, and they knew it. He'd take care of them. That's what he always did.

*   *   *

Captain James Manos came into the interrogation room with the coldest smile on his face Madrid had ever seen on a man. The look said it all, even before he started talking. Madrid knew what was in store for him. He'd been in LBJ for all of twelve hours, and already he'd had a visit from a few of the righteous white boys running his little section of the jail. His face was swollen, his left eye still hadn't focused yet, but it'd take a few days before it opened anyway. The bleeding from the broken tooth had stopped, and his tongue seemed to work, but it hurt, too. The ribs on his right side reminded him with each breath about the parting kick he'd received. He didn't want to think about their next visit.

"Private Carlos Jesus Madrid," Manos began, slapping a thin manila folder on the gray enameled metal table. There were only two chairs in the ten-by-ten room. Madrid was sitting on one of them. Manos took the other by raising one foot up onto the seat, leaning his crossed elbows across his bent leg, staring down at Madrid. He was in tailored green fatigues, with only his name and U. S. Army patches over the slant chest pockets. There was no division patch on his shoulders, nor any rank or branch insignia on his collar tips. The only indication of that was the navy blue baseball cap he wore. On the crown were the silver twin bars of a captain, superseded by small brass letters, U.S. It was the unofficial uniform of the CID.

Manos studied Madrid as if he were a specimen on a slide. "You look like hell," he said finally. "Welcome Wagon call, huh?"

Madrid nodded, and his neck muscles protested dully.

"Well, my friend, there's a lot of that goes on in here," Manos said. "But that won't matter. You won't be here all that long. The charge list against you was good enough to send you to Leavenworth for six years. Up until you stuck that knife into Private Greenberg yesterday. You just bit the big one, Carlos."

He had a look of satisfaction on his face, but there was disgust, too. "You're a sorry excuse, you know? You aren't a soldier anymore. From what I've seen, and know about you, you haven't been one for a long time. You're a punk, Carlos, that's all. A wiseguy dealing in some bad stuff. And it reached up and bit you in the ass, boy."

Madrid looked back, his mind whirling with the repercussions of his own stupidity. He had no doubt that what this arrogant captain was spouting at him was the truth. He was going to jail, if he survived this hellhole first.

"Uh," he began, and cleared his throat. It hurt to talk, and he remembered the fist slamming into the side of his neck the night before. "Can I say something here?"

Manos's foot came off the chair, and he sat down behind the table. "You have the floor," he said. "They read you your rights when you came in, right out of the UCMJ. You remember signing the waiver?"

"Yeah, I remember," he said. He had a plan forming in his head. It took shape as he gathered his wits. If he told it right, there was a chance. "I know something," he began. "Something big, y'know? Maybe I could let you have it."

"What you got is nothing, Carlos," Manos said. "What I got is you, and you're history. You killed a man, Carlos. Kid was just another FNG, looking to dull the experience. You dulled it for him. They're sending him back to his folks in a new green bag inside an aluminum box. But he'll be stateside before you. You're going to spend a little time in this lovely vacation resort, tryin' to keep your ass from being the target of half the good ol' boys in here."

"No, man, listen. I got some information, and it's *big* information. I give it to you, and you cut me a deal. It's worth it, believe me."

Manos listened. He had heard it all before, a thousand times. This lowlife had nothing to deal with, he was sure of that, but he had to ask anyway. Sometimes things came out, useful things.

"Tell me what you think you know, and I'll listen," Manos said. "But that's all, Carlos. Your future is pretty well set, understand. No matter what you think I might be interested in, I've already got you. So talk away, boy."

"We fragged an officer," Madrid began, and it was the way he said it, and the look in the depth of his eyes, that alerted Manos to pay attention. By the time he was done, Madrid had told him everything. Manos sat there for a few moments, then pushed up from his chair.

"Stay here," he said unnecessarily. He walked to the door, opened it, and leaned out. He spoke with someone in the hall, but Madrid couldn't tell who it was, nor what was said. That part of it was answered when another captain came in a few minutes later, along with an enlisted type carrying a pad and a portable tape recorder.

The two new men joined Manos around the table, both of the officers standing while the enlisted man, a three-stripe sergeant, sat down and set up the recorder, checked the cassette tape, and quickly spoke into the small mike, giving the date, time, place, and personnel. It all happened quickly.

Manos spoke up. "Are you willing to tell me that story all over again, Private Madrid?" he asked.

Carlos looked at him, then at the other officer. The name Husta was on his fatigue shirt. Madrid figured he was on a roll, and also that this was his shot, his last chance. "Yeah, man. I'll tell it again. Whatever. We got a deal? You goin' to cut me a deal?"

"No deals, Carlos," Manos said. "Not yet. We have to check this out first. If it doesn't prove out, then we'll know you've been lying, perjuring yourself to buy your way out of a murder rap."

Madrid knew it was bullshit talking, for the record. He also knew what he knew. Let them prove it, then, he thought. "Fine then. You want to play your legal games, that's cool. I know you got to do that, OK? But you go out there, man, you check it out. Yeah, I'll tell it again. You got that thing runnin', man?" he said suddenly to the sergeant. "I tell you, you check it out, you'll see, Captain. I ain't lyin', man. Swear on my mother."

"Get on with it," the other captain said.

"Yeah, sure, sir," Madrid replied. "OK, here it is." And he told it again.

It would be the last time.

*   *   *

He was found late that evening, hanging from the bars of his cell. Madrid had apparently ripped his issue blanket into strips thin enough to use, anchored one end all of three feet off the floor, then sat down, securing the other end around his neck.

"I should have had him on a suicide watch," Manos told his partner, Captain Tony Husta.

"Yeah, well, there's no guarantees," Husta said.

"No matter," Manos said, taking it in stride. "Part of the story has already checked out. There was a Major Ralph Longbaugh killed in an apparent ambush in the Fourth's area of operations a week ago."

"It did have that ring to it, didn't it?" Husta said.

"Let's go find some killers," Manos said.

*   *   *

But Carlos Madrid's alleged confession, as good as it had sounded, quickly died along with him. It was simple rules of evidence, and Manos and Husta had none. The judge advocate general lawyer, USAF Major Carl Stanton, broke the news, though the two captains knew which way it was going in short order. They met in Stanton's office, located in a two-story brick building on the west side of Pleiku Air Force Base. It was an air-conditioned affair fully twenty by twenty-five feet, with real carpeting on the floors, and a mahogany desk. The Airedales knew how to live.

"Look, you guys've been around long enough," Stanton said from his swivel chair.

His starched camouflage fatigues had a nice crease on them.

The U.S. Marine–style uniform was standard issue for the Air Force, while the real boonie-rats had to scrounge them, Manos noted wryly.

"It's open and shut, no offense," Stanton added.

"None taken," Husta said from his position near the wall-mounted air-conditioner. "So why won't you recommend a general court on circumstantial evidence alone? We've got a body, and a confession, and you've seen the interrogation reports of the eight squad members."

Stanton sighed, then pushed back in his chair, tilting it, and laced his fingers behind his head. "Yeah, I read them. All eight of those beady-eyed little bastards tell the same story, which is basically no story at all. None of them have any idea what Madrid was talking about. Sure, they were out on a day-long sweep the same day as the ambush, but their sitreps show where they were all the time—"

"No, they show where they *claimed* they were," Manos interrupted. He wasn't going to take being told no easily.

Stanton acknowledged his comment with a nod, but went on. "Fine, we can discuss semantics any time you want, but the radio logs are convincing. They put that squad two clicks away from the ambush site—"

"Murder site," Husta cut in.

"*Ambush* site," Stanton corrected. He came down in his chair, his hands out in a plea motion. "No, gentlemen, it's an ambush site until you can prove, with hard evidence, that it is, in fact, something else. You have no motive to start with. The Fourth Division is standing down, going home. Why would anyone want to blow away the battalion operations honcho? What's the point?"

"You just said it," Manos countered. "No one takes chances that close unless they have to. But they were still running operations into the field, and that's a hell of a motive, when all you want to do is live long enough to go home."

Stanton's face clearly showed he didn't buy the argument. "You'll not convince a general court of that. What field missions were being run were equitably distributed amongst the brigades, and down through the battalions to company and platoon levels.

Besides, VC Valley wasn't high on the repeat list. MACV-Saigon had ordered that left to the ARVNs."

Husta pushed off the wall, his features mirroring his frustration. "All well and good, but the Fourth was still going in there," he said. He fixed Stanton with his dark eyes. "The line troops hate the valley, Major. There's a reason for that. Have you ever been in there?" The question was rhetorical, they all knew, but it emphasized the point.

Stanton considered not answering, then shook his head. "No, Captain, I haven't. I understand your point, though."

"Do you?" Husta said. "With all due respect, Major Stanton, the court will have to understand, too. They'll have to crawl inside the minds of those grunts to appreciate the absolute fear and hatred they have for that place. And all of that emotion, all of that foreboding, was personified to them by Longbaugh. And that, sir, is motive."

Stanton conceded. "All right, fine. Let's say a general court believes the motive. Where's the physical proof? You both went out there looking for the guns Madrid said they'd buried. You found nothing."

"It was an approximation," Manos interjected. He didn't like the way this was going. "We didn't exactly have a ten-digit map coordinate. Madrid's description was close, we knew that. But the guns weren't there, and we tore up a lot of ground with the engineers we took with us."

"And the squad's M-16s?" Stanton added.

"Conveniently combat lost in a one-twenty-two attack a few nights after the ambush," Madrid said.

"An attack in which three men from their own company died," Stanton said. "Hardly any premeditation there, gentlemen."

"What is it?" Husta said, seeing how this was going to end up. "What exactly do you JAG types need to prosecute eight killers? We know they did it, *they* know they did it. And you're going to let them walk?"

Stanton bore Husta's heated questions impassively. "They're going to walk because you have nothing to convict them on," he said. "Nothing but the word of a doped-up dealer, a loser with a bad track record of his own, who incidentally was trying to deal his way out of a murder-two rap. And when that didn't work, he hung himself."

It was clear by their returned gazes what Manos and Husta thought of Carlos Madrid's alleged suicide. Stanton stared back at the CID officers, sensing they'd arrived at a stalemate. Still, he felt obligated to drive home the statistics for them. "But you've got another problem here. Sure, there have been a few so-called fragging episodes in all four corps areas. The civilian press would like the public back home to think it's a fairly frequent practice nowadays, but it's not. The actual confirmed incidents are far below what's being portrayed on the nightly news."

Manos saw it coming and interrupted Stanton. "You're talking about the numbers, right? We've seen the reports, too," he said, pointing a thumb at Husta and himself. "We investigate fraggings, remember?" He didn't allow Stanton to reply. "In almost all circumstances of a bona-fide fragging episode, the perpetrator has been alone. Only in rare cases has there been more than one killer."

Stanton nodded slowly at the two of them. "That's it exactly, not to put too fine a point on it. You've got a nine-man rifle squad here, who you have to prove to a general court discussed, then agreed, then carried out together a premeditated murder of a battalion staff officer. *Nine* men," he repeated, his doubts obvious.

"We think we can prove it," Husta said.

Stanton shook his head. "I don't. And the JAG commander in Saigon agrees. OK," he said. "Off the record, I agree these assholes are guilty as hell. But what I think and what can be proven are two entirely different things. Right now, they're taking Lieutenant Bill Calley apart for killing almost four hundred civilians in a middle-of-nowhere hamlet. And they'll do it because they have proof. Irrefutable proof. You don't have that. No, gentlemen, there isn't enough here. They walk."

Manos had had enough. "This is crazy," he said.

"The whole goddamn war is crazy," Stanton shot back. "Why should this be any different?"

"So we have no recourse," Husta said. "There's nothing we can do to these men? We just let them go, knowing what we know?"

"That's it," Stanton said. "I don't care for it any more than you do, but it's the law, the same here as it is back in the World."

"You're right," Manos said. "It really is crazy." He shook his head with the thought. "Eight murderers go free. They probably had Madrid knocked off, too. But we'll never get 'em on that one either. Jesus, man, what's next?"

"Nothing," Stanton said. "Oh, sure, we can screw around with them a little. We can separate them, reassign them to different units. When the Fourth finally rotates home, those with time left on their tours will remain in-country. Anyone with time left on their enlistments we can ship to Anchorage or Panama, or whatever hole we can find. But that'll be the extent of it."

Manos exchanged looks with Husta. It was clear between them how each felt. "I'd like to see them before they're released," he said to Stanton.

"What good will that do?" the major asked.

"No good at all, I guess," Manos replied. "I just want to remind them, so there's no mistake about it, that there's no statute of limitations on murder. Whether it's here, or in the States, it doesn't matter. If I find out anything, I mean freakin' *anything* that will let me nail these guys, I'm coming after them. I want them each to understand that. It won't matter how long it takes."

"Something always comes up with fuckups like these," Husta said, picking up on Manos's promise. "Maybe it'll do some good in that respect, leaving them with that notion. There'll be someone watching them, always. Always," he repeated.

Stanton looked at the two of them, his sympathies fully at odds with the system they were all part of. "Do what you need to," he said finally. "But the order's going out today to cut them loose."

"What about our investigation?" Manos asked, tapping his finger on the thick file folder on Stanton's desk.

Major Stanton looked at it for several silent moments, his eyes working with his thoughts. He reached out and nudged it toward Manos. "File it," he said. "It's over."

Manos picked the file up, weighing it in his hand, then stood up, motioning to Husta. "Is it?" he asked. "What about the family? What are you going to tell the major's wife, and his son and daughter?"

Stanton kept his eyes on the file, then slowly raised them. Manos saw the decision set in them.

"They'll be told Major Longbaugh died as a result of enemy action, specifically a Viet Cong ambush. Mrs. Longbaugh will receive his life policy payout as beneficiary, and his officer's pension."

"You're going to lie to them," Manos added, his tone hostile.

Stanton looked incredulous. "Lie to them! The whole goddamn *war* is a lie!" he shouted. "At the five o'clock follies we tell the press we're winning this war, when all we're doing is killing Americans . . . for what? We take a piece of ground and give it right back. Then we go back a week later and do it all over again. Half the country back home thinks we're all baby-killing goons, while the Vietnamese want our money and guns, but not us." He was angry, and his frustration drove his words.

"Vietnam is the biggest mistake we've made in this century. All we're doing is killing Americans, yet we keep trying to convince ourselves we'll win this one yet." He leaned forward on his forearm and kept his hot gaze locked on Manos. "You said we're going to lie to Longbaugh's family. You bet we will. What good will it do to do otherwise? You'd like us to tell them the major was murdered by a squad of miserable screwups, and by the way, we can't touch them for doing it? The man is dead, and his family will have to deal with it the best they can. Why make it worse?"

Manos held his stare, his own anger flaring in his eyes. But his voice was soft as he replied. "They deserve to know the truth. We," and he paused, underlining that he included the three of them in the office, "should respect them enough to give them that. The war may be a lie, Major, but somewhere the truth has to be spoken, even here."

Stanton sat back in his chair, suddenly tired of it all. "You want to tell Longbaugh's family the truth? You think they have a right to it? Maybe, one day after all this is history, and people start to forget, maybe then." He reached out with a forefinger and tapped the tabletop, punctuating his words. "But not now. Not today."

"It ain't right, Major," Husta said, his disgust apparent.

Stanton looked at him, but didn't respond. His face said it all.

"It won't end here," Manos said.

"Don't push it, Jim," Stanton said. "Let it alone, all right?"

Manos held up his palms in surrender. "Yes, sir, no problem," he said. "But it'll come out, sooner or later. That's how these things go."

"Maybe," Stanton said. "Who can say?"

"In time," Manos answered. "As you said, it'll happen in time. It always does."

1980

June 4

Eglin Air Force Base, Florida

It took ten years.

Aaron Longbaugh had been twelve years old in late March 1970, when it happened. He and his mother and older sister received the official version, just as Major Stanton had promised. At the time they didn't think anything ever again could be as bad. Later on Aaron found out differently.

He and his family had been living in their government quarters, the single-story ranch on post at Fort Ord, California. The staff officers arrived that Saturday morning while Aaron had been washing the family's '69 Polara. He watched the olive-drab Government four-door Chevy sedan glide to a stop alongside the tree lawn. He knew instantly what it was, the big round sponge slipping from his hand to plop onto the tarmac while a chill of denial spilled tingling down his back, all the way to his feet.

A light colonel and a major, the latter required by regulation to match the rank of the deceased, slowly exited the vehicle, the major carrying the closed manila folder in his hand. They were in full class-A uniform dress, ribbons bright with color, metal insignia glittering on shoulders and lapels. They walked by him, giving curt nods, their eyes uncomfortable and distant, and knocked on the storm door. His mother answered, and they all stepped inside, Aaron following with leaden feet, leaving behind a hose and a job half-done.

It was over a few minutes later, and their lives were changed forever. His father had died valiantly, in the highest traditions of the service. Stock phrases for something so significant, so direct.

His teenage sister, Laura, ran upstairs in hysterics, while his mother remained stoic, tears coursing slowly down her face as she saw the two officers out. His own stomach turned suddenly and painfully tight, and a sudden roaring in his head drowned out all sound. He watched the two officers, their duty done, march stiffly in route step back to the car and drive away. He barely heard his mother beside him, nor felt her hand on his shoulder. Inside he had gone dead. Weeks later the dam broke, and with it came the pain, but by then it was too late. Things were already on a downward spiral.

Military families seem more prone than others to have at least one alcoholic member. Blame it on the travel, the constant changes, the months and years of separation, of not knowing if loved ones were safe, or where things were going. Years of such abuse had begun for Aaron's mother long before he came along. Marriage to a career soldier only aggravated the problem, which was dealt with by denial all around.

Her husband's death simply centered her on a descending path, providing a final, gentle, fatal push. One year later, after they had moved back to family in Kansas, following a four-day binge, she put the big, ocean-green Polara into an overpass support on I-235.

Aaron's sister, Laura, older by four years, responded to losing their remaining parent by following her own path of destruction. An unexpected pregnancy led to an unwanted marriage. Neither situation complemented the other. She lost the baby to what she claimed was a bad fall, then divorced her abusive, teenage husband, whom Aaron had always thought *was* the bad fall. Laura disappeared one day right after that. Aaron's last note from her came eight months later, from some tiny no-name town in Oregon. Despite more than a dozen attempts to reply to her, he never heard from her again.

He was taken in by his uncle Larry, his father's younger brother, and his aunt Eileen. They lived not far from the big ranch house Aaron's father had planned to retire to in the small city of Lincoln, a few miles northwest of Salina, out in the prairie flatlands. They

attempted to raise him as best they could, and Aaron tried to appreciate their efforts, and love, as the only family he had left.

But it wasn't the same. Not that life would ever be the same for
him, ever again. He was the sole survivor, and despite the best in-
tentions of his aunt and uncle, they couldn't replace those Aaron
had lost. He came to understand that, but there was more to it, he
felt. His father had left him a legacy, one of professional service.
He had worn a uniform most of his adult life, and Aaron strongly
remembered the sense of duty, honor, and country his father had
instilled in him. There was pride in protecting your country, and as
his father had told him over and over again, serving one's country
was the ultimate privilege.

So it came as no surprise that two weeks after his high-school
graduation Aaron announced his decision to enlist. His aunt
Eileen saw it as spooky in a way, maybe even perverse, wanting to
join the same branch of the military that had been the death of his
father. His uncle Larry calmly waved her objections away. He sided
with his nephew, feeling there was something else beneath the decision. Maybe there were some lingering questions to be answered, and old business to be attended to. He knew the bond
between Aaron and his father had been especially strong. Maybe it
would help settle things for the boy.

As a new enlistee Aaron took to the training as an old friend. A
sense of comfort came to him the minute the bus pulled into the
reception station at Fort Dix, miles away from Kansas. As far as
Aaron was concerned it was a lifetime away as well, and he never
looked back. Instead he felt as if he had come home, for the first
time in a long time.

He proved to be a fast study in the basics of soldiering, his training cadre remarking at his natural aptitude. He was simply becoming reacquainted with a lifestyle he had grown up in. Basic
combat skills were absorbed easily, but one in particular he ex-
celled at: shooting.

Aaron had a natural eye and composure for the rifle, melding
his mind and body to it almost as if it were a physical extension of
himself. He set new course records with the M-16A1, finding it almost too easy to hit the required targets. His measured groups
were eye-opening to the range cadre who scored him. After Basic

and Advanced Infantry Training Aaron was assigned to the 173d Light Infantry Brigade, Fort Benning, Georgia. His command presence was developed there, and by the end of nine months in service, Aaron had been promoted to sergeant and made a squad leader.

His ability with a rifle made him stand out, though, and on his first anniversary Aaron was recommended to the U.S. Army Marksmanship Training Unit/USAMTU, coincidentally head-quartered at Fort Benning. The posting was unsolicited by him, and Aaron liked to think of it years later as pure serendipity that he had landed with both feet in the U.S. Army's premier sniper school.

Aaron learned the new trade well, working with his spotter in a two-man scout-sniper team, trained by experienced, battle-proven masters. He and his fellow trainees learned to trade off positions, each acting as spotter and shooter, honing their deadly skills, de-veloping into a gifted team.

Aaron was among the six out of ten to make it to graduation. He finished the five-week course with the coveted "Bravo-4" rating, the designation for Army sniper. His final qualification score was one of the highest ever recorded at the school, missing only three shots in the entire course of fire.

Aaron elected to extend the training into qualifications hard won for both Ranger and Special Forces. But this was the late 1970s, and America was in between wars. Covert operations, hav-ing special interests in some notable and not-so-notable areas of the world, had a special need for scout-snipers. Aaron was put to the real test with assignments to Central and South America, Mo-gadishu, Lebanon, Laos, the old Ivory Coast of Africa, and Soma-lia, middle Europe, and the Middle East.

Either on the direct orders of the government, or at the behest of a friendly ally needing "deniability" for a particularly delicate situation, Aaron did what he did best, conducting operations in long-range killing.

His official personnel jacket remained mute to this clandestine work, while the Pentagon kept track of his true assignments. By 1980 he was a twenty-two-year-old staff sergeant and had forty-

one confirmed kills. It was a job performed for the Greek government that presented him with the biggest opportunity of his life,
and career. Old events came crashing in, while a new enlighten-
ment illuminated a new truth for him, shaking his beliefs, and
forcing a new decision that changed his life again.

*   *   *

Major James Manos reviewed the orders again. "Staff Sergeant
Longbaugh, Aaron R.," he read. He no longer wondered if he was
the son. Manos had already checked the data bank in D.C. to confirm it. Sergeant Longbaugh was indeed the son of the officer
whose murder Manos and his partner Tony Husta had investigated
ten years before. He had never known what had become of the
Longbaugh family afterward.

He and Husta had promised to dog the men of the killing squad
for as long as it took, but some promises just can't be kept, despite
the intent behind them. Times change, careers move on, budgets
shrink, people forget. The two CID officers had been forced to
curtail, then eventually give up any aspiration of following the lives
and activities of the eight men. It had ended without fanfare, just
drifting away, with nothing new discovered, nothing old resolved.
That included any knowledge of the son, Aaron. All Manos and
Husta knew was that the boy's mother had died, and his elder sister had disappeared. What the boy had come to was unknown, until now.

Manos, attempting to build his own professional career in the
Army, had taken a temporary posting to Special Forces, acting as
an intelligence officer, one of a handful assisting in debriefing returning personnel from clandestine, highly secret overseas operations. It was his job to get the initial facts down before further,
more extensive questioning took place. Most such operations were
initiated out of Eglin Air Force Base in Florida. It was one such
task that brought up Aaron's name, and Manos's subsequent curiosity.

The young sergeant's orders indicated he had been used to expedite the release of a highly influential American businessman,
abducted by a right-wing terrorist group in Athens. Overseen by

the State Department, the mission had apparently gone well. Three of the terrorists had died, and the businessman had been rescued.

But more than the mission, Manos was intrigued about Longbaugh. He wondered how the boy, now a man, had handled his father's death. For his part, Manos couldn't shake off the sense of guilt that resurrected itself. The burden of unfinished business settled into the back of his mind as he watched the small group of soldiers disembark from the dark gray C-130 transport. Longbaugh was easy to spot.

He was tall, broad in the shoulder, and moved with the familiar grace of a seasoned soldier. He wore standard camouflage BDUs, the sleeves rolled up in regulation format, showing the muscles of his arms to good effect. The curved bill of the fatigue hat shaded his eyes and face. He carried his heavy field rucksack off his right shoulder with his camouflage Ghillie suit strapped to it. His left hand clutched the handle of a long, flat, dull black rifle case. He walked with his head up and moving, his eyes taking in everything.

Manos stepped up to intercept him and was struck by Longbaugh's similarity to the man's deceased father.

"Sergeant Longbaugh?" he said.

Aaron stopped, put down his load, and snapped off a responding salute. "Yes, sir, Staff Sergeant Aaron Longbaugh reporting as ordered," Aaron said. His dark eyes held steady on Manos.

Manos returned the salute. "Carry on," he began. "I'm Major Manos, Intelligence. I'm to start your initial debrief." He handed over the manila folder of orders to Aaron.

He had been through this process before. He took the folder, exchanging it for one of his own. "Yes, sir, they told me to expect you when I hit Eglin," he said.

Manos accepted the paperwork and indicated a Jeep parked in the shade a few yards away. "Let's get you inside and started on this," he said. "We've got you on a MAC C-141 to Benning at nineteen hundred."

"OK, sir," Aaron said, reaching for his gear. It was routine, just another step in the process. He straightened up with the cased rifle and rucksack to find Manos staring at him. "Sir? Is there something wrong?"

Manos smiled briefly, a touch nostalgically, and said something surprising. "No. You just look more like your father than I expected."

The reply confused Aaron, and he paused a moment more. "Excuse me, Major, but you said you knew my father?"

Manos motioned to the Jeep. "A long time ago, Sergeant Longbaugh. Let's get this business finished. After that," he paused a moment, then looked up at Aaron, meeting his inquiring gaze. "After that maybe we'll talk about how I came to know him."

"Yes, sir," Aaron said, curious about Manos's statement. He fell in beside him as they walked to the Jeep.

* * *

The debriefing on the Greek rescue mission was perfunctory. Manos was through with his questions in two hours' time. He took his time sealing the report in the classified envelope for the courier. Aaron broke the silence.

"You mentioned knowing my father," he reminded him. "When exactly did that happen?"

Manos seemed to wrestle with the question, but he knew he was already past that. The decision to tell Aaron what had happened had been coming on since he had seen his name on the debrief order. It felt right somehow, but there was something else, too, almost as if Manos was violating an oath of some kind. He shook his head. If he was violating anything it was the memory of a murder unresolved, and a minute piece of a tragic war that needed to be put to rest. He slid the sealed package aside.

"My primary MOS is with the Criminal Investigations Division," he said. "In 1970 my partner and I were assigned to II Corps, Pleiku Province."

Aaron appeared to hesitate, and recognition clicked into place. "The Fourth Division's area," he said quietly.

"That's right," Manos said. "Where your father was killed. That's how I came to know him, or of him, I should say. My partner and I investigated his death."

Aaron looked confused. "I'm afraid I'm not following you, sir. My dad was killed in a VC ambush. Why would the CID have anything to do with that?"

Manos paused, looked down at his hand, and flexed his fingers into a fist several times. Then he looked back up and said, "Because your father wasn't killed in a Viet Cong ambush. He didn't die as a result of enemy action at all." He was in control now as he finished what he had waited ten years to say. "Major Longbaugh was murdered in a premeditated action by a squad from Charlie Company, Second Battalion, Fourteenth Brigade."

Aaron reacted with disbelief. "What! What are you talking about! He was killed by the Cong. We got the citation . . . the officers at Ord came to the house . . . they told us . . . they sat there with me and my mother and sister and *told* us!"

Manos felt the anguish, felt the old wound ripped open, and for a moment, just one moment, regretted his decision. But it was too late for regret. Compassion filled him instead, and he reached across to touch Aaron's arm.

"It wasn't the truth, and I'm sorry for that . . . truly sorry. Things were different then, there were other circumstances involved."

Aaron sat back quickly, looking around the room, and took a couple of breaths, composing himself. His chest felt constricted, and visions of that day flashed in his memory.

"I don't understand." He paused, replaying Manos's words in his mind. "Oh, man," he said. "Oh, Christ. Murdered? My father was murdered? Why?"

Manos pushed on, wanting to get it all out now, the injustice of it, the guilt of the eight men in the squad, free for all these years because of a system that didn't work. "It was a fragging," he said. "Your father was the operations officer for the battalion. He set the orders that sent troops out into the field. The war was winding down, the Vietnamese were taking over, our boys were beginning to come home. These guys got it into their heads that all they wanted to do was live to go home. They didn't want to go back into the field."

"So they killed my father for that?" Aaron responded with anger. "That's crazy, Major. It doesn't make sense." He shook his head. "This has got to be wrong. Why are you telling me this?"

Manos nodded slowly, confirming what he was saying. "I understand your confusion, son. I wish there was another way to say it, but it's true. There's no mistake. The ambush was a ruse, part of the plot. After our investigation the decision was made to report the entire matter as an enemy ambush, just as it was supposed to appear. But the men of that squad did it. They killed your father."

Aaron struggled with the news. After all this time, to be told something like this. A murder? "What kind of bastards were these guys?" He said, almost to himself, emotions in conflict. He returned his attention to Manos. "How did you find out about it?"

"One of them turned the others in," he said, keeping the details about Carlos Madrid's story for himself. "That's how we got involved. Captain Husta was my partner then. We were both captains at the time. We investigated the story, cross-checking sitreps, NSA radio logs, confirming the alleged facts of the squad's actions that day. We interviewed the men involved. There was no doubt in our minds they were guilty. We turned over our report to the JAG officer in Pleiku."

"So the Army court-martialed them," Aaron said, presuming it was so. "How much time did they get? How long did the Army lock them away for killing my father?"

Here it comes, Manos thought with dread. The one question he hadn't wanted to hear. But there was no going back now.

"That's the problem," Manos said. "They weren't prosecuted."

"What do you mean!?" Aaron challenged, suddenly incensed. "Excuse me, Major, but I'm not following you here. You just told me my father was murdered . . ." he paused from the effort of saying it aloud, "by a squad of men, but none of them were punished? What happened? You said you investigated it." His eyes bore into Manos, his anger barely under control. "You've been holding back on me, sir," he said. "I think you better tell me everything. In detail. Now."

Manos knew Aaron had the right to know. He also knew he alone had the facts to give him. But he had promised years ago that this day would come. Now that it had arrived he wasn't going to let it pass unfinished.

"All right," he said. "It's time you heard it . . . heard it all." He began to tell Aaron the entire sordid tale, leaving out none of the details, including where he could obtain a copy of the declassified investigation report he and Husta had written. It took another two hours, but by the end of it Aaron had already made up his mind about what to do about it.

It was a natural progression, all things considered. There was a price associated with it, and changes to be made. Nothing comes without sacrifice, he told himself. His father had taught him that. He'd also taught him about duty, and honor. He thought about his father, remembering the words, the years, the love, all memories now. Aaron was his father's son, he thought with painful pride as Major Manos came to the end of his story. What would his father do about this? What would he expect Aaron to do? The answer was there. It seemed so clear, actually. Why question it, since it was the right thing to do . . . the just thing.

When Manos was finished Aaron stood up slowly and reached across the table for his hand. "I want to thank you, Major," he said. "Thank you for what you did . . . for trying." He held the man's hand firmly. "And thank you for the truth."

"Sergeant Longbaugh . . ." Manos began, letting his hand go.

Aaron came to attention, his hand snapping up smartly in a salute. "Please, sir," he said, his eyes straight ahead. "With your permission I need to square some things away if I'm going to make that MAC flight." The words came easily, but his mind was elsewhere.

Manos motioned beyond the closed office door. "What I've told you is still technically classified information," he said, his meaning clear. "Call it for your eyes only."

Aaron stood a moment, and nodded. "I understand, sir. Thank you."

"Look, son," Manos finally said. "If there's anything you need . . . any time. Call me. You've got my number at the Pentagon."

"Thank you again, sir," Aaron responded. All he wanted to do was get away. Get out of that room. There was too much going on, but already things were falling into place. He performed a smart about-face and walked out of the office, closing the door behind him. He felt he had no choice about what he was considering.

It wasn't every day you got handed a new job offer.

1991

May 27

Macon, Georgia

It was a good place to be, Aaron thought, then corrected himself to say, No, it's the best place. He had analyzed obstructions, variations in the dipping hollows of the high grass-covered terrain as it undulated toward the group of white buildings that made up the farm, 567 yards away. There was nothing blocking his chosen field of fire, and the stand of live oak trees he sat under gave fine cover. He had scouted all of the other approaches over the last six months, looking at them through his experienced eyes, taking his time. This was it, he had decided eventually, and had begun to plan the shoot.

He'd been christened Aaron Ralph Longbaugh, his mother's homage to her grandfather, his middle name belonging to his father. In his own mind he was still Aaron, but to those with whom he worked in his "day job," as he called it, he was Frank. He had learned how to create a new identity, how to crawl into a persona completely different from his real self. There are ways to do that, and he'd been taught that aspect of the craft by the true experts. He never reacted to the inadvertent slip if he heard his true name, but that had yet to happen. Nor did he carry over any of the specifics from a prior character into a new one. Each identity he built was fully able to exist by itself, more than complete enough to last as long as it took to finish the job. Then it was discarded, forgotten, buried as surely as his father had been.

49

And it was his father who accounted for Aaron's being here on this rural Georgia hillside. Major Ralph Longbaugh, his emotions, strengths, and love, riding there deep in Aaron's memory. That was all that was left to his son. The war had taken him, and Aaron's mother and sister, forever from his life. The war, and nine men, of whom Jack Linet had been one—the squad leader, in point of fact. He was the sixth of them he had found, each one tracked over the years, viewed and studied in absolute, meticulous detail. The next target, as were they all.

Aaron settled his mind into the task at hand. The shade from the late-afternoon slant of the sun cast mottled shadows under the wide branches, adding to the effectiveness of his clothing. Aaron wore a civilian one-piece coverall that combined patches of differing shades of green and streaks of muddy tan, with an overlay of black web lines. He had covered his exposed hands and face with camouflage stick, smearing it to disguise the highs and lows of his brow, cheeks, and chin. A USMC-style cap in the same pattern covered his head, and he wore it reversed, so the bill didn't block his vision.

He sat next to the base of the wide oak's trunk. A tree-climber's hook had been screwed into the side of the tree at the right height to rest the stock across it. He had taped a roll of half-inch-thick foam rubber around the U of the hook a few turns as a rest. Hard on soft, that was it, one of the many incidental things that made a steady rest. It was a small part of the sniper's craft. With the heavy-barreled rifle resting across the hook, and his upper arms just over his raised knees, legs spread, heels dug in, the position was very stable and allowed him to see over the high grass running slightly downhill from his perch.

He'd had to complete certain precautions after taking each target. He had returned to the big family house in Kansas, now his by default as the sole survivor. There, in the hidden workshop in the basement, he rebarreled the rifle, replaced the bolt, extractor and ejector, and firing pin. Years before he had purchased enough spare parts to make the changes to each rifle he used. Changing out these parts effectively eliminated any forensic evidence common to each killing. He had a second weapon, the accurized M-14 called the XM21. Army snipers had used it extensively in the war.

The same work on the XM21 was more difficult due to the gas port system, but he was able to complete the job.

He'd been careful not to inadvertently lose a shell casing. He left nothing behind, no ballistic or forensic evidence that could be traced back to either rifle. But there was always a chance something would be missed, a crucial piece of evidence left to be found. The postshooting changes to each weapon were necessary. They still allowed him to maintain the same feel to each rifle, although there was a break-in period to let the new parts settle in. A sniper's rifle was unique to its user, down to the nth degree, and he knew them both better than that.

Besides making, in effect, a new rifle for each target, what further bound each target in turn to him was his skill in first finding them, then hunting them down. In that respect there was a correlation, should anyone begin to look into these seemingly unrelated deaths. But it was a risk that existed only because of his decision to do what he had to do. Justice, he had discovered from personal experience, carried a convoluted set of definitions. The one he had chosen worked for him, and that was good enough. He checked the time, preparing himself.

As if on cue, Jack Linet's pickup appeared, coming down the lane from the main highway, a low dust cloud roiling behind it. Linet lived alone, forty-three years old, with a beer-belly that matched his bad attitude. His philosophy seemed to be that since life chose to dump on *him* all the time, why not do the same to everyone else? Consequently, the only relationships he seemed to count as steady ones were with a handful of bad-asses at the plant who thought as he did, and a few regulars at the two beer joints where he hung out.

Linet liked to regale his drinking buddies with boastful tales of "Veet-Nam," as he pronounced it, in his heavy Georgia drawl. And occasionally, when someone doubted his veracity, usually a patron new to the scene, he had been known to discuss the newcomer's disbeliefs with the aid of a sawed-off baseball bat, or a five-inch lockblade knife.

Aaron had pulled Linet's entire record during the time he had been on the Macon PD SWAT team. Linet's wife of fifteen years had finally tired of his beating her and had left him five months before, taking their three kids with her. Some of the reports on the various domestic calls his fellow officers had answered on Mr. and Mrs. Linet simply confirmed his opinion of the man. People rarely, even if given the chance, change. The one-time Army squad leader seemed to solve all of his life problems with violence. This afternoon, that would change.

The pickup rounded the side of the house, curving toward the barn, and came to an abrupt stop, sliding a little on the hard-packed dirt of the side yard.

Aaron shouldered the rifle and settled down behind it, leaning into it, both elbows down over his upraised knees, making bone-on-bone contact, anchoring his position. His left hand was back, supporting the toe of the butt against his shoulder. The scope was dialed up to nine power, and he clearly saw Linet roll out of the cab, his hand coming up to stiff-arm the door shut. At almost six hundred yards the chunk of the door was lost to distance and a gentle swell of a breeze that lifted the high grass, wafting toward the distant figure.

Aaron reached up with his right index finger and rotated the scope's cam lever, bracketing Linet's body between the two horizontal stadia lines in the sight picture, keeping the bottom line on his waist and the top line on his head. Once set, he merely aimed dead-on for wherever he wanted the shot to go.

Linet wore a battered green John Deere baseball hat over his graying hair, though the tractor with the same name on it sat immobile in the barn. It hadn't run in months, as derelict as its owner seemed bent upon being. Ragged-out jeans and a worn poplin shirt, sleeves rolled to midforearm, completed the look.

He started walking toward the side door, construction boots scuffing in the dirt. Aaron hoped for a profile shot, which would present the target's lungs and heart in the same plane, but he was also prepared for an oblique one. Linet approached the house at a slant, angling toward the single step up to the door.

The shooter computed the lead required by the distance, keeping in mind the mild breeze, too. It could blow the bullet completely off target if not allowed for. The distance mandated a chest shot. It was too far for any guarantee of a head shot, though he was confident he could have made it if necessary. But there was no rush, and he wanted to put Linet down with the first one.

Aaron aimed behind him, then slowly swung the crosshairs past the walking man, getting a feel for his speed, then hesitated a split second, ready in case he stopped before pulling open the kitchen door. His breathing adjusted, coming deeper, relaxing him. It became mechanical as he merged his psyche into the rifle, the finger resting on the trigger almost tasting the metal, so fine was his concentration. Consistent repetition honed from tens of thousands of practice rounds made it a unique mix of conscious/unconscious actions. Real-time experience with breathing targets had solidified his confidence.

Four more steps, he thought, knowing how far Linet had to go to reach the door. He had watched him take the same path, the same number of steps, dozens of times. He counted them off, timing his own breathing, matching his inhalations and exhalations, looking for the steadiest moment between breaths when everything was absolutely flat. Two steps more . . . now turn . . . hand comes up for the door handle, and . . . now . . .

The shot went off, a flat crack that whipped across the undulating ground, absorbed by the open spaces. If Linet had had time, all he would have heard from his end would have been a faint pop. But he couldn't, because his ability to hear anything, to say anything, to think anything ever again, suddenly stopped in less time than his next heartbeat.

The bullet took .79 of a second to reach him, hitting Linet in his right triceps as his arm came forward, his hand coming up to grasp the screen door's handle. The 173-grain projectile drilled neatly through the fatty skin and muscle, and out the other side, then penetrated the lateral side of his chest above the seventh intercostal rib space. The round drove in four and a half inches, well into his right lung, then through it, now ten inches inside the chest cavity, and began to yaw, turning ninety degrees, smashing into the left lung, mangling its upper lobe, the bullet spinning about its long axis too at 3,000 rpm, like a miniature buzzsaw. The temporary wound channel ballooned the soft tissues out, creating a chamber several inches wide, violently compressing the fleshy matter, stunning the heart. Then the round, crush-cutting its way, blew a two-inch-wide hole out the other side, taking a chunk of rib out with it.

All of this forensic activity took place in a millisecond. What Aaron saw in the quick vibration through the scope as the rifle sharply recoiled was Linet suddenly stiffen up, his motion frozen, then fall absolutely straight down onto his back, his head thumping hard against the ground. He lay still, then his chest spasmed once, and again, out of synch as the brain fired impulses to the ruined heart down dying synapses, cascading signals to muscles and nerve centers that had fallen off-line. The fingers of his left hand scrabbled in the dirt, then relaxed. His chest rose one last time, and sighed away, the body settling into itself in permanent immobility.

The shooter had seen it before, and the results meant nothing more than whether his bullet placement had been on target. It was all done automatically, this brief critique of his performance. It was habit now, part of the routine: a ritual, actually.

He remained in place, studying the body through the scope. The crosshairs drifted across the body to the head, which was canted slightly toward him now. Linet's hat had been dislodged by the impact of his head against the hard ground. The crosshairs stopped on the top curve of his ear and the second shot cracked out.

The bullet flashed across the distance, striking a quarter-inch off the aim point used, an exceptional shot for that distance. It punched a neat hole going in, sliced through the medulla oblongata cleanly, and erupted through the back-left corner of the skull.

Aaron worked the bolt again, put the rifle on safe, and pushed himself up. He collected both empty shell casings and pocketed them. Carefully laying the weapon down he unscrewed the tree-climbing hook and dropped it into the deep pocket on the side of his left leg. He retrieved the rifle and stood all the way up.

"That's six," he said aloud, and turned to leave. He glanced at his watch and nodded. He still had a few hours before his shift started. Plenty of time, he thought, holding the weapon in the crook of his right arm, muzzle down. He paused, and almost turned to look back. "Stop it," he said quickly, catching himself before his head could move. There was no room for such thoughts. Not ever.

He took his hat off, reversed it to sit the right way, and replaced it on his head. He turned his thoughts to the next part of the process. He began walking back to his four-by-four Toyota truck, parked a mile and a half away, thinking ahead to the change of shift, and roll call. He wouldn't miss this place. He never did. He hadn't come here looking for roots, and a life. This was a mission, nothing else. Once it was over, when all of them were accounted for, maybe he could consider finding a real life. There was still plenty of time.

1994

May 3

Westport, Ohio

Monnell Bennet watched the people come out of the post office with the eye of a professional. Black, twenty-four years old, an Illinois home-boy from East St. Louis, he'd been drifting east since his momma had run him out, tired of his years of misdemeanors and third-degree felonies since he was eight years old. He was bad, a dude to be avoided, righteous in his indignation at life, and why it hadn't treated him better.

He'd learned to take what he wanted early on, and he was doing so again, right now. A chop shop was looking for new bodies, guys in the know, boosters who could deliver the right cars on specs and on time. It was his big chance, and he was being tested. If he delivered, he was in, and on his way. Big things loomed over the horizon for him, he hoped.

They needed a Lexus, the big LS 400 sedan. And there was one out in front of the post office right now. The driver was a white woman, and Monnell was waiting for her to emerge. He stared impassively through his wraparound Oakleys, setting his face to match his attitude: strong, mean, a power on the street. Monnell was in a taking mood.

He slid a hand into his field jacket pocket, touching the butt of the gun resting there. It was a .38 Super semiautomatic, with lots of bells and whistles on it. Monnell didn't know a lot about guns, except what he'd seen on TV and in the movies. Up until now he had relied on blunt-force instruments, and his speed. Just point the barrel and pull the trigger. Some of the custom touches confused him, what with all the levers and buttons and complicated sights. All he knew was the gun was hot, stolen from a gun club, and that it carried twenty rounds in the fat square magazine. It had cost him two hundred hard dollars out of the back of a dealer's van in Indianapolis. It would do the job, of that he was certain.

The door to the post office opened, and the woman came out. Monnell stepped off the curb into the street, his hand closing to grip the gun tightly, keeping it in his pocket. Adrenaline almost danced him across the street, and he smiled as he walked quickly, his vision tunneling in on his target.

*   *   *

Ruth Avery never saw the young black man slide in quickly behind her, but she felt the hardness of the gun stab against her side, and the fast encircling grip of his other arm go across her chest.

"Gimme the keys, bitch," she heard close to her ear, and smelled him at the same time. Myriad odors flitted by, none of them pleasant, and Ruth exploded. Hours afterward, talking to the police, she couldn't explain to them where her flash of courage came from. Mostly it was just plain anger, she told them.

"No!" she shouted, and swung her purse sideways, connecting with Monnell's face.

"Aw fu—" he started to shout when she twisted against him, hit him again, and tried to run away. She almost made it.

Monnell, surprised and stunned, his vision suddenly blurred from the tears, struck back almost by instinct. Ruth's sudden retaliation had hurt him, but he'd been at this sort of thing longer than she had. It was his advantage. He backhanded her once with the gun, knocking her senseless, and she fell into the car, across the front seat.

The woman had fallen too far in to drag out easily, and the keys had dropped conveniently onto the driver's seat. Monnell hopped in, shoving Ruth farther over as he grabbed the keys, slammed the door, and slid the right key into the ignition, all in one fluid motion. He cranked the key hard, shot a quick glance at the woman, and popped the selector into reverse.

Without looking, he tramped down hard on the pedal, and the big Lexus leaped backward out of the angled slot. A blasting horn and chirping brakes announced the pickup behind him he almost rammed. Now other cars were jamming to a halt, voices were raised in quick shouts, and Monnell threw the lever into drive. It felt as if the whole street was alive around him.

"Move, man! Move it!" he said between gritted teeth, and spun the wheel as the car lunged forward, the engine howling under the effort.

All he wanted was to get out, out of town, out of sight, right *now*, goddammit! Monnell flew down the short leg of the town square, saw the signs for I-75, and whipped the wheel, tires screaming as he rocketed out of the square, running for freedom. The entrance to the interstate was half a mile ahead.

Behind him, confusion reigned for the dozen witnesses to the carjacking. One citizen picked up her cellular phone and stabbed in 911, summoning help. It didn't take long.

* * *

Monnell entered the on-ramp doing sixty, toed in a little brake, and shot up the incline, merging quickly into the lane. There was no traffic close by, but he didn't look. He pushed the car up to eighty in seconds, and the Lexus fairly leaped ahead, stable, quiet, powerful, like him. Only things weren't as they should be, he realized.

For the first time Monnell took a breath, calming himself. Beside him Ruth Avery moaned, still sprawled across the seat. He almost hit her again, but saved it.

"Why'd you do that?" he questioned her, wondering at the stupidity of white people. "Oughta kill you right now," he threatened, pointing the heavy gun at her. Then he shoved the big automatic down between his thighs where he could grab it quick, and returned both hands to the wheel.

Monnell looked around, judging his surroundings. He was floating past other cars, but he didn't let up on the speed. Instead, he pushed it up to ninety and started threading from lane to lane.

They'd be there soon enough, cops behind him. He needed to shake the pursuers first, he knew that much. He'd deliver the Lexus later. Things seemed to be crowding in on his mind, making decisions difficult. This wasn't going the way he had planned.

The first blue-and-red glimmers appeared, way the hell back in the traffic, but coming on fast. Monnell watched them in the mirrors and felt his stomach tighten.

"No good, man," he said tightly, flicking his eyes to the speedometer, and saw he was up to ninety-five now. Up ahead loomed the signs for the Carrollton Hills Mall, and he spotted the tops of the buildings half a mile ahead. "Lose'm in the mall," he muttered, reacting to the suggestion from the overtaxed little voice shouting in his head. It seemed like a good idea at that moment. He didn't see it as the trap it would become.

The Lexus shot off the exit ramp, taking the long right-hand bend at high speed, and headed for the parking lot.

Ruth Avery stirred awake then, and started to rise as Monnell skidded the car to a stop, near the high glass doors leading to the building.

He kicked the door open, picked up the gun, and grabbed Ruth with his other hand. "Out, out, out!" he shouted at her, tugging her across the seat and through the opening. Once standing, he switched hands, ignoring the woman's protests as she tried to resist. She was still groggy, and he pushed her hard toward the doors. Sirens sounded behind him, rising in volume, and he chanced a fast glance back toward the entrance ramp and saw half a dozen cruisers careening down for the mall.

"Goddamn it, move!" he shouted at her, shoving and running with her, hitting the center of the bank of tall glass doors, and they were inside.

People, sounds, smells, lights assaulted Monnell's frightened brain. He was in survival mode now, running on almost pure instinct. A young man in a dark uniform appeared in his line of sight, his eyes round in surprise as he recognized the gun, and Monnell saw him start to reach for the handgun on his equipment belt.

Monnell's right hand came up in a sudden jerk, the .38 Super pointed dead center at the guard's chest from less than eight feet away, and he pulled the trigger three times. The incredibly loud boom of the gun going off whacked against his own ears, drowning the echoes that batted off the walls, obliterating the breathy exclamation from the guard as he folded down face-first onto the floor.

People screamed and dove and spun away from him, and Monnell saw nowhere else to go, then there it was, the open storefront, plants and tee-shirts with animal faces on them staring wide-eyed at him, and he shoved Ruth before him into the store.

He pushed Ruth away from him, and she staggered a few steps, tripped, and sprawled down on the floor. Monnell stared around and saw a dozen people staring right back. He raised the gun at them, feeling its new power, relishing the rush, and smiled crazily. He swung the gun at one of them, a middle-aged woman with a name tag. "You. You work here?"

The woman nodded, uncertainty struggling with fright across her face. She started to raise her hands, then stopped, unsure what to do.

"Close the security gate," Monnell said, pointing the muzzle at the metal box on the wall near the entrance. Two buttons, big as fifty-cent pieces, were on the box. The edge of the chain-link gate extended down six inches from the ceiling above the entrance.

"Do it now, bitch!" Monnell said, motioning with the gun. "Move!"

The woman walked stiffly but quickly over to the box and hit the lower button with her palm. The gate started to descend, closing off the twenty-foot-wide entrance to the store.

"Get back there," Monnell ordered, again directing her with the gun, all the time casting glances out into the mall. The body of the security guard lay on the floor, unmoving. Monnell felt the rush heighten. It was his first-ever kill. But oh, man, what a thrill! The gun felt like the power of God in his hand.

"That's what I got," he said, showing them the big stainless steel pistol. "I got the power! And it's gonna get my ass outa here." He had a plan now, so he thought. If not a real plan, then the means to get one. He had the gun, and he'd shown them he knew how to use it. They'd listen now, wouldn't they?

"You damn straight," Monnell said aloud, replying to his inner voice, so full of itself now. "They'll listen, all right."

* * *

But it didn't happen that way. Four hours later, and Monnell was running out of time. He'd run out of patience, too. "No! No! No!" he shouted into the phone. The hostage negotiator was trying to bullshit him again, and he wasn't taking any of that. "I tol' you fuckers I want the helicopter and the money now! I tol' you the same thing two hours ago! Now I ain't tellin' you no mo'!" His voice remained tight, his emotions wound up to match, his control badly frayed.

Monnell stood behind the column of rock, covered from any view from the front, holding the cellular phone in one hand, the gun in the other. On the floor before him lay all the hostages. He'd had them barricade the back door into the store. There was no way in, and no way out. His thumb flicked the lever back and forth, absently playing with the gun while he considered which one of his victims to use. His eyes fell on the young white boy, barely out of his teens.

Monnell smiled, but his eyes were blank, focused elsewhere, burning with a distant light. He held the cell phone to his lips. "You fucked with me fo' the last time. *This* is how serious I am!"

He dropped the phone, and grabbed the hostage's shirt behind his neck, lifting him one-handed. His legs weren't set, and the weight of the boy pulled him off-balance. Monnell took a step forward, holding on, keeping both of them upright. He pressed the barrel into the back of the kid's head, never hesitating. The boy was chanting something, fear rising in his voice.

Monnell tightened his hand around the gun's grip and pulled the trigger. Nothing happened. The hammer remained back, frozen in place. Monnell hesitated, confused, expecting the boom like the first time, and started to turn the gun to look at it, wondering why . . .

His head exploded from the strike of the .308 bullet fired by the police sniper in the second-story movie theater facing the store's front. Monnell and the hostage both fell to the floor. The hostage survived. Monnell's question, like his career, died without an answer.

September 8

Trans Patriot Insurance, Hamilton, Ohio

Vanessa Lin Tau eased her 1995 medium metallic blue Blazer LS into her assigned parking space. She switched off the engine and paused to check her makeup in the lighted mirror set into the reverse side of the sunshade. The face that looked back bespoke her Vietnamese heritage. Perfectly white teeth were revealed behind her full lower lip, her upper lip ending with a slight upward curve accentuated by her smile. High cheekbones complemented her small chin and thin nose, drawing attention to her deep brown eyes, seemingly slanted by the delicacy of the hooded fold over each one. Long, dark lashes lent the right touch to features clearly Oriental, as did her ebony hair, worn long in the traditional way, down to her midback, her bangs softly framing her face.

Vanessa was not tall by American standards, but was so for a Vietnamese, at five feet five inches. She had also filled out considerably more than was usually seen on women from her country, with full-bodied attributes her mother, Lai Mhinh, kidded her about, but of which the older woman was inordinately proud. Her daughter had become Americanized quite well since they had all arrived in California fleeing from the invasion by the North in 1975.

She was four years old then, but hadn't picked up her American name until the Tau family had resettled in Columbus, Ohio, with relatives who had managed to get out a year earlier. The middle of five children, one of whom remained buried near the family home in Bong Son, she had acclimated to a new lifestyle rapidly, as young children do anywhere. She attended Roman Catholic parochial schools while her parents rebuilt their business lives around the successful restaurant they started.

Three years after their arrival in the States, they all swore their oaths as new American citizens. Despite it all, though, her parents never gave up the dream of returning one day to a free Vietnam.

That same dream fueled a determination in Vanessa and her siblings to succeed. She had received her business degree at Ohio

University and was currently working on her masters at Miami University in Oxford, which was one reason she had accepted a position as claims adjuster for Trans Patriot Insurance in 1991 after receiving her BA degree. The company covered the cost of the advanced degree as part of the in-house bootstrap education program. In her case, it was money well spent. She had learned the claims trade well, with every sign of making it a career.

She locked up the Blazer and followed the winding sidewalk into the side entrance of Trans Patriot's office.

There were forty-two people staffing the office, with technical types, such as underwriting, sales, and claims making up a third of them. Clerical support accounted for the remainder. Vanessa was one of four claims adjusters, who all worked pretty much their own schedules. Their supervisor oversaw their work from the Cincinnati office, while each of the adjusters was required to spend one day a week there, reviewing caseloads.

She entered the building and made her way across the large central room to her cubicle, greeting a few people along the way. Vanessa dropped her purse and briefcase on the floor beside her desk and turned on her PC to check her phone messages. Each workstation had its own fax software and individual inkjet printer as well. It was only part of the massive computer system used by Trans Patriot, and was almost beyond the cutting edge of the industry.

She logged on, pulled up her Windows display, and clicked on the phone icon on the bottom of her twenty-one-inch monitor. The smaller window opened and listed half a dozen messages. She noted those that needed a return call and jotted them down.

Next she clicked on her diary icon, showing the files she wanted to review that day, then pushed the ALT/TAB keys to check for any new assignments. There were two new cases waiting for her. The parent office system in Cincinnati had had the first reports received, consisting of the actual paper reports generated by the insureds, imaged into the computer, and reproduced in perfect, three-dimensional color, exactly as received. The claim file was created then, with the originals kept in Cincinnati, but hard copies could be printed at the branch office for the adjusters to use while completing their field investigations.

Vanessa left the information on her monitor and turned in her chair to pick up her purse and put it into the bottom drawer of her desk. Then she called up the new cases assigned to her. Several different headings appeared.

"So let's see what these are," she said under her breath, keying in the first reports on each new case. She scanned the information displayed quickly, noting the contact people and appropriate telephone numbers.

Her day was partially scheduled already, but she always left room to fit in the new priority calls, like this. The first case she read was a lawsuit resulting from a police shooting involving the Westport, Ohio, PD's hostage/rescue team. The summons and complaint was a wrongful death claim by the family of the suspect, Monnell Bennett, involved in a hostage situation.

The shooting lawsuit needed immediate looking into, she decided. The actual shooting incident had happened four months before. The suit had been filed by a Cincinnati attorney named Julia Chandler Disare. Vanessa knew her name immediately. Disare was a firebrand, formerly with the ACLU, who had struck out on her own practice half a dozen years before, compiling a long list of high-profile cases. She had won her share and was no stranger to the federal court and civil rights cases. In fact, she carried the reputation of being formidable in prosecuting 42 USC 1983-style cases, suing under the civil-rights statute.

The complaint included all the expected counts: violations of Monnell Bennet's First, Fourth, Fifth, Twelfth, and Fourteenth amendment rights as guaranteed under the United States Constitution. The police were alleged to have, under the color of law, of course, exercised a policy and practice of excessive and deadly force when they shot and killed the plaintiff in such an outrageous manner as to shock the public's conscience.

The police department and the municipality were also named as defendants, including the mayor, city council, Chief Daniel Tusca, and almost his entire staff, including the two-man sniper team, Sergeant Nathan Samm and Corporal Jerry Lanier. The allegations against the insured and the city were based upon their respective positions as employers, for failing to train and properly supervise the officers involved in the shooting.

The summons and complaint, or S&C, ran on for fourteen counts, covering eighty-nine numbered paragraphs, and asked for five hundred thousand dollars in compensatory damages per count, plus a million dollars in additional punitive damages per count, as well as a declaratory order from the court forcing the city to revamp its police policies and procedures.

"Reaching for the moon, eh, Julia?" Vanessa said under her breath, and moved on to the other information attached to the lawsuit.

Preliminary information on the Loss ACORD form sent by the local agent for the City of Westport Police Department, a Dayton suburb, indicated the deceased, Monnell Bennet, had been shot and killed by the Westport SWAT team at the Carrollton Hills Mall, the new megamall location near the town. The description triggered her memory of the incident. She thought she had seen something about it either on television or in the paper.

Vanessa knew she would need the basics right off: get the S&C assigned to a defense attorney as soon as possible. There were only twenty days from day of service to get an answer filed, or face a default judgment, and she noted ten of those days had already run. She immediately thought of Rose, DiPratta, and Welles in Dayton. Arthur Gabel was there, and he was one of the best.

"Good deal," she said, deciding that issue. She would call him straight off and fax over a copy of the S&C. She'd also need the full in-house police field report, to include any additional investigations by either the Dayton PD or the Ohio State Police, who often were brought in on serious police cases to investigate further. The Ohio Bureau of Investigation always investigated police fatality cases, she knew from experience. Set up much like the FBI, the OBI was the premier law-enforcement entity in the state. Many other states had equivalent agencies, and perhaps a separate shooting review board report as well. As to the deceased subject, she needed the death certificate and formal autopsy report, besides his complete civil and criminal background.

Once all this information had been collected and reviewed, she would schedule her interviews with the SWAT team members involved, along with the chief and other appropriate superior officers and training personnel.

The city attorney was the best contact for setting up her first round of calls. She found his name, Charles Kedrick, and number on the Loss ACORD report. Vanessa pulled up her day's schedule on the screen and saw where a few changes would fit the police case into her day's activities. Once the schedule was rearranged, she printed it out and started making her telephone calls.

"Westport Municipal Building," the receptionist answered.

"Yes, Vanessa Tau, Trans Patriot Insurance," she replied. "We have your police liability coverage and just received a new notice of claim. Is Mr. Charles Kedrick in?"

"I'll connect you," the receptionist said.

And here we go again, Vanessa thought. She was anxious to get started. It promised to be a good day.

September 8
Westport, Ohio

Charles Kedrick looked at the pretty Oriental young woman sitting across his rather deep desk, silently appraising her. Kedrick fit the standard description of the corporate attorney: sixty-dollar haircut artfully covering the thinning spots over each temple, highly starched white shirt, striped tie, and a three-thousand-dollar suit. There was an expression of annoyance on Kedrick's face. He got right to the point.

"What do you know about police shooting cases, Ms. Tau?" he asked, referring to her Trans Patriot Insurance business card. He had the air of a man with more important things on his mind than wasting time talking to another rookie adjuster.

She had seen the look before on white-collar paper shufflers who rarely, if ever, bothered to actually read the policy provided to them by TPI's broker. Most of them conducted the occasional foray into an insurance claim involving their municipality with a general liability/this-is-a-slip-and-fall-claim attitude. Few had the slightest clue how a police professional claim was investigated, and how the defense of one was handled, once a lawsuit appeared. She kept her expression mild and her voice pleasant.

"A police liability claim," she responded, stressing the word liability, "requires specific investigative procedures for the initial claim reported. And since many of these claims also result in litigation, the investigation must be conducted with an eye toward defending such litigation somewhere downstream." She fixed him with her eyes, but kept any smugness out of them. "Are you asking how many such cases I've handled, Mr. Kedrick, or is it something else?" Her inference to her sex remained unspoken, but the tone of her delivery was clear and recognizable.

Kedrick reconsidered his initial assumption and dismissed his sexist thoughts with a wave of the hand. "Just asking the question, Ms. Tau," he replied, changing his tone. He was more than familiar with the arguments for affirmative action. His initial impression of the young adjuster shifted accordingly.

"Who were you going to assign the defense to, Ms. Tau?"

"Do you know Arthur Gabel, with Rose, DiPratta and Welles in Dayton? They handle most of our cases in this jurisdiction."

"Art Gabel?" Kedrick replied, his voice sounding pleased. "Sure I know him. He was a couple of years ahead of me in law school. Good man."

"I've already faxed him a copy of it," Vanessa said. "He'll file the appropriate notice of appearance and answer the S&C. There are a few things he'll need right off," she continued, "which is partially why I'm here."

"Yes, well," he continued, as if nothing had happened. "What is it you'll need from us?"

"Well, first off," she said, "I'd like to have the entire police field report, to include any additional investigation from the shooting review board, if you have one. The notice of claim forwarded to us from the agent wasn't complete."

"We have such a board," he acknowledged, beginning to take notes of his own.

"Next, if there was any review by an outside source, such as the Ohio Bureau of Investigation, I'd like to see that, too. The OBI often gets assigned police fatalities. They provide a third-party look into potentially serious cases."

Kedrick added the note, while his opinion of Vanessa continued to improve. This lady knows what she's doing, he thought, and added aloud, "I'll see to all of that. As it happens the OBI was called in, although I don't think their final report is in. From preliminary information passed along to us, they seem to back up our officers in the use of deadly force in this case. I presume you'll be wanting to interview the officers involved, and the chief."

"I'd like to speak with them, yes," Vanessa said, "especially those on the SWAT team, besides any other officers who were at the scene. There won't be any formal statements, written or recorded. The privilege of protected work product has taken a few hits by the judiciary in the last two years. We've gotten away from doing anything discoverable. If suit follows, the officers' depositions will be taken at some point. That will do for the record. I'd rather get a feel from them about what happened out there and how they tell it."

Kedrick openly smiled now, the last of his initial misgivings over her qualifications faded away. "I'll make the arrangements, Ms. Tau. Anything else?"

She shook her head negatively. "No, I think all of that will be a good start. Oh," she remembered, "if you have the autopsy report and death certificate, I'd like copies, too."

"I'll check on that," he replied. "I believe we have those in the file."

"Good," she said, and gave him a pretty smile. "Depending on how things go, we might decide to bring in an independent police investigator, possibly even an expert. There may be specific procedural questions that we need to tie down. We often refer these matters to experts in those areas. Will that be a problem here?"

"I think we have a winning case here, Ms. Tau. The deceased, this Monnell Bennet, had a record, a rather long one, actually. Bennet was a three-time loser, a felon. We'd like to not have to pay anything simply because the right decisions were made out there."

Kedrick leaned back in his chair and toyed with a pen, turning it over as he spoke. "Westport has a population base of roughly sixty-three thousand citizens," he said. "To protect them we've got a forty-two-man police force. The SWAT team, as you called it, consists of twelve police officers, with Lieutenant Dean Barlot in command. There are three four-member units or tactical teams. One is the shooting team, consisting of two long riflemen and two spotters. The other two teams are entry teams, with one of them also the command and control unit. Lieutenant Barlot heads up that one. Each team has a sergeant, and the rest of the members are corporals." Kedrick paused a moment, then continued.

"Getting an assignment to the tactical team is considered a promotion, due to the extra skills and training necessary for the position. We like to compensate those officers who qualify with a promotion to corporal, or higher. As to Lieutenant Barlot," he went on, "Dean's been with us a dozen years now, came up from Kentucky, master's degree in criminology, actually had three years with the FBI until he caught a bullet in the chest. They let him go, and we picked him up."

He stopped playing with the pen and slid it into his suit jacket pocket. "He's got a good crew under him, Ms. Tau. He thinks they did everything right out there, and I tend to agree."

He started to push back from his desk. "It's tragic that a couple of people died, but I don't see where there was any choice in the matter. Bennet forced the issue, as I understand it. Shall we get started? I'll take you to Chief Tusca and get you situated."

"That'll be fine," Vanessa said, reaching down to retrieve her briefcase beside the chair.

They left Kedrick's plush office, Vanessa preceding the city attorney, who politely ushered her through the doorway. "This way, Ms. Tau," he said, motioning to the right.

"Vanessa," she replied, giving him her preference, and added, "Thank you."

"Thank *you*," he replied. They had both scored points. It was a good beginning.

*   *   *

Vanessa sat at the long table in the conference room, Chief Daniel Tusca opposite her, Kedrick beside him, and Lieutenant Dean Barlot, the SWAT commander, beside her. Introductions had been made, and now Vanessa studied the two new men.

Chief Tusca was in his early fifties, tall at six foot three, and thin, like a distance runner. His short hair was salt-and-pepper gray, offsetting his hazel eyes. He wore a dark gray suit and looked more like the administrator he had to be than the policeman he was. However, the Beretta 92 Compact L snugged into the holster over his right hip reminded her who he was for real. His face exhibited years of outdoor life, with a fine web of creases, deeper about his eyes and mouth, which turned down at the edges. In fact, she noted, his facial features seemed to droop slightly, as if he was beginning to melt. She quickly decided it was just gravity taking over, that and the rigors of thirty years.

Lieutenant Barlot was black and appeared to be in his midthirties, the years carried well on a solid football player's physique. He had the muscled neck typical of such men, sloping into heavy shoulders. Barlot's clean-shaven face bore the marks of prior hard contacts, with a short scar that bisected his left eyebrow and a nose thickened from an old fracture. His black hair was military short, lending his features a no-nonsense appeal, which was accented by a thick mustache. His eyes were muddy brown, but intense at the same time. They studied her with a casualness that was deceptive. Vanessa felt no detail really escaped them.

On the table lay several bound or stapled stacks of reports, representing the entire in-house file on the shooting. Chief Tusca was explaining the reason the members of the team weren't available for the meeting with Vanessa, which had been planned for that afternoon. He had referred to them as the HRG team, and Vanessa had interrupted him for a clarification.

"HRG stands for Hostage/Rescue Group," Chief Tusca replied. "Unfortunately it's a sign of the times, but in these politically correct days, the letters SWAT put people in mind of militant cops with submachine guns shooting anything that moves. We borrowed the hostage and rescue part from the FBI, which has the Hostage/Rescue Teams. Anyway, it reads better in the papers."

"We've got to be sensitive to the public," Kedrick added in deference to the chief's explanation.

"Like a bunch of damn public relations jerks, you mean," the chief said bitterly. He turned back to Vanessa. "So there you have it," he said. "I had to loan them out last night for a combined situation with the Dayton PD. We belong to a joint task force with five other municipalities, sharing narcotic, hostage/rescue, and special assets. Luckily, last night's situation resolved itself, with the negotiators calming things down. No one hurt, and everyone went home safe." It was obvious such a resolution was his preference.

"Unfortunately, my officers have been up twenty-six hours straight and need the rest," Lieutenant Barlot interjected. "We'll have to reschedule your interviews with most of the members of the team involved in the Bennet incident."

Vanessa waved her hand, a quick ripple of her elegant fingers. "No problem, Lieutenant. It'll give me time to digest these reports first anyway, and get some of the preliminary things out of the way. I would also like to see the site of the shooting, if possible."

"I can arrange that," Barlot said. "If you'll let me know how soon you'd like to get out there."

She consulted a pocket-size notebook, her adjuster's weekly planner. "Actually, tomorrow morning would work for me," she said. "After nine o'clock. Can you have an officer ready for me?"

"How's 10:00 A.M. sound?" Barlot replied. "Sergeant Samm will be available then."

"That will be fine," Vanessa said, thinking ahead. She could be finished with her first call of the day easily by then. She gathered up her copies of the field reports. "In the meantime, I'll start on these. It looks good so far, Chief," she said, referring both to the reports and to the briefing the chief had given her on the incident.

"I think so, too," he confirmed, hesitating. This was the first time the chief had had to report a fatality to Trans Patriot Insurance. The prior insurance carrier for the Police Department hadn't been all that efficient, in his opinion. The few claims his department had produced before had been the usual conglomeration of false arrest and excessive force allegations, and some employment-related issues like failure to promote. None of them had carried any major exposure. Now this had happened, and he wanted to know going in how TPI would treat his people.

"I know that insurance is a business, just like anything else," he began. "Sometimes insurance companies throw money at claims to make them go away, without regard for the facts." He watched her for a reaction.

Vanessa stopped arranging the papers inside her opened briefcase before her, and answered him. "You'll find TPI doesn't do that," she said. "We take every claim on its individual merits and defend accordingly. We don't have a company policy of making cases go away simply to keep the accountants happy. If it's defensible, we defend it, all the way through trial, if necessary."

"Charlie says Arthur Gabel's going to defend this for us," the chief said. "I've heard of him. He's done good work for some other PDs in the area."

"We're comfortable with him, too, Chief," Vanessa said. "He doesn't waste time, or money. Chances are, we might get this dismissed on a motion. We'll see how that works out. A lot depends on the black-and-white facts."

"You'll be interested in Bennet's record, then," Lieutenant Barlot said. "Monnell Bennet was plenty familiar with the justice system, as it turns out. He was on parole this last time, for aggravated assault on his ex-wife, in violation of a court-ordered restraining order, and for A&B on two of the officers who were called to the scene. He hurt one of them pretty badly. But armed robbery was his true calling. Bennet served nine years of a twelve-year sentence for that. A real sweetheart."

"Not a lot of jury sympathy, is there?" Vanessa said.

Chief Tusca smiled wryly. "You'd think so, but who knows. His ex-wife is one of the potential plaintiffs in this, you know. Along with his parents. Seems like Monnell was really a good family man," he said, the sarcasm apparent.

"Yeah, once he was dead they suddenly all suffered selective memory loss," Barlot added. "Funny how much they miss him, now that he's worth a few potential bucks."

"We still take them on the merits, one case at a time," Vanessa said in response. She couldn't fault the skepticism in the officers' attitudes. Insurance claims have a way of finding the true depth of greed in normal, everyday people. She'd seen it a thousand times.

"That's nice to know, but you'll still settle a claim if you think it warrants it, won't you?" Chief Tusca said.

"If the facts justify that decision, yes," she confirmed. "Not because it starts getting too costly to defend it further. That's not how we do business, Chief."

"We don't either, Ms. Tau," he said. "And I'm glad we share the same philosophy."

"It's the only way to do it," she agreed. She closed and latched the briefcase. "I'll look forward to seeing you both tomorrow, then," she said, getting up from the table.

"And Sergeant Samm," Kendrick added.

"Him too," Vanessa said.

"You'll like him," Chief Tusca said. "He's pretty good at this racket. I've been in law enforcement nineteen years, and I've seen few better than him, especially for SWAT work. I think you'll be impressed."

"I'll take that on the plus side, Chief," she said, extending her hand. "Thank you for your time, and I guess we'll continue this in the A.M."

"My pleasure, Ms. Tau," he responded.

As they walked out Lieutenant Barlot fell in beside her.

She looked up at him. "I really am on your side here," she added, offering a small grin.

"Just what I wanted to hear," Barlot said, responding with his own smile. "None of us enjoy getting sued for doing our job," he said. "And that's all this is about, in the end. We were just doing our job."

"Lawsuits, unfortunately, are a sign of our times," Vanessa said. "People don't like accepting responsibility for their own misfortunes. It's become too easy to look for someone else to lay the blame on. Police are excellent targets, no pun intended," she went on.

He merely inclined his head in silent reply.

"What we'll have to show a jury, if it goes that far," she continued, "is exactly what you just said. You and your team were just doing your job. In my experience, when you finally get right down to it in front of a jury, it becomes that simple to understand. And for what it's worth, most juries come away believing in the police. But we've a long way to go to get there," she added.

"I know," Barlot said. "I'll do all I can to help you on that score."

"That's the name of the game, Lieutenant," she said.

He motioned down the hall. "I'll see you to your car, then," he said, and waited her to begin walking.

"It should be an interesting case," Vanessa said, walking beside him, thankful to be back on neutral ground.

"They always are, Ms. Tau," Barlot replied. "They always are."

* * *

Vanessa went on to complete a call on a new worker's compensation claimant, taking her statement about the lower back sprain she had incurred on the job. A late lunch was followed by an activity check on yet another worker's compensation, or WC, claimant, a metal worker recovering from surgery for a comminuted fracture of his left lower leg.

It was late afternoon, and she had no reason to return to the office. Her scheduled calls often kept her away from the office for days at a time, depending on where and how far she had to drive each day. Using her company-issued cell phone, she made her final call to her supervisor in Cincinnati, who informed her he had nothing hot on the night's agenda. She'd check her office e-mail with her laptop PC once she got home.

By 5:30 P.M. she was on Route 73, heading back into Oxford, where she shared a two-bedroom apartment with her roommate, Danielle Klein. Vanessa attended night classes for her master's degree in finance three times a week at Miami University. Danielle, or Dani, as she preferred, was a twenty-six-year-old double major, the first one in history, the second in sociology. Dani was a 4.0 student, and enjoyed the benefits of a full scholarship in both fields.

Vanessa arrived, parked the Blazer in the small lot behind the six-unit building on the corner of Spring and Beech streets, and went in, hanging her keys on the small rack tacked on the inside wall beside the door frame.

"Hey, Van," Dani called out, crossing from the kitchen in the back of the apartment to the small dining room. She carried her dinner, a Healthy Choice frozen meal, which she had just finished nuking in the microwave.

Dani was a pretty brunette, taller than Vanessa by two inches, with the slimness that came with distance-running, an activity Dani had been involved in since high school. She routinely ran half a dozen marathons each year, including both New York and Boston.

"Hey, yourself," Vanessa replied, dropping her purse beside her briefcase. She ambled into the dining room and cast an eye toward her roommate's dinner. She shook her head and walked into the kitchen, saying over her shoulder, "I don't know how you can eat those things."

"Mind over fat, girl, that's how," Dani said, blowing on a forkful of turkey-something. "And you'll be doing Bruno's again, I suppose," she added. Bruno's was an Oxford icon, a pizza parlor that had been around for decades, in the same hole-in-the-wall store on High Street, uptown. Its claim to fame was the olive oil–laden pies they made there.

Vanessa nodded as she opened the refrigerator door and took out a diet Coke. "Maybe, I don't know yet. I might amble over to the Res," meaning Shriver Center, what used to be called the old student Reservation building, over near the south quad. It had been nicknamed the "Res" for years, and the old name had stayed, even after the major renovations that turned the two-story building into a campus showplace.

She took a glass down from the cabinet next to the refrigerator, filled it with ice, and walked back out, joining Dani at the little round table. She held up the can, saluting her friend before starting to pour its contents into the glass. "Well, you'd better inhale that if you're going to make your class."

"I know," Dani replied around a mouthful. She swallowed quickly. "Landau'll have my ass if I'm late again. I don't know why I signed up for a night class, even if it is extra credit. It's not like I need more hours."

"Maybe eighteen credit hours during the week wasn't enough," Vanessa kidded. She took a sip, smiling as she looked back. "And they say we Orientals are perfectionists."

"You are, but the class is so damn interesting, and I'm late," Dani said in a rush, stuffing the last bite into her mouth. "Sorry," she apologized, pushing back from the table.

"It won't do any good to eat it that fast, you know that," Vanessa said, keeping her face serious.

"Yes, Mother," Dani teased, cleaning up after her hastened meal. Moving fast, she collected her backpack and jacket off the living-room couch. Her twenty-one-speed mountain bike was leaning against the wall just inside the door. She waved once and propped the door open with her hip so she could push the bike through. "See ya at nine, Van."

"I'll be here," Vanessa replied, and watched her out the door. She took a sip of her soda and looked around the apartment. It reflected their mutual tastes, with Dani's yuppielike leaning toward natural oak and basic solid colors offset by Vanessa's cultural background. There were some fine Oriental screens and pictures up, providing a small visual anchor to Vanessa's past.

Vietnam was a long time ago for her, both in time and in her memory. But she remembered what it had been like, despite the distance. Sometimes she missed it. One day, she thought, letting her emotions center inside. Someday, she added.

Vanessa rose from the table, and carrying her drink with her, walked into her bedroom and sat down at the desk there. She turned on her laptop PC, tapping into the office's system. After checking her e-mail, she started working on her claim file field reports. It'd been a typical day in her life so far.

September 8

Upham Hall, Miami University

He stood in the dark of the arch, just outside the yellow glow of the coach lamps that lit the curved walls. Without their intrusion he could make out the stars through the tops of the trees across the quad from Upham Hall.

His hand came up with the cigarette and paused, the slow-burning tip vibrating slightly. He focused his eyes on it, willing the minute twitching to stop. It slowed, then stopped altogether, and he smiled ruefully into the darkness.

"Big fucking deal, you can make your hand stop shaking," he said to no one. Professor William S. Landau took another drag, held it longer than he needed to, and exhaled slowly, blowing the smoke out in a thin, steady stream. It dissipated into the night.

He bent and tapped the still-burning tip against the flagstones of the terrace, tamping it out. Straightening, he held the stub with his index finger and thumb, and quickly flicked his middle finger across the burnt end, spilling the final shreds of tobacco out of the paper. He rolled the husk of paper into a tiny ball and slipped it into his pants pocket.

The entire act was done absently, without thought, an ingrained habit, learned years ago, and never forgotten, although the purpose for it was long since over. It had once been a small lesson in field craft, as in how not to leave a trail for the VC to find. It was called field-stripping your smokes. The cigarette itself was another habit, almost a relic: an unfiltered Camel, just like the fourpack he used to find in the box of C-Rations.

The cigarette was a killer, he knew, according to all the statistics. But he'd made it through Vietnam, so what's a little cancer now, he thought. The attitude marked him as a survivor, but he knew that, all too well.

It's getting worse, he told himself, then frowned, his eyes shutting tight for a few seconds. No, he thought too quickly. Let's not get into that now. Instead he forced his mind back into his lecture notes. Class started in ten minutes, and he welcomed it, as he always did. For the next hour and a half he would ramble to the two hundred students who had signed up to take his night lecture class. For them it would be history, verbal descriptions of things having little meaning to them, a generation removed.

For Landau it would be a perversion as he immersed himself back in the war, and the Highlands, and the times that were, indeed, changing for America then. But he wouldn't think about the names, the ones who hadn't come home. And he wouldn't think about the other thing. Especially not that.

He turned back into the arch and pulled open the heavy door. Making his way to the north end of the building, and the lecture hall on the far wing there, he walked with head down, concentrating on the old and worn blocks of brick-colored tile on the floor, keeping his eyes occupied. His brain he kept tuned to his presentation, but his subconscious kept at it, the part of it he couldn't control, not anymore. It remembered, like the humorless thing it was. It never forgot, not in twenty-five years. And it hadn't let him forget, either.

Landau wondered how the others were doing now, Linet, Perriman, Aceto, and the rest. Were they dealing with it as he was, which was basically by not dealing with it at all? Did they carry guilt the same way he did, a leaden, misshapen lump settled low inside, a cancerous thing insinuated through him, so entwined in his body and his brain that there was no way of ever removing it? He hadn't spoken to any of them since he'd flown back to Oakland in August 1970.

It was like yesterday to him.

*   *   *

The Fourth Division was standing down that late spring of '70, packing up to go home. They thought they had pulled it off, the fragging of the major. They'd looked over their shoulders for weeks after it happened, but no one came after them. It'd gone down as an ambush, just the way they had planned it. Carlos Madrid's arrest had given them all a scare, but Linet had taken care of that, too. Already he had begun to bury the deed deep in his mind, covering it over with other worries, other concerns.

Then came the day he came back from the PX to find two Military Police NCOs and an Army CID lieutenant waiting for him. They arrested him on the spot and drove him down to the chopper pad where they literally *threw* him onto a UH-1 H slick. He was flown out to Qui Nhon on the coast of the South China Sea, manacled, and placed in the stockade. The next day he was flown out again, this time on a big C-130, down to Cam Ranh Bay, where he was locked up in another stockade. All this time no one spoke to him, telling him why, but he knew.

They let him sweat for a whole day, alone, before a CID captain came in to see him—Captain Manos, dressed in the usual faded green jungle fatigues. Instead of a boonie hat, he wore a dark blue baseball cap. Fixed just below the crown were the letters U.S. in highly polished brass. Below that were the twin silver bars denoting his rank. The hat was the trademark of the Criminal Investigation Division. His greeting was direct and left no doubt that it was over, for all of them.

"Madrid, Archer, Madison, Roselli," Captain Manos said, taking a chair opposite Landau at the empty table in the small concrete block room. "Burris, Aceto, Perriman, Linet," he continued, his eyes boring straight into Landau, letting him know there was no mistake. "And finally, Private William S. Landau," he finished.

Landau felt the guilt drop over him like a heavy, dead chill.

Manos saw it in his eyes and smiled. "You thought you had it planned so well, didn't you?" The question was rhetorical. Manos obviously had all the answers. He shook his head. "It was Carlos Madrid," he began, and went on to tell the tale of the squad's undoing. It seemed pretty simple, when he was done. They'd considered the possibility, right up until Madrid hung himself in his jail cell. Or was supposed to have.

The investigation had speeded up after Madrid's confession. Captain Manos, given the case, quickly compiled more evidence, even though he and Captain Husta hadn't been able to find the VC weapons Madrid had described. Still, it seemed like enough. Manos reached out and touched all eight of them, locating and arresting them one by one. He had tried to break them down, but heavily coached and threatened by Jack Linet, they'd all held to the same story of denial.

Landau had resisted Manos's grilling as well as the rest, although he knew if the CID captain succeeded in making his case against them, death, if not life in prison, was imminent.

Then the Army had sprung the big surprise on them, really out of left field. They let them go, each of them. For the good of the service, they were told. They were never told the real reason. All the hoopla over their arrest, the threats of a general court-martial, all slammed to a halt. It left him confused, wary, and wondering, all at once.

He didn't care what the reasons for it were. Landau listened with the other seven as they were threatened again with court-martial, this time if they ever breathed a word about the incident to anyone, or ever saw each other again. An incident, they called it, he remembered, unable to shake the irony of the simplistic word. We *killed* a man, murdered him outright, and to the Army it was an *incident*. What it was, was another bit of insanity in an insane war. None of it made sense.

But one thing did, though, and that was Captain Manos's promise. He would find a way, he had told them. He made it clear that he knew what they had done, and that he would never give it up. Sooner or later, he had said, looking carefully at each of them, sooner or later, this would all be resolved. He would never forget them.

Nor was any further sense made of it when his tour finally ended, and he hitched a ride on a C-123 down to Saigon and boarded the stretched Douglas Super DC-8 at Tan Son Nhut. The Freedom Bird, they called it, the one flight every man and woman doing time in Vietnam dreamed of from day one. And he was on it, finally.

And the bitch of it, the absolute total mindblower of it all, was that he really *was* free. He had, they *all* had, committed murder and gotten away with it. It was amazing, but he was going home, with an honorable discharge and nothing to worry about.

That attitude lasted less than six months, once he was back in the World, safe again with his family in Bordentown, where he had grown up. He never talked about his tour, least of all the murder. It seemed easier to stamp it down, smother the entire lost year in some dark pit in his soul and keep it there. But it came out on its own, usually when he was alone, when his guard was down, then it was there, biting at him.

The emotional aftermath of the Vietnam War was given a new label, posttraumatic stress disorder, PTSD for short. Most vets had it, most vets handled it, and most vets assimilated back into the society that had sent them, some putting their lives back together painfully over the years. How it was handled varied widely amongst the millions of men and women who went, but almost all of them had it, to some degree.

Landau was no exception, but he carried two burdens. Guilt was the first, but it was augmented by something that made his guilt worse: cowardice. He had murdered a man, something that was not part of everyone else's tour of duty. He had gone along, hiding his cowardice in the herd frenzy of Linet and the others.

Could he have stopped them? The answer was lost to him, since he'd never made an attempt. He had swallowed his morality and hidden it behind a false bravado, and a rehearsal of imagined wrongs, directed at a man he barely knew, in truth. No, he hadn't stopped it. He had gone along, and when caught and accused of it, had expected to have to pay for it. But that hadn't happened. There had been no jail time, no judgment, though there certainly had been a verdict of sorts. But they let him go, and he had finally decided there had to have been a reason for that.

The answer was atonement. It was what made sense of it all to Landau, and it took him over a year to realize it. Even if it wasn't true, he grasped the idea, seeing it as a way for him to handle what was tearing him up inside. How to atone for it came fairly easy. He returned to Princeton, got his teaching degree, went on to a Ph.D., and began teaching history to young minds, the same age he was when he became a killer.

The choice of curriculum seemed more than appropriate, even though he was fully aware of the irony. He majored in U.S. history, and teaching it was what one who had failed to learn by it did. That he had failed was without doubt. It remained to be seen if he could make up for it in any way. This was to be his penance. Doomed to relive the era he had helped to create, he was also doomed, by choice, to teach it.

And it had worked, hadn't it, all these years? Sure it had, Landau finished the thought. Sure it had.

He pulled open the lecture-room door and stepped inside. He caught the eye of one of his grad assistants, who came over and nodded.

"All here, Professor," she said, indicating the filled seats in the amphitheater. Landau's U.S. History/Twentieth-Century American Warfare class was popular, especially his six-unit segment on the Vietnam War.

"Very well," he replied, giving her a quick smile. "Let's get to it." He strode down toward the podium, aware of the eyes upon him. He took his position behind it, adjusted the mike, and tapped it, the thumping returned from the ceiling-mounted speakers telling him it was on. He gazed out over the two hundred faces looking back.

"It's nice to see you all again," he began.

* * *

Aaron Longbaugh watched Landau from a seat in the back row, over on the right side of the hall. He'd been here before, and despite his age, didn't seem out of place in the crowd of younger faces. Older people often took college classes, and a quick look around the hall confirmed several others like him in attendance. No one gave him more than a cursory glance.

He sat quietly, apparently absorbed in Landau's presentation, letting the man's habits and mannerisms settle into his mind. It was part of the process, getting to know each man on the list before he killed him. He filtered out Landau's words, shutting out the sound as so much patter. How ironic that the seminar should be on Vietnam. Aaron controlled the anger that roiled beneath the surface, his eyes locked on Landau standing at the podium far below him.

Had Landau bothered to get to know his father before he murdered him? He thought not. Aaron had read all of it in the CID report, read Landau's own words as he and the rest tried to refute the accusations against them. Their collective denials sounded like a lame justification for what they had done. It didn't hide their guilt, in the end. The two investigating officers, Captains Husta and Manos, had been convinced the squad members had done the killing. Aaron knew it was true. Manos's and Husta's report was the foundation of his work.

Aaron subsequently spent a lot of time learning about each man on the squad, but not out of any curiosity about them. No, he took the time to learn who they were only because it was required for the job. To kill them the way he had started out to was to do so as a complete professional. Each man was a specific part of the overall mission he had set himself to complete.

Like a trained athlete he went over the scene of the projected shoot in his mind, replaying the specifics, reinforcing the act before he actually did it. He had learned to do it years ago when he worked for special operations. It was nothing more than a professional's technique, used to eliminate errors, perfection through repetition.

He let his mind's eye work on the image, and it came easily while Landau spoke.

* * *

Aaron lay in the orchard, lost in the mottled early morning shadows cast by the gnarled apple trees above him. The mild breeze coming from behind his left shoulder still carried some of the warmth of Indian Summer. This time he wore his complete Ghillie suit. The suit consisted of layers of long strips of forest-colored cloth, individually hand-sewn to a one-piece coverall. The finished garment, shaded in multiple greens and browns, effectively covered his entire body, breaking up and softening the human outline into something totally natural that seemingly belonged to the forest.

Beneath him was a thinly padded mat in a matching camouflage print. His body was a small hump at the base of a tree. As always the exposed parts of his face and hands were covered with matching shades of camouflage stick. He rested with elbows on the camouflaged ground-cover cloth beneath him, eyes to the rubber sockets of the 20X60 mm Zeiss binoculars. The German-manufactured binoculars were mechanically stabilized, providing a remarkably clear and vibration-free image at that distance. Beside him the 40-XB rested on its bipod, barrel canted upward slightly.

Landau's house seemed quiet, as expected. It was barely seven in the morning, and the early light, coming from his left, illuminated the northern exposure of the house and the killing zone clearly. It was a weekday morning, and Landau, per his schedule, would drive in to the campus early. Once there he would begin his day by spending three hours in his office on the third floor.

Landau's home was a modest three-bedroom brick ranch, built to last in the late fifties. A large oak stood in the front lawn, shading that side of the structure, while half a dozen Italian cypress trees lined the concrete drive leading to the detached garage on the north side. The construction of the house was solid, as they had meant it to be. Landau lived there alone. No family, no live-in, no pets.

He had considered doing the shot on the campus, but there simply hadn't been any convenient positions to set up a successful blind. The Miami campus was thickly wooded in spots, with too many buildings that drastically reduced the clear distance for the shot. The reduced range also made a successful escape and evasion difficult.

No, Landau's house was the better choice. The best feature was its isolation. Route 73 was a long, hilly two-lane blacktop that ran for miles before entering the east side of the city. The few homes along the roadway were set well back from its edge, some as far back as a hundred yards or more. Lot sizes ran to four or more acres, with lots of open space between homes. Landau's house was one of these. For the owner it offered some seclusion, yet ready access to the campus and town. But those same features confirmed Landau's imminent demise.

It was the details, Aaron thought, moving the binoculars a bit. The garage set it up, actually. It stood alone, beside and slightly beyond the back of the house. A long concrete driveway connected the garage to the highway. There was a side door, but by habit Landau always left by the front door, locking it behind him before passing down the length of the house and turning the corner to walk to the garage.

He lowered the glasses and checked the time. A few more minutes, he thought, and put the binoculars down. He picked up the rifle, set it down before him, and snuggled into the butt stock, right elbow cocked, his hand back, supporting the toe of the butt. He found his spot weld, flipped the safety off, and waited, both eyes open, watching. The scope was run up to nine power, and he readjusted to the difference in magnification settings between it and the binoculars. He had set the external cam already for the distance, dialing in the needed trajectory for the 173-grain match-grade bullet. He was ready.

The door opened and Landau appeared. Aaron picked up his magnified image easily, tracking him as he stepped down the single step to the sidewalk. His breathing had been regularly spaced in anticipation of his target.

The shot whacked concussively, the rifle punching back in recoil barely felt, and his eye came back to the scope, looking for the target, knowing the shot was good. It punctured Landau's chest under his left nipple and tore a long hole straight through the lung's lower lobe. It yawed up and to the right, still spinning about its axis at tremendous speed, tumbling around until it was base-first, ripped out of Landau's ribcage behind the arm, cutting through the jacket's sleeve, and whacked into the thick brick wall of the house.

Landau felt the impact as a blinding, numbing, smashing sensation, stunning his diaphragm. He took a hesitant, staggering step, then dropped in a jarring heap to a sitting position, his back to the porch step. The pain hit, bone deep, a hot, burning sensation that spread across his chest.

He tried to raise his left hand to his side, but through the haze of pain saw his hand lying uselessly beside him, palm out. His entire arm was numb with heat. Slowly, his head bent as he struggled to make his diaphragm work, to drag in a breath, and saw the blood welling on his shirtfront, and the torn fabric from the bullet's entrance. He knew he was mortally hurt, but his brain struggled with the deluge of alarms flooding in. His other arm pressed down, palm flat to the concrete, supporting him, and began to push, seemingly moving by its own volition. "Get . . . up," he gasped to himself, trying to fight the cascading pain. "Got to . . . get . . . up . . ."

Aaron gauged the results of the first shot. Landau was down, but definitely not out. He chambered another round and moved slightly, bringing the crosshairs to his face, noticing Landau's head was tilted downward, as if he was looking for something, and his right arm was down, pushing, beginning to lever his body upward.

He settled the intersection of the fine wires on the bridge of Landau's nose, allowing for the tilt of his head, right through the skull. The point of impact was a two-inch circle.

The second shot cracked flatly over the long distance and struck half an inch off target, near the inside corner of Landau's right eye, smashing through his sinuses, transecting the base of the brain, and ripping into the medulla oblongata, the brain stem, obliterating it in spectacular fashion. Three-quarters of Landau's head exploded, most of the cranial contents spray patterning across the red brick and white screen door. His face was the only part left, and with nothing behind it, tilted back on neck muscles made rigid from traumatic shock to leave his sightless eyes staring up at the clear blue of the morning.

Aaron observed the results of the second shot with professional satisfaction.

"That's seven," he said quietly, and prepared to leave. The vibrations he felt inside, the tightness in his stomach, were the results of the adrenaline bleeding off, nothing more. "That's it," he said aloud, and pushed up.

The body on the stoop settled a bit, while the dark pool beneath it spread without a sound. . . .

He came out of his reverie to the sound of Landau's voice. The image of his intended target's imagined death was crystal clear. It wasn't the first time he had thought about it. There was nothing to change, either. It felt right, all the details as he expected them to happen.

And it will happen, he thought. He had already made it happen with Perriman, Roselli, Archer, and Linet. Similar images had included Aceto and Burris, though other fates had decided their demise. The reality of each shooting was the physical manifestation of his skill. The military had taught him well, and the irony of using that blooded experience was a bittersweet thing to him.

The other matter bothered him, though, and would have to be dealt with. The lawsuit had come at exactly the wrong moment. It wasn't the first time he had been involved in litigation as a result of his day job, as he often thought of it. He knew how the process worked, though. He had plenty of time before the requirements of the suit would affect him. The intricacies of the wrongful death litigation would take months, leaving him with a comfortable window in which to work. The Landau hit would occur as planned, all in order. He'd be long gone before any problems with the lawsuit arose. He was too close to resolving his life's work to allow any outside forces to stop him.

The thought brought up the other variation. Michael Madison, living almost next door in Indiana, remained. Aaron had taken the Westport PD position because of the city's proximity to his final two targets. It was the same situation he'd been presented with in the beginning, with Paul Roselli on Long Island and Louis Archer in New York. There he had been able to score twice before moving on. It hadn't really mattered which one he started with.

Now he had the reverse situation. There was an importance in the exact manner he ended it. One of them should know who he was, and what had happened to the others. And by rights they should go in a particular order, Aaron believed. He had spent considerable time already, stalking Madison, observing his daily routines, where he lived and worked, finding out about the man. Aaron had decided on the details of that shoot, too, playing and replaying each part, each movement in his mind exactly as he had just done with Landau.

The choice of the last target was biased toward the professor. Bill Landau had always seemed a cut above the others, despite being just a squad member. Jack Linet had been their leader, but in rank and experience only, Aaron had decided. Landau had the education, and in that respect was more worldly than the others. That he had ended up actually doing something positive with his life had come as no surprise. Most of the others had been born losers, and stayed that way.

He would have to decide soon. His participation as a defendant in the lawsuit did add a factor that had to be dealt with. Even though there was no immediate danger to him, there would be background checks into the professional careers and private lives of all the defendants. He couldn't stop it, but he would have to be careful when people started looking. His record looked good, but it was possible to discover that it was all fabricated. He had counted on no one even bothering to check on his credentials. It had been the one risk to his mission that he had always lived with. So far he had managed to preserve the secret of his true identity. The one other time he had been caught up in a lawsuit, he had managed to slip away before his background had been checked. He would simply have to do the same thing here.

Aaron checked his watch, closed the notebook he had been unconsciously jotting in, and got up to leave. He had a few hours before the shift change. He let himself out through the door quietly, not looking back, while Landau continued speaking behind him. The door hissed closed, abruptly cutting off the sound of his voice, the thumping of the door echoing in the small lobby.

By then Aaron was gone, into the night.

September 9

Westport, Ohio

Vanessa arrived a little past nine in the morning and immediately went to Chief Tusca's office, as arranged. She wore a light blue blouse, buttoned to the neck, and a tan pants suit. Her long hair was pulled back into a ponytail, and she wore stylish walking shoes, her normal footwear. Adjusters spent long hours on their feet, and today promised to be no exception.

The secretary ushered her into the chief's office, and Tusca rose to meet her from behind his desk, his hand outstretched in greeting.

"Ms. Tau," he said, taking her hand and directing her to one of the chairs facing his desk.

She accepted the seat, and they exchanged quick pleasantries. Vanessa kept her briefcase beside her on the floor.

Chief Tusca checked his wrist and said, "Sergeant Samm will be here any minute. I called him last night to tell him about the meeting."

Vanessa began to acknowledge him when the secretary stepped into the office. "Excuse me, Chief," she interrupted, "Sergeant Samm is outside."

"Speak of the devil," Tusca quipped, and strode over to the door. "Nathan," he called out, "would you come in here for a minute?"

Vanessa rose to meet him and paused, taken by the tall officer who walked in. For a moment she thought he was Lieutenant Barlot, so similar in height and physique was he to the HRG leader.

Sergeant Samm's skin color was actually medium brown, and he had a handsome, mustached face that looked back with a mild smile tugging at the corner of his mouth. His dark eyes glimmered underneath long lashes, and his hair, what she could see of it, was close-cropped along the sides.

He was five feet ten inches tall, with a medium build and flat stomach. Vanessa noticed the fabric of his sleeves was tight across his arms, visual proof he kept himself in good shape.

Vanessa smiled and put out her hand. "Officer Samm, my pleasure," she said.

His eyes swept quickly over her, a rapid appraisal. Then he returned her handshake and smile. "*Chao, co, manh yoi' comh?*"

The traditional morning greeting in Vietnamese took her completely by surprise, and her interest in the man took an immediate upswing. She slowly smiled. Still holding his hand, she said, "*Toi manh yoi', camh oung?*"

He answered her in English. "I'm fine, and it's a pleasure to meet you." He released her hand, his brief smile abruptly fading. "You're about to ask the obvious," he said, "right?"

She nodded. "Forgive me for being taken aback," Vanessa said. "It's not often I'm greeted in Vietnamese. Most people don't even know what I am to begin with, but you . . ."

Chief Tusca answered for him. "Nathan is fluent in several languages," he said.

Nathan waved her back to the chair, which she took. "They're sort of a hobby of mine," he explained. "I found an affinity for them in high school and carried it into the service. I know Korean, Spanish, and Polish, with a touch of Farsi in there, besides Vietnamese."

"And how did you know I was Vietnamese?" she asked.

"Bone structure," he said simply. "No offense, but Vietnamese are finer-boned than, say, Koreans, who tend to have broader features, and are usually physically taller. Japanese seem to be darker, and again, a little taller. It wasn't a guess, actually," he admitted, "I did know your name, too."

She eyed him with a bit more intensity. There was something about him, a self-control that pleased but intrigued her, at the same time. "Would you have known my background without my name first?"

He regarded her a moment, with that same crooked smile. "What do you think?" he replied.

"I think we need to start calling each other by our first names," she answered. "Vanessa's fine with me."

"Sounds good," he said. "You can call me Nathan, or Nate. I'm not particular."

"Well," she said, turning the conversation back to business, "looks like we'll be working together on this shooting case for a while. Should we be going?"

"Absolutely," he answered. "The chief says you want to see where it went down?"

"If you would," she said. "I've got to include the physical description of the location and get the time line of the events down for my field report. If we have to bring in an expert on procedures later on, it'll be easier for him."

"Understood," Nathan said. "I'll try to keep this interesting for you. Police work can be boring sometimes."

She looked at him for a second. "I doubt that anything about you is boring," she said.

He didn't reply, but indicated her briefcase. "We'd best be going," he said, then, to the chief, "This'll probably take a couple of hours, and we've got that debriefing on the situation yesterday scheduled for two o'clock?"

"OK, then," the chief said. "I'll speak with you two later."

She left with Nathan, and as they walked down the hallway in the municipal building, he asked, "Do you want to ride with me or take your own vehicle and follow me out?"

"Actually, I've got other calls after this. I'll follow, if that's all right."

He held the glass door to the parking lot open for her and pointed toward a white Ford LTD patrol car parked near the entrance. "I'm right there. I'll wait for you to join up. It'll take about fifteen minutes to get to the mall," he said.

"I'm parked around the corner," she said. "It's a medium blue Blazer."

"I know," he said, and left her there as he walked to the cruiser.

She turned toward her truck, wondering. How did he know? she thought. Officer Samm was a walking mystery, at the moment. But an attractive one, she added, unlocking her car door. She suppressed the smile as she started up and drove after him.

* * *

Carrollton Hills Mall reflected the current notion that bigger was better, but monstrous was better still. The mall was a huge Y-shaped structure, each arm like a letter S, four stories of fashion, fun, and food, joined at a hub in the center that contained a respectably sized indoor theme park that rose through all four stories. Fast food courts radiated off the park on each level, while the center of each floor was open from floor to ceiling, a veritable jungle of plants, trees, waterfalls, and running streams providing a stunning vista of ersatz Brazilian rain forest meandering the length of each wing.

Nathan turned in near the end of one of the huge wings and into the parking lot.

He pulled the cruiser into an empty space and waited while Vanessa eased in alongside him. He was waiting for her when she climbed out of the Blazer.

Nathan pointed back toward the parkway. "The suspect, Bennet, came in from this side, in the victim's car. He stopped right about there," he finished, pointing to a spot near the curb.

Vanessa nodded once. "I read the field report last night," she said. "He dragged the car owner into the entrance over there, didn't he?"

Nathan stood looking down at her, his face serious. "Yeah, I don't know why he held on to her. I guess because she fought him when he first grabbed her back in Westport." He shook his head. "You don't know why a suspect will do what he does, sometimes. Bennet was armed, he could have shot her right there, but didn't. Instead, he struggled with her, raised enough fuss so that one of several witnesses called 911 on her cell phone, and the chase, as they say, was on."

Nathan crooked an elbow up, leaning against the top of his cruiser. "If we'd had a chopper maybe we could have stopped him out on I-75. The highway patrol's bird was involved with a pileup north of Dayton and couldn't get down here quick enough." He looked around, taking it in, remembering. "As it was, we didn't have enough ground units up ahead we could have used to block him. Let's go inside," he said. "I'll show you how it finished up."

"All right," Vanessa said, and fell in beside him. She glanced over at him and said, "Your Lieutenant Barlot seems very intense about his job."

"You have to understand about Dean," Nathan said. "He works under double pressure, being the officer in command of the tactical unit, and being black. It means a lot to have the position he has, and he didn't get it because of some affirmative-action requirement. He earned it, all the way, just like the rest of us on the team. He's one hell of a shot," Nathan said, and his eyes sparkled a bit. "He's almost as good as I am. Dean's worked on SWAT and tactical teams for years. His background credentials are impressive. I've seen a lot of people in this business, and he's one of the best."

She slowed down, then stopped, turning to face him. "He sounds like a tough boss to work for."

Nathan looked back at her with an odd expression, a mixture of amusement and curiosity. "Tough is the only way to be when you consider the stakes involved." He held his look. "It's simple, really. When we do it wrong, somebody may die. When we do it right," and he held her with his eyes, "somebody may still die."

Vanessa returned his gaze for a long count. Then she set her briefcase down, clasped both hands close to her chest, and bowed slightly. "I understand," she said, and straightened.

His vision shifted, giving her a quick but close onceover, top to bottom, and back again, just like back at the station.

She allowed his inspection of her to take place. She'd expected it, actually, the thought also surprising her a bit. What's going on? she said to herself. You're getting awfully forward, girl.

She picked up her briefcase and started back toward the entrance. Nathan walked along beside her. "Why Vietnamese?" she asked suddenly, changing the subject. "I mean, of all the Oriental languages you could have chosen, why that one?"

"I had a cousin," he said, looking ahead, "Freddy. My mom's older sister's son." She heard the change in his tone as his voice grew softer. It was the first overt change from his slightly aloof manner with her.

"He was ten years older than me, but we were pretty close. Anyway, he was Air Force, crewed on an RB-66. That's a big twin-engine jet bomber."

Now she was positive what he was going to say, but she let him continue.

"He was shot down over Haiphong in 1971." He glanced sideways at her. "It was a long time ago, but I've had an interest in Vietnam ever since. It just seemed to come together, what with the way languages come to me. A couple of us in the department lost family in the war."

He brightened. "So, and if it's not being too forward, what about you? You still carry a trace of accent about you, but there's an awful lot of Ohio in there."

"Oh, you mean my valley speak?" she kidded, deliberately ending with a rapid-fire upward lilt. It brought a smile from Nathan.

That's a positive sign, she thought to herself. Aloud, she continued. "We came over in 1976 from Cambodia. My father got us out of Vietnam in '75, after the fall, and we spent a year in the relocation camp before we could get over here." She told it easily, without regrets. It was the way she was used to explaining it to people. She kept the special emotions inside, rarely letting them out. "The rest is hard work and holding on to a dream. I'm still working on that. But you're right," she added, "about family loss, and the war. It was a long time ago. You just don't forget it, not when it's that close. I know."

"Nor should you," he agreed. His reply surprised her.

They neared the bank of tall glass doors leading into the mall. As she slowed down, Nathan leaned over and pulled one of them open for her.

"Thank you," she said automatically, stepping in ahead of him. He followed and the door closed behind them. They paused together, looking around. He pointed off to their right, all business again.

"Bennet dragged her that way, flashing the gun. That's where the mall security guard tried to stop him. He didn't make it."

Vanessa knew that. The suspect, armed with a semiautomatic pistol, had shot the guard three times, killing him instantly. It also sent everyone within hearing to the floor, screaming. Bennet apparently panicked even more then.

They continued walking, slower now as Nathan described the situation to her, his hands pointing out locations and positions.

"The shooting was his biggest mistake. There wasn't any doubt later on what he was capable of. He took Mrs. Avery into Wild

Lives over there, and ended up barricaded inside with a dozen hostages, including Avery."

They were opposite the store now, which retailed shirts, backpacks, and home decorations, all with animal themes. The front of the store was almost completely open, a twenty-two-foot-high expanse of it. Imitation rock walls served to frame both sides of the entrance, and the interior was designed to mimic the look of a tropical jungle.

"You can see the problem," Nathan said. "No straight aisles, nothing that open. The shelves and clothing carousels are scattered around the floor, some free-standing, some in groups along the walls. Those rock pillars go all the way up to the ceiling, and they're pretty solid. They give a lot of cover. Bennet had all of the hostages down on the floor in the back, almost wedged around him. He had dropped the security chain wall down over the front of the store, which kept people out, but also kept him in. He wasn't going anywhere. But he had already killed someone, and he had plenty of ammo, as far as we knew."

Nathan's eyes were moving, constantly taking in everything going on around them, and for some distance down the length of the wing of the mall they stood in.

Vanessa spoke up. "He had some sort of military gun, didn't he?"

Nathan shook his head. "No, that's not right. He had a target pistol, what they call a race gun, built on a high-capacity frame. It could hold twenty rounds when fully loaded, and it was. That's why he had seventeen shots left. That pistol was a three-thousand-dollar special custom piece, a hot gun, which Bennet bought for two hundred dollars on the black market. It was one of twenty that had been stolen the month before from a gun club in Indianapolis. The Feds tracked the gun back and rolled up the guys who had ripped it off."

"So it was an assault weapon," she said, and was surprised when he laughed. The sound was short, without humor.

"I see you read the Dayton reporter's description of this," he said. "That's a typical media screwup, and a hot button for me," he continued. "That was no assault weapon, since there isn't any such thing. It had more than the magic ten rounds mandated by the

Crime Bill, plus it was built on what is called the Government Model. Because of that, the reporter decided to perpetuate the media myth, and called it something it wasn't. I guess he didn't know enough about guns."

Vanessa heard the condescension in his tone, but let it go. She didn't feel like getting into an argument over gun control at the moment. She stepped a few paces away and did a slow turn, taking in the layout.

Nathan pointed up at the second level. "I was inside the movie theater lobby up there," he explained. "Bennet had barricaded the back service door, so we couldn't get in that way. We tried the ceiling crawl space, but it wasn't deep enough over the store for us to get there. Mall security kept track of Bennet and the hostages on the video cameras in the ceiling, so we knew where he was the whole time."

"But you had the negotiators here, too, didn't you?" she asked.

"They were here," he concurred, and he shrugged a little. "But Bennet had made up his mind before they started to talk to him. I guess killing the guard started it. It happens that way sometimes . . ." he trailed off.

"You're talking about the first-blood syndrome, aren't you?" Vanessa asked.

He nodded. "It sounds too easy to say it, but that's how it goes with some of them. Once they've pulled the trigger, or cut someone, or beaten in somebody's head, they change, just that fast." He snapped his fingers quickly to emphasize his point. "It becomes easier for them. Bennet was no exception. He wanted to kill another one."

"And you stopped him," Vanessa said.

He turned his head to look down at her, fixing her with a calm look. His face was benign, but she saw something move deep in his dark eyes. "Let's get something straight," he began, holding her eyes with his. "I didn't come here to kill anyone. A situation developed, and I'm trained to handle it, just as every member on the team is. We practice to pull that trigger one time, to put the round exactly where it has to go to stop the assailant. It's a Catch-22 deal," he continued, without looking away. "Working a special tactics team, being a long gun shooter, a superior marksman, is the only job where you rehearse how to stop a man with one shot. Sometimes that means having to kill, but you'll never hear anyone on a tactical team testify to that. We train to stop, period. Immediate incapacitation. But inside, you know what that can really mean. Then you hope like hell you never have to. But if it becomes necessary, you do it. Without hesitation, Vanessa, but you do it. It's the last option, the very last chance. Clear?"

She broke contact first, feeling the heat on her face. "I'm sorry," she said slowly, wondering how she had managed to get off on the wrong foot with this man. "I didn't mean to imply that you had . . ." she struggled with the words, "had *murdered* Bennet. I think I understand why it happens sometimes. I really do. I've handled a lot of police liability cases, OK? I know this happens. It's not pleasant, but it happens."

Nathan's face softened, and his eyes seemed to follow. "It's a job, Vanessa, only that. It takes a certain mindset to do it, and there is a great deal of satisfaction in doing it right. When you have this kind of responsibility, the lives of real people in your hands, you have to feel it, here," he said, his fingers thumping the center of his chest lightly.

"You like it," she said, and instantly knew it had come out wrong.

Nathan studied her with narrowed eyes for a moment. She felt uncomfortable in his unwavering gaze, and her eyes almost faltered and looked away, but she held them on his.

"Look—" she started to say, when he interrupted her.

"Yes, I like it," he said, "but maybe not for the reason you think. I like it because of who I am, and what I can do. It's a special accomplishment, Vanessa, an exacting skill. You have to be good enough to put a small particle of metal into a hole the width of your finger, and you have to be able to do it on demand." He held her attention. "That hole is going to appear in the body of another human being, and you're doing it to stop that person, to keep him from hurting someone else. It takes an ego, sure, no question about it. You have to be cocky and sure of yourself. A sniper is the best, the absolute best there is in his trade. He has to be."

Now his eyes softened for the first time. "Because if he's not, people will die, the wrong people."

She nodded her understanding. It was obvious he felt a special pride in his profession, and she was chagrined that he thought she had challenged him on it. This wasn't going the way she had imagined it would, and that bothered her, too.

She set her briefcase down and sat down on a nearby bench. Nathan took a few steps over to stand beside her. She looked up at him, and let her belief in herself, and in her desire to do the best job for her insured, overshadow other concerns. Vanessa indicated the empty space beside her, and said, "Please."

He sat down next to her, still a head taller than she. Then he surprised her by stating what she was about to say.

"We've gotten off to a bad start, I think," he said.

Vanessa nodded vigorously. "We seem to," she replied. "It wasn't my intent to put you on the defensive. I do this for a living, the same as you. I've seen enough police cases to know that you guys do a great job, and get almost no credit for it."

He nodded. "True enough," he said. "But I'm the one who should be apologizing. I take my job pretty seriously, too, especially after a situation like this, where people died."

Vanessa wondered what shoppers passing by thought of the two of them, the short Oriental lady and the tall black cop sitting together. It might have looked odd, but she didn't care.

"This is great," she said. "I've known you for an hour or so, and already we've apologized to each other half a dozen times." She favored him with one of her brightest smiles, and held out her hand. "Friends?"

For the first time that morning, Nathan genuinely returned her smile. "Friends, definitely," he said. "Care to start again?" He didn't wait for an answer, but offered her his large hand. "Hi. I'm Sergeant Nathan Samm."

Vanessa took his hand firmly. "Vanessa Tau, Trans Patriot Insurance. I'm one of the good guys, believe it or not."

"I am, too," he said. He dropped her hand and settled back into the seat.

Vanessa took a breath, glad the awkwardness was over between them. She turned her attention back to their purpose for being there. "Do you want to continue with this?"

"No problem," he said, twisting around slightly, and just like that the detached aloofness was back. The change in his manner caught her up short, seeing how quickly the personable side of him disappeared, replaced by the professional. It was as if he had thrown a tiny switch and now was all business once again.

"My spotter, Corporal Jerry Laird, and I were in the lobby of that movie theater up there," Nathan said. "We had a pretty good view down over the glass railing into Wild Lives, and Bennet. The theater people had a small cherrypicker cart in there. They'd been using it to hang some big posters along the lobby walls. We used it as a gun platform."

He stood and pointed down to a bank of escalators rising slowly through the suspended foliage to the second floor. "Let's go upstairs, and I'll show you the setup."

Vanessa rose and walked beside him, listening as he continued his replay.

"The problem was, we had the security fence in the way," he said as they stepped up onto the rising staircase. He turned sideways and rode up that way, talking as they went. "If we had to take a shot, it had to be between the open spaces of the links and crossbars."

They emerged onto the second floor, which repeated the rockplanter dividers of the main floor. The sound of gently rushing water as it spilled down the raised median between the lush plants echoed slightly off the high walls. Canned music drifted overhead. Nathan walked with her toward the movie theater entrance. Shoppers continued to stroll by, most of them ignoring Nathan and Vanessa.

They stopped in front of the theater's ticket sales office, a circular glass-sided structure with six separate windows. Vanessa gazed down toward Wild Lives and tried to place the hostages according to the report. "You said you and Corporal Lanier were on a raised platform?"

Nathan pointed out the spot inside the lobby, off to one side. "Yeah, right over there," he said. "We had the cherrypicker up about ten feet in the air, far enough back in the shadows so that it was difficult to see us, but high enough to clear the top of the guard rail."

Vanessa walked over to the rail, a clear glass affair four feet tall, topped with a solid brass runner six inches wide, and about as deep. She looked down at where the suspect had held the hostages in the back of the store. She could see customers and shoppers clearly as they browsed or stood patiently before one of several registers scattered about the floor. She wondered if any of them realized what had happened there just a few months before.

"But Bennet was making demands, wasn't he, threatening to kill the hostages?" she said.

Nathan came up beside her and looked down. "The situation was deteriorating quickly. Bennet was in the back, just over there," he said, pointing at the spot. "He stayed pretty much behind that rock outcropping, waving the gun around."

"When was the decision made to shoot?" she asked.

"The decision had already been made, and the order given, a few minutes before I took the shot," he said. "Lieutenant Barlot called it. He saw how the situation was going and knew the negotiators were losing Bennet. He was over the top, and all the indications were he was going to execute one of the hostages. Anyway, the lieutenant realized we were down to the wire and gave the order." He looked at her. "Let's go back downstairs," he said, and headed for the escalator. Soon they were back at their initial point across from the store again.

"You have to read people in this line of work," he began, explaining it to her with care. "A police sharpshooter can't fire without authorization. We don't enjoy the luxury of the battlefield, where every hostile target is free to take."

She hung on his words, feeling his calm through his voice. He sounded completely detached from the scene, but not, both at the same time. It was a curious mix, and made her wonder even more about the temperament of men like him.

"I know about the liability problems," she said. "That's what we deal with all the time."

He nodded, the broad flat brim of his campaign hat accentuating the movement. "That's part of it, sure," he replied, glad she was following his replay. "You've got to worry about overpenetration, and whether a civilian will be hit by your shot." He waved his hand around, including the entire mall. "In a place like this, you have to know exactly where that bullet's going to go before you send it."

His eyes returned to hers. "But more important, and this is the big one, Vanessa, before you shoot, you have to be convinced that it is, without any doubt, the last resort. There simply is no time left for any equivocation. It's one shot," he said, "one chance to end it, and it has to be right on."

She realized in that instant the depth of Nathan's commitment to his job and his profession. She felt a strange comfort from the feeling it left with her. "And that's how it was here," she said, meaning it as a question, but it came out as a statement. The outcome of Nathan's single shot had long since been concluded.

"Yes, it was," he said, then continued. "Bennet had reached the end of his string, and the negotiators had lost him. He was out of control, screaming at them through the security fence and the cellular phone they'd been talking to him on. Then he made the move that resolved it. He reached down and dragged up one of the hostages—"

"That would have been Jim Myles, one of the store clerks," Vanessa interrupted. Myles was a nineteen-year-old cashier working part-time in the store. It was his misfortune to have been there that day.

"That's the guy," Nathan concurred. "Bennet jerked him up to his feet, still profile to us, almost completely hidden behind the column. He brought the pistol up and jammed it against Myles's head. It happened in a few seconds. His intention was clear.

"Jerry was watching through the spotting scope, and just as Bennet shoved the muzzle against the back of Myles's head, he shifted forward a few inches. The move pulled Bennet forward, too, enough to clear the column. I had him in the scope, and there was no choice then. It had to be a brain shot, as he had the gun against Myles. There was no one beyond them, no overpenetration problem. In that circumstance what you want is instant incapacitation."

He stopped for a moment, gazing across at the store, remembering. Vanessa could see his face reflect the pictures his mind gave him. "That's when he tried to do it, and when Jerry saw it.

Bennet's finger pressed against the trigger. But he had been play-ing with the safety before, pushing it on and off, over and over again. I could actually see the movement, and Jerry almost shouted out. 'The safety's on!' he said, and I saw it, too. Bennet had flipped the safety on while playing with it, and the gun wouldn't fire. He froze, just for a split second, and that's when I took the shot."

He turned his face toward Vanessa. "Right here," he said, touch-ing his index finger to the side of his head, just above his right ear.

"But wasn't that risky?" Vanessa asked. "Couldn't Bennet's fin-ger have twitched on the trigger?"

Nathan shook his head. "That's a good bit of fiction, but it doesn't happen that way in the real world. A head shot will literally explode the cranial cavity in about one-half-millionth of a second. That's faster than the brain sends messages down the same route. I knew Bennet would be stopped instantly."

Vanessa was quiet for a few moments. Nathan had described it calmly, but she had seen death before. She had been there when the bodies were loaded into the ambulances. Still, his detailed ac-count affected her, reinforcing her opinion of the grave difficulties of his occupation. A person had died inside that store, but in the end, other people had lived, too.

"I can't imagine doing what you do," she said, meaning it as the compliment it was. She held police officers in high regard. Nathan Samm was turning out to be no exception. "How do you handle it?" she added, not trying to be facetious. "I mean, the responsibil-ity you have, the . . ." she searched for the right word, and he bailed her out.

"It's a cliché," he said calmly, looking away from her. "Fiction would have you believe the marksman is supposed to agonize over his actions, the decision to kill a man."

She was surprised by his coolness, and crossed her arms. "And you don't?" she asked.

"Never," he replied. "Not with the first one, not with our bad guy here, either. It's a mindset, Vanessa," he said. "Call it a skill, or mental preparation, whatever you like. To do this job you *must* im-merse your mind in the task. Don't misunderstand me," he said quickly, seeing the reaction forming on her face, "people don't stop being human and turn into paper targets. You know what they are." His voice took on a measured cadence, and Vanessa felt drawn into his concentration. "The entire time you have your sights locked on, you know," he added softly. "That's a life out there, and with just a few grains of metal you can remove him from consciousness forever."

He pointed at the storefront. "You rationalize it at a level I can't really identify for you," he said. "What I can tell you is that not everyone can do this job." He smiled briefly. "But each of us is capable of doing it. I've seen plenty of what one human can do to another. The extremes would amaze you, and frighten you to death."

Vanessa seemed to be considering his words. "And you're obviously one of those who can."

He tipped his head in acknowledgment. "Yes, ma'am," he replied. "Sometimes it's necessary. Is there anything else you'd like to see?"

She looked around and answered, "No, I don't think so. I can incorporate all of this into my writeup. The plan view and photos in the police report were detailed enough to help fill out the descriptions." She looked up at him. "I appreciate your taking the time to cover this with me. It clears up the questions I had."

"No problem," he said. "So you do this sort of thing a lot, walk the ground like this?"

"If I can," Vanessa said. "It helps to see where claims happened, especially serious ones like this. As I said, you can focus on the details, and then there's that touch of reality. Claims are real, and what happens to the people involved is more than just words on a piece of paper, or a fax. It's something I try to keep in mind when handling the file."

"So what happens now with the lawsuit?" he asked.

"The usual preliminaries," Vanessa said. "Attorney Gabel will file his notice of appearance on behalf of all of the named defendants, then he'll file an answer to the complaint. That's all pretty stock. He'll have copies of everything I get from you and the PD. It'll help him lay out his strategy." She paused for a moment. "At some point, probably in a few days, maybe a week, Gabel will want to talk with all of you, to get your perspective on the shooting."

"You mean to see if all of our stories are straight?" Nathan replied.

Vanessa caught the tone in his voice. "No, not quite. It isn't our intent to see that you all tell it the same way. Gabel, as *your* attorney, not TPI's, needs to know each one of you. He'll want to find out how you speak, present yourselves, whether you get shaken on cross-examination, how you may do when your depositions are taken. At some point he may want to see your personnel files, track your backgrounds, things like that. What he's looking for is anything that will bolster the defense's position, and anything adverse that the plaintiff's attorney might be able to use against us."

Nathan seemed concerned. "What kind of things?" he asked.

"Oh, like a history of excessive force, or a disciplinary problem, whatever. If it can be used against you or any of the other officers, to attack your credibility, we need to know about it and plan how to defeat it, or not worry about it, or keep it excluded from the case."

He was quiet for a moment, taking in her reply. "And this is normal routine," he said, "checking into our backgrounds?"

She eyed him, wondering about his questions. "Sure it is. You don't have any skeletons in your closet, do you?" Vanessa asked with a grin.

"None that I know of," Nathan replied, then asked another question. "When will all this work start up?"

"Probably any time," she answered. "Gabel sets his own pace on cases like this. The suit is in U.S. district court, and we'll abide by their rules of procedure. Still, it will take some time. Background checks are routine, and usually done early on. He'll be doing the same thing with Bennet, through discovery. He'll draft a series of requests for production and interrogatories, all aimed at finding out everything he can about Bennet's life all the way back to the womb. And from what I've seen so far, there's a possibility a motion to dismiss may be granted. The facts so far seem to support the defense's side. The plaintiff's estate has included civil-rights violations. If we can show there's no basis in fact for those allegations, we may get them dismissed from the overall suit. That would knock a big hole in their case."

Nathan considered her last words. "So you think there's a

chance Gabel may get this whole thing dismissed?"

She nodded. "There's always a chance for that. I'd say the chances right now are better than even. We'll know more about that after discovery's run a little longer."

She saw relief on Nathan's face. "I know," she said, "you'd rather not have to go through a trial. Most people feel the same way."

"If it happens that way, yes, I'd prefer it," he said. "All of us would. We don't need the exposure of something like this."

Vanessa nodded again. "No one wants adverse publicity."

Nathan shook his head negatively. "That's part of it, of course. Ours is a special tactical unit, and often the public gets mixed signals on how we work, and why. But at the same time, we're not as visible as regular patrol officers, Vanessa. The less the public sees our faces, the better. You understand?"

"I think so," she said, trying to see his point. "I'm sure Mr. Gabel will do his best for you guys."

He checked his watch. "If there's nothing else, I should be getting back."

"And I've got other calls to make," she said.

"Come on, I'll walk you out," Nathan said, and fell in beside her.

So we've gone from embarrassing each other to respecting each other, sort of, she thought, and kept the smile that tugged her lips inside instead. She watched Nathan out of the corner of her eye, wondering what it was about him that made her think of him . . . how? her inner voice asked quietly, prodding her. Don't get involved, she silently admonished herself. He's just doing his job and you'd better just stick to yours. But still . . .

She shifted her briefcase and continued beside him until they reached their cars.

They quickly said their good-byes, and Nathan waited beside her four-by-four as she put her briefcase inside, then helped her climb in. She started up, and slid down the driver's side window.

"Seatbelt," he said, nodding toward her.

"I always do," she said, reaching for it.

"Good," he said, and his eyes twinkled. "It's the law, you know."

She regarded him a moment, then said. "Listen, if I need to talk with anyone about this . . ."

He reached back and fished out his wallet, then dug out a business card. "Here's my number at the station, and my home number's on the back." He pulled out a ball point pen from his uniform chest pocket and wrote quickly across the bottom of the card. "This is my pager number," he said as he wrote. "I don't give it out to everyone." He finished and straightened, presenting the card to her. "But you're an exception, and you may need it. You can call any time."

For a second she toyed with how he meant that. Call any time, she thought. Oh, stop it, her little voice said. Aloud she said, "Thank you, for this," as she tapped the card, "and for this morning. Really. You were a big help."

His fingers came up and touched the stiff brim of his hat. "Tell my lieutenant," he said. "I can use all the brownie points I can get."

"I will," she said, sliding the transmission lever into drive. "Seriously," she added, confirming it.

"You look like that kind," he replied, and stepped back. "A serious type, I mean."

She looked at him, a quick appraisal, and nodded. "That's me all right. Very serious."

"Good," Nathan said, and waved once. "Have a nice day, Ms. Tau."

"You too, Sergeant Samm," she said, and drove away. Glancing up toward the rearview mirror, she watched him stand there, then turn and head toward his squad car.

"Nathan Samm," she mused. "You are one *interesting* man."

* * *

That afternoon Vanessa sat at her desk at the Hamilton office, entering the results of her day's appointments. Pulling up the *Bennet* v. *Westport PD* claim file, she started transcribing additional notes from her mall investigation with Sergeant Samm. She referred to the police report several times, coordinating details with her own information.

She paused after a while, caught up in an incongruity she had noticed before. Insurance claims was a peculiar line of work. Incidents happened involving people and physical, dynamic events. A man's hand was amputated by a machine, an elderly person fell down a moving escalator, automobiles collided head-on at high speed, and fires turned safe homes into raging pyres. But after the fact, an insurance company took all those details and reduced them to black characters on a white page. The elimination of the human touch was the same in any business, Vanessa noted.

It had happened here with the Westport PD reports. The hostage crisis at the shopping mall had resulted from heated emotions barely under control, fear and pain, anger and passion.

Two men had died, another had come close to death, an elderly woman had been assaulted and terrorized, along with a store full of innocent shoppers. She shook her head. But it was the absence of violence in the descriptions and lab reports that were now spread out across her desk that seemed so out of place. But that's how it is, she reminded herself. Maybe that's how it becomes manageable, too. You have to separate out the emotions of this job, or you can never get past it and do the job.

A case in point was the section she had come to that described Nathan's one and only shot: "The open vertical space between the (steel) links of the security fence measured two and one-quarter inches," she read, just under her breath. "The elapsed time from when the suspect (Bennet) attempted to fire his own weapon, and the fatal shot by the HRG sharpshooter was taken, was one point eight seconds."

Vanessa paused, and looked down at the second hand of her watch, counting the seconds. She thought about it, how intense it must have been, yet how coolly, almost detachedly, Nathan had described it to her. She considered all of the police reports she had read as an adjuster, and the cases she had investigated, and the officers she had met. None had been anything like Nathan. Sure, most had the same professional's outlook on their jobs, but none had shown the same calmness.

She knew that being a police officer was similar to any other occupation, in most respects. Those who did well learned the job through time and effort, but few were born to the work. Skills were taught, and practiced, until they became finely honed. But there was a difference, she thought. Nathan impressed her with being a natural at his occupation, as though he had been born to it. Thinking of him this way seemed odd, even ridiculous. How can someone be born into killing? The idea was absurd. Then she remembered his eyes, and the way he carried himself, and she reconsidered her feelings.

No, he *was* a natural at doing what he did. It was no exaggeration, no show of macho virility. Nathan Samm was completely at home as a sniper.

It made Vanessa wonder again why she thought she was attracted to him. She tried to push it aside, but the feeling remained. There was something there, something about him. If for no other reason, she told herself, I'm going to find out what that something is.

September 14

Westport, Ohio

Aaron felt the water from the hose running down his arm, the texture of the sponge rough but slick with soap as he stroked the sides of the big Dodge, squatting beside the car. His dress shoes squeaked, soaked clear through, but he didn't notice it. He knew it was a dream, in that curious way that happens even as real-life sensible things warped strangely within the sleepscape. He saw from the perspective of the twelve-year-old child he was then, yet through the eyes of the adult man he was now.

The strangeness was comforting, because he knew what was next. He'd had this dream before, not frequently, just sometimes. The first time it frightened him, but now he knew what to expect, and the familiar anticipation tugged at the corners of his mouth. This time the two officers wouldn't be there, wouldn't be delivering the feared telegram from the secretary of the Army. This time there was a change. It was going to be all right.

The olive-green staff car glided to a stop at the curb, and he almost jumped up to run for it, but that wasn't how it went. Wait for it, his unconscious mind coached him, and he let the sponge drop from his hand. It slid down his trouser leg, staining the navy blue uniform black, and landed atop the toe of his spit-shined Oxford.

He ignored it, because the driver's-side door was opening, he could see the top corner swing out from the edge of the roof. He felt the grin spreading wide on his face again.

His father stood up out of the car, class-A dress greens sharp, ribbons blazing in full day-bright color on his left chest, eyes shining from under the shadowed edge of his hat's bill, its gold braid flashing.

So straight and tall, Aaron remembered, looking up at his father walking up the driveway toward him, hand outstretched to reach out for him, to welcome him, coming closer, and . . .

* * *

He woke with a start, and the grief slammed away the artificial warmth of the dream. He's not coming back, the voice whispered, as if it really needed to. He's gone, Aaron. He's never coming back.

"Shut up!" he groaned back, pulling himself upright. He sat in bed, breathing hard, deliberately, willing the ugliness away, trying, as he always did, to recapture just for a few more seconds the lingering warmth, the love of the memory. But not this time. It was gone again. The closeness it had brought, the way it should have been, all gone. He hated it, hated the way it had come over the years, always the same, always with the promise that could never be for him.

His father was dead, years ago, long ago, and that was the certainty of it. In the beginning Aaron had tried to make sense of it, to fit it into something he could draw from. The only thing that made sense to him was that it had to be a reminder, reinforcing his mission. Avenge his father against the men who had taken his life. Keep on doing what he had sworn to do. He'd bring his father home the only way he could. Finish the mission, he told himself. That's what it's all about. Finish it, and he'll be home, at rest.

He fell back, throwing his arm over his eyes. Just once, he thought. Just once I'd like to go all the way. He's going to tell me something, I know it. God, but I'd really like to hear it, just the one time . . .

He drifted off, but nothing else came that night. He didn't understand it, not yet. One day he would. And it wouldn't be what he expected it to be. Not at all.

September 21

Dayton, Ohio

"OK," Arthur Gabel said, flipping the legal-sized pages over. "The interrogs look good. Let's get them off to Julia Disare ASAP. How're our answers to her batch coming along?"

"Almost done," Jeff Ravenni, his associate, replied. "I'm waiting on the personnel files on the Westport cops. Kedrick's not responded yet with those."

Gabel nodded at his paralegal, Maxine Hyett. "Max, you want to give Charlie a jingle? Tell 'em we need those files, OK?"

"Yes sir," Hyett said, jotting a note.

"Ask him about the policy and procedures manual, while you're at it," Ravenni added. "He's late with that, too."

Gabel cocked an eyebrow, his warning radar up and running. "Any reason why Charlie would delay sending this stuff?"

Ravenni shook his head. "I don't think so, Art. It probably just got lost in the shuffle. I haven't seen anything they'd want to hide, if that's what you're thinking."

Gabel glanced back at his own notes, then flipped the pad onto the desktop. "You're probably right, Jeff. But we've got a police department here, and it wouldn't be the first time we've been stonewalled on discovery because they're covering something up. It's happened before."

"As I said, I don't think it's the case here," Ravenni said. "These guys look pretty straight, and I didn't get the impression off of either Chief Tusca or Lieutenant Barlot that they're hiding anything over there."

"Just the same," Gabel said, "push Kedrick for those files."

"Yes sir," Hyett said.

"All right, on the personnel reports, you want the usual routine?" Ravenni asked.

"Absolutely," Gabel said, "especially the prior service hires in the batch. We don't want any Indians in the woodpile."

Hyett listened to their exchange, hearing the undercurrent. It prompted her to ask, "What's the deal with the personnel files, besides the obvious? I mean, I know that if an officer has had some problems at Westport, we need to know about that." She was still new to the business of researching the defense on a big-money case. Her inexperience showed in the question.

Ravenni looked at Gabel, who nodded for him to go ahead. "The significance goes beyond what may be there with Westport. We're interested in any prior service, too. It's a syndrome you'll run into all too frequently. Most municipalities fail to check the backgrounds of cops they hire from other jurisdictions. Usually budgets are tight, and if the officer's resumé contains the right letters and such, no one bothers to check."

"That's right," Gabel said, "which is often a problem for us. I can't tell you how many times I've ended up defending some cop on an excessive force case, then he transfers down the road to another PD and starts the same trouble all over again. Cops like that rely on the fact that no one is checking up on them. They're playing the odds, hoping to slide through. More often than not they beat the system. Chiefs and sheriffs are just glad to get someone they think is experienced, and doesn't look like Jack the Ripper."

Roselli laughed. "Yeah, and sometimes they *are* Jack the Ripper. All the city planners need to do is request the prior hire candidate provide a letter from his old chief stating he's eligible for rehire at any time. Then follow up on that. Call the old chief and find out if the letter's for real. We'd save a lot of problems that way and weed out trouble-prone cops before they become *our* problem. Which reminds me," he continued. "There are four prior service types. Chief Tusca, Lieutenant Barlot, the HRG commander, Lieutenant Warrington, the department's training supervisor, and Sergeant Samm. They all came from outside Westport."

"OK. Let's take a look at all of them when the files arrive. If they're clean, we may let it ride. On the other hand, if there's anything in anyone's background that can screw up our strategy, I'd rather we find it, and not Julia. You know she'll be looking for all the dirt she can find."

They briefly discussed some of the witnesses from the store and the mall. Satisfied all was moving smoothly, Gabel rose from his chair, signaling the end of their meeting. It was just beginning, but he felt comfortable with the case. And that was always a good sign, this early on.

September 23
Middletown, Ohio

Vanessa sat there listening, watching the claimant recite his version of the accident while the small tape recorder took it all down for her field report.

"So I was tryin' to pull the jammed piece out of the break when the guard kicked back, catchin' my hand . . ."

The claimant, a young black machine operator, had fractured his left hand on a hydraulic press at a factory that made railroad steel forgings. He continued answering her questions as she prompted him. Occasionally she referred to her interview guide in the small pocket-sized binder beside the tape player.

As she neared the end of the session her thoughts floated back to Nathan Samm. He really is an attractive man, her little voice offered, and she almost shook herself, angry with her daydreaming. She forced her mind back to the recorded interview. To her inner voice she thought, Not now! Let's finish this statement first, all right? Aloud, she asked, the claimant, "And to the best of your knowledge, Mr. Jenkins, have your answers to my questions been correct, to the best of your ability?"

They finished up quickly and Vanessa soon found herself back inside her Blazer. She set about checking her planner for her next call and verifying her travel route on the folded map she kept on the passenger seat. Satisfied with her plans, she started the engine, then sat for a minute before driving off.

I've got to stay focused, she scolded herself. I've been thinking of Nathan way too much. It's not like I've never met an attractive man before, so what's the deal now?

"And he's a client," she said aloud, "besides a defendant in a lawsuit I'm working on. I don't have time for this," she finished.

Exactly right, she added. Never, never mix business with pleasure.
It won't do either of us any good, she argued silently, and more
than likely will compromise handling the claim he's involved with.

She gazed out her side window, lost in her thoughts. She knew
all the pros and cons of taking her work home, or worse, getting
personally involved with someone she was supposed to be working
on behalf of. It was never a good practice, and in a real sense could
interfere with her investigation of the claim. So it surprised her
even more, as levelheaded as she was trying to be—no, she reminded herself firmly, *had* to be—that she couldn't shake her
growing feelings for Nathan Samm.

"What's happening here?" she mused aloud in a quiet voice.
"Why now, and why him? It's not like I'm really looking for a relationship just now. I've got my work, and my game plan. I just
can't . . ." She shook her head in frustration, because her little
voice was back, comfortably whispering counterarguments in her
ear. Because it happens this way sometimes, it said. And if it is
happening, do you want to ignore it, walk away from it? It might
be worth the effort, and the time. What if, it finally said, fading
away at last. What if . . .

"All right," she answered it, sliding the selector into drive, surprised with the firm tone in her reply. "All right, if that's what you
want. We'll see about it . . . or him. Let it run, see where this may
go. Who knows?" she said, pulling out into the street. And way
back in her mind, a faint echo came back. Who knows indeed?

She focused on her driving, but a part of her, a small but significant part, significant because it was now aware, stayed with the
new face. Nathan Samm, she thought. What's going on with you?
Then the thought turned a bit, and prompted her with a new perspective. What's going on with me? it said. She had no answer, but
she wanted to find one. She *needed* to find one.

Vanessa drove on, anticipation leaving a warm spot inside her.

September 28
Oxford, Ohio

The Westport PD case became an important claim file for Vanessa to handle. Discovery was in the hands of Attorney Gabel, but she had to stay in touch with him, approving specific discovery requests and obtaining additional information to assist in his planning the defense of the officers, the police department, and the other municipal defendants. But there were other claims and cases to work. That was the nature of claims adjusting.

Mostly her daily routine remained the same: scheduling appointments with claimants and insureds and balancing those hours against her time in the office. Occasionally she carried some work home, where she attended to it when not running off to her night classes.

Wednesday evening found her so occupied at home, sitting at her bedroom desk with her laptop PC and microcassette recorder. She wore faded jeans and a red Miami U tee-shirt, her long hair loose down her back. She was working on the last of a handful of field reports. Her head was fully into drafting a coverage position letter to an insured when the thought came to her, suddenly interrupting everything else.

Sergeant Nathan Samm, she said silently. She stopped in mid-sentence, microcassette recorder close to her mouth, seeing him again. Tall and good-looking, she thought without any admonition, or embarrassment, comfortable with her thoughts about him now. She smiled to herself, and Dani Klein, sitting at the head of Vanessa's bed, reading her own class notes, commented about it.

"Either you've had an exhilarating day, Ed McMahon's knocked on our door with ten million, or whatever just flitted across your little mind is so illegal you could bottle that look and make a fortune."

"What?" Vanessa replied, realizing she'd been spoken to.

"Uh oh," Dani said, dropping her spiral notebook and hitching down closer to the foot of the bed. "I've seen that look before, roomie. Not on you," she was quick to add, "but on others, sure enough."

"I don't have any look," Vanessa said, quickly wiping the smile off her face. She was still sorting out where the flash of the police officer had come from, and better than that, why.

"No use denying it, Van," Dani said, scooting closer to her until she was perched on the edge of the mattress. She crossed her long legs Indian-style and held her ankles, arms straight. She gave Vanessa a knowing look.

Her face was mock-serious, but her eyes were alive with curiosity. "Who is he?"

Vanessa tried to save the moment with a quick denial. "I don't know what you mean," she began, trying to sound earnest, but her face flushed delicately, and she looked down for a moment. "Damn," she said then, and swiveled her chair toward Dani. "Was it really that obvious?"

"Obvious?" Dani replied, rocking back suddenly, still holding on to her ankles. "I thought we'd had a power surge just then, girl. The whole room lit up with that goofy smile of yours."

"It wasn't that bad," she countered, then, "was it that bad?" and, "Oh, God, it *was* that bad."

"Like I said before," Dani confirmed.

"And it just popped in there," Vanessa said, as if her roommate were no longer there.

"Hey, don't go spacy on me until you tell me who this guy is, OK?"

"All right," Vanessa said, giving up any further pretense of working. She put the cassette recorder down and stood up to lie across the foot of the bed. Propping her head up with her hand, she thought for a moment, then said, "He's a cop I met working a claim file a few weeks ago. Sergeant Nathan Samm."

"Oh, a cop. This sounds good already," Dani replied, an anticipatory smile on her lips. She stretched out to face Vanessa on the other side of the bed, mirroring her position. "And . . .?"

"And I don't know," Vanessa said. "He's tall, and a little older—"

"No problem there," Dani interrupted.

"He's got a great personality . . ." and she saw her roommate frown.

"Uh oh," Dani interrupted. "That's what you say when there isn't much else to say, you know?"

"Stop it," Vanessa said defensively. "I didn't mean it that way. It's just that he has this . . . way about him," she finished, not certain she liked her own answer. Nathan was more enigmatic than she cared to admit.

"So what's he do, this Sergeant Samm?" Dani asked, enjoying her friendly interrogation.

"He's on the insured's city SWAT team," she said, then corrected herself by saying, "HRG, actually. That's short for Hostage/Rescue Group. It sounds less threatening."

"But almost as dangerous," Dani replied. "So what, like he's in charge of it, something like that?"

"No, he's what they call the long gunner, the team's sharp-shooter. He's one of two they have."

Dani paused, and her face became serious for the first time. "Wait a minute. You mean he's the sniper? He's the one who kills people?"

"It's not like that," Vanessa said quickly, surprised by her sudden defense. "Yes, he's the one who may have to shoot, but only when there's no other option. It's not like every time they get called out he kills somebody."

Dani's interest remained morbid, though. "I've never known a SWAT team member before."

"You should see it from my side," Vanessa said. It really was odd, in its way, but strangely comforting, too. "I had very much the same reaction the first time I met him. It was just another part of the day's business, you know? And then there he was, with his uniform, and so tall, and good-looking . . ." she trailed off, aware she was smiling again.

"And single, I hope?"

"As far as I know, or I assume so."

"You didn't ask?"

"It didn't exactly come up," Vanessa said. "I was investigating a police shooting claim, after all. Asking a cop for his marital status isn't something that occurs naturally."

"Sorry," Dani said. "I'm just being nosy."

"Well, there is something else," Vanessa said, not sure how her roommate would take this one. She forged ahead anyway. "He's black."

Her statement left Dani unfazed. "I don't have any problem with that," she said. "Do you?"

"No, no, not at all," Vanessa said truthfully.

"OK then, so what's the deal?" Dani prodded. "What is it about Nathan Samm? Anything there?"

Vanessa shook her long hair, sending it rippling over her shoulder. "Maybe," she said. "But to tell the truth, I'm not sure I really *want* there to be anything. I mean, he's nice, in a sort of detached way, but I get the feeling there isn't time for anything but his work."

Dani assumed a more interested expression. "Why do you think that?"

Vanessa rolled over on her back and replied to the ceiling as she thought about it. "He has a coolness that underlies his whole demeanor," she said. "It's like he knows how to be personable, and charming, when he has to, but he can turn that off in the blink of an eye." She turned back to face Dani, bouncing slightly as she crooked her head on her hand once again. "There's an intensity there, and he guards it. I don't think he allows the time for relationships." She stopped. Why was she so intrigued by him?

"What is it about Officer Nathan Samm that leads you to the opinion that he doesn't let people get close?" Dani asked.

"Sergeant Samm," Vanessa corrected, "and I didn't say he doesn't let people close." She felt a little off-centered by Dani's questioning. She was also frustrated by her own vague feelings concerning him. Issues were always resolved quickly for her. She rarely had to second-guess herself, her motives, or her emotions. Now here she was challenged over her initial impression of a man she barely knew, and certainly no one she had considered in more than a business way. But there was something there, way back in her mind, that told her otherwise.

"I don't know," she said. "Look, I met him on the job, just like I've met a thousand men before. It's just that I've never been affected by someone like this before."

She shifted a bit, crossing one long leg over the other for balance as she lay stretched out, facing Dani. "I think there's an attraction here. At least that's what I'm feeling inside."

Dani nodded in agreement. "I know what you're saying."

"The problem is," Vanessa went on, "I'm not sure I *want* there to be an attraction. I mean, I'm not really looking for anything along those lines right now. I've got a job, and school. I'm not sure *I'm* the one with any time to give for this sort of thing."

"And Nathan?" Dani offered. "You said before he doesn't seem to have any time, either."

"He's very intense about his work, that's clear, so much so that any personal stuff seems to be on the surface sometimes. His focus is his job."

"So play it by ear," Dani said, and rolled off the bed. "At best you've got an interesting situation. That's all. I wouldn't try to make a big deal over it." She walked toward the bedroom doorway and paused. "Think I'll get some ice cream. Want some?"

"In a minute," Vanessa replied, almost to herself. She lay on her back, staring up at the off-white stucco swirls of the ceiling. So, Nathan Samm, what am I going to do about you? she thought silently. But this time, her tiny voice remained quiet.

September 29
Seaside Heights, New Jersey

Colonel Jim Manos sat quietly in his nylon fabric beach chair and watched the darkness overlap the eastern horizon. The small deck extended out a dozen feet from the back of the house, solid on the eight foot-thick pilings that kept it a couple of feet above the sand. It gave him a clear view of the shoreline for a quarter-mile in either direction.

The incoming tide carried the swells steadily up the beach a hundred yards away, thumping down into froth that slid back into the next set. An early fall breeze rushed across the sand, caressing his face as it passed, leaving a salty chill.

His two-story wood-sided, weathered house cast quickening shadows that pushed the night past him toward the water. Manos had lost track of the time, barely aware of the change of day's ending light to darkness. Occasionally he reached up to adjust the bill of his fisherman's ball cap, or light up another Winston, smoking it silently while the waves provided the only sound to accompany his thoughts.

It was the tenth night of his thirty-day leave from D.C. He was back in the CID, based in the Pentagon, reunited with his old Vietnam partner, Tony Husta. They'd both made grade, too, carrying the silver eagle of a full colonel on their collars. Manos and his wife, Marie, had come up to their New Jersey beach house to spend their leave time. He didn't usually take any time off, but he'd skipped too many years, and his accrued leave was piling up. His boss, Brigadier General Polchuski, had told him in no uncertain terms to "get out of town, James . . . and don't come back for at least a month." Manos had taken the heavy hint. Besides, he needed the vacation. It had been too long since the last one.

He had been enjoying himself, doing little projects that had been put off around the house for too long, not worrying about the demands of a schedule. Until the evening news story had come on the television right after dinner, resurrecting old memories.

It involved a man in prison and an old letter, lost in the mail for twenty-six years. The man, a Jason Rupert, had once been an Army specialist fourth class in Vietnam. His squad leader, Sergeant William Morse, had died when a grenade exploded in his one-man hooch one night. There had been a lot of bad blood between the two men, and Rupert had been accused of doing it. The Army had tried him in a general court-martial, which sentenced him to forty years in Leavenworth, Kansas.

Then the letter showed up. Written by the supposedly murdered man to his wife, lost in the mail over two decades, it had been discovered and delivered, revealing the bitter truth for the first time. Sergeant Morse wrote to his wife about his despondency over the war, and his fright, his inability to lead, and his sense of cowardliness. He told her he was going to end it by taking his own life, and prayed she would forgive him.

The widow, now remarried, took the letter to the military authorities, who reopened the case. A new look at the facts determined the authenticity of Morse's threat and subsequent suicide. The conviction against Rupert was dismissed, and he was released with full back pay and benefits, based upon promotions he should have earned. A grateful Mr. Rupert acknowledged he felt no anger or remorse against his old squad leader, or the Army.

"What good will that do now?" Rupert was heard to say to the reporter as he walked out of the prison gates. "The war's over. It's all been over for a long time. I just want to go home," he said, just as his wife ran into his arms.

Manos was taken by the story, remembering his own participation in the Longbaugh case. He thought of the son, Aaron, and his chance meeting with him over fifteen years ago now. He had never run across the young sergeant again, nor had he checked into his records. As far as Manos was concerned, he had fulfilled his final duty to him by telling him the truth about his murdered father.

That brought up the question that at the time he had consciously avoided: why? Why had he told the son anything at all? Because Aaron had the right to know, he answered himself silently. But was that it, really? Funny how time can alter perspectives, Manos thought, knowing what was digging at him. He'd been given a golden opportunity to right things, wasn't that it? By some odd serendipity the murdered man's son appears, coincidentally trained by the same Army to kill people in a precise, straightforward manner. And there was Manos, the man who knew the truth.

"Truth?" Manos repeated aloud. "Was that what was behind this?" Come on, he derided himself, admit it, if you want to venture into the so-called truth. The kid was a weapon, a tool to be used. You *wanted* Aaron to know what had happened, because you wanted him to correct the problem. That was it, wasn't it?

Manos had never quite faced it head-on like this, but once done, he knew what he had done. He had launched his own personal avenger on eight men who had done the killing. He had taken advantage of a loaded weapon and turned him loose, hoping Aaron would follow some form of natural progression.

"Natural progression," he said ironically. "What a nice, bland, safe description." He huffed, dismissing the thought. It was all moot, anyway, wasn't it? Nothing had happened after he had met Aaron. He hadn't heard about anything happening to those eight men.

But that brought up another issue, and a possible reason why he hadn't heard. He and Tony Husta hadn't followed up on their promise to keep in touch with the suspected killers. They had tried for a few years after the war ended, but even that fell apart over time. "There's your natural progression," he chided himself. "That's how it goes. What was once important loses its importance with time."

Indifference? he wondered. No, not that. Not indifference. Tony and I tried, we really did. It just happens. There's no excuse for it, and no other way to explain it. Now it came back to him, digging away at his sense of unfinished business.

"Goddamn Army," he mumbled. None of it had made any sense to him, nor to Husta. They'd been told to kick the squad free, letting them go back to the World, and to freedom. Now, twenty-five-plus years later, it was still hanging there, twisting in his mind's eye. Justice had been revoked, the guilty had gone free, and murder had been ignored

So, he wondered, where were they now? If Aaron Longbaugh had done anything to avenge his father, Manos was completely in the dark about that. Maybe it was time he found out.

Manos flipped his finished smoke expertly into a number-ten can hung on a short post at the edge of the deck. It bounced against the inside rim in a minor shower of red-orange sparks and disappeared.

And that was what it came down to in the end. Years of doing the job had left him with a curiosity, and a desire to know things. He hated a project left unfinished, and the killers of Major Longbaugh certainly fell into the classification. He wanted to know, needed to know, for himself. Especially for himself. He wanted to find out how they had lived with what they had done. Had it gotten to them, as it had him? Were they eaten up by replays of the ambush? Did the picture of Longbaugh's shattered and shredded body haunt them as it did him? Not knowing was eating him up, piece by piece.

"Want some company?" Marie said beside him.

Manos jumped at his wife's soft voice. She had come up beside him silently, or so he thought.

"You've been out here for two hours, hon. Anything wrong?" Marie Manos, late-forties, middle-age hips softening her once-slimmer self, took the empty beach chair beside her husband. She watched his profile in the dark, the lights from their house providing enough illumination for her.

He saw the concern in her eyes and sighed. He reached for her hand, squeezed it, and a faint smile appeared. He turned his head to look out at the breakers. "I've been thinking," he said.

She squeezed back with both hands and leaned forward to rest her elbows on her knees, watching him. "It's Vietnam, isn't it?"

Manos shifted to face her. "You know me pretty well, don't you?" he said. She didn't answer, but let him get it out.

"There's some unfinished business, Marie," he said. "I need to know what happened. It's time."

His wife was no stranger to the story, especially in the last few years. She knew the entire sordid tale. Manos had withheld little from her concerning his career. She had gone through too much with him, had raised their three kids with him, had seen him from duty station to duty station. There was no reason for secrets between them. So he had told her everything about the killing, and the mutinous squad, and the Army's critical failure to punish their murderous act. She knew their names at least as well as he did. It had become her husband's sole obsession, but so far, he'd done nothing about the problem. But it occupied him all the time, an unseen cancer that ate and ate, demanding time and suffering from him, without offering a cure.

She knew the answer to curing the cancer. It had to come from inside himself. He was a good man, with principles and a sense of right and wrong, and had always been that way. It was part of what had drawn her to him so many years ago. It was also what made the pain of this thing so hurtful to him. Now she wanted him to face it, once and for all, and take care of it. It had been with the two of them far too long.

"I think you're right, dear," she said. "I think it's time."

He lifted her hands to his lips and kissed them, rubbing his affection into them a moment. "I'll make the call in the morning," he said.

"Whatever you say," she replied, and still holding his hand, turned to gaze out toward the near beach. "I'll be here for you," she said. "You know that, don't you?"

"I know that," he answered.

They sat that way for a long time. Finally he said, without looking at her, "Thank you."

"Thank you," she replied.

* * *

He started the next day. Over a cup of coffee in the small bay window of their kitchen, Manos dialed the number for the office on the fourth floor, D-Ring of the Pentagon.

"Colonel Husta," his old friend, still his partner, said.

"Tony? It's Jim."

"Hey, Jimmy," his friend replied, "tired of your vacation already? The old man hears you been calling he'll be ticked off."

"No, man, I ain't coming back right away. I'm calling on something else."

"I'm all ears," Husta said, his curiosity aroused. "Go ahead."

"Did you see the piece on ABC last night on the Rupert guy and his release from Leavenworth?"

"Yeah, I did," Husta said. "Pretty weird, huh? Remind you of anyone we know?"

"Longbaugh," Manos said simply. "I think it's time we found out what they've been up to, Tony."

Husta paused, feeling it again, that connection they had between them. It had started back in Vietnam, the seeming ability to know what the other was thinking. It had continued after the war, one of the unique facets they shared that kept them in the groove. He knew exactly what Manos was talking about.

"I thought you might be calling on something like that," Husta said. "I've kinda been having the same thoughts myself."

Manos chuckled. "It's true, you know, Tony. Some things never do change." His voice sobered. "They've been on my mind a long time."

"Like about twenty years' worth?" Husta interjected. "You told them, *manolito*. You said you'd never let up, never stop looking. But you have . . . we have," he corrected. "The promise was to ourselves, too. Ah, hell, maybe it was easier to forget about it, leave it behind with all the other memories. Vietnam wasn't exactly a big win for us, was it?"

Both men were silent, feeling the years. Vietnam was unfinished business for a lot of people, the ones who had been there, at least. Husta broke their mutual silence first. "We should let them know we're still around, you know?"

"Yeah, and that the statute never runs on what they did," Manos replied. He felt his commitment rising again, letting it fire him up. He had been coasting with this, despite the way the murder haunted him. They'd exhausted all of their leads years ago. There had been nothing for them to chase down. But now, maybe if they prodded them, shook them up after all these years, maybe something would happen. They thought they were safe now, didn't they? They really thought they had gotten away with murder.

And what of Aaron? Manos wanted to find him, too. It seemed time to see what happened to all of them, perpetrators and victims alike. Or were they all one and the same? He shook the thought aside.

"I hear you," Tony said. "Give me a couple of days, unless you're in a rush or something," Husta said. "You want me to call you there?"

"There's no rush, and here will be fine."

"Hey, *no es problema*. I'll pull our old report and do a little checking."

"We owe it to ourselves, Tony. Carlos Madrid, rest his sorry soul, was telling the truth. We had them, we really had them."

"I know, man. I feel the same way, but you know that, too. Hey, we need a challenge like this. It'll be a pleasure to fall all over these bastards again. I'll call you."

"Yeah," Manos replied, feeling it coming together. Time to fulfill the promise, he thought, and aloud he said, "Thanks, Tony."

"Hey, we're in this together. Let's go hunting," Husta said, and broke the connection.

October 5

TPI Office, Hamilton, Ohio

Vanessa had been back in the office only half an hour. She had completed six calls and had planned the office stop to add to the file notes on her appointments before heading home. When her phone rang, she took the call on the second ring. "TPI, Vanessa Tau," she answered, her eyes still on the monitor screen.

"Vanessa? Jeff Ravenni, Art Gabel's associate."

"Oh, Jeff, hi," she said, turning her attention fully to the phone. "What's up?"

"The *Bennet* v. *Westport* case," he said. "We've got some interrogatories we're working on, and there's a couple of things we need, background checks on some of the people over there. A few of them are from out of state. Rather than hire an independent adjuster, I thought maybe you could ask TPI's respective branch offices to check on this stuff for us?"

Vanessa nodded to herself. "Sure, no problem. We can do the work just as easy, and get your answers quicker. What is it you're looking for?"

"It's the personnel files on some of the officers in the department. Art wants to run down their prior service with the other places they worked before coming here. Why don't you come by the office and pick them up in the next day or two, if that fits in with your schedule?"

She glanced at her desktop calendar and checked quickly. "How soon do you need this done?" she asked.

"There's no particular rush," Ravenni said. "Answers aren't due for another sixty days or so. But we finally got the files from Kedrick yesterday, and I'd like to get this part out of the way."

Vanessa checked her schedule the next couple of days. "How does Friday look to you? I could stop by your office, let's say around three, three-thirty, though."

"That'll be fine," he said. "I'll have the files ready for you then."

"So how goes it so far?" she said, wanting to know, but unable to avoid a quick thought about Nathan Samm at the same time.

"Not bad so far," Ravenni replied. "There've been no surprises yet, but it's still early. We've got a ways to go before it gets really interesting. Art is thinking about a motion to dismiss the '83 counts, though."

Vanessa approved his last comment. Eliminating the civil-rights allegations from the complaint was often nothing more than an initial tactical move. When the court actually paid attention to the motion's arguments and granted it, though, it could have a tremendous effect on the plaintiff's case. Losing this part of the case could gut the damages prayed for, as well as cutting off the plaintiff's attorney's fees.

"When might he be filing the motion?" she asked.

"Maybe by the first of December," he said. "We ought to have the research into the case law we need done by then."

"Keep me informed on that," she said. Research hours meant serious additional costs. As the file handler she was the one responsible for approving request like this.

"I was completing a status report for you to include the research request," he said, reading her mind. Ravenni knew the rules, too.

"OK," Vanessa said. "Give me a quick rundown on what you've got in mind, and I'll get back to you. Anything else on discovery?"

"Art's been thinking about filing a motion in limine to bifurcate the case," he said, "splitting up the municipality versus the individually named defendant officers."

Vanessa hadn't seen that tactic before, and asked, "What's the advantage there?"

"Well, it's just a gambit for now," Ravenni said. "But what that will do is, presuming there's something in the actions of the officers that could hurt us, by bifurcating their part of the case away from the allegations against Westport itself, we eliminate discovery and evidence concerning them from both discovery and trial."

She began to understand. "So if we can't get the civil-rights claims dismissed, we could limit the information plaintiff's camp could get relative the officers, and the city, right?"

"Something like that," he said. "There are other reasons for a motion like this. It's all tactics at this stage. Art will decide later on if he wants to pursue this line."

"All right, I understand," she replied. "I'll see you on Friday afternoon then."

"Appreciate it," Ravenni answered, and hung up.

Vanessa replaced her handset, and finally allowed her little voice to speak up. It nudged her about Nathan Samm, and the fact that if she wanted their relationship to advance, she had better get serious about making the next move. It certainly didn't seem to be coming from Nathan's side. Yes, but *is* there a relationship? she asked herself. Or am I caught up in some wishful thinking?

When she thought more about that last, she smiled inwardly. No, there had been something between them back at the mall, she was sure about it. They'd stumbled around with each other at first, but all of that social probing had initiated something. He's interested, too, she said confidently, and a warm shiver tingled through her middle, carrying promises of things only sensed so far. Her smile widened and now graced her full lips.

"All right then, Sergeant Nathan Samm," she said aloud, softly. "Let's see if this really does go anywhere." She returned to work, part of her mind busy with her next move with the tall police officer.

October 5

Seaside Heights, New Jersey

Jim Manos's eyes jerked open at the sound of the bedside phone, and he was instantly awake, his body reacting to a lifetime of rude, late-night telephone calls. Some things never did change.

"What the hell," he said, reaching out for the phone. Marie nudged him with her shoulder, rolling over.

"Jim . . . who? It's midnight . . ." she said thickly.

"I know," he started to say to her, and into the receiver he said, "Manos . . . who's this?"

"Tony," came his friend's clipped reply, and Manos heard the no-nonsense sound in it. It caused him to rotate up to sit on the edge of the bed.

"Tony? What's going on?" He didn't have to ask where his friend was. He had to be calling from his office at the Pentagon. But why?

"Those eight guys in the squad, the Longbaugh killers," Husta continued, giving it to Manos straight, "six of 'em are dead, Jim."

The news thudded into place, but it took him a few seconds to comprehend what he'd just been told. Realization shook the last vestiges of sleep from his head. "Holy shi—" and he remembered Marie, hovering behind him, becoming more awake herself. "Wait one." His mind swirled, and he blinked a few times. "Dead? How, when? Talk to me, man. What's going on?" His mind repeated Husta's message, but it didn't lessen its surprise. The answer he expected to hear was running through his head.

"What's going on is, I pulled up the file, and started the usual checks, you know, local PD records, individual state networks, NCIC and NCISR networks. I'll tell you about those in a minute. Then I threw in utility and finance companies, all the public-record sources first. It's funny, but none of these guys ever strayed too far from their roots, you know?"

Manos heard the rustle of paper over the line as Tony continued. "Here, let me run down the list, at least as far as I have now. It covers quite a span of time. Uh, first one in 1982, September, Max Perriman in Illinois. Then in the spring of '84 a double-header: Paul Roselli on Long Island in March and Louis Archer in April, Long Island City, Queens." Husta paused a moment and added, "Archer was the only one with witnesses, if you want to call them that. I'll explain later. It picks up again in June of 1985: Hector Aceto in Texas; then in '87, February, John Burris in Wisconsin." He stopped, letting Manos ponder the names. "And the latest, but probably not the last, their fearless leader, Jack Linet, May of 1991, Macon, Georgia."

"Jesus, Mary," Manos said, this time forgetting Marie. She touched his shoulder, communicating her questions and concern with that quick touch. He nodded at her and spoke into the phone. "How'd it happen? And I'm presuming by what you've said so far that their deaths weren't random acts." He had to ask the question, but the feeling he already knew was building, winding tighter inside. He was pretty sure he already knew what had happened.

"Wait'll you hear," Husta said. "But two of them seem out of profile with the other four. Aceto died in a construction cave-in, and Burris died of leukemia, supposedly Agent Orange–related. Natural causes, if you want to classify them as such."

Natural progression? Manos's little voice mocked him. He thought he heard it coming but asked the question anyway. "And the other four?"

"Shot, my friend. All four of 'em, and all the same way. Long distance, two shots apiece: center mass and head, in that order. The weapon used fired a 7.62, match grade round. The killings were real smooth. No one saw anything, no one heard anything, and the cops came up empty each time. They're carrying them as open-unsolved homicides." He paused a moment. "Well, actually that's not completely correct. Jack Linet's killing finally triggered an inquiry out of Georgia. Seems the Macon PD ran their case through NCIC and turned up enough similarities to Perriman, Roselli, and Archer to make some phone inquiries."

"And?" Manos asked.

"Apparently they've got people still digging. With the Army connection popping up in their records, and the fact they were all sniped, Georgia's interest in the shootings must have turned on the other jurisdictions too. They're all running further investigations, but there's been nothing new from any of them on the net for a while. Maybe the time in between the killings has thrown them off. Personally," he added, "I don't think the time between is all that significant. It's kinda hard to miss the connection, eh, mano?"

Manos sighed. It was true. It had happened, just as he had (*hoped*) feared. Still, he couldn't believe what he was hearing. In his mind he saw them, younger faces from his last memory of them, arrogant and smug, thinking they'd pulled it off. "Wait a minute," he said, his mind working on the news. "You said there were witnesses in Louis Archer's case."

"Yeah, well, seems our boy Louis turned into quite the bad-ass when he got back to the States after Vietnam. By 1984 he had quite a sizable drug operation going. Still made his own deals, though . . . apparently didn't trust anyone. He was whacked out right in the middle of a buy, in some freight yards in Queens. There

were four people besides Louis, and according to the NYPD report, none of 'em heard a thing. Archer took one right through the
face. He'd been wearing body armor, believe it or not. The second
one was in the head after he was down. Homicide sided with the
narcs who had been watching Archer for months. They all figured
the deal went south, and the competition took Archer out, as a
warning or some kind of power play. In any event," he continued,
"no one was ever arrested for it."

Husta paused. "The homicide investigations on the others par-
alleled each other, as far as they went, but they didn't make any
connections. I don't have all the details yet, but I presume they did
the usual background checks. If they ran across a military service
record on any of them, they wouldn't have found much. We saw to
that." His tone reflected the quandary that faced him.

Manos heard the frustration in his friend's tone. Husta was still
struggling to make sense out of it. The news had shaken him, not
because he wasn't used to hearing about violent deaths, but for another reason, a darker one. He had entertained a similar fantasy on
occasion, one that began, Wouldn't it be nice, wouldn't it make
things so much cleaner if they all died somehow . . . ? Then he had
set the wish in motion. Hearing that it was really happening
chilled him a little.

"So they have no suspect?" he said, knowing the question was
rhetorical.

"No they don't," Husta replied, and Manos heard the emphasis
he gave to "they." "At least we have something they don't, and
that's the tie-in. And the motive," Husta said. Husta wasn't in the
mood for any hypotheticals this night. He'd already spent several
hours considering what to him were the obvious facts. The motive
was clear to him and Manos. "Somebody knows about these guys,
Jim, and knows what they did, and what they got away with. He
has the connections to find them, and the expertise to take them
out, one by one. That much is certain. The why of it seems pretty
clear. He's balancing the books."

A picture of the young man floated into Manos's head, a familiar face, a close resemblance to his dad. He glanced at Marie,
whose face showed her astonishment as she realized what her hus-

band and his old friend were really talking about. She started to say something, but Manos quieted her with a gesture.

"There's a real pro out there," Husta continued, "and he could be anything . . . civilian, police, military-trained, active or ex. Personally I'm leaning toward the military angle. Most cop sharpshooters, the SWAT guys, don't do much shooting beyond a hundred meters. Urban situations don't present that many long shots, which is not to say they couldn't do it. But military snipers do. None of these hits were less than 350 meters out, even Archer's out in that rail yard in Queens. He was well inside the city. The shooter fired from five hundred yards away, the police figured, based on a reconstruction of the shoot."

Manos heard the confirmation in Husta's tone. His partner felt the same way he did, worked the evidence the same way. There didn't seem to be much doubt here, either. Tony knew about the kid. He'd just laid out the preliminary facts. The obvious was left to the man who had set the kid loose.

"Which leaves the son," Manos said finally, feeling uneasy, "Aaron Longbaugh, a military-trained sniper."

"Indeed it does," Husta said. "Aaron Ralph Longbaugh, an impressive name. You met him, didn't you?"

"Yeah," Manos said slowly while his mind whirled in high gear. "Down at Eglin, when I was doing the black ops gig. I told you about running into him. It was pure luck."

"It seemed odd to me too, when you mentioned it. And you told him about the murder." He was quiet a moment or two. "You know, Jim, back then it seemed like the thing to do. What happened after that doesn't take much of a stretch of the imagination."

Suddenly Manos wasn't so sure. "Look, Tony, let's not fall into the same trap of circumstantial evidence that cost us the first time. We've no proof the kid's been doing this." The thought that what he had revealed to young Aaron Longbaugh could have launched a killing spree that had lasted over a dozen years sat cold and hard in his stomach.

"Yeah, you're right," Husta replied. "We have a hell of a long way to go before we can prove anything here. And to tell you the truth, my friend, I'm not all that certain I want to find out. I mean," he said, and Manos heard the irony in his words, "the possibility that justice is finally falling down on these bastards does my heart good. Despite the years, and the fact we couldn't put the case together tight enough to nail them back in-country, you and I both know they were all guilty as hell. I can't bleed for them now."

Manos closed his eyes a moment, Husta's comments making an almost audible click inside his head. It began to make sense, in an all-too-familiar manner. He chased the brief flash of guilt away.

Husta picked up on his partner's silence. "My feelings exactly, Jim. It all goes together, doesn't it? The kid's old man gets blown away and the guys who did it get off. The Army conveniently comes along and trains the kid to kill people from a long way off. Then the truth of what happened to his father falls into his lap."

"That's a poetic way of putting it," Manos cut in. "It didn't exactly fall into his lap. I gave him the goddamn story!" Another detail fell into place. "Oh, man," he said. "I even told him how to access our old investigation, to see it for himself. That's where he got the information on where to find them." He knew they were on the right track, but it didn't make him feel any better about it. He had unleashed a killer, justified or not. The responsibility was his.

Husta took a few seconds to answer. "Yeah, mano, I know. And if it had been me that ran across the kid I'd have done exactly what you did, too. He had the right to know. There was no one better, that's for sure. And," he continued, "there was no one better to have told him, either."

Manos wasn't entirely convinced. His guilt was getting in the way again. "So if there was ever a motive to exercise what he'd learned, he sure as hell got one from me. Only this one got out of hand," Manos said. The realization of what he'd started, and what was being done now, had left a sour taste in his mouth. Self-recrimination rolled oily low down in his mind.

"So where's he now?" Manos asked tiredly, hoping against hope that Longbaugh was still in the service, but not sure he wanted to hear the answer.

"No idea," Husta told him. "But the timeline does suggest certain conclusions. You met with the kid June, 1980. I found out he left the service three months later. Then he flat disappeared. I mean, like he fell off the face of the earth. Nothing. I've got computers from Florida to Alaska looking as we speak, but so far, zip."

That brought Manos around. "But the first killing was September, '82, two years later, Perriman in Illinois. That's no coincidence, Tony."

"I agree," Husta said, "but that's a lot of time from when he left the Army and when Perriman bought it. What did he do in between?"

"I don't know," Manos said. "So the kid goes deep cover, and he's hunting these guys one by one. But why is he taking so long? This has been going on for years, from what you said. Why didn't he take them down one after the other? Why the delay? It's been over a dozen years now. That's a long time to be hunting."

"Yeah, it's a long time, but I don't know why," Husta said. "We have to find out what he's been doing, how he's been getting around. Unless the kid won the lottery somewhere, he has to be doing something to finance his search. How's he getting by? And there's another bit of evidence to consider. Remember I said the caliber used on these four shootings was a 7.62? Well, the bullets used were all the same weight, too, according to the police reports. 173-grain stuff."

"You lost me, Tony. What's the significance of the bullet weights?" Manos asked.

"Something I looked up," Husta replied. "Most tactical teams these days shoot match loads, Sierra boat-tail stuff. It doesn't matter who the ammo manufacturer is, most of 'em use the Sierra bullet. It weighs 168 grains. The 173-grain round was loaded by Lake City Ammunition Plant. It was the big match load in Vietnam, mano, the only one all the branches issued to field snipers. Both the Army and Marines used it."

"The shooter is using twenty-five-year-old ammo?" Manos asked.

"No, just the same weight bullet, probably hand-loaded. But don't you see? It fits with the kid. He's using a period bullet to kill these guys. Divine justice and all that."

"That's a bit of a stretch," Manos said, his mind working on the information, but it made sense in a strange way that bothered him. "Have any of these other police departments asked the FBI to run a profile on the suspected shooter?"

"Not that I've seen so far," Husta replied. "But it's only a matter of time before it's done. So where does that leave us?" he continued. "Right or wrong, don't we have an obligation to try to find him, and stop him?"

"I thought you wanted this to go on until . . ."

Husta laughed softly at that. "C'mon, James. We've worked together a long time, especially on this one. Why do you think we're so good at it?"

Manos knew the answer. He also knew it was the only way he could ever be straight with himself about the killers, and what was happening to them now. "We're so good at it because we *are* good," he replied. "It has to do with that outdated stuff about duty, and honor, and country."

"You got that right," Husta agreed. "We're the last of a dying breed, the good guys in white hats that really give a damn about what's right and wrong. We have to find him, Jim."

Manos rubbed his closed eyes with his free fingertips. Tony was right, and he knew it. "Yeah," he said tiredly, feeling totally exhausted. He'd heard too much, relived too much, and worse, knew what was about to take place. They had to go hunting again, this time for a kid who maybe, just maybe, didn't deserve to be in their sights. Then the irony of that thought slammed into him, and he winced from the awful truth of it.

But he shook it off and worked the phone receiver in his hand. "All right, Tony. We go after him, or whoever," he added, needing to say it, holding out the hope, no matter how slight, that Aaron Longbaugh wasn't the one, but not believing it, not really. But there was that other problem, not yet resolved. He offered it to Husta. "And after we prove that it is him, and track him down, what then, Tony? What do we do about him then?"

His question met with a long silence.

"I don't know, Jim. Honest to Christ, I don't."

"Looks like my vacation just ended," he said. "I'll be in D.C. tomorrow."

Husta heard the decision made. He didn't feel all that much better, either. "I'm sorry, Jim. I didn't want it to go this way."

"No one did," Manos replied, seeing all of the casualties parade across his memory. "But we do what we have to."

"Yeah, we'll do that, all right," Husta said heavily, and added, mostly because it needed to be said, "we still have to look for other possibilities. At least until we know for sure."

"Yeah, I know," Manos said. "Nothing's a lock until we have all the proof. Frankly, Tony, I'm hoping we'll find someone else."

The silence between them was palpable. Both knew what they were really going to find.

"Me, too," Husta said finally, not believing it. "I'll see you to-morrow."

"Sure," Manos said, and hung up. An idea was forming in the back of his mind, something about turning this over to the Feds. Maybe they could help, or something. He realized with a savage turn that the "or something" was for them to do the dirty work for him. Find the kid and bring him down. He grimaced at his cowardice. You started this, he chastised himself. Now it's up to you to finish it . . . all the way.

"So be it," he said. He turned to Marie, sitting anxious but quietly with the covers around her knees. "You're not going to believe this," he began.

He was wrong, because she did. Even more so, she got out of bed when he was done explaining Husta's call and started packing for him. "I figured it might be something like this," she said. She had been through a lot with her husband. This was no different. "Just watch yourself, OK? I'd like to have a real vacation some year."

He knew she was only half-joking. But it wasn't all that funny in the first place.

Not at all.

October 6

Miami University, Oxford, Ohio

The memory tugged at William Landau for a moment, and he felt that nostalgic pang for something he almost wished he still had. Adrienne had been one of his grad students, and their affair had run heavy for half a year before grinding to a slow-motion, painful end. But they'd been overly cautious, even to the extent of renting the apartment in Somerville, a few miles outside Oxford, for their clandestine meetings.

That was where they'd had their last argument, and where it had finally come to an end. Adrienne was gone four months now, but he'd held on to the apartment. He sighed. A girl he didn't have and an apartment he didn't need. Beating himself up seemed to be his way of life.

Landau sat back and turned his chair to face the single window in his corner office. He gazed down at Spring Street, watching the kids and cars go past. Young life, he mused silently, just a little envious. When I was their age I was getting shot at, he thought, letting the memory come in.

His face sobered, and his eyes took on the peculiar long-distance stare of those who had been there and had seen and done far too much. His view turned inward, though his eyes still tracked the movement outside his window on the wooded campus below. The feeling was still there, heavy and black now, and in his mind's eye it took on the familiar sheen of old rusted metal, covering his soul like a shroud, imprisoning him. It silently contained him, a self-constructed manifestation of his own silence all those years ago, when he should have spoken against their plan, instead of letting Jack Linet cajole and prod and push them until . . .

He bolted back into reality, the image of the shroud fading, leaving behind its promise he'd never be free of it, never break out of it, never regain his freedom from the murder, nor forgiveness for it either.

He'd made his choice then and made his choice of atonement afterward. Unable to bring his guilt into the light, he would continue to relive it through this method instead, teaching the next generations about his times, and his mistakes. Maybe they'd learn not to fall into what had snared him, he thought. He truly thought he was making a difference. And doing so kept him in this Purgatory of his own making, a masochistic continuous reveling in the memories that refused to leave him, blood-spattered and horrific.

But was it enough? he sometimes argued with himself. Was he

doing enough penance? It was all self-imposed, after all. He'd decided the level and effort of repayment. Maybe he was being too le-
nient with himself.

But he knew how much he had bled inside, how much he had
given up to that terrible memory. It had ruled the course of his life
ever since, and wasn't that payment enough?

"Not until it's done," he answered himself again. His voice
sounded tired and washed-out. And when will it be done? the
small voice threw at him, demanding as it always did, cutting him
a little bit more.

He considered the question as he reached for the pack of
Camels and shook one out. He took his time, tapping one end
against his thumbnail, then reversed it and stuck it between his
lips. When? he thought, holding the ancient Zippo before the
smoke. "When there's no more left to give," he said, and spun the
wheel. The flame touched the tip of the cigarette, and he snapped
the lid closed.

He exhaled the smoke toward the window, trying to let it go. He
allowed only so much time each day for this reverie. It wasn't therapy, not as most people would have thought it. It was part of his
penance. Landau's lips thinned with the real question that pushed
itself to the front. It wasn't a matter of being enough, not really. It
was the question of forgiveness. Was that an option left to him? He
didn't know, because he didn't know who had the power to forgive.
Certainly not their victim. Major Longbaugh was buried and cold
far too many years now. As to the others, the members of the
squad, he didn't care to guess. How could they forgive, since they
were the participants, the executioners?

Which left himself, curiously enough. He didn't consider how
he could remove himself from the others, since he was as guilty as
they were. But he saw his involvement as different. He'd had the
education, hadn't he? Given that, it should have been up to him to
have stopped the killing. But he hadn't. No, he'd done less than
that, he'd gone along, without one word, one syllable in protest.
He'd wanted Longbaugh dead just as badly as Burris, and Aceto,
and Roselli, and all of them. They shared in the decision, and in
their mutual damnation.

So who was left? he asked. The answer came back, as it had for

all these years, in silence. There was no one left to forgive. No one
left.

October 7

Westport, Ohio

"So what d'you think?" Corporal Jerry Lanier asked. He placed the
long aluminum rifle case carefully into the trunk of the cruiser. He
and Nathan were on their way to a neighboring police department's firing range. A special products event had been scheduled
by the Cincinnati office of the FBI to demonstrate a new rifle, the
.300 Winchester Magnum Interdiction Rifle, a special tactical
sniper's piece from Arms Tech, Ltd., a Phoenix, Arizona, company.
Lieutenant Barlot and the rest of the Westport HRG team had already left for the demonstration.

Sergeant Nathan Samm loaded the black canvas duffel in next,
then paused to regard his partner. "You've never been sued before,
have you?" he asked. Lanier's expression provided him the answer.
"I didn't think so," he said, and leaned one hand on the edge of the
raised trunk lid.

"Look, I've been down this road a couple of times," he said. "I
know, reading those lawsuit papers make us out to be worse than
Jesse James or something, but that's just verbiage."

"Some verbiage," Lanier said. "Bennet's lawyer makes us sound
like we plotted to blow him away, and waited until he was un-
armed, down on his knees, praying for deliverance." He was
plainly worried about being named a defendant in the litigation.

"That's all it is, Jerry," Nathan said. "What it boils down to is
whether the attorney can prove any of her allegations, and the
truth of it is, she can't. It was a good shoot. You know it, I know it,
the OBI knows it, and the review board knows it."

"Yeah, well, if everyone knows so damn much, how come the
courts let this stuff get filed in the first place?"

Nathan motioned around with his head. "Hey, it's America,
babe. You can sue anyone for anything, seems like, and *we*," he

said, punching his partner on the arm, "protect them so they can. It's the people's divine right."

Lanier heard the irony in his voice clearly. "And it's still their right even when it's us that gets nailed?"

"Especially when it's us," Nathan said. "It's the American way." He looked down and made a quick visual check of the contents of the trunk. "It comes with the job, partner," he said, and closed the lid. "Let's get out to the range. I'd like to see if this new rifle is as good as the printed hype we received on it."

Lanier stood beside the car a moment. Something Nathan had said before came back to him. "You mentioned you'd been down this road. You mean you've been sued before?"

Nathan dismissed the question with a wave of his hand. "Yeah, a few years back. It was no big deal, another hostage situation. Actually, it went down similar to this one. We took out the bad guy in a fast-food joint. It was a good shoot, too." He continued to hold Lanier with his eyes. "Just like this one," he added.

"How'd it turn out?" Lanier asked.

Nathan grinned quickly and tossed him the car keys. "Justifiable shoot," he said. He paused looking over the top of the car at Lanier. "Coming, Jerry?"

"Yeah, sure," Lanier said. Then he added, "I feel better now."

"That's good," Nathan said, opening the door. "Just don't sweat the small stuff. That's what our attorney is supposed to do."

"No problem, Nate," he said. "Let's go see what this new rifle can do." He opened up his side and slid into the driver's seat.

October 7

Four Mile River Shooting Range, Northwest of Cincinnati, Ohio

The single echo of the last shot whapped back at the open-air bleachers and the eighty police officers sitting there. They all looked beyond the Arms Tech company shooter, lying prone a few yards in front of the bleachers on a shooting mat. He pulled the empty magazine from the bottom of the receiver, looked to make sure the bolt was locked back and the chamber was empty, and rolled away from the rifle, leaving it canted barrel up on its bipod.

It had been a full day of shooting, with all members of their representative tactical teams taking turns with the half-dozen rifles available for them. Most of them had been favorably impressed with the gas-operated semiauto weapon. All were flatly amazed with its long-range accuracy, easily matching the best bolt actions they were familiar with.

In the bleachers behind the firing line, all eyes were directed toward the barely discernible target at the twelve-hundred-meter line. This final event was to show the tactical team members the extreme limits the rifle was capable of reaching. In the real world it would be a rarity for any of the police shooters to take a shot beyond one hundred yards. Urban distances were usually measured within the limits of a single block. Residences and commercial buildings were far too close together for anything longer than that.

But the need for precision, for surgical accuracy, remained just as important for police sharpshooters as for the military scout-sniper. The Arms Tech weapon had proven more than capable of multiple-shot, single-hole results at the typical police tactical distances. That it could replicate that performance well beyond a thousand meters spoke volumes for its inherent accuracy.

The company shooter, Curt Lamanna, had tried to fire as tight a group as humanly possible. They waited while the team in the target pits marked the results and called the score back to the range master. The announcement came over the PA system.

"Ten shots, all in the X, center ring," the range master called out. He was stationed in the elevated shack behind the firing line, some twenty-five feet above the ground. Inside the shack, he listened to the report of the group size and shook his head. "Unbelievable," he muttered under his breath, then keyed the mike. "Total group size is four inches," he said, and a round of whistles and rumblings swept the crowd. "We'll run the target back for y'all," he said, and shut off his microphone. "Carlos Hathcock himself would be pressed to do better." His reference was to the retired U.S. Marine shooter whose ninety-three confirmed kills in Vietnam had become almost legendary.

"I've seen Hathcock," the Bureau agent beside him replied, pushing up from his seat. "He *could* do better, back in his day. Even now, I wouldn't bet against him. But aside from that, you're right. That's some kind of shooting."

Down below the tower, the officers in the bleachers were slowly climbing down, milling around the last seat, some of them going over to the tall shooter to speak with him. Another Bureau representative, wearing a short jacket with the letters FBI emblazoned across the shoulders, stepped up onto a portable podium, tapped the microphone, and waved at them for their attention.

"Gentlemen, on behalf of the Cincinnati Regional office, I'd like to thank you for your attendance at today's demonstration and exhibition. The Arms Tech Interdiction Rifle, in its proprietary .300 Winchester Mag caliber, has recently been approved for Bureau use. As some of you are aware, units are already being issued in the field. This is a battle-tested weapons system that can hit farther, faster, and harder downrange than any .308 load. It is capable of delivering multiple rounds on target faster than a bolt action in any thirty-caliber. You've seen what this precision weapon is capable of. We hope your departments will consider acquiring the system."

Nathan Samm and Jerry Lanier made their way to the bulletin board to check their scores. Several other officers joined them, and the usual bantering over group sizes and course times rippled through the group as they checked and found each other's scores. The comments were good-natured, and several had bested the Arms Tech shooters. Samm and Lanier were among that minority.

"Hey, pard, we did all right," Lanier said, looking at their posted scores. They'd consistently outshot the civilians at each phase of the difficult course.

"Yeah, but not by much," Nathan replied, seeing how close the measurements had been at some of the ranges. "Those boys are pretty good, too."

"I guess," Lanier replied, "for a bunch of legs." He tapped the column of numbers. "Let's go take a closer look at those pieces," he said, and with Nathan a step behind, began working his way out of the crowd. They headed for a line of picnic tables upon which several rifles rested, set up in various displays to show off their best features. The two of them found the rest of their team at one of the tables, hefting a couple of the new rifles. Lieutenant Barlot held one of them to his shoulder, peering through the scope of the unloaded rifle.

"So, Lieutenant," Lanier said as he approached, "are the city fathers going to buy us a couple of these things?"

Barlot let the rifle down, clearly admiring its lines. He handed it over to Lanier with a smile on his face. "Why bother, Jerry, after looking at the scores you and Nathan put up?" The city was in fact considering such a purchase for the HRG team.

"Aw, boss, but Christmas is coming," Lanier said, and took his turn examining the weapon.

* * *

Fifty feet away, two men stood observing the tactical team officers. One was Kevin Parsons, who owned his own company, ASP, Armament Systems and Procedures. He was a big man, close to six feet, and solid in a way that suggested he was familiar with the gridiron. He wore a sport coat and tie, and ignored the slight breeze that touched his thinning hair.

The other man, slightly smaller in stature, was Thom Castlebank, who ran his business out of Atlanta, Georgia. His features were benign, his salt-and-pepper-bearded face lending a professorial appearance to a man who had twenty years' experience in special weapons, both in their operational use and in training. As an instructor in weapons of this type, he was in a class by himself.

Both gentlemen had been brought in as consultants by Arms Tech for their national promotional tour of their sniper's rifle. Parsons and McLoughlin acted as experts to field specific questions concerning the use of the rifle in a multiplicity of tactical situations, both rural and urban.

"Interesting crowd," Parson said, looking over the policemen milling around.

"They always are," Castlebank replied. He was watching Lieutenant Barlot's group pass around one of the rifles nearest them, and saw a few of them chuckle at a comment Barlot made. They were too far away to hear what had been said. There was something familiar about the group, he thought, but Parsons was speaking to him.

". . . see the new suppressor AWC's got now?" Parsons was saying.

Castlebank turned his ear to his friend, but his eyes were drawn back to the group.

"You mean for the .308?" Castlebank asked, his tone a little preoccupied.

"Yes," Parsons said. "It's tiny, compared to what's being used out there. The example I saw was only five inches long, and . . ." He noticed Castlebank's attention was not all there.

Immediately Parsons's eyes sharpened, more from ingrained habit than any other overt reason. "What's up, Thom?"

Castlebank realized he had been distracted. He nodded at the tactical team, with his hands in his pants pockets. "Nothing, I guess, Kev. That group over there," he said, and shrugged once. "The tall guy looks familiar. I've seen him before, I think. Can't be sure," he said, squinting to see better, but the gesture didn't help. "Maybe another training gig, but where . . . ? Ah," he said, and turned away. "Maybe not. Dressed in camouflage they all start looking the same after a while."

"I know the feeling," Parsons replied. "Truth is," he added with a wry smile, "between the two of us, we probably *have* trained a few of these boys over the years."

"Probably right," Castlebank said. "Now what's the new AWC suppressor about?" he asked, forgetting the Westport team for the moment.

* * *

Aaron handled his surprise well. He didn't think any of the others had noticed his concealed reaction to seeing Thom Castlebank. He'd instantly recognized the man. Their paths had crossed seven years ago, when Aaron had been in Wisconsin, tracking John Burris before the man had died of leukemia. Aaron's SWAT team had gone through a training session on CQB, close-quarters battle with the new Heckler & Koch MP-5 submachine guns they'd just received. Castlebank had been one of the instructors.

The problem was immediate, but manageable, he knew. He couldn't leave, not without attracting attention from his teammates. But more important, he had to avoid his former instructor. The last thing he needed was to be recognized as one of his former personas.

Maintain, boy, that's all, he cautioned himself. Stay cool, but keep away from Castlebank. He ambled away from the display table with the rest of the team.

Aaron stayed with the group, using the other bodies as much for cover as anything else, keeping them between himself and the older man, who now seemed to have forgotten about him. For a few moments he thought it was over. Castlebank had been staring directly at him, and Aaron knew he had remembered. He also knew he had looked different then, and hoped that the changes to his appearance now, and the intervening years, would cast some doubt with Castlebank.

Still, the best course of action was to stay away from him and find a natural way to leave. He would also have to come up with a way to skip the reception and dinner that evening. He dare not risk another brush with the man.

October 7

Dayton, Ohio

Vanessa checked the packet of files waiting for her with the receptionist. "These are all of them, Elena?" she asked the older woman, who looked up from her PC monitor.

"Yes, Ms. Tau," Elena said. "Mr. Ravenni said it was just those four, I believe."

Vanessa slid each file down to read the names, speaking aloud as she did. "Tusca, Warrington, Barlot, Samm." She paused upon finding Nathan's file amongst them. "I didn't know Nathan was from outside Westport."

Jeff Ravenni happened to stroll out of the hallway into the reception area just then, and overheard her remark. "Hi, Vanessa," he greeted her, and motioned to the stack of files. "I see you've got the personnel files."

She returned his greeting with a smile and held up the top folder with Nathan Samm's name on it. "Interesting getting Nathan's file here. I assumed he had been with Westport for a while."

Ravenni explained. "Sergeant Samm has been with the PD about three years, but he came from out of state. His file shows an impeccable record, though. I don't think we'll have much to worry about him, or most of the others, either. They all look pretty clean, from Chief Tusca on down, except one." His brow furrowed a bit. "The only one that looks a little off-center is Lieutenant Barlot. There's a discrepancy in his record, but you'll see it. Have your people check him out as close as they can, OK?"

Vanessa reshuffled the stack and found Barlot's file. "Anything special I should be concerned about with him?"

Ravenni leaned an elbow against the reception counter, feet crossed at the ankles. "Barlot's been with Westport about four years," he said. "He was in Alabama before that, on a SWAT team near Montgomery. His record's light."

She looked confused. "Light? I'm not sure what you mean by that."

"Maybe nothing," Ravenni said. "But for a guy with over fourteen years' experience, there's not a lot showing there. You get the feeling there ought to be more to see. Maybe there is, and it's not there for a reason."

"You think he's covering up something?" Vanessa asked.

"I'm not sure," Ravenni said, pushing off from the counter. "That's why we're giving him to you to check out," he smiled.

She returned his smile with a wry one. "And if we do find something in his past?"

"Let us know right away," he said. "I'd rather find out on our own before Julia Disare does. It could require some damage control. And tell your people to be discreet, OK? Julia's style is to send out a PI to do the same checking. And she's got a couple of ex-Feds she uses. They're pretty good at finding things, if you get my drift."

Vanessa repacked the folder and slipped the big rubber band about the package. "I'll get these off to the respective branch offices immediately," she said. "And I'll tell them to complete the checks quickly, but quietly."

"That's the idea," Ravenni said. "Thanks, Vanessa."

She waved with her free hand. "No problem, Jeff. I'll let you know what we find out soon."

He walked off down the hallway. She hefted the package. This ought to be interesting, she said. It'll also give me a chance to learn a little more about Nathan. She smiled to herself, then said goodbye to Elena. The prospect of getting a step closer to Nathan was appealing. Especially since she planned to take it further than that, and soon.

* * *

Back on the interstate Vanessa realized she would pass by Westport on her way to her office. She decided to make a quick stop by the police headquarters and see if Nathan was available to answer a few of the background check questions. It didn't take her long to find the duty sergeant's desk.

"Yes, ma'am?" the sergeant said, eyeing her appreciatively through the thick glass at the visitors' window.

Vanessa offered her business card for him to see, and identified herself. "I'm with Trans Patriot Insurance, and I'm working on a lawsuit involving several Westport PD officers. Is Sergeant Samm in? There's a couple of things I need to go over with him."

Satisfied with her credentials, the desk sergeant checked a large acetate-covered chart on the wall beside him, and after a moment, shook his head.

"Afraid not, Ms. Tau. Sergeant Samm is in the field today."

"Oh," Vanessa replied, a bit disappointed. It had been a chance thing anyway, deciding to come to the station. She really should have called ahead. "That's all right. Will he be back any time soon?"

"Don't think so," he said. "Would you like him to call you?"

"Would you?" she said. "He can call the number on my card."

"No problem," he said, and she heard the tone of dismissal in his voice.

"Fine," Vanessa said. "But if it's after six, he can call my home number," she said.

"And that would be?" the sergeant asked.

"Sergeant Samm has it," she replied, and turned away. Let him figure that one out, she thought to herself.

Back in the Blazer, she paused a moment, looking vaguely at the building. She had been genuinely disappointed that Nathan hadn't been there. Had she really wanted to see him over the lawsuit business? Just that?

"So?" she asked aloud, challenging her little voice. "A girl can't call a man on occasion?"

Sure, it answered. Whatever you say. Geez, she thought, this is getting ridiculous. She backed the Blazer out of the parking slot and glided down the street. In the back of her mind she had already decided that if he didn't call her by 9:00 p.m., she was going to call him. She figured it was time to put her inner voice to the test.

October 10

The Pentagon, Washington, D.C.

Colonels Manos and Husta were in the midst of a problem. They'd put together all the latest information they could on the eight murder suspects from the old Fourth Division squad. Modern law-enforcement computer networks made the task of reconstructing their individual lives for the past two decades relatively simple. The information gathered confirmed an unremarkable and consistent thread to most of their lives.

Almost to a man they had walked the fringes, sometimes stepping over the line into brushes with the law, problems with booze or drugs, a series of short-lived jobs, or a combination of all of that. Some were wife-beaters, some couldn't keep a spouse, and a couple had spent some serious time behind bars. But through all of their sordid records, they all shared a common thread.

"Losers," Husta said at one time, shaking his head in tired disgust. "Damn near every one of them. They came back to the World, fell into a hole, and pulled the lid closed after them."

Manos agreed, slapping a pile of printouts onto the thick stack. "Pretty sad group of assholes, no doubt about it," he said. "They didn't have much going for them before Nam, and sure as hell had nothing going afterward."

"Yeah, it's interesting in one way, though," Husta said. "The only one who showed any promise is Landau. And he really sticks out from the rest."

"Professor William Landau," Manos said, leaning back in his chair, fingers laced behind his head. "Who'd ever have thought a murderer would end up teaching college history?" His mouth twisted, as if he'd just tasted something sour.

"He and Michael Madison in Indiana are the last ones. Taking any bets on who goes next?"

Manos lowered his arms, coming upright in his chair. "I thought we were trying to stop that from happening," he said.

"That is the mission," Husta said, "but you have to wonder. These guys have been targets for a long time, judging from what we've seen so far. You have to figure young Longbaugh's long since checked them out. It's like he's taking them at his leisure. I still haven't figured out why there is so much time between them. But you also know sooner or later he will catch up to them."

"Like I said, that's what we're supposed to stop, right?" Manos got up from the table and began to pace the small conference room. "We can take these guys one at a time, or together," he said. "Either way we're going to have to let each of them know they're being hunted."

"The problem is which one to protect next," he said. "There seems to be a window of time here, but I have the feeling that the next one's going to be soon. Jack Linet was the last one, in '91, remember. I think Longbaugh is due for another by now."

"Right, but which one? If we split up and try to cover each of them at the same time, we might warn Longbaugh off. On the other hand, if we go together, we leave one of the potential victims unprotected."

"Unless we go with option C," Husta said. "Call in reinforcements."

"The Feds," Manos said, his reluctance apparent.

"Hey, I don't like it either, but we're a little thin here. The old man already turned us down."

Manos grunted in acknowledgment. They had gone to their boss, General Polchuski, and laid out what they had found, and suspected, about the eight men. In a scene eerily reminiscent of twenty years before, the general had turned down their request, citing circumstantial evidence problems. "Get me some hard proof," he had said, "and I'll give you a team."

Further arguments had gotten them nowhere, despite what they knew was happening. The only points they had gained were a limited operating budget for themselves. "Work on it, just the two of you," the general had said. "I can squeeze some appropriations for you, but that's the best I can do. You have to bring me something more than this."

Now they were getting to a critical stage. They couldn't go too thin on this, not with lives in the balance. But their only option, as they had argued before, was to go outside the CID. At least with the Bureau, they'd have some more manpower, if nothing else. And Jim Manos had a contact. They proposed the idea to the general, who recognized the advantages of associating with their sister agency in the effort. He gave his approval to at least talk to the Bureau about the case.

"I'll call Pete Jovenall," he said.

Husta nodded. "I don't see where we really have a choice," he said. "Pete's good, and he owes us a few favors. He'll respect our jurisdiction on this one, too."

"Until we decide to turn it over to him, if we ever do," Manos concurred. "If Aaron Longbaugh is the shooter, then he's ours, and he remains ours. Pete'll have to accept that, or no deal."

"I agree, Jim, but let's keep our options open, too. This might get a little sticky."

"I think we're already there," Manos said. "Let me set up a meeting with Pete." He reached for the phone. "How about the metro station on the Mall?"

"OK by me," Husta said.

Manos dialed the number. He knew it by heart. The two CID officers had worked with the Bureau agent several times over the last six years. When he picked up on the other end, Manos said, "Pete? Jim Manos . . . fine, yeah. Listen, I have something for you, my friend." He began to explain the story.

* * *

Peter Jovenall stared up at the curved ceiling of the metro tunnel. It never ceased to amaze him how big the station was. And they're all over the city, too, he thought. All of Washington must be honeycombed with tunnels.

His eyes dropped, and he swept them over the crowded floor below them. He and his partner, John Paraletto, were on the upper floor near where the long escalators deposited and picked up passengers. The two agents were waiting to meet with Jovenall's Army CID associates.

"Husta and Manos know I'll be here too, right?" Paraletto asked.

"Yeah, no problem," Jovenall said, scanning the people around them too. "After what Jim started to tell me over the phone, I told him I thought it would be a good idea to let you in on it. I think he's got something we'll both be interested in."

"You sure these guys're on the up and up?" Paraletto asked. "The last thing I need right now is some kind of ridiculous domestic cloak-and-dagger routine. The Bureau's getting more than its share of bad press, with all the Senate hearings and leaks about crime lab screwups."

Jovenall waved off the question. "Manos and Husta are OK, John. I've known Jim about six years now. We've worked a few cases together. They've always been straight with us, hard as that has been on occasion. The Pentagon's still one big pain in the ass, but you already know that."

"Yeah, I already know that," Paraletto repeated. He'd spent his time in the service, back in the late sixties and early seventies. He'd done one tour as an Army helicopter pilot, flying copilot with Luther Sitasy, who worked at Trans Patriot Insurance out in Phoenix. Paraletto's few years in the military had forever soured him on how it worked, or frequently didn't, he remembered wryly. Consequently he had worked hard at putting those years behind him.

"There they are," Jovenall said, indicating with his chin the two men in civilian clothes who had entered the lower lobby off the train that had just arrived below.

Tony Husta paused, casually looking around, and spotted the two agents on the second floor. He motioned to Manos, and they strolled over to the escalator and stepped on, riding it up.

Jovenall and Paraletto waited for the two men to join them. As they neared the top of the escalator, Jovenall pushed off the railing to take Manos's proffered hand first. "Jim, glad you could join us." He handled the brief introductions.

Husta looked eye to eye with Paraletto, not an easy task as the big agent stood six feet two. But height was all they shared. Paraletto outweighed Husta's 180 pounds by forty more.

"Shall we get down to business?" Jovenall offered.

"Let's walk a bit," Husta said, and the four of them formed a loose formation and began to stroll toward the exit.

"There was a fragging episode in Two Corps, March of 1970," Husta, began. "A squad from the Fourth Division, near Pleiku, ambushed and murdered their battalion operations officer," and he proceeded to tell both agents the full story. He also went on to describe the judge advocate's reaction, and how their case against the eight men was denied for lack of any hard evidence.

They emerged outside and ambled in the direction of the Mall, taking their time. All four men casually kept track of their surroundings, looking for any overt eavesdroppers. None were expected, but the act of looking was ingrained, long since automatic in nature.

"So what happened after that?" Jovenall said.

Manos picked up the story. "The world continued," he said. "The war ended, and we all came home. I arranged a transfer to Special Forces, one of those moves supposedly good for your career, you know." The group neared the front of the Freer Gallery of Art. "I was stationed at Eglin AFB in 1980, doing after-action debriefs on classified overseas missions, when the kid showed up, totally out of the blue."

"What kid?" Paraletto asked.

"Aaron Longbaugh, the dead major's son," Manos said. "By then he was also in the service, fully Ranger and Special Forces qualified, and assigned to special ops."

"In what capacity?" Jovenall asked.

"As a sniper," Manos replied, his tone serious. He went on to explain what had happened between them at that unusual meeting, leaving nothing out about his telling the young sergeant the truth of his father's murder.

Manos looked at Paraletto to find the big man regarding him with a peculiar look on his face. His eyes were focused and intense. Nothing spoken in the last twenty minutes had gotten past him.

"So we have a vengeance thing going," Paraletto said.

"Without embellishing it too much, that describes young Longbaugh pretty well," Manos agreed.

"And there's not much doubt between you two that Aaron Longbaugh is the suspect?" Paraletto said.

Manos glanced at Husta. "There's always the possibility that it's someone else. Hell, given the facts, you can build a fairly solid hypothesis that the killer is someone else. Maybe there's a rogue JAG type out there, or a buddy of Major Longbaugh's from the Fourth Division, or whatever." He looked back and forth between the two agents. "Tony and I considered a few possibilities, some of them pretty far out, some not so bad. But the facts come back to the kid, and my meeting with him, and when the first killing occurred."

"Yeah, the time line appears right," Paraletto agreed. "But I'd feel better getting a profile run up on this. I'd like our behavioral-science people in Quantico to take a look at this. We'll need to consolidate all the individual homicide investigations out there."

Manos nodded to his partner. They had expected this approach, despite their convictions already. All the bases needed to be covered on this one. Especially on this one.

Paraletto continued. "So how do you want us to split up the labor?"

Husta answered. "There's only two of them left, Landau in Ohio and Madison in Indiana. There's also some family territory back in Kansas to go over. Jim and I would like to handle that end for starters. Can you guys cover Landau and Madison for now?"

"We ought to be able to do that," Jovenall said. "I suppose you've considered protective custody?"

"We have," Husta said, "But if they don't want the protection, there's nothing we can do about that. The evidence isn't enough to keep them under wraps. And they're hardly going to confess to a murder-one rap now." He smiled wryly. "It's turn about, actually. Twenty-five years ago we couldn't convict these guys for lack of solid evidence. Now we can't keep them alive for the same reason."

"And they might not believe us anyway," Manos added. "Once upon a time Tony and I tried real hard to get these guys convicted of murder. There's no love lost between them and us. Plus, the last time we saw all of them alive, we told them we'd be back, that we'd never rest until we got the proof we needed against them. They might think this is all a ploy. They'll take some convincing, and to be quite frank about it, I'm not exactly looking forward to sitting down with either Landau or Madison again. Part of me hopes the kid gets to them before we do."

"There is one other thing to consider, too," Jovenall said. "As I understand it, these eight men were ordered to keep away from each other. No communication of any kind. After all this time, you don't really believe they've done that, do you?"

"What are you driving at?" Husta asked.

Jovenall's eyebrows went up. "Simple. That one of them is the bad guy. Maybe he's afraid someone in the squad was going to eventually rat out on the rest. So he's taking care of that, over time."

"On the installment plan," Husta said, thinking about it. "It could happen. Not likely, I think, but a possibility. We're pretty sure they arranged to have Carlos Madrid knocked off in his cell at LBJ. That establishes a precedent, but I still don't think one of them is going after the others."

"I agree with Tony," Manos said. "You're betting that Madison and Landau know about the other deaths." He shook his head. "I don't think so. We've only done some preliminary checking, but they've not done anything to suggest they know. Neither has relocated, or disappeared, or changed their patterns to suggest a reaction to a threat like this. Madison's still working at his job at the local town newspaper, and Landau's still at the university. That suggests they're still in the dark. If one of them is the killer I'd be very surprised."

"Then they'll need some convincing for their own sake," Paraletto said. It was his first brush with a documented fragging episode from Vietnam. He had heard about them before. Stories like this were rampant during the war. But this . . .

"And if either one of them refuses protection, or help, do we let them go, or keep on it?"

Manos shoved his hands into his jacket pockets. "We have to stay on them, until we catch the kid."

"Or whoever," Jovenall added.

"Hey, benefit of the doubt," Manos said, "but you're right. Still, much as I'd like to just walk away until he, or whoever, takes them out, we can't do that."

"I know," Paraletto said. "I just wanted to get the game plan on the table." His mind was still working on what was needed. "Who've you got running down the kid's background and whereabouts?"

Husta flicked his thumb at Manos and himself. "Just us," he said. "Times are tough, and so's the money. Jim and I are the total investigation team."

"Not anymore," Jovenall said. "Now you have us. We can get some more manpower in on this. We can set up shop on the last two targets, Bill Landau and Mike Madison."

"Tony and I have the book on Aaron Longbaugh," Manos offered, "and we'll start running down this thing from that angle. Maybe we'll find a way to intercept him. We still have two bright lights out there."

"Yeah, and someone who wants to turn them off," Husta said.

"And one other thing," Manos said. "We keep calling him a kid. Aaron was twelve years old in 1970 when his father died. He's thirty-seven now."

"Yeah, we're all getting older," Jovenall said.

"This case has added years to my life already," Manos replied. "I think it's going to add more before this is done."

"So let's go to work," Paraletto said. He liked the CID men, and the straight-ahead manner between them. He also recognized that they operated like a smooth machine, with all the subtleties of two people very comfortable with each other. He had no doubt what they wanted to do.

The four men strolled off, the beginnings of an expanded plan forming. The two agents, new to the case, considered how and where to begin, each motivated by procedures and a certain protocol in matters like this, but unable to distance themselves from the morality of the story. Sometimes, things worked themselves out because that was the best way. Maybe finding the killer and stopping him wasn't the best way to go about this one. But their pride and their duty to the job mandated otherwise. They'd do what needed to be done to find Aaron Longbaugh, or whoever it was out there.

Manos and Husta came at the case from a different perspective, one more personal. This business had taken a lot from them a long time ago, and had left unsettled feelings and a load of unresolved issues. Now there was more added to the pile. They were convinced they knew who the avenging killer was. But like the agents, their agenda had long since been set. They, too, would find Aaron Longbaugh, and stop him.

But none of the four men were entirely convinced it was the best choice. Indeed, the only fact they did know, and agreed on, was that it was their only choice.

October 10

Trans Patriot Insurance, Scottsdale, Arizona

Gordon Hatton called up the diary list of files yet to be worked, and they appeared instantly on the monitor's screen. He tapped in a macro command, and the list disappeared, replaced by a three-dimensional computer image that showed his desktop, viewed edge on, with his in-box on the side. A stack of file folders rested neatly in it, and the pile was over a foot in height, all of them expandable folders. The depiction was as if he were looking at an actual picture of his desktop. The image represented the files he had to go through.

"Not a normal one in the bunch," he mumbled, and shook his head. "Man, I hate disc-pro audits." Disc-pros were discovery procedural audits, a survey of law firms' efforts on the defense of a particular case. Gordon correlated all the discovery performed over the life of a case against an established protocol. All he had to do was check off what he found in the file. Trans Patriot's system then ran a comparison of legal expenses incurred against the work reported, and that against the actual invoices received. The final tabulations were incorporated in the law firm's permanent file, which was reviewed quarterly by TPI's in-house legal audit division.

He called back the file he'd been working on and clicked on it to attach his initials to the closing checklist. Then he pulled up the next one off his diary list, noting this one was from Trans Patriot's Macon, Georgia, branch office.

He'd completed four similar audits already, and figured he would be through with the rest in a couple of hours. This was but one of his tasks as one of the managers in the Professional Liability Department. A few years before Gordon had worked for Luther Sitasy in the Policy Limits Division. The two of them had been promoted up the line, still in the same overall division. Luther was now the vice-president of the division, with several other departments reporting to him, including the professional liability group.

Gordon's primary responsibility remained the policy limits cases, the section that Luther used to manage. But his duties had been expanded as well. It kept his mind on the present, which was what he preferred.

Gordon pushed back from his desk and stood to stretch, taking deliberate care with his legs. They still bore the scars from the fiery explosion that had almost killed him five years before. Norman Bloodstone had set the trap, turning Gordon's entire house into a natural gas bomb.

Bloodstone, a former TPI investment broker, and Dana Quinn, employed by the company in the same job, and Bloodstone's lover, had created a deadly scheme to murder policy limits claimants, freeing the million-dollar reserves on those files for use in their own investment scam. They had thought that Gordon and

Luther Sitasy had discovered their scheme, and attempted to kill both of them. The explosion at Gordon's home had left him with third-degree burns and multiple fractures of both legs, plus deep-tissue burns of his lungs, which had cost him the surgical removal of the right one. He spent thirteen months enduring skin grafts and painful therapy before he was able to return to work again.

The same explosion took the life of Sheri Moradilo, Gordon's fiancée, and her young niece, leaving him with additional emotional scars that had yet to satisfactorily heal.

Bloodstone's subsequent murder attempt on Luther also failed and led to a bloody confrontation in which Luther eventually shot Bloodstone to death, after the killer had taken the lives of three police officers.

Gordon's return to Trans Patriot over a year later had brought with it many difficulties. Still, he had accepted the promotion to manager, a minor but deserved plaudit from the company.

The injuries to his legs caused Gordon to favor the right one, and he took care with it, propping his foot on the pulled-out edge of a desk drawer. Bent over, he massaged the leg from the knee down, absently gritting his teeth against the residual pain as he did so.

After a few minutes he returned to his chair, and the waiting file. It involved a four-year-old police wrongful death action for a township east of Macon. The named insured's police SWAT team had shot and killed a man acting irrationally, threatening neighbors in his small development. The suspect had been high on PCP and cocaine at the time and had attacked several officers trying to talk him down. He had used a heavy-bladed hunting knife, badly lacerating two of the officers before a SWAT team sharpshooter had killed him.

The case had gone to trial and resulted in a defendants' verdict. The plaintiff's estate had appealed, and the decision by the appellate court had just come down, again affirming the U.S. district trial court's findings. This time the plaintiff's side had given up, and the matter remained resolved.

Gordon paged through the computer-replicated file just as if he had the actual file on his desk, reading it from back to front, taking note of the discovery conducted by the defense firm. The computer program isolated each page of the file individually as a separate, three-dimensional image, including the back side of the paper if additional information was on the reverse side. It turned the pages with a simple click of the controlling mouse.

He had gotten past the field report by the GBI, the Georgia Bureau of Investigation, when he came across the newspaper accounts of the shooting, lawsuit, and trial. He read the articles from three different publications in detail, two from Atlanta, and one from Macon.

One page had a brief column, and its small size hinted that it had been fitted in just to fill the space. It depicted the dead-end investigation of yet another local, and unsolved, murder.

After four years, police still have no clues in the murder of Jack R. Linet, Gordon read to himself. Linet, a long-time resident of Macon, was found shot to death outside his rural farm home May 27, 1991. He had been shot twice, once through the body and once through the head. Police surmised the shots came from a distance, though they could find no evidence to confirm that theory.

Linet, estranged from his wife, Lucille, and their three children, had no known enemies. Mrs. Linet had been questioned initially, but cleared of any suspicion. She has since remarried, and has moved to Dalton. Police are still looking for anyone who may have information related to this investigation. Any such person may call the Silent Witness hotline at 1-800-9-SILENT.

Gordon glanced at his desk clock and read on quickly. One page included photos of the deceased plaintiff's family and their lawyer after the defense verdict had come in. Another article on the same page contained pictures of the officer-defendants. A few of the officers had left the force before the trial, he noted. It was another by-product of litigation. Once sued, it wasn't unusual to see a cop choose to leave the department, rather than subject himself or herself to the legal grind.

He swept over the photos quickly and continued, checking off the appropriate items on his list. Fifteen minutes later he was finished and signed off on the file, signifying it was in order.

Gordon called up the next one, glancing at his small digital desk clock again. He had a lunch date with Luther at 1:00 p.m. Time for one more review before lunch. He started reading the next one, ironically smiling at the quick thought that claim files were his job security, after all.

"Yeah, right," he said under his breath, and continued reading.

October 13

Trans Patriot Insurance, Hamilton, Ohio

Vanessa Tau dialed the number while scanning the papers on her desk.

"Westport PD, Sergeant Mason," the male voice answered.

"This is Vanessa Tau, Trans Patriot Insurance," she said. "Is Sergeant Samm in this morning?"

"I'll connect you with the HRG's extension, ma'am," he said, and immediately put Vanessa on hold while he made the connection. She listened to a soft-rock FM radio station on the phone while waiting for the transfer. The line was picked up just before B. J. Thomas sang about what he was hooked on.

"HRG, Corporal Doyle," the new voice said.

She identified herself again and asked for Nathan. There was a series of clicks, then his voice.

"Vanessa? This is a pleasant surprise. How've you been?"

She felt the smile tugging on her lips. "I'm fine, Nathan, thank you. Actually, I'm calling on business," she said. "Those background checks we discussed last time. Art Gabel asked if I could expedite them a little. He'd like them sooner than he initially said."

"Is there some reason for the rush?" Nathan asked.

"Not really," Vanessa replied. "He just wants to incorporate the information into the responses to some of the discovery motions plaintiff's counsel has filed. It's pretty routine."

"I'm familiar with the process," Nathan interjected, and Vanessa had the feeling she had interrupted him in the middle of something.

"Oh, well then," she said, continuing, "I'd like to set up a time to go over some of the questions with you, if that's all right."

"I see," he said. He was quiet for a few seconds, and she imagined him checking his calendar. "No problem," he said. "How soon would you like to meet?"

"How about this Friday night?" she said easily.

"That'll be a problem for me, but next Friday's open," he said.

She quickly thought ahead and replied, "Next week is fine. In fact, it'll be even better. I have a couple of heavy tests coming up in the middle of the week, and I really have to study for them. By Friday I'll be ready to relax."

"Terrific," he said, sounding pleased. "Where would you like to meet?"

This was turning out better than she had hoped, but she kept her fingers crossed anyway. They could do a little business and maybe have time for something a bit more personal. It would be her best chance with him so far. "I finish for the day around five, and then I've got to get back home and get cleaned up," she started to explain.

"Why don't I pick you up at your place?" Nathan said. "There's no sense in your driving halfway to Dayton, and I'm sure there's some place in Oxford we could go."

His offer pleased her. Maybe this *was* a good idea, she thought. Smiling openly now, she said, "How's seven-thirty sound. You have the address?"

"Never leave home without it," he said, and they both laughed. She enjoyed the sound of his laugh. It fit him, she thought, but he was still speaking.

". . . ven-thirty will be fine. I'll see you then. We can go over those questions, then you can show me around the campus."

"You have a deal, Nathan," she replied. "You're sure this is all right with you?"

He made no reply for a few moments, then said, "I wouldn't miss it, Vanessa. See you next Friday."

"I'm looking forward to it," she said. "Bye." She hung up the receiver. That wasn't so bad, she said to herself. Then she sat back in her desk chair. Oh, man, what are you doing? she asked silently. This definitely wasn't like her. But how else was I going to see him again? It's fine, she told her little voice, don't worry about it. Just watch yourself, she heard softly, as the voice faded quietly away.

October 14

Connersville, Indiana

Connersville sat astride the crossroads of state routes 1 and 44, a rural community that never quite reached big-city status. It wasn't much different from any other farm-belt town in the state. Small-town politics and regional attitudes, with the local Grange putting on the annual Fourth of July picnic and barbecue. It was a comfortable, slower-paced life-style, but Connersville had seen its share of the big world.

Its sons and daughters had been venturing out into that bigger world, meeting challenges, and passing their new knowledge and skills back to the town. Connersville denizens were adventurous when they chose to be. Consequently they knew about life, yes indeed. And occasionally they met the country's call, for pride and duty were home-grown traits, not to be shirked. Returning survivors had brought back their experiences to be shared and examined by those who remained behind. Often those experiences were assimilated to become a permanent part of the fabric of life there, influencing the people and the times. Most times that influence was positive, adding to their heritage.

Sometimes, though not often, an individual would bring back something he never shared with the others, dared not, for the experience was frightening and destructive, a sordid reminder that even the city's own offspring were capable of doing the worst and bloodiest of crimes.

Mike Madison carried such experiences in his pressured mind. He sat on the bench in the square, his brown-bag lunch forgotten beside him, his stomach so knotted up that solid food was out of the question. Maybe tonight, he told himself. Maybe I'll get some soup down, if Alma will just stay the hell off my back. Or maybe it'll just be me and a cold silver bullet. Coors had become almost a staple in his life, anyway.

Then his subconscious nudged him with the irony of the beer's nickname he'd used. He jerked his head up, his eyes sweeping the rooftops for potential sniper sites. Sitting on the bench was risky, he knew. It could happen right here, he said to himself, looking around. Goddamn death wish, he thought, and not for the first time. Oh, sure, he had considered doing it to himself, especially in the last few weeks. He had cause, after what he had found out about the others.

Why not? he argued. Take the Ithaca pump and stick it under his chin. That'd take care of the problem, wouldn't it? Why wait for it, or him? He dragged his eyes down from the edges of the rooftops. Maybe he's not here yet, Madison said. But he's coming, his little voice answered, speaking the one thought that had become a constant for him. *He's* coming, whoever *he* is, and that's for certain. He's coming, and he'll kill you, it said, just like he's killed all the others. Six of us, so far, Madison thought.

The missing name jolted him a little. Madrid, he remembered, Carlos Madrid. Funny that he didn't consider him as one of them anymore. After his arrest the CID guys had shown up, and they all knew. But Linet had seen to that, cutting off that source, leaving the junkie dead in his cell in Long Binh.

"We shoulda been there, too," Madison mumbled aloud, under his breath. He'd taken to talking to himself too much, he knew, but ignored the singular habit. Talking to his wife, Alma, was a waste of time, and besides, they had nothing to say to each other anymore, it seemed. More often than not whatever communication they had now started after his fourth beer, and usually ended up with his hands on her, just tuning her up, he liked to say.

"And maybe she deserves it, too," he countered the edge of guilt that tried to push its way inside his head. He pushed it right back out and looked around nervously. Worrying about what, and who, was nearby was another habit that had worsened, too. His paranoia was well-founded, though. He had good reason for it.

"Six of us," he repeated, seeing their faces, deliberately ignoring Madrid again. "All dead, all 'cept Landau and me." He thought of the letter he'd sent to his old squad mate, the big-time professor not that far away in Ohio. It'd been fairly easy to find him, with the contacts Madison had on the newspaper. That was also how he had confirmed the whereabouts of the others, and eventually, what had happened to them.

He'd stayed away from contacting any of them at first, as they had been ordered to do. Eventually the years had piled on, and he'd almost succeeded in burying the incident, and the squad. But it had always been there, lurking in the blackness, jumping sometimes, unheeded. Other times it ripped into his mind often enough to tell him that no matter how he tried, no matter how much time passed, it would always be there. To worry him, to goad him, to torture him with its existence, giving him no peace.

Six months ago he had finally, reluctantly, relented. He'd made the first attempt to find them, starting with Max Perriman. Instead he'd found Max dead. It surprised him, but wasn't unexpected. Life goes on, things happen. It don't mean nothin', he'd thought at the time. Then he'd found the second one, and the worry had begun. Then the third, and fear had prodded worry aside. And now he knew. He'd turned to Bill Landau as his final hope. The two of them were all that were left.

"He'll come," he said, thinking of his plea to Landau. "He'll come, and we'll figure out what to do." Madison glanced around again, unable to stop himself from doing so. He ought to get going, get back to the shop. He worked on the big presses at the paper. Beside the huge machines, surrounded by their slamming, syncopated sounds, comforted by their sliding and whirling oiled parts, he felt secure and safe. They were solid, and reliable, and functioned because he kept them that way.

His hands and fingers carried the permanent marks from his years around them, caring for them. Black ink that traced every minute age line on his skin, following the prints of his fingertips, the life lines on his palms. Madison looked down at his hands, turning them back and forth, seeing the years in them, wondering at the good they had done, and the bad.

"Ah, fuck it," he said, louder than he intended. The letter carrier emptying the blue mailbox at the corner looked over at him quickly, distaste crossing his face.

Madison saw him, and recognized him. "And you too, Jake," he called out, unable to check the sudden vindictive, angry edge to his voice. "Fuck you, too, man," he said, and pushed up off the bench. The speed of the anger inside him left him shaky and surprised. He had to get away, walk away from Jake, and anyone else who might be nearby. If he didn't he knew that he wouldn't be able to control his hands. They'd reach out, and begin to hit, and hurt, and strike, and squeeze . . .

Alma's bruised features blipped into the forefront of his mind, and he groaned inwardly. He'd done that last night. He'd meant to get out, get away from the house and his wife, before the redout, before he lost it again, but he hadn't quite made it, and there she was, harping on him, shouting at him again, with the same old bullshit line, baiting him, pretending to be worried, but he knew better, he knew what she *really* thought, and he'd . . .

Madison kept walking, his pace throbbing in time with the pulse beat in his head. His fists were balled tightly, his thumbs working hard over the first knuckle of his index fingers. He kept his hands thrust tightly into his jacket pockets. He didn't trust them in the open, where they might get out of control. He didn't like getting out of control, but it seemed to be a way of life for him now.

Ah, Jesus, what's happening to me? he cried inside, but he knew the answer. Someone knew. Someone had found out, and he was coming for them, getting them all, hunting them down one by one. Who was it? he asked, easily for the thousandth time. Who wanted them badly enough after all these years? Captain Manos, or maybe his buddy Captain Husta? They knew, he remembered. They told them all that it wasn't over. The two CID officers would keep digging until they had the proof. And then they would come for them.

No, it wasn't them, Madison said, still striding down the sunlit street. Manos and Husta wanted to see the eight of them tried and convicted. They wanted the goddamn system to get them. No, they wouldn't be up for killing them, no matter how much they wanted them, or hated them.

It was someone else. It had to be someone else. Someone who knew it all, who had that special knowledge of the fragging he and the others had pulled off. But he hadn't a clue who it could be. No one knew but the Army, and they'd forgotten. His harried mind returned to the letter, mailed the day before. Yeah, that's it. Landau will know what to do, he thought, nearing the newspaper building's entrance. Madison remembered how intelligent Bill had been, back when they were young, before they'd decided to murder . . .

He reached for the door handle and paused. Madison cast his

eyes around behind him one more time, then pulled the door open. Not yet, he thought, entering the building, not today. The Ithaca twelve-gauge appeared in his mind, and he pushed it aside. Not that, either, he decided. Landau'll come. He'll come, and we'll figure this thing out. He'll come. He has to.

October 21

Oxford, Ohio

Dani Klein cast an appraising eye on Vanessa's attire. Slowly she looked up and down, taking in her salmon-colored Land's End denim blouse, fitted stone-washed jeans, and brown and taupe Windjammer moccasins.

"Stylish, without being too dressed down," she commented.

"You think so?" Vanessa asked. She had worried over her selection. "It's not going to be that kind of date," she said. "I'll take Nathan over to the Res, and we'll talk a little business. Maybe we'll walk through the campus a bit. Nothing special."

She wore her hair down, knowing its length helped give her height. She filled out the blouse fine, she thought, without attracting too much attention to that particular area. The slim jeans accentuated her graceful legs. Not bad, she thought, trying to be honest with herself. She leaned forward to check her eyes, thinking she had used the right amount of eye shadow.

Dani watched her go through her routine, and nodded. "Killer combo, girl. Now tell me again that this is a working date."

Vanessa glanced out of the corner of her eye. "It is. I really need to get some of this background information on Nathan finished up. We'll be working . . . mostly." Her tone suggested she had been waiting for such an opportunity for several weeks.

"Well," Dani said, checking the wall clock, "you've got about fifteen minutes." She reached for her jacket and took it off the hallway table. "I'll be at the library for a few hours. If you end up back here . . ."

Vanessa blushed. They had a prearranged signal if one or the other ever wanted some privacy in the apartment. The Venetian blinds in the living-room window would be left six inches from the bottom sash. So far in the entire time they had been rooming together, only Dani had taken advantage of their agreement, and that had been only the one time. "Oh, I'm not worried about that," she said. "I don't think that's going to be an issue tonight."

Dani put her jacket on. "Just the same, watch yourself. He might have other ideas."

"I don't think so," Vanessa said. "We're just going to have a good time, that's all."

"I hope so," she replied, and walked to the door. "Have fun," she said, and opened the door, then stepped back inside. "He's here." She came in all the way with Nathan Samm behind her.

Vanessa saw him and smiled openly as she went to meet him.

"We sort of ran into each other in the hall," Dani was saying, unable to hide the admiring look on her face as she perused the big man.

"Nathan, hi," Vanessa said, offering her hand to him.

Nathan took it firmly, but gently. His dark eyes smiled down at her.

Introductions were made all around, and Nathan shrugged. "I'm a little early."

"That's fine," Vanessa said.

There was a pause of a few seconds as the initial newness faded, and Dani moved toward the door again. "Well, it's a pleasure finally meeting you, but I have to be someplace else right now," she said. She raised both eyebrows in silent approval to Vanessa. The door closed behind her.

"Did I pass inspection?" Nathan asked, smiling.

"Absolutely. With flying colors." Vanessa said. She crossed the room to the closet, where she took out her jacket. "On these background interrogatories," she said, getting back to the business of the evening, "we're looking to see how your prior service record appears, if there is anything that the plaintiff's camp can use to hurt the defense, or discredit your testimony. The primary interests are in training and supervision," she said, accepting his help as she shrugged into the jacket. "In this case, Bennett's attorney has brought such allegations as part of her attempt to show the plaintiff's civil rights were violated."

"I thought it was something like that," Nathan said, nodding his head. "I've been through this before."

"Oh?" Vanessa responded. "How did you do? Any problems?"

"No, no problems," he said. "We won."

"Good," she said, picking up her purse. "Would you like to tell me about it? It could affect this case."

"There wasn't much to it," he replied. He pulled out his keys. "I'll tell you on the way."

*   *   *

They were in the main cafeteria in the basement of Schriver Center, which looked out over the beginnings of the south quad. The booth was designed with tall sides all around, both to provide privacy and to promote studying.

They sat in the deep booth, sipping sodas, trading questions and answers. Vanessa felt she had been doing most of the answering, though. She had meant to go over the list of questions Jeff Ravenni had given her for Nathan's background check. The list was identical to the ones she had already sent out to the Trans Patriot Insurance branch offices for Lieutenant Barlot and the other defendant officers who had worked out of state before coming to the Westport PD. The list read like a standard interrogatory and covered the basics, such as education, prior employment history, and occupational training.

At first Nathan had scanned the half-dozen legal-length pages quickly, then returned the list to her. "These questions seem pretty thorough," he said. His manner was noncommittal, but she noticed an edge of concern in his voice.

"They're meant to be," she replied. "The information requested is fairly routine, but is designed to uncover any skeletons hiding in the closet, so to speak."

He smiled. "I understand," he said. "Attorney Gabel is trying to find out if he's got a bunch of trigger-happy storm troopers as clients."

Vanessa heard a touch of bitterness in his statement, and it furrowed her brow. "You seem concerned, Nathan. Is there a problem with the questions, or with Mr. Gabel?"

He waved a hand and sighed, looking around. "It's nothing, I guess, Vanessa. I just don't like being on this side of it, being sued for doing my job." He returned his eyes to hers. "I'm sure this is old hat to you, dealing with lawsuits every day. Being on the receiving end, though, let's just say it's not pleasant."

Her face showed her sympathy. "I know, it's rough going into a claim like this, but that's why we've brought in Arthur Gabel. He really is one of the best defense attorneys in the business. And given the facts of this case, I think we're going to win this, a full defense verdict all the way down the line. Unless Arthur gets it dismissed first."

"A dismissal would be fine with me," Nathan said. He motioned toward the list again. "Why don't I take them with me and fill in the questions for you? I can mail it back to you then."

"Sure," Vanessa said, understanding his needs. She felt he wanted to have a more active part in the defense, rather than just sitting there waiting for things to develop. It fit his character, she thought. "Just don't take too long. Arthur will need these back in order to respond to some interrogatories the plaintiff's camp has sent."

"No problem," Nathan said. He sat wedged against the back wall, his long arm on the table, and watched the goings-on. "This is nice place," he said. "It's not what I imagined it would be."

Vanessa took a sip of her Coke, and asked, "And what did you think it would be?"

"Oh, you know," he said. "Kids jammed in everywhere, blaring music from the jukebox, a haze of cigarette smoke covering the room."

She laughed aloud. "During finals it's wall-to-wall students. But the loud music and smoking are out. This is, sad to say, the nineties. Didn't you go to college?"

He shook his head. "Never had the chance," he said. "Things after high school kind've got out of hand, and I had to get a job." He looked around the big room, enjoying himself. "I thought about going one day. So far, I've been busy doing what I do. Just never found the time, I guess." He looked across at her. "That's a bad excuse, isn't it?"

"Not if it's true," she said.

"I don't know," he said, turning around more, and resting his elbows on the table, crossing his arms. "You're going to school, and holding down a full-time job at the same time. I admire that. I just don't know if I could do the same thing, what with the time constraints of my work."

She considered his response a moment. "You could find another job," she suggested.

His eyes sharpened. "Not too likely," he said, and shook his head. "I'm sort of caught up in things, just now." He leaned back, and toyed with his soda cup. "It's all I know, Vanessa," he explained to her. "I've been doing this a long time. It's become important to me to continue doing the job." He relaxed a little, and made a motion with his hand.

"Of course, if I intend to keep on going, I'll probably need to get a college degree sooner or later. As you said," he acknowledged to her, "it's the nineties. Degrees are required if you want to go anywhere. And I intend to do that."

"Go somewhere or get a degree?" Vanessa asked.

"Both," he replied.

"Looks to me you're already going places," she said. "You have a responsible job, with a great future in it."

He smiled wryly at that. "Do you think so?" he said. "I've had times where I've wondered about that."

She considered his remark, and the dangerous side of his job, and nodded. "I can imagine," she said. "I was speaking to the need for your position. Law enforcement is a necessity in our world. It's sort of like that old cliché about death and taxes."

"Can't argue with that," Nathan replied. "Still, finding the time to expand on *my* needs is the problem."

"You'll find a way," she said.

"You sound pretty sure about that," he said with a grin.

"There's always a way," Vanessa said. "Besides, you look like the sort who always gets what he wants, sooner or later."

"I do, huh?"

"Indeed," she said, eyeing him closely. "And if that's true, why are you still single?" She had meant the question lightly, but she really did want him to answer.

Nathan paused, wondering where the abrupt change in the conversation had come from. He said as much in reply. "That one came out of left field."

"I'm sorry," she apologized quickly, realizing he had taken it a bit more seriously than she had intended. "You don't have to answer. It's just that you seem to have it all going for you. You've got a prestigious job," and she ignored his sudden smile at that, replying, "no, it's true. Being a police officer still carries a great deal of respect."

Nathan acknowledged her summation. "If you look at it that way, I guess you can say that. But availability presumes that the one available is looking, correct?"

She hadn't considered the possibility. "You mean you're not?" she asked.

He took a sip, studying her over the cup's rim. "Maybe," he said. "You've seen the stats, I'm sure, though. Cops have one of the poorest track records for relationships. Look at the divorce rate. I don't know if I have the right to expect someone else to attempt to put up with the kind of life I lead."

"You won't know until or unless you try, will you?" she replied. "Like you said before, it's not all ugly out there. There is a sense of balance going on. Relationships and marriages do last, despite the statistics."

"All right," he conceded, "but what if I never met anyone I wanted to take the time to know more about?"

Vanessa leaned against the edge of the table and crossed her arms. The move tightened the material of her blouse against her breasts, and she saw his eyes flicker down quickly. The look pleased her, especially now that she had him talking about himself. That was what she wanted.

"There are a lot of maybes you can fall back on."

He raised his soda cup and inclined his head slightly. "Touché," he said.

"So which is it?" Vanessa asked again, sensing she was pushing it, but wanting an honest reply.

"Do you always do that?" he said, echoing her earlier question to him. He crossed his forearms on the table and sat forward a little, a small smile on his lips.

"Do what?" Vanessa asked.

"Go for the throat like this," he said.

"As you said, it comes with the job," she said. "I learned a long time ago that if there's something you want, you have to decide how much you want it, then find a way to get it. But the key is to do it, not just sit around and talk about it." Her face sobered, and her eyes got distant. "It was that kind of thinking that lost my country," she said. "America taught me to work for the good things in life."

Nathan pushed back from the table. "We seem to have gotten a little heavy here."

"You don't like going this way, do you?" she said. "This is not the first time you've started to draw back when the discussion gets deep. I have to tell you from a woman's perspective it makes talking to you difficult at times, not being sure where the line is."

Nathan looked down at the tabletop as he digested her words. It had come out pretty fast, she realized, and had sounded a bit harsh, too. She hoped she hadn't angered him, and was about to say that when he answered her.

"I hadn't realized that before," he said, still with his eyes lowered. "Maybe it's an unconscious protective reaction . . . a defense mechanism. I've spent too much time divorcing myself from those everyday emotions, I'm afraid." Nathan raised his head but looked past her shoulder. "I've never let anyone get close to me," he said. "It's always been too . . . risky, I guess you'd say. For both sides."

"Are you uncomfortable with me?" she asked, her eyes softening.

He turned his eyes toward her. "In the beginning," he said, "the first time we met, yeah, a little."

"And now?" she smiled. She felt his eyes lock on hers, and a delicious tingle started at the base of her throat.

"Now, I feel very . . . relaxed . . . being with you," he said.

"I'm glad," she said, not sure what else to add to that.

"Weren't you going to show me the campus?" he asked suddenly, steering them back to neutral ground.

"Why not?" she said, accepting his change of topic, but unable to avoid the feeling of disappointment that nudged at her. She pushed out of the booth. "Let's walk if you'd like," she said. "We can come back for your car later," she added.

Nathan slid out and stood beside her, and helped her on with her jacket. "Truck," he corrected. "And walking sounds like a good idea."

"Truck," she acknowledged with a smile, and slid her small hand over his as it rested a moment on her shoulder. She caught his eyes and held them for moment before he deftly withdrew it. "That way," she said, motioning for the exit. He seemed more animated now, she thought, walking with him for the doors. I hope he stays this way. She had found out more than she had expected to. There were still unanswered questions, she realized, but she had finally answered one. He was definitely worth finding out about.

* * *

Dinner had gone well, with both the meal and the conversation remaining in a light vein, one complementing the other. Vanessa tried to pull him out about himself, but seemed to spend more time talking about herself. Afterward, they strolled through the lights of Oxford before returning to the campus, taking their time. They angled down the gentle slope past the bell tower and Roudebush Hall toward a large three-story building with an arch in the middle.

"That's Upham Hall," Vanessa said, "It's been used by both the biology and English departments for years." She pointed ahead. "We can cut through the arch. That'll take us to Maple and back to the Res, and your truck."

He paused on the terrace as they cleared the arch and looked up at the night sky. "It's peaceful tonight," he said, and she detected an underlying tone, as if he were melancholy over something. "Being here is an escape, isn't it?" he asked, but Vanessa had the impression he wasn't speaking to her.

He stood with his hands in his pants pockets and slowly panned around. "It's a good place to hide," he said after a few moments. "The world out there doesn't exist here. Nothing that makes it hard matters in this place, does it?"

His observations surprised her, especially coming from left field as they seemed to have. "You have an interesting way of seeing things," she said. "You're right in a way. College life isn't the real world. People who come here prepare themselves to go out into the big world, but the truth is, the biggest challenge is finals week. It doesn't compare to doing the nine-to-five routine. Seeing both sides as I do, I've come to appreciate ending my day back here, having a few classes to go to, where I can really let my mind open up and leave the day-to-day stuff behind."

"That's kind of what I was feeling, I guess," Nathan said.

"Yes, but it's all fantasy," Vanessa continued. "Sooner or later the ride ends, and that other reality starts. A final exam won't pay the light bill."

"I understand that," he said, and waved his arm around. "But until that time comes, Vanessa, you can exist here, safe from that other world out there, where no one knows who you are."

She heard his tone change again, this time to a hint of harshness, as if he was accusing her of something. She looked up in his eyes. "You mentioned it before," she said. "This is a good place to hide. Do you want to hide from something, Nathan?"

He returned her steady gaze, and they stood that way for several long moments. Vanessa felt a shiver deep inside and stepped closer to him, tentatively touching his arms, waiting for a response from him.

His hands came up slowly, fingertips lightly touching her temples, sliding down softly as they outlined her face, and she tilted her head up slightly, feeling the tingle inside again, warming her in anticipation.

"No, I don't," he said. His hands steadied on both sides of her face, and he brought his face down, nuzzling her cheeks in small movements.

His touches were in counterpoint to the rush inside her, sweet syncopation to the beginnings of that peculiar visceral thrill tightening below her stomach until she gave over to it, her eyes closing, his breath close against her lips, parted slightly for him, and they met his in a kiss that started soft, then harder, longer, and the tingling warmth suffused itself through her, and she held him to her until they parted.

"That was very nice," she whispered against his face, her eyes still closed, head down, not wanting to let go yet, not just yet.

"Any ideas?" he asked, his voice above her, muffled in her hair.

She pushed back from him, her eyes holding his. "I have a few," she said. "Why don't we go get your truck. Otherwise it's a long walk to my place."

Nathan didn't say anything for a long beat, then another, and another. She saw the decisions flitting back and forth far back in his eyes. When he started to speak, Vanessa touched her fingertips to his lips.

"Don't say no, if that's what it's going to be," she said softly. "Just hold me here instead. But if it's yes, take my hand, and walk with me. OK?" She took another step back, releasing him, and waited, fighting the nervousness in the pit of her stomach. Oh, God, what if he says no, what if he just turns and walks away, what if he . . .

Nathan held out his hand to her and half-turned, and she saw her answer in his eyes. Silently, her heart jumping, she took his hand in hers.

"Which way?" he asked.

There was only one answer. "Home," she said.

* * *

Vanessa closed the apartment door quietly behind the two of them and led him into the living room. A single lamp on a corner table provided a comfortable glow. Dani wasn't home yet.

"Wait a minute," she said, and crossed the room to the front window, removing her jacket at the same time. She dropped the jacket over the back of the long couch under the wide window, then lowered the Venetian blinds to within a few inches of the sill, and adjusted them, letting in the glow of the street lights.

"What's that for?" he asked.

She turned to him, and shrugged nervously. "Something I didn't expect to be doing tonight." She turned toward the bedroom, hesitated a moment, and said, "I'll be right back."

Nathan nodded slightly. "I'll be right here," he said, and watched her go. She shut the door quietly behind her. He crossed over to the big window, and rested his arm against the wall nearby, looking out through the slant in the blinds. He leaned his head against his forearm, and stared quietly at the street below. He was still in that position a few minutes later when Vanessa came out of her bedroom. His entire body registered her presence, as if his very skin could hear her approach. She stopped beside him, and he sensed the warmth and promise of her as her arm slipped around his waist.

"Something on your mind?" she asked, her voice questioning. He remained looking out and down, and she felt the nervousness in him, the tenseness in his back muscles, and instantly knew what his problem was. My God, she thought silently. He hasn't been with a woman in a long time. She pulled back from him slightly, and he turned then.

"No, not really," he said, facing her now, and looked a little surprised. "You changed."

She heard the appreciation in his tone. "It seemed appropriate," she replied. "You like it?"

Nathan looked at her, dressed in a royal blue silk robe, belted at the waist, that covered her completely. The dim light from the street angled across her in thin strips, illuminating the rich blue. He knew she was naked underneath. Her long ebony hair fell across her shoulders and back gracefully.

"I like it very much," he said.

She still felt his nervousness. She reached a hand up to his cheek. "I didn't know," she said.

"What?" he asked, not understanding.

"You," she replied. "How long it's been for you."

His grin was quick, almost boyish. "Damn. Am I that obvious?"

"Enough," she said, trying to keep the moment light. She didn't want to embarrass him any further than she thought he already was. Then she saw the indecision in his eyes.

"Hey, Nathan. It's all right. Look, I understand, really." She slid her hand down to his. "If you don't want to be here—"

"No, that's not it," he interrupted her. His head motioned outside. "Some people out there may not understand."

"What concerns people out there makes no difference to me," she said. "What happens in here does. Are you bothered by being here with me, Nathan?" She watched his eyes for several long seconds, not sure what he was thinking.

"No, I'm not," he said. "I want to be here with you very much. But . . ."

"Are you breaking a regulation or something?" she asked. "Isn't a police officer allowed a private life?" She had a sudden feeling she had touched on exactly what his problem was.

He gave her that quick grin again, his eyes softening. "There's no regulations involved, Vanessa. This is personal."

"I was hoping you'd say that," she said, "because it's personal with me, too. But you're still a bit tense. That's all right, too," she said, dropping her voice softly. "Let me help you with that." She untied the sash around her tiny waist, then took both of his large hands in hers, holding them between hers as if in prayer. She touched his fingertips to her chin, and slid them down her throat, then lower, parting the slick fabric of the robe. She drew his hands inside, encircling her.

Nathan felt the warmth of the skin on her back, and pulled her closer. She tilted her face up to meet him, and their lips touched. She reached up to wrap her arms around his neck, which pulled her robe open more. He moved his hands around to her front, and tentatively touched the sides of her full breasts.

"Oh, Nathan," she responded.

The heat from his touch radiated into her, but she sensed how cautious he was being. Her heart went out to him. He's more nervous than I am, she thought, her own emotions rolling now.

She pulled back from him, and slid her hand down over his, pinning him to her breast. She wanted him to know it was all right. She raised his hand to her lips and kissed it. Looking into his eyes she said softly, "Come with me, Nathan," and stepped back, pulling him gently along.

She paused in the doorway, knowing what lay ahead, knowing how she wanted it to be. Nathan stood before her, holding her hand, seemingly content to let her make the next move.

"All right?" she asked. She wanted him to know this, as well. If he wanted to, he could stop it. But he had to make the choice.

His hand squeezed hers. "Yes, Vanessa. This is very much all right."

She didn't say anything more. Instead she turned and walked into her bedroom. He followed close behind.

* * *

She was above him, raised on one arm, looking down, a silhouette in the faint light from outside. "Don't move, Nathan," she whispered, dark eyes glittering. "Can you do that? Keep your arms down," she said, her voice soft but heavy with intent. "You can't touch me, until I say you can."

"What?" he started to question, but she shushed him with her lips, and it began.

Vanessa touched him with her entire body, slowly and deliberately, the myriad points of contact forcing him toward tactile overload. Her lips caressed the lids of his eyes, closing them, letting him concentrate on the stimuli that cascaded across his energized nerves. Her hair drifted featherlike across his shoulders and chest while her mouth worked down the features of his face. Her legs caressed his carefully, smoothly, gliding across him.

Nathan's breath caught, held, then escaped in a low moan as she continued down his torso. His hands ached to hold her, and he started to lift one when she stopped him with a light touch, returning his hand to the cool surface of the sheets.

"Sshhh," she whispered, a long exhalation of breath, "not yet, Nathan." She shifted. "Soon, my darling . . ."

He moaned again, frustration building with his reawakened ardor, and he tensed, almost quivering with need.

"You like this?" she said.

"Oh, God," he sighed, then, the urgency in his tone tightening his voice, "let me touch . . . just a lit . . . just a little . . . please . . ."

She judged the moment, and the effect, and slid up along his body, molding herself to him, her hands finding his face, kissing him deeply.

"Yes," she mouthed around him. "Now, Nathan, touch me now . . ."

He reached for her, almost exploding, but checked himself at the last possible second, determined to show her as much pleasure as she was showing him.

"That's it," she said, nestling her face alongside his as she gave in to his ministrations. "That's the way, my love . . . that's the way."

They came together carefully, breath by breath, touch on touch, closing toward each other's center, so aware of the other's needs, yet needing the satisfaction of their own inner self that cried for the passion of release. They took and gave equally, exquisitely sharing all that they were, all that they imagined, until fantasy became real . . . so completely real . . .

*   *   *

"I'm going to have to leave soon," he said beside her.

"I know," she said. It was hours later, and they hadn't slept. They had come together again, the second time with more gentle holding than anything else, but even that had been intense. She stirred inside with a newfound awareness.

"I don't know what to say," he began, and she felt a stab of fear, until he finished with "except that I want to see you again."

She relaxed, happy with the thought that he had expressed her sentiments exactly. "I was hoping you would say that," she said. "I've been thinking about you a long time."

"I know," Nathan said, stroking her hair spread across his shoulder.

"You knew?" she said in surprise, raising up on her elbow to look at him.

"I kind've had that impression," he said, smiling back at her.

"Oh, God, now I'm the one who's embarrassed."

"No need," he said. "No one noticed, I guess, but me. I'm a trained observer, remember."

She popped him on the chest with her fist. "Don't give me that," she said in mock anger. "You let me go through all of this, knowing all the time I was interested in you, without . . ."

"Until tonight, I wasn't sure myself if what I thought I saw in you was real, or not," he interrupted. "I haven't had much experience in this sort of thing, Vanessa."

"Yes, I know," she said.

"Now I'm the one who feels obvious," he said, shifting until she lay beneath him again.

"Really?" she asked again, wondering what he was doing, then she felt him, and smiled.

"Really," he said again, moving to her.

"Yes," she said, sighing.

October 22

Miami University, Oxford, Ohio

Bill Landau carried his battered briefcase in one hand, and his packet of mail in the other. His steps echoed up the stairwell as he made his way up to his office. Landau enjoyed coming in to the office on weekends, rather than working at home. His office seemed more comfortable sometimes, and the building was quiet on Saturday mornings.

He unlocked the door, and dropped the mail on the desk, surveyed the papers in his in-box, and bent to put the briefcase near his desk chair. His mind was already organizing the morning's projects when he dropped into the chair and picked up the stack of envelopes.

Landau quickly riffled through them, separating the couple of large manila ones containing academic trade publications into their own pile. The rest appeared to be the usual correspondence, mostly business, but he paused with the next letter. He'd scanned the Indiana return address before his eyes froze on the name, and he actually felt the color drain from his face.

"My God, Mike Madison," he said aloud. He had known only one man with that name in his entire life. And almost every day for the past twenty-five years he had thought of that name, and those of the rest of the squad.

His fingers trembled as he tore open the edge of the envelope and pulled out the single-page letter. Not wanting to, not even wondering why Madison would be contacting him, Landau began to read the carefully typed words. It didn't take long, but he had to stop and go back a few times to reread the letter. When he was finally done, he sat back slowly, aware his heart rate had accelerated, his pulse thumping almost audibly in his ears.

"Jesus . . ." he whispered, and brought the letter up to read it again, this time slower, getting the feel for Madison's curt but brutal words. "There's no way," he said aloud. All the times he'd thought about Madison, Linet, Archer, and the rest came rushing in. How had they coped, were they surviving the years of guilt the same way he was? He spun his chair toward the windows, staring at the cold-bright morning. The glare hurt his eyes, and he turned away, fighting the rising panic within.

"It can't be," he said, fear cold and tight inside him, seeing their faces again, remembering the first bond that had brought them together, that peculiar brotherhood of combat.

Landau looked at the letter in his hand, then tossed it disgustingly onto the desk, as if the feel of the paper could somehow infect him, the letters skittering off the page and onto his hands. It can't be happening. Who is it? Who could know about us?

A new chill shivered down from the top of his scalp, a fatal illumination he couldn't escape, bright with certainty. He knew who it was. The thought fairly leaped across his guilty mind.

"Husta and Manos," he said, remembering the truth in their accusing stares, and their promise the last time he and the rest of the squad had seen them. Why hadn't he thought of them more often? he wondered. His mind had no immediate answer. Now they were back. They hadn't been fooled by all of Jack Linet's posturing, by all the lies they each had sworn to. Husta and Manos had promised to keep after them. It was their final parting shot to them, before the Army scattered them to the four winds, and he had never seen any of the others again, never heard from them, never called them . . . until now.

Landau's eye slid to the telephone, and he paused, his fright pumping away. He picked up the letter again. There are only two of us left, if this is true. Me and Madison. Mike! he cried inside, fear overriding the sense of duty to a brother, striving for a piece of the old feeling they had once shared.

He had to call him, he decided. He had to hear it from Madison personally. Maybe this could be explained. Coincidence, fate, life's peculiarities. Hell, he thought, there were a thousand explanations. It could be Madison's own paranoia running out of control. That he could sympathize with. Oh, yes, he knew *that* feeling pretty well.

His hand picked up the phone. Madison's number was at the bottom of the letter. Landau dialed, tapping the buttons absently, his mind whirling with the words he needed to say as the electronic burrs sounded in his ear. Landau felt his fear twist to anger, and that felt better, yes indeed, that *was* better, because it gave him a focus, a target to vent against, and . . .

"Hello?" the voice said suddenly, and his mind warped back across the years, seeing Private Michael Madison's face clearly, as they all were in his memory, unchanged by time, young men with old men's eyes, the stigmata of death on their faces.

"Mike? It's Bill Landau," he said, launching right into it, not knowing how it would go, letting the words tumble out, steamrolling over the man. "I got your letter. What happened, man? How did you find me . . . ?"

"Nice to hear from you again, too, old buddy," Madison said, his voice a monotone, the sound grating Landau to a stop. "It wasn't hard finding you," he continued, and Landau heard the long, tired sigh. Then Madison chuckled, but there wasn't a trace of humor in it. "Man, I was surprised to find you were still alive, considering . . ." and he trailed off.

Landau recovered quickly, his memory triggered by Madison's voice, sounding so like it had all those years ago. "God, Mike. It's been so long . . . so very long." None of the usual pleasantries seemed appropriate. It wasn't that sort of reunion call. "What made you start looking?"

"Curiosity, that's all," Madison replied, seemingly more animated now. "It's been a rough time for me," he added. "Thinkin' about the war, and . . . what we did. I've thought of you guys every damn day since I came home, y'know?"

Landau shuddered, hearing himself in Madison's words.

"It's been tearing me up, Bill," he continued, without having to specify what "it" was. "The first few years I kept looking over my shoulder, thinkin' they were comin' to bust me . . . all of us." Landau heard that odd laugh again. "Crazy shit, huh? But after a while, when nothin' happened, I figured, well hell, man, maybe they gave up on us. But it never went away, that feeling that someone was always out there, always watching. Hell of a way to live, man, but I guess you'd know too, wouldn't ya?"

"Yes," Landau answered, his mind whirling with their mutual fear.

"So that's how it's been for all these years, until I had to try, you know, to see how the rest of you were handlin' it. I figured, maybe

I could talk to the guys, maybe I wasn't the only one with the night-mares. So I started looking." His voice flatlined again, and Landau felt it. He glanced at the letter as Madison continued.

"I couldn't believe the first one, Bill. Max Perriman. You know how we used to hang together, talkin' cars and girls, makin' plans about gettin' back to the World . . ." and Landau thought of the young face, unable to see Perriman dead in his mind's eye.

"He was shot, man, that's what the newspaper article said. It blew me away, y'know? Like a bad dream at first, but then I thought, OK, it's just bad luck, a sign of the times. The odds had to catch up to at least one of us. Some irate husband, maybe a rob-bery, or a fight, whatever. It can happen, but the article said it was a rifle, and from long range. That's military shit. So I checked up on Pauly . . . Roselli, man, the wiseguy in New York." He was abruptly quiet, but Landau already knew what he had found.

"Same thing, Mike. I read it in your letter. There's no mistake? The articles had it right?"

"Yeah, yeah, no friggin' mistake, Bill. I doublechecked, as far as I could get with it. I didn't have the official records, just the local stories, stuff I could access from here. But still, there was that con-nection. All long-range rifle shots. Cops don't do that, not even SWAT teams. They don't have to shoot that far. I'm talkin' about hundreds of meters, real pro stuff. Only two outfits train for that, the government, and the military." He calmed down a little and continued. "They're all gone, man, he got them all, except Aceto and Burris, the lucky bastards. Nam got Johnny Burris . . . the big C . . . Agent Orange. Ate him up, from what I could find out," he said, and Landau heard him drift away. He almost called to him when Madison came back on the line.

"And Hector, Jesus, man. Crushed to death, buried alive in a ditch. Goddamn swingin' a pick in the sun, humpin' his back for a living. He didn't do so good either, ya know? The shooter missed them, but the odds didn't. Either way, it doesn't matter, does it? They're just as dead as the others."

"How did you get this information?" Landau cut in, surprised the two of them were talking as if they'd last seen each other the day before. Time had vanished for the moment.

"My job," Madison said, "at the paper. I asked some of the reporters to show me how to access the computers upstairs. I work on the big presses, see. But I'm not a reporter. So I asked around. It didn't take too long."

"Look," Landau said, picking up a pen and pad of paper. "Give me the newspapers and the dates of each . . ."

"Killing," Madison said for him. "It's all right, Bill. I had a hard time saying it, too . . . at first. Wait a minute," and Landau heard the receiver being put down. Madison was back a few moments later. "I thought you might want this stuff. I kept it handy . . . here it is," and he read off the list of articles he had found on his scan of local papers. The brief news articles on each murder sounded bland, meaningless epitaphs for the victims.

Only we're the victims now, Landau thought as he copied down the information.

Madison raised the question he had posed in his letter. "What are we going to do, Bill? They're out there, and they're coming for us. I don't want to wait for it, man. I can't stand the waiting, you know? But we can't go for help, right? Who're we goin' to tell? The cops? That's a laugh. We're *murderers,* man. We fragged Major Longbaugh, and that's murder one in anybody's book. But we all knew that goin' in, didn't we? Who knew it'd ever lead to this . . ."

Landau heard it, the plea in Madison's voice, and the fear too. The latter he was familiar with, and it ripped into his soul, forging a new bond between them, more pervasive than even their mutual guilt. "I'm sorry, Mike," he said again, meaning it this time. "What do you want me to do?"

"You feel it, don't you, Bill?" Madison replied. "This is real. It ain't bull. They're all gone, just like I said there. They know, man, and they're comin' after us. That's why I wrote to you, see. To let you know, because you're family, man." He was quiet for a few seconds, and Landau anguished as he imagined what he looked like now, sharing the panic and fright he had just learned himself.

"And," Madison went on, his voice shuddering with an intake of breath, "because I don't know what the hell to do. I thought you might. You always knew more than the rest of us, back then," he said.

Landau almost cried out with that, wanting to shut out the bitter irony of Madison's words. *It wasn't enough to keep us from murder!* he all but screamed out. *I never tried to stop it . . . !* He swallowed it with difficulty. Saying it would do no good. And wouldn't change it, not at all. The past, *their* past, had long since been set.

"Uh, I don't know what to do, right at the moment," he said, lacking anything more substantive to say. "You kind've hit me out of the blue with this," he added.

"Yeah, I figured it would get your attention that way," Madison said. "And like I said, this ain't made up or nothin'. I checked it out. Aceto and Burris are the only ones who missed out, near as I can tell," he said, his voice lighter for the first time, and Landau could almost see him shaking his head.

"I guess it doesn't matter," Madison continued, and repeated himself. "They just took another way to end up in the same place. What's the difference?"

"We're not taking either way," Landau said determinedly. "We have to come up with a way to beat this."

"Yeah, that's what I was thinkin', man," Madison replied, sounding more enthusiastic with new hope. "I was hoping we could get together, you know. Talk this over, see how we can stop them, what the options are . . ."

"You say that as if you know who it is," Landau said.

"There were only two who knew besides us, man," Madison said, his voice dropping to a whisper, as if he was afraid to be overheard. "Those two CID captains, Manos and Husta. Remember them? I bet they sure as hell remember you . . . and me, too."

Hearing their names come from someone else clarified the equation for him. Who else could it be? And if it was true, then the trouble was even worse than he had considered. What if they were still in the service? Jesus, man, they were CID. They had all the connections, all the means to find them, and to take them all out. The CID was like the CIA, or the Feds. Yeah, it could be them. Still, something didn't set right with that idea. The uncertainty renewed Landau's panic, but he kept it out of his voice.

"Look, Mike, I don't know. It doesn't all fit, man. Why would the

CID want to kill all of us off now? They had plenty of reason to keep us before, years ago. They couldn't make their case and kicked us loose. So why now? What's changed?"

"Hell if I know, man," Madison said. "I've been tryin' to figure that out, too, and I keep slammin' against a blank wall. Yeah, years ago, it would've made sense to me if they'd tried us, or threw us into Leavenworth. But then it came to me," he said, his voice rising with his certainty. "They took it personal, Bill, that's what it is. We are all loose ends that need to be cut off. They couldn't get us before, much as they wanted to. So the two of them waited. They're lifers, man. They're the big green machine. That's how bastards like them think. They figure enough time's gone that no one will look twice at what they're doing. Who'll care anything about us? So they decided to start after us. It has to be Manos and Husta, Bill. Who else'd know, or even care?"

Landau thought it made sense, too, up to a point, but it was off-center just a little. Something was missing from the equation. The problem was he couldn't see it. He wasn't capable of reasoning much better than Madison, right at the moment. "OK, I grant you it could be them. Let's take that for an operating premise. The why of it we know. They want us taken out for the fragging. All right, fine. I want to check into a few things, get a better feel for this." He felt it then, the old edge coming back. It was strange, but it didn't seem out of place, as if it had always been there with him.

"Sure, sure," Madison agreed quickly. "That's why I wrote you. But we don't have a lot of time. When d'you want to get together? Name the place, man, I'll meet you there."

"Soon, Mike. Let me do some looking of my own, OK? Then we'll get together, plan it out."

Madison picked up on it. "I hear you, man. We need an operations plan. We're goin' back in-country, huh? We did it to all them Victor Charlies, and the NVA, too. Put 'em into a box. Even Major Longbaugh," and he laughed again, harsh and tight. "We put him in a box, too, didn't we?"

Madison's raw-tinged voice cut into Landau. He'd thought he remembered, but he had forgotten what it was all about, how they had really survived the war, the true cost of combat. But you never left a buddy behind, either. He and Madison were the last. If that was true, then they'd make a fight of it. A new idea nudged its way up.

"I think I see how it's been going down. They used the years against us. They knew we wouldn't talk to each other, that we'd lose touch. They counted on us staying away from each other. We wouldn't know when one of us was taken out, and it almost worked. Only now we know, you and I."

"You bet your ass we know," Madison confirmed soberly. "I just hope it ain't too late."

"Just maintain," Landau replied, gathering strength from his old squad mate. "I'll call you in a couple of days, Mike." He paused a moment. "Look, in case you try to get me at home or the office here, and get no answer, let me give you another number where I might be." He gave him the Somerville apartment number.

"OK, got it, sure. But not too long," Madison said. "Don't wait too long. We may have to move out, y'know. Secure a safe place. If the shooter knows where we live and all . . ." His voice faded. Then, "Be seein' ya, Bill. Oh, one more thing." He paused a few seconds. "Get yourself a gun. Keep it around, close by, like. And take care of yourself, man."

The suggestion brought a new reality that settled down over him. So we're back to that, he thought. It had to happen, sooner or later. He could do it, though, he realized. If he had to go down that road one more time, he knew he could do it. There was no other way. "Yeah, I'll do that. You be careful, too, Mike," he said, but he was speaking into space. Madison had broken the connection.

Landau let the dial tone drone in his ear a long time before slowly replacing the receiver. Survival, that's the name of the game, he said to himself, and remembered the old phrase, when it had been too much, when things had gotten too deep to react any other way. "Fuck it, it don't mean nothin', drive on," he said aloud, staring at the phone. He had a lot of plans to make, and the clock was running.

October 23

Westport, Ohio

Aaron was still awake, an unusual situation for him. The end was coming, he could sense it. But he'd been dragging it out, taking too long, he realized. There were only two of them left now, separated by a relatively short distance. There was no reason to procrastinate any longer.

But that's what you've been doing, he told himself. It's been getting longer after each one. And you know the reason why, his little voice answered his own unspoken question. It was the job, and the duty, and the commitment. He enjoyed doing it, the sense of value it gave him, of contributing. As if his life had meaning . . .

"Ahh!" he growled, sitting up in bed. He knew where his mind was going with this. He didn't want to hear it again. There was no comparison between the two tasks, being a cop versus his mission to avenge his father. There was a valid purpose to both, he argued silently. Taking out these eight men has just as much importance as anything I've ever done wearing the badge. Why else did I go into the service, and why else was I chosen for the sniper school? Reasons, he argued, there were reasons. Hell, it was more than that, it was destiny. This was meant to be, from the start. He lay back down, pressing his palms against his eyes, trying to shut out any further discussion from the deep place in his mind.

And look at the cost, it said, despite his efforts. Look at what you've come to in this. How far will you go to complete it, this blood work? How much will you hurt . . .

"Stop it!" Aaron almost shouted. He lay staring at the ceiling now, his eyes flicking rapidly around, seeking an answer that wasn't offered. "I'll do whatever I have to, whatever it takes," he said aloud. "I owe it to him. I owe it to my father. Oh, God, oh damn," he said, his throat suddenly tight with the pain of it, the loss growing from the very center of his chest, hot and heavy with age. "I'm sorry," he cried softly, meaning it for the memory of the man who couldn't hear him, would never hear him again, but it went deeper than that, he knew, and that hurt as bad. "I'm sorry," he said again, and rolled his head to the side, letting it come, letting it pour out, not fighting it this time. He was tired of fighting it, holding it back. He was just . . . so . . . damn . . . tired.

"Dad," he finally called out, but the room was empty, and no one heard him. After a while, he calmed down, and remembered, pulling it up, needing to feel the why of it again. It began with the first name on the list: Max Perriman.

* * *

He couldn't have done it from inside the military. He needed mobility and autonomy, neither available to him as long as he wore the uniform. But that was the key, he decided. He could wear another kind of uniform, for a position that would allow him access to each intended target. The position was perfect, since suspicion would be easily diverted. No one would suspect that he had an ulterior motive at all. He would become a cop.

Aaron's duty assignments had occasionally teamed him with FBI and CIA personnel. He picked up a few things about law enforcement, filing the information away for future use. At the time it had been done without conscious thought of ever having to use any of it. Now he saw the advantages of developing that information further.

As a police officer he would have access to the vast data banks and the other technology available to find the men he sought. The idea solidified as he put it together and took it apart, analyzing all the pros and cons, advantages and disadvantages. He was a skilled operations planner and approached his idea as if it were any other mission. The main differences with this one were specific: Completing the task would take a long time, years, in fact. He considered the level of commitment carefully before accepting it. He understood the job would effectively remove him from any close, personal relationships. Having one could jeopardize his mission, besides taking valuable time from his task. Finally, having considered all the intense ramifications of what he was about to do, he realized the most important reason. This was personal. This was about blood, and life, and love. Reasons like these superseded any rules, or theories, or laws, for that matter.

Aaron left the Army three months later. He enrolled in OPOTA, the Ohio Police Officer's Training Academy, located in London, Ohio. It had the well-deserved reputation of turning out top-flight graduates. He remembered with a touch of nostalgia Sam Faulkner, the tall, bald, thin defensive tactics instructor. Faulkner had seen to Aaron's training, not knowing what the young ex-Army veteran had in mind.

After graduation, Aaron phonied up a new resumé, showing his training credentials as having been completed not in Ohio, but in Illinois. With his experience working for the CIA, obtaining a set of false identification papers was relatively easy. The important thing was he had real school training, which would be obvious to whoever saw him. With luck, though, they wouldn't bother to check to see if his background was anything but what it purported to be, that of an experienced police officer. He knew that if he picked the right department, preferably one a bit underfinanced and in need, he could pull off his deception. If not, he'd move on until he landed with the right one.

But his first assignment was Illinois. Call it the luck of the draw, but Illinois it was, for the simple reason that Max Perriman lived there.

Aaron worked patrol for six months, learning the new job, all the while tracking his target. His new identity was ready, and at the end of his self-imposed time limit, he turned in his resignation, claiming police work was not what he had expected. None of the arguments from his chief could dissuade him, and he was reluctantly let go.

But he stayed in the area, finalizing his move. Aaron had sent out applications, under his new alias, to other police agencies and had received a solid bite with the Carthage PD, only twenty miles away from Max Perriman's town. Now he contacted the city's human resources office and obtained an interview. Shortly after that he was offered a job.

In six months he applied for a posting to their SWAT team. Normally he wouldn't have been eligible until he had been with the department for at least a year. But the need was there, and the city had voted for the position. He gained a reputation as a cool head, reliable in a crisis, stable and professional. It was the image he wanted, and he worked hard at it. His cover as a lawman, performing his sworn duty to safeguard the public, was a supremely ironic counterbalance to his private, premeditated actions. There he was, projecting one persona, while his mind worked in the shadows, stalking the first on his list, Max Perriman.

He observed the man, finding a middle-aged, obese insurance broker with thinning hair. Perriman was working on his second marriage and a dead-end career, but he had his own little diversions. He had a nice collection of child porno he kept in his office, and liked the company of children, normally around twelve or thirteen years of age. He often hung around near the town's middle school, offering the occasional ride home to a hapless boy or girl. A few complaints had been reported to the police, and discreet inquiries had been made. Nothing had come of them, though Perriman had garnered a short police record in spite of it, with a few DWI arrests and couple of petty larceny busts.

Aaron reviewed the record, disgusted at what Perriman had become. Was it the guilt, he wondered? Or had he become complacent in his guilt, secure in the belief that the system had forgotten about him? The physical changes were apparent, and the reality of what the man looked like now forced Aaron to readjust the mental picture he had formed of his target. Certainly his deviant behavior was a change from the days of his youth. It was a bit of a learning experience, and he realized he would have to be prepared for similar changes in all eight of them. Still, how they appeared and what they were involved in, whether it was quirky, illegal, or otherwise, had no affect on what they had done when they were younger, and dangerous. He wouldn't allow what they were now to change what they had been then, when they killed his father.

Did any of them ever wake up sweating from the nightmare, driven by the sure knowledge of what they had done? Manos had told him he and Husta had seen little remorse in any of them. It didn't matter. They knew they were guilty, and he knew it, too. He didn't care what they might feel. They had acted without caring then; he would act the same toward them now.

Perriman's home was in a cul-de-sac. The house was a clone of its neighbors, in slightly better condition. The problem with the location was it left no real opportunity for the shooter to set about establishing a decent blind. Aaron needed distance, both for security reasons and for the justice of it. Perriman's demise had to be totally unexpected, the required end to his life.

The better location was his place of work, a small office at one end of a small strip mall. A dry cleaner's vied with a movie rental place, a take-out-only pizza shop next to a similar Chinese restaurant, and an electronics parts store.

Perriman's insurance brokerage seemed to do average business. It also had a back door, leading out to the small rectangle of asphalt behind the strip, where Perriman preferred to park his nine-year-old Honda.

There was open acreage backing the strip shops, as well, a large section of commercial-zoned property that had been recently bulldozed clean. Beyond the freshly turned and graded earth was the beginning of a stand of trees, the last remnant of what had once been a huge plot of forest. Now it was reduced to a narrow finger of maples and ash studded by thick underbrush, with new housing going in beyond it. Narrow as it was, it was enough. The trees allowed an unobserved line of sight to the back of Perriman's office.

Aaron surveyed the setup, looking for positions, and found one 307 yards out, in a stand of poplar trees. He verified the approaches to the hide, noting terrain and elevation factors, working out the details carefully. He fitted in his reconnaissance on his off-duty hours, careful not to attract any attention. To his fellow officers he was cordial and pleasant, easily playing the part of the professional he really was. He kept his socializing to a low level, cautiously disguising his after-hours activities.

The surprising thing that occurred through all of his careful preparations was that he found a real affinity for police work. As with his primary avocation, the ability to perform with the badge turned out to be something he truly enjoyed. He found himself capable of existing within each life, but able to separate them as if neither affected the other. The mindset of a cop, and more specifically one on a tactical team, was akin to the mental conditioning he had developed as a military sniper. SWAT work had its own requirements, distinct from but in some ways identical to his former military role, yet he found no difficulty in making the transition.

He took Max Perriman on a quiet September night when the

moon was full. Max had the habit of working to eight o'clock on Tuesday nights. He'd sit at his desk doing paperwork, hours after his partner and their one secretary had gone home. Then Perriman would close up the office, set the security alarm out back, and leave. Aaron had observed the same routine for months before deciding.

There was no great challenge to it, really. He had already selected the M-21, and had fitted it with an original Sionics M14SS-1 sound suppressor. The rifle was an exact reproduction of the XM21, the Army's premier sniping system in Vietnam. He felt it was more than fitting to use it to take down the first target on his list. Aaron had replaced the 3X9 Redfield ART/MPC scope with a night-vision sight, another original, the AN-PVS4 Starlite scope. Both the Starlite scope and the sound suppressor had been obtained from special operations contacts Aaron had made in the service. The rig made for an efficient and accurate combination for night use.

He waited for Perriman to come out, briefcase in one hand, keys in the other, and pause to lock the back door. Then he walked six paces to the left to the alarm box, mounted at shoulder height. Aaron watched him through the rubber eyepiece of the night scope, whose 4X magnified, light-enhancing mechanics turned the view into an odd luminescent limegreen. The batteries gave off a thin, high-pitched whine, partially overlapping the distant traffic noises.

Perriman paused in front of the small gray metal box, and Aaron settled the inverted dash-T shaped reticule on the center of his back, below the scapula ridges. His breathing had been steady for the past few minutes. He exhaled, and the image locked on in the brief space before his diaphragm pulled in the next breath. He pressed the 2.4-pound trigger and put the 173-grain bullet through Perriman's heart from exactly 307 yards out.

The report from the suppressed rifle had been a flattened, slightly sharp crack, barely audible. He brought the scope back on his target for the followup shot.

Perriman had fallen heavily against the wall, face-first, then slid down, his body collapsing to the right. He ended up on his right side, facing the back door of his office, illuminated by the hundred-watt spotlight fixed over the door.

It was a bright, clear picture, green cast and all. Aaron settled the reticule on the base of Perriman's skull and sent another round cracking flatly over the distance into the back of his head, centered on the brainstem.

The second shot wasn't just insurance. Aaron knew the first round had killed him instantly. In combat a kill was recorded when the sniper actually walked up and touched the body, literally stepping on his victim. But this wasn't the battlefield, and Aaron couldn't afford the luxury of getting that close to them, much as he wanted to. But there were to be no mistakes, nothing left to chance.

He unshouldered the rifle and snapped down the toggle switch on the left side of the Starlite scope, turning off the system. The thin whine died quietly. Then he shifted from his kneeling position slightly, cradling the weapon in the hollow of his thigh, butt on the ground. With both hands free now, he brought up the 45X power spotting scope hanging on the padded strap around his neck. Aaron had taken only a few moments to observe the results. It wasn't the first time he had killed a man, but it was the first of *them* to fall. He allowed the satisfaction to swirl around briefly, then clamped it down. There would be time for that later. He put the kill behind him with a professional's ease. It was time to return to his other job.

He checked his hide quickly, making sure he'd left nothing behind. Both shell casings had been caught in the small nylon bag attached to the right side of the receiver, and he removed them and slid them into his shoulder patch pocket. His Toyota pickup truck was fifty yards away in the shadow of the trees, and he had no trouble retracing his steps back to it. In minutes he was gone.

The killing went unsolved, as he knew it would. There was no motive, no clues to follow, and no leads. Interest in the shooting carried only a one-time mention on local television, and soon fell off the local newspapers.

He stayed on the full first year as a cop, then turned in his resignation, telling them he had received a better offer in another town. He hadn't, but they didn't need to know that. It was time to move on.

*   *   *

Aaron relocated to New York in 1983, obtaining a position on the Valley Stream PD SWAT team on Long Island. His surface identity and credentials had been perused and accepted fully, but as he had expected, no serious followup was made to determine the veracity of the resumé.

He had taken his time, lining up the second one, Paul Roselli. It took five months to scout out the man, and Aaron found the beginnings of a common profile. Roselli had been no stranger to the law, either. Roselli had low-level connections with the local wiseguys, the same ones he had professed to admire back in Vietnam. Several arrests with no convictions for bookmaking and extortion confirmed that Roselli was trying to live up to his own perception of his reputation.

In the light of day he worked at a small electronics subcontractor shop out in Nassau County. The industrial park covered several hundred acres, surrounded by thick woods to screen the sights and noise of the Southern State Parkway that ran past on the north side of the complex.

Aaron had found a hide twenty yards inside the tree line, a reasonable shot a few paces over four hundred yards across the tarmac of the wide-open parking fields. He took Roselli down on a cold night in late March 1984. Roselli worked the earliest of two shifts, coming in at 2:00 a.m. There weren't many people around, since most of the other businesses in the park didn't run late-night shifts.

Aaron watched Roselli step out of his glitzy '82 Buick Riviera. Aaron lay prone behind the 40XB, in a clear area under the wide branches of a fir tree. He had had to remove a few lower branches to accommodate the hide, but the resulting view was free of obstructions. He steadied the rifle on its bipod legs, his elbows serving as the base anchor points to lock in the weapon. He bracketed Roselli in the scope's horizontal ranging lines, and returned his firing hand to the stock. His breathing slowed and steadied, as even as a machine, as he timed the man's movements. The crosshairs sought the exact spot on his back as Roselli turned to lock the Riveria's door.

The magnified image through the ART/MPC scope paused, and his finger touched the trigger, breaking its one-pound pull. The rifle bucked almost straight back, seemingly at the same moment the .308 caliber projectile broke Roselli's spine at the eighth thoracic vertebra. The bullet broke up on the heavy bone, the central core careening off to perforate his left lung. The smaller piece of the front of the projectile ripped through the left ventricle of the heart, stunning it immediately. His leg seemed to collapse, dumping him sideways awkwardly, and he came to rest on his back, partially under the car, looking in Aaron's direction. His hands fluttered toward his chest, then dropped, his fingers vibrating as his heart died and the brain fired damage control messages that were too late.

Aaron had already bolted the gun with a sharp backward stab of his thumb, catching the spent brass with his shooting hand and dropping it beside the rifle in a smooth, practiced motion. Taking his time, he moved the crosshairs to Roselli's upper lip.

He fired a second time, driving the bullet through the facial bones to traverse the bottom of the brain and obliterate the medulla oblongata. The match-grade bullet exploded out the back of the dead man's skull, taking a softball-sized hunk of bone and gray matter with it.

Again there was no instant moment of jubilation, only the satisfaction of a job well done. He didn't even stay to observe this time, but quickly packed up the weapon and left, as quietly as he had arrived, leaving no trace behind.

Louis Archer came next, and Aaron found the former RTO had immersed himself deeply in criminal pursuits, even more so than some of the others.

Archer had gotten into the black-power movement at first, doing all the militant things popular in the early seventies. He had tried to remain true to whatever cause he had nurtured in his mind those years away from home. The grandiose ideas of the new black revolution had worked until he'd discovered the real power behind the movement. Cocaine, heroin, and crystal meth, it all came and went, leaving tons of money behind in the hands of those willing to run it. And Louis Archer was more than just willing.

Success had aged him, adding forty pounds to his broad-shouldered body, thick fat sheathing muscles that remained powerful, even if softened by abuse. He sported a pencil-thin beard and mustache that outlined his heavy jaw and chin and had shaved his head, adding menace to a visage that seldom smiled anymore. His eyes now radiated power derived from ability, and money derived from his varied street-valued products.

Aaron had been following him as long as he had Roselli. He knew the NYPD's Narcotics Division had an undercover unit working on Archer, along with the DEA. He had made careful contacts in the old-boy network from his Army days to find out enough about Archer to know the narcs were building a case against him, in hopes of making another try at bringing him down. He had become a fairly big fish in the drug-trafficking arena since his return from the war.

Inside of a dozen years he had built a hard-hitting, midsized organization that dealt death and drugs in equal measure. Arrested twenty-three times since 1973, he'd managed to plea bargain down the four occasions the authorities had enough evidence to convict him on. Archer had spent a total of only five months in county lockup. Police knew he was guilty of a lot more, but proof was hard to come by. Archer was guilty in point of fact, which made Aaron's decision on how and when to kill him easier.

The opportunity came in the middle of April, when Archer and two of his henchmen were to complete a buy for several hundred pounds of Colombian coke. The transaction was to take place in one of Archer's favorite places: a vast rail yard on the west side of Long Island City. The connection was a two-man team from Bogotá, possibly a notch or two worse to deal with than Archer himself.

The meeting promised to offer Aaron the perfect setup. Having learned about the buy through his contact in the DEA, which was going to stake it out with an NYPD team, he had arrived several hours early, setting up in a warehouse 396 yards away. He was using the XM21 again, with the sound suppressor and Starlite scope.

The choice of weapon had been decided by the events. A drug deal would move quickly, and fast followup shots could be required. Although he had no intention of taking down anyone other than Archer, Aaron was taking no chances.

The presence of the other four hoods would make the killing seem something it wasn't. The similarity to his father's murder was more than appropriate. Archer and the others had covered it up with the trappings of a Viet Cong ambush. It was fitting Archer's death would look like a drug deal gone bad.

Aaron had been in place for four hours when Archer's big black Mercedes punctually arrived at midnight, undulating solidly over the multiple sections of track that reflected dully in the half-moonlight. The car stopped a few yards away from the waiting Colombians, who exuded nothing but cautious contempt for Archer and his two cronies as they emerged slowly from the darkness of the car. The group stood in a loose formation, and even from his distant perch, Aaron could sense the tension amongst the five men.

The sniper's hide had been set up using a small work bench Aaron had positioned two feet back from the shattered window he observed the meeting through. He settled into the position, stock firm into his shoulder, both elbows over the upright back of the chair so that his upper arms, not the point of bone, anchored his position. His left arm was bent with his hand supporting the toe of the butt plate.

He adjusted his breathing, quieting his mind as he held the dotted-T crosshairs on Archer's impassive face. The Starlite scope was only four power, but it provided more than enough magnification for the distance. Aaron knew underneath the black leather trench coat Archer wore a heavy ballistic Kevlar vest. He raised the sight's reticule until it settled on the point of his chin, then raised it an inch. His breathing fell into the familiar syncopated rhythm, and he began the squeeze . . .

* * *

Louis Archer stood there, hands in the open, letting his underling do all the talking. He returned the hostile glares of the Colombians with a baleful look of his own. Don't show 'em nothin', he thought, mindful that appearances with these people were every-thing. He had plenty of heat under his coat, as did his two men. He knew the Colombians would be packing, too, and was mindful not to initiate a challenge that would end with them all going to guns in a flash. He had the money, and that was the motivating factor. They had the product, and getting to it to arrange for its trans-portation was the sole issue at the moment.

"What it is," he said, interrupting his man, "is that the price was set a month ago, see. Am I right or are we just strokin' each other? 'Cause if it be that, well hell, man, I got plenty of stuff at home can stroke me widout this shit."

One of the Colombians smiled softly then, and made a gesture, and suddenly Archer's head snapped downward, and a mist sprayed over them, barely covering the solid thunk of the bullet strike.

The round had whacked into Archer's face a finger's width below his bottom lip just under his teeth, and had broken apart from the impact. The heavier portion drove deep, through the soft underpalate, across his throat, and ripped through his spinal cord at the fourth cervical vertebra, exploding out the back of his neck. The second piece glanced upward, piercing Archer's tongue, then the roof of his mouth, and plowed into the bottom of his brain. He died in a millisecond, his legs giving way as if the bones had turned to liquid. He pitched forward, his face slamming into the ground with a thick slap.

The four men around him froze. Then they started to hunch down, crouching as their brains screamed the warning to them, and four hands swept toward hidden weapons, intent on instant retaliation, when the second shot hit.

Archer had fallen with the top of his naked head exposed to Aaron, who sent the insurance shot squarely into the middle of that smooth surface. His head exploded with a wet crack, shower-ing its contents over the ground and the four hoods.

They jerked and flinched instinctively, guns out now, but a sud-den uncertainty caused an odd pause in their combined herd men-tality. They'd heard the unmistakable sound of both rounds striking home, and the high supersonic cracks. But they had no di-rectional reference. The accuracy of the gunner, and the quickness of the shots, was clear evidence that a pro was covering them.

Stunned, the four survivors looked at each other, then at the body, waiting for the next round. Nothing happened as they waited, instinct guiding them now. Slowly they backed away from each other. None were positive they weren't going to be next, but they weren't about to start anything now. Mutual self-destruction was assured at that close range. All they wanted to do was get out of there. The deal was forgotten.

The NYPD narc undercover team, closer than Aaron, had seen the entire sequence through their night vision scopes. "Goddamn!" one of them shouted. "It's a hit! They blew Archer away!"

"Stay down until the tac-team finds out what's going on," the lieutenant in charge ordered. He jumped on his radio right away.

Confusing orders overlapped the net, as they always do when things go wrong. In a few minutes it was clear, though. Louis seemed to have been the only target.

"Maybe they didn't like how things were going down," the lieutenant observed. "I guess we'd better round those bastards up."

"Where the hell's the shooter?" his partner asked, scanning the distant buildings with his own scope. "I can't see anything out there."

"Call the backup," the first one said. "Maybe they can get someone over to that side of the yard."

"What side of the yard?" the partner asked. "The guy could be anywhere out there."

"What the fuck does it matter?" the lieutenant said. "The Colombians probably did it. They like blowin' people away. I think our boy Louis just became a lesson."

Aaron watched them gather up the shaken survivors and leave, and looked once more at the fallen form. He wasn't worried about the undercovers finding his hide until he was long gone. He put the rifle on safe, and turned off the Starlite scope's switch, listening to the small whine fade away. "That's three," was his sole commentary.

* * *

He stayed with the department six months afterward, following the progress of the investigation into Roselli's and Archer's deaths.

Both efforts came to a grinding halt three months later, as he knew they would. Their cases joined the open/unsolved files, and the homicide detectives went on to other matters. It left him free to move on, without any suspicions raised from leaving too close to the shootings.

Aaron turned in his resignation and moved to Texas in late '84, going after Hector Aceto. There he applied for and got a job with the Medina County Sheriff's Department, eventually working his way onto the SWAT team.

Once again he developed the working profile on his next target. Hector Aceto didn't disappoint him. He'd married twice, though neither one had lasted. Now he lived with a woman, a hooker, appeared to be branching out into dealing crack cocaine. He had a record of criminal assaults too, some gang-related. All indications were he was escalating his bad-ass attitude, and it was only a matter of time before he went into the big leagues and ended up in a federal prison.

Aaron had been on his latest job a year and a half before deciding the time was right. He had completed his preparations and had chosen the day when fate reached in to disrupt his plans. Two days before the chosen time, Aceto died when the walls of the ditch he was working in for the utility company in San Antonio collapsed.

The missed opportunity upset him, but there was nothing he could do about that. Life had its own way of doing things, and he had had to remind himself of that more than once before. Prepare for every eventuality, he had been taught, and Aceto proved that axiom. Some things would be out of his control, and he didn't dwell on it. There was other work to do.

He stayed through to the spring of 1986, making the most of his opportunity to further his law-enforcement career. Nothing on his agenda was wasted time or effort. He resigned when it felt right, his new identity and resumé prepared, and moved north to Wisconsin, and the next one on the list. He managed to land a position with the PD in Janesville, a few miles south of Madison, where he had found John Burris.

No one within the command structure of the Janesville Police Department bothered to check into his background. All they saw was a level-headed, SWAT-experienced officer. What they wanted was exactly the same. It underscored his manipulation of the system, and he was careful to give them honest service for the opportunity they'd given him.

* * *

Six months later, just after the new year of 1987, Aaron was ready for former private Burris. Once again, though, fate stepped in. Burris fell to another agenda. He had died of lymphatic cancer in the VA hospital in Madison, another statistic of Agent Orange.

Aaron had known about the disease, but the prognosis had given Burris more time. A sudden downturn in his condition had collapsed the window, taking him sooner than anyone had predicted. This time he allowed the frustration to rattle around for a while, getting it out. He was primed, ready to go, and had to bring himself back down, keeping the long-term plan always in mind.

* * *

Time had passed, longer than he had anticipated, and the new year had come and gone. It was 1989, and the mission called again. He hadn't felt as if he were ignoring it, not at all. There was an internal rhythm to it, and he was content to let it happen on its own.

He had located the squad leader, Jack Linet, in Macon, Georgia. He was simply the next one on the list, another purely random choice. And he had joined the others, becoming number six in the process. Afterward, when things were quiet, Aaron had moved on, secure with his next location: Ohio, and possibly the end of his life's work.

* * *

Aaron came out of his reverie slowly, feeling drained. He was at once ashamed at losing control and for not having revisited those same emotions for so long. He had pushed his grief down, keeping it isolated deep inside, where it couldn't affect his performance.

This time it had come from another source, triggered by a need he had kept hidden. He knew what it was, and why the emotions had come. His father's loss had been the first of several tragedies for him. His mother had been next, all too soon. His sister had faded away, unable to control the ill fortune of her own making.

Loss, the singular experience it had been for him, remained all-encompassing. Aaron felt an attachment for his aunt and uncle and their attempts to offer him the comfort of family. But they were gone from his life too now, shortly after he had gotten out of the service.

By then he was well into his mission. Aaron sighed, letting his concentration shift back to the job, reining in the control so necessary for this last action. He'd already taken a chance, one he should have passed up. But he could change it. He pushed the thought away, intending to revisit it later. For the moment he had to concentrate on the two targets left. So be it, he decided. He knew which one of them would be next. And which one was to be the last.

October 23

Carefree, Arizona

Kevin Parsons was quietly in awe. He and Thom Castleback stood under the massive full-size aircraft propeller suspended from the ceiling of the huge game room. Luther Sitasy, their host, and John Paraletto were close by. Luther had been conducting a tour of his mansion for his guests.

"That is for real, I take it?" Parsons asked, pointing upward at the propeller.

"Absolutely," Luther replied, and explained. "It's off an F4U-4 Corsair, a Hamilton Standard hydromatic, four-bladed prop, all thirteen feet two inches of it."

"How did you get it up there?" Castleback asked. "It must weigh a ton."

"There's a couple of steel beams in the ceiling to carry the weight. They run all the way down into the floor. It's powered by an industrial-strength electrical motor, with the rheostat control on the wall over there. You can even change the blade pitch to change the air flow."

Parsons shook his head. "I feel like an idiot, offering you a job that first time we met at Quantico. I had no idea . . ." and he looked around the vast room, filled with priceless antiques and two regulation pool tables.

"Yeah, well, it wasn't important then," Luther said, meaning it. "All this comes from an annuity I receive from my family's shipping business. Call it my inheritance. It allows me a certain lifestyle, and I can still do what I want to do."

"An admirable quality," Parsons said, turning to his host. "But given all of this, the question sort of presents itself."

Luther smiled a bit through his salt-and-pepper beard. "You mean, why do I work?"

Both Parsons and Castleback nodded, curious for the answer.

"I need to be productive," Luther said. "Doing something of my choice. All this," he motioned with his head, "comes from a birthright. But it's not what I wanted originally. I had to go my own way, and it took a while before that idea set in with my family. Now, it's all right. And this place, the income, is just . . . there. To be used or not, renewed each year. I finally decided to use it, that's all. But the day job at TPI, that's mine. It's what I do. I enjoy the work," he finished modestly.

"I applaud your attitude, Luther," Parsons said.

Luther nodded once, and said, "We'd better get back to the women. Jackie's probably thinking I've gotten you all lost in the mansion."

He led the way to the back of the house until they emerged through the French doors opening onto the magnificent patio that ran the length of the back side of the home, providing a grand view of the lush ten-acre estate.

"Finally," Jackie greeted them in her soft Louisiana accent, turning from her discussion with Cathy Paraletto. They were seated by the big built-in barbecue grill. "I was about to send in the dogs to find you."

"We got a bit carried away, I guess," John said in Luther's defense.

"You have a beautiful home, Mrs. Sitasy," Parsons said to her.

"Jackie, please," she corrected, and added with a smile, "and thank you."

"I'm very impressed," Castleback added, "especially the shooting range in the basement."

"You know something about firearms, Mr. Castleback?" Jackie asked.

"You could say that," he replied. "And call me Thom, if you would."

Gordon Hatton ambled over from the patio.

"I didn't get a chance when we were introduced before," Castleback said, turning to Hatton. "What is it you do with Luther at Trans Patriot?"

"I'm one of the managers in the policy limits section," he said. "I get to oversee the really weird cases we get."

Luther grinned at his friend and associate's glossed-over explanation. "It's a little more complicated than that, but Gordon's like a right hand for me."

"You know," Castleback said, "Kevin's done work for insurance companies before, but I've never really seen how a company like yours operates. Is there any chance I might be able to stop by while we're out here?"

"Sure, why not?" Gordon said. "I'd be glad to show you around the shop. You'd get a chance to see what the public never does, not that they would ever want to."

"Listen," Castleback said, "any corporation that does as well as Trans Patriot does intrigues me."

"When are you leaving Phoenix?" Gordon asked.

"We'll be here through Friday morning," Castleback said.

"My time is yours," Gordon said. "What's good for you?"

Parsons spoke up. "If you don't mind, I'd like to come along, too." He and Castleback exchanged looks, going over their mutual schedules. "How's Wednesday morning, say around ten or so?"

"Fine," Gordon said, including Luther in his answer. "Before you leave here I'll give you directions to the place. It's easy to find."

"Great," Luther said. "Now that that's settled, let's check on dinner. C'mon," he said, and turned to attend the grill, smoke drifting out from under the edge of the four-foot-wide arched metal top. He paused, whistled once, and motioned beyond the pool, forty yards out. His whistle was responded to by black-and-white dogs that came racing out of a stand of date palms. They slowed as they neared him and milled around his legs, waiting for the obligatory ruffling of the fur on their necks.

Luther scratched each in turn, then pointed toward Jackie. "Go on now," he said, and they trotted off in her direction.

"Starsky and Hutch," John grinned, and took a sip of his drink. "You always did go for unusual names. They look a lot like Khanh, though."

"Same breeder," Luther replied with a touch of nostalgia. Khanh had been his pet five years before, a big ebony black lab and shepherd mix. He'd been killed by the murderous Norman Bloodstone while trying to protect Mikki Sitasy, Luther and Jackie's daughter. "I wasn't going to get another one, not after ol' Khanh," he said. "But Mikki talked me into it. She missed him. I did, too," he said.

"How is Mikki? She's doing well since she transferred to Tulane?" John asked.

Luther nodded. "She's got another year to go on her master's in communication, then she's off and running. She's a lot like her mother," he said, nodding toward Jackie. She worked at the local NBC station as a news producer.

Jackie raised one hand, palm out. "It was Mikki's idea to change her major. It seems to be working out for her. And she's got family close by. Big Nick, Luther's father, has had her over to Houston a few times, so she keeps busy. I'm glad," she said, but her pride in her daughter's accomplishments was evident.

"She's a lucky girl," John said, and for a moment he and Luther exchanged glances, remembering just how lucky Mikki had been. Bloodstone's wild shot when Khanh had leaped on him had struck the young girl in the side, severely damaging her liver. It had taken her over a year to heal satisfactorily from the injury, but she still had residual complications. Her decision to change majors and pursue her master's degree at her parents' old alma mater was motivated as much by a need for a change of climate as by anything else. She'd taken the time and distance to settle her own issues left from her brush with death.

Jackie caught the look between the two men but kept her feelings inside. Instead she said to Luther, "The steaks need to be turned, I think, hon."

Luther raised the curved metal lid and allowed the smoke to roil out as he checked the meat cooking there. "About ten minutes," he called out, just as Myoshi came out from the kitchen.

"We're ready when you are," Jackie said, and nodded at Myoshi Arutaka, the Sitasys' housekeeper. "Aren't we?"

"Ready, Mrs. Sitasy-san," she said. Normally the cooking duties fell within her bailiwick. She had an understanding with Luther that occasionally he was allowed to use the outdoor grill. This was one of those occasions. Having close family friends over warranted a major outlay of Arizona hospitality. And the Paralettos were as close as anyone could be with Luther and his family. There was a commonality amongst the group, which accounted for the way conversation drifted back to discussions of shop talk.

"Luther said you're out here on some big-time drug interdiction symposium," Gordon said.

Parsons and Castleback pulled out chairs from the circular glass-topped table and sat down, drinks near to hand.

"Ah, it's a public-relations thing," John said, waving his hand. "The director came out from Washington with the DEA's people to help the president on his latest antidrug policy. I'm just a spear carrier on this one."

"So, anything interesting going on, or is it all classified?" Castleback asked.

"Only the usual," John said to him, "although there is a new one we're working on. Lute, you might like to hear this one."

"Sure," Luther replied, taking a chair near Gordon.

John sat down as well and put his drink on the low table beside him. "This isn't classified or anything," he began, inclining his head at Castleback. "The CID brought us a new one—"

"What's the CID?" Gordon interrupted.

"Army's investigation people," Luther answered, "the Criminal Investigation Division. Sort of like Bureau people in uniform."

John nodded and continued, "Anyway, it looks like they have some sort of rogue shooter out there, tagging a group of guys who used to be in the same squad in Vietnam." He saw he had the group's attention, including the wives. "They're pretty sure the shooter is the grown son of a major who was fragged in a mock ambush back in 1970, Fourth Division's area. The squad supposedly did the fragging, but the investigation team couldn't get anything more than circumstantial evidence back then. The JAG types didn't prosecute 'em."

Gordon put his hand up. "I don't want to sound stupid, but what's fragging mean?"

Luther answered him. "It was a phrase the press made more popular than we did. It came from a nasty situation where you rolled a fragmentation grenade into the hooch of someone you didn't like. Usually a superior officer, platoon sergeant, or squad leader. Later on it meant any method . . . shoot 'em, cut 'em, whatever."

He glanced at John. "It wasn't as widespread as it was reported to be, at one point. There were a lot of myths about Vietnam."

"Fragging," Gordon repeated. "Sounds pretty descriptive. And they let them go?" he asked, amazed.

John's big hands spread wide. "They couldn't make a case," he said. "Not enough to assure a conviction. So they walked."

"Where's the son come into this?" Luther asked. Old memories had been stirred for him. He and John had been stationed in the Central Highlands, home for the Army's Fourth Division.

John smiled a little, but it wasn't meant to be humorous. "This is the part that seems to be mostly conjecture. The son grows up and enters the Army, just like his old man. The Army trains the kid to be a sniper. He learns it so well he ends up attached to a special operations group, doing little jobs all around the world, all hush-hush stuff, very sensitive.

"So years later, around 1980 or so, the kid is back in the States, being debriefed from his latest trip across the pond, and guess who the debriefing officer is?" He didn't wait for any of them to answer. "One of the original investigating officers in his father's supposed ambush. He recognizes the kid from the name and sits him down after the debriefing and tells him what really happened to his father."

"I think I can fill in the rest," Luther says. "The kid quits the service and goes after the surviving squad members."

"That's the current theory," John confirmed, "or at least, it's the best theory we have at the moment. Facts and conjecture seem to point to the son. He got out and flat disappeared. But it looks like he found his first victim in '82 and went on from there. The kid bagged four, all shot from long range. Two others have died over the years from unrelated causes, but we think he was stalking them, too. There's no evidence he did, but by the same token there isn't any to say he didn't. The shootings were very smooth and very professional. He'd learned to do it that way. Nothing left behind. No evidence, nothing forensics can match to anything, zippo."

"Nothing?" Gordon asked. "What about ballistics, that sort of thing?"

"Well, sure, there's that kind of physical evidence. It looks like he's using the same caliber weapon, but none of the bullet fragments can be matched from case to case. Quantico is running down the tests since we obtained the field reports and physical evidence from the various police departments involved. Preliminary information indicates different guns so far. And he's not in a rush. The first one was done in '82. The last one was in '92."

"That's a long time in between," Parsons said, interested in the story, "presuming it is the son doing it. Why so long?

"We don't know," John said. "You'd think if he was on a real vengeance kick he'd have found them sooner and done them in, one after the other. Dragging this out doesn't fit the expected profile."

"Is Quantico building a profile?" McLoughlin asked.

John nodded. "The behavioral science boys are working it up. They seem to think that the reason there's so much time between killings is that the shooter has something else he's doing during that time."

"What, you mean like trying to find the next victim?" Gordon asked.

"No, more like another activity of some kind," John replied. "Like a job, or something. It explains how he's able to move from location to location and finance his search. Tracking these men over ten years has cost money. Either the shooter has something going for him, or he's being financed by someone else. We have to look at all the angles."

"What about a connection amongst the squad members, something they've all been involved in, instead? Maybe that could account for them getting tagged," Luther said.

John nodded. "Already thought of it. The Army people are checking that, but it appears none of them have talked to each other since they came back from Nam."

John took a swallow from his drink. "These cases are scattered all over," he continued. "The first one was in Illinois, the next two were in New York, and the last one in Georgia, Macon, I believe. Jack Linet was his name."

"Linet?" Gordon repeated. "That sounds familiar for some reason."

"Really?" John replied, curious. "Why?"

"Beats me, John, but I'm pretty sure I've seen it before," Gordon said, and shrugged his shoulders. "Can't remember, but I'm sure it's recently," he said again, his brows furrowed in thought. "It'll come to me, or maybe not."

The conversation had returned to John's explanation of the case he was on when Luther noticed Parsons smiling.

"What's so funny, Kevin?" Luther asked, wondering if he'd missed something.

"Sorry, I didn't mean it to be funny. I remembered something you said a long time ago," Parsons replied. "Murder and mayhem in the insurance biz," he said, including them all with his answer. "That was one heck of a deal you and John were caught up in back then. I was just thinking how odd all of that came out of some routine task you do every day. Good thing it never happened again, though."

"God forbid," Luther said, meaning it. "Once was enough."

The mood around the table had suddenly thickened. "I think we can eat now," Luther said, and pushed himself up. As he turned he caught John's eye, and he paused. John's silence said it all. Not again, Luther thought silently. Not again.

October 24

Connersville, Indiana

Mike Madison saw Ted Hays, the shop foreman, coming toward him, a dour expression on his face. What now? Madison thought, checking the counter on the side of the huge press. The noise of the massive machine was horrendous, which accounted for the protective electronic earmuffs all the printers wore. Bigger publishing companies could afford the high-speed, and much quieter, computerized presses, but the *Connersville Times* still relied on the same ancient machines it had for the last fifty years.

"Mike!" Hays hollered at him, waving his hand for Madison to approach.

Madison acknowledged with a nod, took a step back from the press, and leaned his head close to Hays's face.

"Visitors!" Hays shouted in his ear, and jerked his thumb over his shoulder. "They got suits, Mike!"

He brushed past Hays, who fell in behind him. They proceeded down the narrow hallway, then up the single flight of metal stairs at the end of the press room, ascending to the main floor. Madison pushed open the heavy metal door, held it for Hays, and let it slam shut.

Madison pulled off the muffs and absently scratched his ear. "So who are these guys, Ted?" he asked.

Hays studied him for a moment or two, then said, "Federal agents," unable to hide the curiosity in his tone. "You in some kinda trouble there, Mike?"

Federal agents? Madison echoed to himself, and to Hays he said, "Not that I know of. Where are they?"

Hays jutted his chin forward. "Front office, Dave's office." He meant David Kindelbok, director of personnel.

Madison left Hays standing there with hands on hips and made his way through the building to the front, stopping to knock on Kindelbok's door frame. "You wanted to see me, Dave?" he said, leaning in. He took in the two men waiting inside, one in a gray suit, the other in navy blue. Both in their mid-thirties, dark hair, bland faces, and sharp eyes.

Dave Kindelbok came around from behind his desk, casting a furtive, nervous look at his two guests as he approached Madison. "Mike, yes, come on in. These gentlemen—"

"Agents Ruberry and Mitchell," the one in the blue suit said, interrupting Kindelbok. He was holding out his identification toward Madison. "Mr. Kindelbok, thanks for the loan of your office. Could you excuse us just a few minutes? We'd like to talk to Mr. Madison alone."

Kindelbok looked more concerned than he had a moment before, but he nodded quickly. "Ah, certainly . . . sure," he stammered. "Take your time, and uh . . ." he paused midway between Madison, who stood staring at the two agents warily, and the agents themselves, who seemed poised to block Madison from leaving the room too quickly. No one was paying him the slightest attention. Kindelbok eased out of his office and closed the door softly behind him.

"What d'you want with me?" But he already had an inkling, a nasty rush forming in the back of his mind. Agent Ruberry clinched it.

"Major Ralph Longbaugh," he said, and Madison's day came to a crashing halt.

*   *   *

They had begun by explaining his right to counsel, especially as this was under military jurisdiction. They weren't going to question him or accuse him of anything to do with Major Longbaugh's alleged murder in 1970.

Instead they simply relayed the information Colonels Manos and Husta had provided John Paraletto and Pete Jovenall. Madison remained mute throughout this introduction, while his mind worked on the problem. He finally replied with, "No, I don't need no freakin' attorney, least of all some JAG type from the Army. It was JAG lawyers tried to send us all to jail over this back in-country. I'll tell you now what I told them then." He was warming up to it, falling into character. "I don't know nothin' about any so-called murder. Didn't then, don't now. It was all a scam, put up by Carlos Madrid. He used to be one of us, see, but they busted him for dealin', and for knifin' a new kid. Carlos tried to deal his way out of that, too, and come up with that crazy story about how we all supposedly lit up the major." He looked at them both. "Lies is all it was. Still is."

Neither agent seemed affected one way or the other, and that sunk in on Madison. His face hardened suddenly, seeing he was getting nowhere with these boys.

"So I'm supposed to believe there's some whacked-out gunman out there, pissed off at me for supposedly shooting his daddy," he said. "That's a load of crap. Charlie blew the major away, or didn't you guys read that part of whatever freakin' report you have? Asshole had a habit of ridin' the highways at five o'clock every afternoon. That was Chuck's prime ambush time. So he got careless and paid for it. But Carlos Madrid tried to lay all of that on us, buyin' his way out of that murder rap."

He paused, shaking his head. "I never could figure that little spic out. Why he wanted to screw us all like that." He looked at the two agents, his eyes angry. "And I'm supposed to buy the idea that you guys are here to protect me from this maniac, huh? You goin' to park yourselves out to my place, keep me and my family prisoners in our own home, while we all wait for this guy to show up? Is that pretty much the deal, now?"

His protestations and flip attitude had slid easily off the hard veneers of both agents. Mitchell said as much.

"Look, it's very simple, even for a jerk like you. Talk all you want, deny whatever you want. It makes no difference to me. Just know *someone* popped four of your old Nam buddies, nice and clean. And now he's coming after you. And until we get him, Agent Ruberry and I and a few more agents, are going to keep you, your wife, and your kids safe and sound. How you decide to accept that is your problem. But," and his face tightened a bit, mostly around the eyes, "if how you accept that becomes a problem for us, then there are alternatives to how you'll wait out this problem. Give it some thought, Mr. Madison."

For all his bluster, inside Madison was ricocheting between

emotions. Obviously the government knew what he had already discovered and had passed along to Bill Landau. It was all true, and the shooter was headed his way. Not only that, but now his wife and family were going to be told what he had hidden all these years. He vowed to maintain the line, no matter what. It was all a frameup, that was the best way to handle this. Blame it on that poor bastard Carlos Madrid. The story built rapidly in his head, making more sense as he went along with it.

That's it, he repeated to himself. Just maintain the story, keep telling it, and hope these Feds catch this rogue shooter out there. He still wasn't sure the agents weren't part of the deal, trying to set him up so the shooter could take him out nice and clean. But he had no choice.

The one thing he did understand was that if he gave even the slightest hint that he actually had joined in the murder of Major Longbaugh, that his ass would be thrown in jail faster than he cared to think about it. And as soon as he landed there, he'd be visited by Manos and Husta again, and they'd try him for murder one, just like they had promised him all those years ago.

"All right," he said, "may as well get going." He stood up from his chair. "Looks like I don't have much choice in the matter."

Ruberry motioned toward the closed door. "No choice at all," he said.

"It's for your own protection," Mitchell added, his face completely deadpan. "Of course, you can reject federal protection. It's one of your rights," he finished.

Madison looked at him. "Yeah, right," he snarled, and reached for the door.

And as he predicted, the rest of his day was no better. Quite the opposite, actually. By the time midnight had rolled around, his day, and his life, had been knocked pretty much upside down. But he was still alive. One thing he had to do, though. He had to call Landau, let him know what was going on.

* * *

As it turned out Madison didn't make the call to his friend. The Feds had politely refused him access to his own telephone. "Not until this crisis is over, Mr. Madison," Agent Ruberry had told him. "We'll monitor all calls for you and your family. For your own safety," he added.

"My own phone!" Madison had ranted. "You're cutting me off from using my own goddamn phone?!"

Ruberry had merely nodded with a slight smile, while Madison's wife had looked on with fearful confusion. She didn't understand this situation at all: federal agents in her home, saying that her husband was in danger from someone wanting to kill him. Why? For something that happened way back in Vietnam? What could that be about?

But when she had tried to confront Madison about it he had turned on her savagely, telling her it was nothing, to forget it, she wouldn't understand.

He was lying, of course, and she knew it. She could see the fear in his face, despite his anger and threats. It *was* important, but whatever trouble her husband was in, he wasn't about to tell her . . . not now. At least he wouldn't start hitting her over it. The presence of the agents seemed to have a restraining influence on him. That was something, she thought. She accepted the small blessing amidst the confusion of the bigger issue, and tried to push aside her fears. But it was hard. Whatever was going on was very serious. And her husband was scared, really scared.

Maybe there is a God after all, she thought, at once elated and ashamed at the thought. But she couldn't help it. Something bigger than all her pleading words and arguments had its hold on Madison.

She just wished she knew what it was.

October 24

Oxford, Ohio

They planned it as a triple-pronged movement: three two-man teams, one team each for William Landau's house, campus office, and lecture class. They all arrived at their designated locations at the same time, synchronized with Agents Ruberry and Mitchell's apprehension of Mike Madison. It would have worked, if Landau had been at any of the locations.

The team at Landau's home found the house empty, the professor's car still in the garage. The agents who knocked on the door to his office found it unlocked when they tried the knob. There was no one inside. And finally, the team that arrived outside Upham Hall found the notice taped to the hall doors stating the professor's day and night class schedule was canceled for the rest of the week.

They each reported their findings in turn to Agent Peter Jovenall at the Cincinnati regional office. He didn't take it well.

"Son of a bitch was quicker than us!" Jovenall ranted to John Paraletto.

"I don't suppose there's another reason Landau's gone?" John asked rhetorically. All the possibilities had to be covered before they cranked up a more definitive search for the missing man.

"None," Jovenall said. "We checked with Landau's department people. He has no scheduled time off. Landau called in yesterday to tell them he would be gone a week or so. Another prof in the department is covering his day classes; the night lectures for the grad students have been canceled outright."

"That answers that question," Paraletto said. "If Landau knows what's going on, it's a good bet he got it from our boy Madison."

"Works for me," Jovenall said. He huffed once and looked up at the acoustic ceiling tiles, a wry smile twisting his lips. "Should have known this was going too smoothly. Now we'll have to find him the hard way. Damn, I hate it when they rabbit like this!"

"Hey, part of the job description," Paraletto said. "So we do it the old-fashioned way. But we better find him fast. Aaron Longbaugh's still out there." He caught Jovenall's eye to emphasize his concern. "And he's been watching Landau a whole lot longer than we have. It's a good bet *he* knows where Landau's run off to."

"If he's out there," Jovenall added, "and *if* it really is Longbaugh. But you're right. The shooter's probably already studied Landau, Madison, too for that matter, until he knows them better than they know themselves. And where either of them might run to, given the chance."

"Yeah," Paraletto said. "Looks like Landau just took his. Let's find him."

The two men fell to the new task, summoning in their troops, outlining what needed to be done. Of the two last potential targets of the sniper they had secured one, taking him out of the game. Madison was well-protected now.

But Landau had thrown a new figure into the equation with his sudden attempt to flee. It was a rash move, both agents believed. Amateur moves like this always upset the routine and allowed even graver consequences to occur. Their problem had just doubled in complexity. Not only did they have to intensify their search to locate the shooter, but they also had to find his final target. They both knew what would happen if they were late on either solution.

October 25

Connersville, Indiana

The new day's light came as a hazy gray at first, defining the horizon's shapes. Treetops became perceptible silhouettes to the naked eye, standing in their single lines, planted for windbreaks generations ago to guard the rural fields. Farms, once the area's only occupants, now shared their individual acreage with scattered groups of newer subdivisions, giving the developments the appearance of having sprouted up from the older fields, an odd sort of modern crop.

Aaron observed the occasional lights that marked the few early risers in the development off to his left, half a mile away. The lights didn't bother him, nor were they his concern. His concentration instead was on the two-story brick farmhouse straight ahead, slightly downhill from his position in the tree line. He lay on the shooting mat, the Remington 40-XB before him on its bipod. Raising the laser range finder, like a large monocular scope, he sighted on the small metal box and tapped the button under his fingertip. The distance appeared along the bottom edge of the viewfinder as red digital numbers in both yards and meters. "Eight hundred sixty-three yards," he read aloud. It was a considerable distance, but the new morning was calm, with hardly any breeze. His confidence wasn't bothered by the range.

He set the range finder down beside him, returned his eye to the 60X spotting scope, and resumed his silent vigil on the house. Michael Madison would be coming out in another forty-five minutes or so to collect the morning's paper. The delivery man, not yet arrived, would stick the paper into the metal mailbox mounted on the ornate cast-iron pole next to the highway. That was the ranging target for Aaron. Madison would walk the length of the driveway to the box, his usual habit. It was a long, solitary walk. Aaron planned on taking him at the mailbox.

The two-lane blacktop that led into the newer development ran past the farmhouse's property line, which sat back from the road 150 yards. A narrow gravel lane came off the road at a right angle and ran directly back to the lone house, connecting with the two-car garage bay on the home's left side. Close-cropped grass covered the generous expanse of acreage between the highway and the house. Madison and his family had lived in the home for twelve years, Aaron knew.

Aaron knew the exact layout of the house, the number and placement of all the rooms, how the driveway curved around the back of the house to form the patio that ran under the elevated deck, the furnishings, and the decor. He'd been inside the place twice, both times when Madison and his wife had been in town at their respective jobs, and Madison's three teenage children at school. He'd taken note how the former grandeur of the home had faded, the signs of abuse and neglect apparent in the nicks and holes, the cracked window on the east side repaired with a square of cardboard. The shabbiness of the interior contrasted with the well-groomed exterior, as if what went on in the house were being hidden from the outside.

"And it is being hidden," Aaron mumbled absently. He knew about the domestic complaint calls, the number of times the town cops had driven out to the place and hauled off Madison for whacking his wife one too many times, or bouncing his middle son off the walls. He knew about the DWI arrests and the jail times. It's always the same story, Aaron thought, no longer surprised by the similarity amongst the men he had hunted so long. Booze and

abuse, he thought, playing the system, bad-asses and bad attitudes. None of them ever changed. None of them ever seemed to
want to change. Except Landau . . .

Aaron shook the name from his head, remembering Louis
Archer instead, so heavily into illegal drugs, and Paul Roselli, a
low-level mobster. The rest weren't that much better, he thought.
All of them had their problems, which included a certain need
to rebel, to fight back, to sneer at life in general, yet demand better than they deserved to get in the same breath. They were all the
same, he'd decided long ago, all from different places once upon a
time, but how alike they had turned out. All of them save one.

He was the exception, almost glaring in comparison. A college-
level professor, single, living quietly with not so much as a traffic
ticket in fifteen years. Why him? Aaron wondered. What was it
about him that turned him in a different direction from the rest?
Why hadn't he chosen the pattern for self-destruction like the others? Education? Was he above the rest because of his intellect, because he was a class step above them? Hardly. He'd gone along
with the rest when they decided to murder his father. He hadn't so
much as lifted a finger to stop them, had he? No matter what he
was now, or what Landau thought he had become, Aaron knew
him for the murderer he was once, and would always be. In that respect there was no difference. He was exactly the same as Mike
Madison, whose life was minutes away from ending.

Aaron turned away from the spotting scope and rotated his
head, stretching his neck muscles to relieve the tension in them.
He took a breath and calmed himself down. None of them were
worth saving, least of all Professor William Landau. He was perhaps the worst of the lot, when you came down to it. He could
have stopped it, Aaron knew. He could have persuaded them not to
take the step that had damned them all. It was too late now. Way,
way too late.

He checked his surroundings surreptitiously, satisfied he had
chosen a good hide. The edge of the tree line provided plenty of
cover in all directions. He lay behind a large fallen tree, its aged
trunk suspended at a near-horizontal angle a few feet above the
forest floor. Aaron's view from beneath the trunk was perfect, and

its bulk effectively masked him from view, not that anyone had the faintest hope of seeing him at this distance. Still, he was in full camouflage gear, including his Ghillie suit.

He started to put his eye to the spotting scope again when he noticed the car approaching half a mile away. Aaron watched it with mild interest. It wasn't the newspaper delivery man. He drove a late model Ford pickup. The car was a break in the routine, that was all.

Until it slowed and turned into Madison's long driveway. The car was a four-door dark red Chevy Caprice, and a sudden realization came to him. What it suggested was impossible. Aaron shoved the thought down, keeping his eye on the slowing car.

It glided past the house, then stopped at the garage. Three men got out a few seconds later, and Aaron studied them, noticing their suits right away, and the way they moved. The feeling crystallized with a sudden chill. The implication was worse.

* * *

Special Agent Peter Jovenall looked around before closing the car door. It was his first visit to Michael Madison's house. He felt the anxiety associated with guarding Madison, now that Landau had escaped their protection.

The team of agents from Cincinnati had descended on the man the day before. Madison's anger and confusion had crashed into almost pathological denial once they had told him what they knew about him and the other eight men, and Colonels Manos and Husta, and Aaron Longbaugh.

Madison's denials to the contrary, the federal agents, acting under instructions from Jovenall, set up watch in his house. Madison had taken in random snatches to pacing the basement, where they were keeping him, his wife, and his kids—his wife frightened, unable to believe what the agents had told her. The tension in the house was palpable to them all.

"How's Madison taking it?" Jovenall asked Agent Mitchell, the driver.

"Like an asshole," Mitchell replied. "Still denies knowing anything about anything. He also claims he doesn't know anything about the other shootings of his old squad mates. Except we found copies of newspaper articles he'd pulled from around the country. He knows all right. What's the current news on Landau?"

"Still looking," Jovenall said. "We've got the profile on him and have already checked the known possibilities. Apparently he didn't head for the home ground back in New Jersey. We've covered all the transportation means, including the rental agencies. No dice, but he could have a second car we don't know about."

Mitchell shook his head. "His running sort of resolves any lingering question of his possible innocence in the fragging, doesn't it?"

Jovenall nodded in partial reply. "I don't think there was ever any doubt about his involvement. Hell, about any of them. Jim Manos has been in this game a long time. He had 'em, way back then. They did it, including Landau, and Madison, here," he finished, motioning with his head at the house. "Let's go meet the bastard."

* * *

Feds! Aaron almost shouted the word, but kept silent with an effort. He couldn't believe it, but experience, and the appearance of the three men, said otherwise. Federal agents, Aaron thought, his mind whirling. There could only be one reason for their being here now, at Madison's house. As impossible as it seemed, there was no other explanation. He'd been found out!

A thousand messages ran helter-skelter through his head. Warning bells went off even as he rifled his memory for the mistake, the one time he had screwed up. Images shot by one after the other, details reviewed, then discarded for the next, his eyes flickering back and forth as he worked rapidly on the problem. It took only a few moments, but he came to the conclusion that there had been no mistake. He had been too careful, painstakingly so.

It had to be something else then, a variant he hadn't considered, an outside chance he should have seen. But what?! his warning voice shouted silently. He looked around quickly. Take care of business, he commanded himself, setting immediate priorities. First is survival . . . to use the alternate plan. Fade out of here, then close down the apartment in Westport. Move to the backup place.

He always had a second place to go to, a secure one. This was the first time he had been forced to use it.

A new thought tumbled into place. If they were here at Madison's they had to know about Landau, too. That meant there were agents camped out on his doorstep. Were they using Madison and Landau as bait for him? Quite probably. This was no good, no good at all.

Aaron rolled away from the rifle slowly, ready to begin breaking down his sniper's hide. He would need to be extremely cautious. With protection around Madison they would know he was a target. That presupposed they had set up a counter-sniper operation to look for the source of the threat . . . himself. Aaron stopped and went back to the spotting scope. He began searching potential positions a counter-sniper team might set up at.

Taking his time, moving with an absolute economy of motion, Aaron studied where the threat directed against him might be. Light continued to brighten as his visual search continued. It took over an hour, but he was finally satisfied there was no counter-sniper team deployed out there. At least, not yet. But if they hadn't done so, they would. They couldn't afford not to.

Damn it! So close to finishing this. Why now?! Letting it go was not an option, not even a consideration. Two targets left. Aaron had planned for something like this. He could not allow a distraction to enter into the picture.

He pushed aside all further thoughts about what he'd just seen and began to retrace his steps from the hide. Expect the unexpected, he reminded himself. He kept his head and mind in professional mode, working on the problem as he went. Experience was on his side, experience and skill. He was going to finish the mission.

October 25

Trans Patriot Office, Hamilton, Ohio

Vanessa caught herself daydreaming again and realized she had read the same page of the claim file on her PC's monitor several times. Snap out of it! she told herself silently, but still she couldn't quite erase the small smile on her lips.

The Friday night date with Nathan had been pretty incredible, she had finally decided in a peculiarly warm way. She'd woken Saturday morning hours after Nathan had gone home. Alone in her bed, she listened to Dani up and making noises in the kitchen. She allowed herself the luxury of staying covered, hands bundled under her chin, eyes closed, reveling in the aftereffects of the night before. A sudden shiver tingled down her back, across her shoulders and chest, and her stomach tightened in unison with both nipples, surprising her. She almost moaned aloud softly, so intense was the rush, but she sighed instead.

She recalled how he had responded to her the first time, and beneath the obvious sexual desire she had sensed an urgency, and not just blood-driven. No, there was something else there, a real . . . need, she decided. He had needed her, in the truest definition of the word, pulling from her all she had to give him, and yet striving for more. It was an intense urge, couched in his passion. She had sensed Nathan had an emptiness that she could fill, completing him. The explanation for the feeling seemed too extravagant at first, as if she were merely applauding her own ego. But it wasn't that at all, she argued silently. It was nothing she had ever experienced before.

It was as if a new door had been opened for her, and she realized she loved him, just that quickly. The thought whirled around the flashes of him in her mind, then settled down over her inner being, close and comfortable, finding its place within her, and she knew. This *was* the one. She had no doubt of it, and with the acceptance of it came an almost profound sense of belonging. She yawned in pleasure, feeling just a bit smug with herself. I'll call him later today, she decided, and threw the covers back, preparing to meet her new day.

But she hadn't been able to reach him at the station, and he hadn't responded to the voice message she left on his home phone. She stifled her disappointment by a long talk with Dani, who had already guessed the reason for her elated mood.

Dani nodded. "Apparently you've gone well beyond the smitten stage with Nathan." Her face sobered a little, despite her shared delight in her friend's happiness. "Are you sure about this, Van? I mean, really sure?"

"Oh, Dani, that's such a loaded question. Right at this moment, I have to say yes, without a doubt. But when I look ahead, I mean, way down the road, he's still there, you know? It just feels so right." All at once she looked vulnerable, and positive, and perfectly satisfied with herself.

Dani hugged Vanessa. "I'm so happy for you, Van," she whispered in her ear. This was serious business. Vanessa was head over heels for Nathan. Still, it had happened so fast. Dani couldn't shake a vestige of concern. Watch and see how this goes. Maybe it really is all right.

Vanessa let her feelings drift around him for most of Sunday, and when she couldn't stand the wait any further, dialed his pager number. Nathan had returned her call an hour later.

"Hi, Nathan," she answered, smiling openly. "Sorry about using your pager, but I wasn't sure you would call."

"*Sin loi*,'" he said in Vietnamese, meaning sorry about that, in a literal translation of a rough, vernacular phrase. "I was hung up on the job . . . couldn't get to a phone. I did receive the messages you left at the station though."

She was relieved by his explanation and his use of her native language. He'd been doing more of that, she noticed. "*Ngoi' lam*," she replied, praising him. "That's all right, I thought it was probably something like that." She paused, suddenly feeling awkward. "Listen—" she began, when he started to say at the same moment, "I'm sor—" and they both laughed. The sound of his voice soothed her, and she bowed her head, holding the receiver close with both hands.

"So how've you been doing?" she asked. "Are you all right?"

"I'm fine," he said. "Just some work on the street, that's all. A typical day," and he realized she wasn't asking how his day had gone. "Oh, hey," he said quickly, feeling foolish. "No, I mean . . ." and now she laughed again at his embarrassment.

"It's OK," she said, letting him off easy, "I'm still recovering myself. I did want to . . . thank you, again . . . for a beautiful evening."

"Well, you're entirely welcome," Nathan replied. "I had a pretty special evening, too." He was silent a moment. "Uh, actually,

Vanessa," he began, and panic flared inside her, until he continued, "I'm not sure how you're feeling over all that we . . . all that happened between . . ." and he faded off again, and she heard him say, faintly, as if he was covering the receiver with his hand, ". . . ah, hell . . ."

She waited, not wanting to interrupt him, but dying to anyway, her pulse kicking higher. Please, please, she pleaded silently inside, hoping he was about to say it.

She heard a heavy sigh from his end, and then he said, "I guess I'm not very good at saying things to you yet."

She smiled openly, and her heart gave a solid thump. It was all right now. "You said some very nice things Friday night," she offered.

"I hope so," he said. "I suppose we could compliment each other a few more hours," Nathan said.

"We could," she replied, playing with the phone cord, idly twisting it about a finger.

"I'd like to see you again," he said, almost in a rush.

Yes! she thought, and replied aloud, "I was hoping you would want to, Nathan."

He was silent a long count, and she almost thought they had been disconnected, when he came back on. "Vanessa," he began, his voice so low and serious she was afraid of what he would say next. "Vanessa," he said again, a bit stronger, "I've never . . . *never*, wanted to know someone more than I want to know you."

She realized the double meaning of his words and relished the feeling it left in her. "I feel the same way, Nathan," she managed, her own voice turning softer.

"Are you sure?" he asked. "Are you sure about me?"

"Yes," she answered, positive in her reply. "Why wouldn't I be?"

"You know what I do," he said, his voice serious, all business again. "But you don't know who I am."

"I know enough about you for now. The rest will come. For now, it doesn't matter," she assured him. And it didn't, as far as she was concerned. "Isn't that what this is all about now, finding each other?"

"I suppose it is," he said, then, "Vanessa?"

She waited, but the silence dragged on. Then he said reluctantly, she thought, "It'll keep."

She paused now, wanting to say it, wanting it to be right, but not sure the moment was exactly right. "All right," she said instead.

"You be careful out there, Vanessa."

"You, too, Nathan," she said. "Bye."

You should have said it, her inner voice scolded her. You should have told him. Afraid of the words? No, not afraid of the words, she thought back. There'll be time. We're just beginning, that's all. Just beginning, she repeated, but her little voice was gone.

October 25

Lincoln, Kansas

Jim Manos directed the Dodge Intrepid rental car down the long rural road while Tony Husta checked their bearings. Lincoln was just ahead, according to the Grange signs they had passed a quarter-mile back. Kansas remained just as flat as they had come to expect since picking up the rental car at the airport in Salina.

The first visual sign of Lincoln appeared as a couple of church steeples and the obligatory whitewashed municipal water tower on the horizon. The Longbaugh family residence was still six or seven miles beyond that. The town's population was barely over thirty-six hundred. It should be easy to find the man they had come to see.

They already knew that Aaron's uncle Larry and aunt Eileen had passed away some years before, and they were the last of his known family. Aaron's older sister seemed to have dropped off the face of the earth. Their records indicated that Aaron had inherited his father's home in Hutchinson, though. The family attorney, Russell Lancola, was still around. He might be able to provide them with some information on Aaron. Both men doubted that Aaron had contacted Lancola, but it was a potential source all the same.

They'd set their appointment with the lawyer the day before. He'd expressed surprise at their request to meet, understandably, as Husta had given no specifics about their purpose for coming there. They intended to keep those specifics under tight rein until they had a better feel for Lancola. They also wanted to check out the house, in any event. Lancola might be able to give them access to the property.

Husta referred to the directions Lancola had given them over the phone as they glided into town.

"What's the number?" Manos asked, looking at the buildings they were passing slowly.

"Two-one-zero," Husta said and pointed. "There it is."

They neared a two-story brick building. Manos pulled up to an opening between two pickup trucks. He shut down the Dodge and they started toward the main entrance. Outside, a glass-covered brass case mounted to the wall near the door contained the directory. They paused at the base of the steps to check it.

"Main floor," Manos said, noting the attorney's office number. He pulled his sleeve to check the time. Both men were in civilian clothes, business suits. They didn't want their uniforms to trigger any questions they weren't ready to answer yet. "Time's OK," he said.

"Let's go see the man," Husta replied, and led the way up a short flight of steps and through the front door. Husta pointed to the left and they continued. Lancola's office was the last of three offices on that side of the building. He pushed down on the polished brass handle and entered the office.

Lancola's secretary-receptionist, a thin-faced older woman with glistening ebony hair in tight curls, took their names and gave them a detailed onceover before announcing them. Her voice was as thin as her form, with a heavy western drawl. She nodded once to the reply she received in her earpiece and motioned them toward a darkly oiled door standing slightly ajar.

"Mr. Lancola will see you gentlemen now," she said. She remained at her desk and watched them expectantly.

Manos nodded to her. "Thank you," he said, and led Husta through the doorway. A dark wainscoting ran around the room, with cream-colored walls above it. A large, oval broadloom rug covered the majority of the hardwood floor. Floor-to-ceiling book-shelves, jammed with legal texts, covered the narrow wall to their right.

The owner's desk was opposite the door with the street-side window behind it. The old-fashioned rollup shade was all the way up, providing a view of city life passing by outside. A couple of high-backed chairs covered in brass-studded leather were in front of the desk.

Russell Lancola rose from behind his impressive, heavy teak desk to greet them. The lawyer extended his hand, taking Manos first, then Husta. "Mr. Manos, Mr. Husta," he said in a gravelly voice. The strength of his grip surprised them both. Lancola was of medium height, with a thick barrel chest and stomach to match. He wore a black suit with a white shirt and bolo tie. His round face and head were deeply tanned, with a fan of dark creases at the corner of each eye. Manos judged him to be in his late sixties or early seventies. His head was covered by close-cropped black hair, shot through with gray all over, as were his heavy brows. His most arresting feature, the one that now appraised both men, was his dark, ebony Indian eyes.

His eyes looked at them, not missing any details, but giving nothing back either. Manos immediately felt the intelligence behind them, and the quickness. Lancola answered the unspoken question.

"Lakota Sioux," he said, and added a slight smile that revealed startlingly white teeth.

Lancola paused, continuing to look at the two men. "And if you two gentlemen are civilians, I'll eat my Stetson."

Manos glanced at Husta, then back to the lawyer and replied, "You have a sixth sense, Mr. Lancola."

The lawyer turned back to his desk and motioned to the two leather-covered wing chairs placed before his desk. "Please," he said. "And no, I've no sixth sense, Mr. Manos. Just a huge amount of common sense. You two have a look about you, that's all. Definitely military, I'd say, probably Army."

Husta was impressed. "You sound a little familiar with the service. When were you in?"

"The big one," Lancola said, leaning back in his chair. "I was in the Third Army with George Patton, '43 to '45. Drove a truck in the Redball Express." The Redball Express had been Patton's motorized supply line that raced along with his armor, stabbing its way across Europe. His face sobered, signaling the end of the preliminaries. "So you gentlemen want to know about young Aaron Longbaugh, eh? Might I inquire why?"

"How long have you been the family lawyer to the Longbaughs?" Manos asked.

"Forty years," Lancola replied, his eyes displaying his curiosity. "I started with Ralph and Lawrence's father, Jeb Longbaugh. He started a sharecrop farm back in the Depression years. When I began my practice after the war, Jeb was one of my first clients. We did a little business over the years . . . no one else would take him on. Wasn't until after the Korean fracas that the old man hired me permanently as family counselor." He paused again. "My turn. What's your interest in the Longbaugh family, and Aaron?"

Manos answered with another question. "Have you heard from Aaron recently?"

Lancola had enough experience to know Manos was doing some preliminary pumping. He ended it quickly. "You sound like a cop, Mr. Manos, and since you've not denied the Army connection, that'd put you in military intelligence of some kind. I'd guess neither of you are regular Military Police. You've the look of officer material. So why would the Army send a couple of officers out to the middle of Kansas looking for a guy who hasn't been in the service for fifteen years?"

"You should have been in intelligence yourself," Husta interjected admiringly. "I think your common sense borders on being clairvoyant."

Lancola nodded slightly. "You learn things by the time you're my age, sir." He leaned forward, the chair protesting softly. "And I think it's time for you to tell me just what is it you've really come for. I've not heard any denials as to your occupations. If Aaron is in trouble, I need to know what it is, and how bad. While you're at it I want to know exactly who you both are. Fair enough?"

Manos and Husta exchanged glances. An understanding passed between them. Manos reached inside his suit jacket and removed his wallet. Opening it, he handed it across the desktop to Lancola.

"Army Criminal Investigation Division," he said. Both men waited while Lancola studied their identification cards and then handed them back.

Husta put away his wallet and asked, "What do you remember of the death of Major Ralph Longbaugh?"

Lancola's eyes narrowed slightly. "He was killed in a Viet Cong ambush, driving down some highway."

"That's what the family was told, sir," Husta replied. "But it's not correct."

Lancola's interest was full up now. "Are you saying he wasn't killed, or that he was and his death was something else? Nineteen seventy was a long time ago, gentlemen. Why are you bringing up this old pain now?"

"Because it concerns Aaron Longbaugh," Manos interrupted. "At least, we're convinced it does. The official record is that the major was killed that afternoon in a VC ambush. Under the circumstances at the time, it seemed best to leave it at that. There was nothing to be gained by letting the family know otherwise."

"And what it this 'otherwise'?"

"That Major Ralph Longbaugh was murdered by a squad of nine men from a Fourth Division platoon," Manos answered. "It was a so-called fragging incident, made to appear to be the work of the VC. It wasn't. It was a premeditated and executed murder."

Lancola's eyes closed momentarily. He opened them slowly, paused, and shook his head. "This is astonishing news. Assuming for the moment what you've related is true, what was the reason? Why was this done?"

"It was the end of the war," Husta replied. "The troops were going home. No one wanted to die for nothing. Major Longbaugh was the operations officer for his battalion. He cut the orders for field operations. These men presumed that eliminating him would stop the orders, at least long enough for them to get home. No more chances to die."

"You asked why," Manos added softly. "They did it out of fear."

Lancola took in what they said, his mind working on the unsettling news. "So what became of these nine men?"

Manos continued the story. "In 1970 Tony and I were the case officers on this thing. One of the nine men, Carlos Madrid, rolled over on the others. He told us everything. The day he confessed, he was found dead in his jail cell, hanged. The evidence he told us about, the Viet Cong guns and equipment used, was never recovered. And once confronted and interrogated, the remaining eight men stuck to the same story. They didn't know anything about any murder."

Lancola sighed heavily and sat back in his chair. "Circumstantial case, right? Your dying declaration from this Madrid became worthless." He stared accusingly at them. "There was no prosecution then, was there?"

Husta shook his head, confirming the question's answer. "The JAG rep said he couldn't take it up for a general court. There wasn't enough to convict on. He had no choice."

"And the eight men?"

"Discharged, sent back to the States, admonished not to see each other, not to communicate in any way," Manos said. "And we told them we'd never stop looking, either. One way, some day, we'd get them all for the killing."

"This is what you want to see Aaron about, then," Lancola said, misjudging why they had come. "To tell him the truth, after all this time."

"No," Manos said. "Aaron already knows the truth. I told him myself, in 1980."

Lancola was surprised and started to say something, but Manos interrupted him.

"He already knows, Russell, and he's been doing something about it. Aaron got out of the service in 1980, not long after I told him the truth about his father," he said. "Do you know what he was doing while he was in?"

Lancola shook his head.

"The Army trained him as a sniper," Manos explained. "He was attached to a special operations group eventually and sent to certain trouble spots around the world." He held the lawyer with his steady gaze. "They used him to kill people, Russell. And he was very good at it."

The two intelligence officers saw understanding dawn on the old man's face. Husta nodded. "After Aaron left the service, things began to happen to these eight men. Between '82 and '92 six of the eight died. One from an accident, one from leukemia. The other four were all shot from long range."

Lancola's eyes snapped from Manos to Husta and back again. "Aaron?"

"We think so. It fits that way."

The lawyer passed a gnarled hand over his head. "What proof do you have?"

Husta huffed. "That's part of the problem. Right now it's all theory and opportunity. Aaron has motive, and means, at least we think so. He certainly has the skills. After he got out of the service, he disappeared. We've tried to locate him any number of ways. He flat vanished, but then, he knows how. We trained him to do that."

"Why now?" Lancola asked. "What generated this interest in events that began in 1982?"

"In 1970, really," Manos corrected, "with the major's murder. But call it the evolution of things. Over the years official interest in pursuing these eight men lapsed," he said, barely shrugging his shoulders. "Suffice it to say after a while no one cared." He looked at his partner. "We didn't forget," he said. "Sometimes you don't get to do all that you promised to do . . ."

Lancola nodded his understanding. "So you decided to go looking, something like that!"

"Something like that," Manos agreed.

"And you turned up this information on the murdered men."

Manos nodded. "There were enough similarities that we couldn't ignore the obvious, which is that someone knew what they had done, despite the Army's inability . . . no, *our* inability, to prosecute them way back when it happened."

"But you changed that, you said," Lancola mentioned. "You told Aaron himself back in '80?"

"That's correct," Manos said. "Purely as coincidence, I was his debriefing officer on a mission he had completed overseas. I knew who he was. His name was too unique to be just a coincidence. It was a tough decision, Russell, but I made it. I told him everything . . . all that we suspected, every fact we had, and Madrid's confession."

Lancola rocked slowly in his chair, his eyes stern now. "How did he take it? Hearing what you told him must have been brutal for him."

Manos glanced at Husta. "He thanked me for it," he replied.

"And now?"

"I think I turned that kid on to a vendetta," Manos said, his tone reflecting the conflict he still carried.

"I disagree with that statement," Lancola said. "The Army seems to have turned him into a killer. If he is the one behind these murders, then he's doing what he was trained to do."

"Murder is still murder, Mr. Lancola," Husta interjected.

"No doubt, sir," Lancola told him, "but sometimes there is a rhythm to life. That appears to be the situation here."

"Wait a minute," Husta said. "You're condoning what Longbaugh's doing?"

"Presuming it is Aaron, you mean?" Lancola answered, his eyes probing back.

"Presuming so, yes, fine," Husta replied, anger tinting his words.

The lawyer tented his hands, fingertips together, elbows on the desktop. He studied Manos and Husta carefully over his hands. "Aren't we discussing a double standard here?" he said, not answering Husta directly. "The law is written to handle situations like this. I have the impression from you two gentlemen that you've spent your careers, if not your entire lives, dedicated to the belief in that system, of right and wrong, yes?"

Manos nodded for the two of them.

"As I suspected," Lancola said. He brought his hands down. "And when the system failed to respond, to right an obvious, egregious wrong, I submit you found another way to get it done." He held Manos's eyes with his own. "You knew exactly the deadly skills Aaron had. You were his debriefing officer, after all. And there he was, delivered, so to speak, into your hands. What a perfect time to tell the son the truth of his father's death, a dishonorable death at the hands of nine cowardly men."

Manos felt chilled, hearing his innermost fears expressed aloud for the first time, and from an independent source. His silence told

Lancola how close he had come to describing the guilt Manos carried.

Lancola leaned closer, his broad chest against the desk edge. "It's interesting, don't you think? Your finding the son by chance, as it were. You must have asked yourself why bother to tell him at all? Young Aaron had already endured the death of his father once. Yet you were ready to have him go through it again. Why?"

Manos returned the lawyer's accusing stare. "Because he deserved to know. The truth needed to be told. His father's memory deserved it, too."

"Are you satisfied with that?" Lancola asked. "I admit the question is possibly rhetorical, but considering why you are here, in the official capacity you seem to have come looking, it still needs to be asked." He paused. "If you're right, and it is Aaron doing this, you supplied him with as good a motive any man ever needed. Are you sure?"

Manos didn't flinch. He had agonized over his part too many times, but it always ended the same. No matter what followed, given the opportunity to change it, he wouldn't. He'd still tell Aaron the truth. "Yes," he said firmly. "I'm sure. Aaron . . . deserved to know."

Lancola held his eyes a moment longer, then nodded. "Good," he said. "That tells me something." He leaned back in his chair. "Now we can proceed. Whoever is killing off these men, whether it's Aaron or not, he is doing it freely. You may have supplied Aaron with a reason, Colonel Manos, but acting upon that reason was a decision only he could make." He sat back. "For the record, I'm still not willing to accept that it is Aaron Longbaugh who is behind this, as much as you two may believe it. What I am willing to concede is that the deaths of these men seem apt, all things considered. You two are convinced, of course, that your description of the squad's act of premeditated murder against Major Longbaugh is also accurate?"

"I don't think there's much doubt about that," Manos said.

"Then the circle is being completed," Lancola said. "And yet you want to find him, and stop him?"

Manos shot a look at Husta. "Yes, we want to find him. As to stopping him . . . let's say we haven't completely agreed that is the way to handle it. A better solution would be if he simply stopped, on his own." Manos glanced at Husta.

"If it's Aaron, and if we catch up to him," Husta added, "we'd like to . . . arrange it . . . so that he can stop this. Before it's too late." The implication was clear.

Lancola gazed back, his reaction unreadable. Inwardly, he hadn't expected their answer. He had a new admiration for the two of them. He also had a better idea what his two visitors were after now. "What can I do?"

"Can you get us access to Major Longbaugh's home?"

"I can do that," Lancola said. "For what it's worth." He cocked an eye at them. "If you expect to find some evidence to use against Aaron there, I think I'd better accompany you. It's in his best interest that I be there, you understand."

Manos nodded once. "Fair enough."

Lancola's brows furrowed. "I have to ask this, and there is a reason. Are you positive about why Ralph was killed by these men? That they were afraid of him? Could it have been because of something else?"

Husta seemed puzzled. "Such as?" he asked. "I'm not sure what you're asking."

"Remember I said that years ago no one here would represent Ralph's father? It's because of his unique status in this community," Lancola said. "Lincoln isn't much bigger now than it was back in the twenties and thirties. People sometimes have narrow ideas about things, and about other people. I know," he sighed. "Being Indian, or Native American, to use the more popular term, has been difficult for me. I grew up with prejudice. If you don't mind my saying, I'd venture to say both of you are no strangers to similar prejudices. I built my practice on honesty, and a lot of work. People trust me, now. It wasn't always that way.

"It was the same way with Jeb Longbaugh," he continued. "People weren't willing to accept him and his family, not at first. He stood out, was too different, in those days. Later on it got easier."

"In what way?" Husta asked.

Lancola looked at him, his eyes never wavering. "You know the answer, sir, which is why I asked the question. I'm aware of the racial tension that existed in the military in those days. Much of what happened here in the States carried over in Vietnam. It was a particularly ugly time for America. Could Ralph's murder have been racially motivated? Because the Longbaugh family was black. The first black family to move to these parts."

Manos and Husta had long since considered that theory. They had also long since come to a decision about it. Manos answered for them both.

"No, sir," he said. "Major Longbaugh wasn't killed because of that. I'd bet on it."

Lancola considered his reply. "All right then. Let's see about getting you out to his house."

October 26

Trans Patriot Insurance, Hamilton, Ohio

Vanessa was on the way out of the office, after stopping by after her second call to drop off some machine parts she'd collected as evidence of a possible product defect. The phone rang just as she started out of her cubicle. "Vanessa Tau, Claims," she answered.

"Vanessa? Charles Kedrick."

"Oh. Mr. Kedrick." She recognized the city's attorney's voice. "How can I help you?" She glanced at her desk clock quickly, calculating where she had to be next.

"It's what I can do for you," he said. "I'm relaying some news. I've already discussed this with Arthur Gabel this morning, actually."

"What is it?" Vanessa asked, his mention of Gabel getting her attention.

"We've lost one of the defendants in the Bennett case," he began, and added, "well, not really lost. Lieutenant Dean Barlot, the HRG commander, has left the Westport PD."

"What?" Vanessa said, remembering her first meeting with the tall black officer. Barlot was a defendant in the lawsuit, and a critical witness. He couldn't just leave. "When did this happen?"

"This morning, I'm afraid. Dean gave notice, pretty short-term I have to tell you. He said it was something that had been in the works for some time, a better offer with another agency, hefty promotion, all of that. He was going to tell us about it, with appropriate notice, he said, but there apparently was a problem, and he had to leave right away."

"Where's he gone?" she asked.

"Washington state," Kedrick said, "near Tacoma. He apologized for the bad timing, but he promised us he would be available for depositions and the trial, of course."

"Is that all right with Arthur?" she asked, "I mean, I've never had to deal with this kind of thing before. Can Arthur handle it like this?"

"Oh, sure," Kedrick said easily. "This sort of thing happens all the time. Usually there's more notice, but it won't be a problem in this case. Besides, plaintiff's counsel hasn't set any depositions yet. We've still a long way to go. When we get around to the depositions, we'll arrange to bring Dean back here, or we can depo him out there. At that point it's merely a logistics problem. 'Course, Art's planning to file a motion to dismiss based on qualified immunity of the officers and the city officials. If that's successful, that'll be the end of the case, barring an appeal. Should we have to try it, the city will pay for Dean's attendance at the trial. Anything he needs to review or sign off on can be mailed out. It won't be a problem," he repeated.

"Well," Vanessa replied, taken by surprise by the news. "I guess if Arthur is OK with this, I have to be."

"Really, it's no big deal," Kedrick assured her. "Things happen this way sometimes, that's all."

"It all happened this morning?" she said. "And he's already gone?"

"Right," Kedrick said. "Chief Tusca's going to have to interview for Dean's replacement. There won't be a lieutenant's review board for several more months. The city council will have to schedule a special session to approve a replacement and the promotion, unless we hire someone from the outside. That part of it is a budget issue."

"Will that happen?" she asked, thinking of Nathan, "I mean, hiring someone from the outside?"

"Not likely," Kedrick said. "HRG is special to the chief. He'll want his own man in place. Nathan Samm's got a good chance at it. We'll have to see."

"Will you let me know how it works out?" she said.

"Certainly," Kedrick responded. "I just wanted you to know what happened this morning, that's all."

"I appreciate the call," she said. "Thank you, Charles."

"My pleasure, Vanessa," he answered, and broke the connection.

"Wow," she said under her breath. "Interesting morning." She gathered up her briefcase and purse and headed out. She'd already planned on calling Nathan later on. This could be his lucky day.

October 26

Days Inn, Covington, Kentucky

The motel room contained a small table in the front corner with a single chair, a long bureau upon which the television sat, and two double beds. Bill Landau lay on the bed farthest from the door, the television turned to CNN, the volume down low. He had half his attention listening to the news, half-expecting to hear something about Madison, or himself. Panic had a pretty good hold of him, he knew, but still, something had happened, of that he was certain.

He had tried to call Madison the day before, but the man who answered the phone had been noncommittal, in a businesslike way. Madison wasn't available, the man had said.

Landau's paranoia had gone up a notch, and he had called his friend at the *Connersville Times,* eventually finding himself speaking to a Mr. Kindelbok, head of personnel. Kindelbok spoke in rapid, hushed tones, as if he was parlaying the biggest secret in the world.

"Madison's been taken into custody!" he had said, and Landau's heart had thudded once, painfully, then kicked into high gear.

"Yep. Couple of FBI agents showed up here and took him away. Just like that," Kindelbok went on, his tone suggesting he was glad it was Madison, not him. "Is there a message you want to pass on to him?" he asked. "I can get it to him. They gave me special access," he added, which Landau suspected was a lie. He hung up on the man instead, and left his house in a hurry, his mind in overdrive, all sorts of possibilities whanging around inside his head.

All he knew was that if the Feds had grabbed Madison, things had just gone downhill in a big hurry. That meant they were after him, too, and that was the last thing he needed. He fled almost blindly, wanting to get as far away from Oxford as he could until he could calm down and think.

He had ended up in Covington, across the Ohio River from Cincinnati, and checked into the first nondescript motel he could find. That was the day before, and safe behind the closed and double-locked door, Landau was coming to terms with his fright.

First order was to find a place they wouldn't think to look for him, at least not right away. He couldn't stay in the motel, that much he knew. They'd find him soon enough there. He had a better place in mind, the apartment in Somerville, south of Oxford.

Landau stabbed the power button off on the remote, and the television blinked off. He felt his head being compressed, as if giant hands were squeezing themselves on both sides. He rolled off the bed and went into the small bathroom, where he shook three Bufferin out of the bottle near the sink and swallowed them down.

Landau walked back into the room and saw the gun lying on the table in the corner. It was a new purchase, the result of Madison's last warning to him. He walked over to it and picked it up. The Browning Hi-Power 9 mm was distantly familiar. He had carried one in the war. Landau pressed the magazine release button behind the trigger and caught the heavy loaded magazine as it dropped out of the butt. He set it down on the table and racked the slide back, locking it open.

The gun felt good in his hand, giving him a sense of confidence he needed. Not safety, his little voice prompted. Confidence in the thirteen rounds it carried. You won't be safe until . . .

"What?!" Landau said suddenly in the empty room. "Until what?!" He heard the fright in his own voice. Instinctively he looked at the closed door.

You know, the voice answered, mockingly. It's started, now. They'll be coming for you. *He'll* be coming for you.

"Who will?" Landau asked aloud, this time much more quietly, because he already knew the answer this time. It wouldn't be the authorities. Not the FBI, or the CID. Not this time.

"Ahh!" he growled, and picked up the magazine, thrusting it home in the butt of the pistol. He thumbed down the slide release and felt the comfortable jump of the gun as the slide thumped home. He left the hammer cocked and pushed up on the thumb safety. He held the weapon up in front of his face. "Let him come," he whispered, looking at the Browning intently, focusing on the power it radiated. Inside he felt the weakness, but the gun bolstered him, painting his fright with a thin bravado.

Landau suddenly groaned and slowly put the gun down on the table. He shuffled backward until the edge of the bed caught him behind the knees, and he sat down heavily. He folded up, head bowed, and his hands slid over his eyes, now squeezed tight, fighting back the desperation, and the tears.

"Why?" he managed through clenched teeth. "Why now?"

But he knew the answer. That was the real certainty. And running away was fast becoming no option at all.

October 26

Trans Patriot Insurance, Scottsdale, Arizona

Gordon Hatton indicated the spare chairs in his office to his visitors, Kevin Parsons and Thom Castleback. Outside it was afternoon, but six stories below ground in the midst of the huge Trans Patriot complex only the clocks gave away the time of day. Scheduling problems had delayed Parsons and Castleback's arrival until after lunch. Once they were there, Gordon had taken them on a shortened tour of the vast facility. They had just finished, and both men found themselves amazed over the size and intricacy of the complex.

Gordon logged onto his PC while his guests quietly busied themselves around his office. Castleback motioned toward the fifty-gallon salt water aquarium set into the wall beside Gordon's desk.

"In lieu of a window, I presume?" he asked.

"Exactly," Gordon replied, pulling up a claim listing based on his diary count. "Some people need more than artwork on the walls. It's a nice touch," he said.

"So this is where you do your thing," Castleback said.

Gordon turned back to his keyboard. "Yep, as exciting as it all sounds, this is pretty much it," he replied, somewhat deadpan. "You spend most of the day reading files on the PC. Almost all of the administrative and clerical functions required are handled by the system." He called up a file diary at random. "Just to show you," he said, typing in commands and using the PC's mouse, "this is the closed file unit I've been working on lately."

Castleback and Parsons had come around to stand behind Gordon as he continued paging through the file with the mouse, giving them a running commentary as he went. "I was looking at this one a few days ago," he said. "This is some of the background stuff on the underlying claim, which includes a few newspaper articles, as you can see."

"Macon, Georgia," Castleback read. "A police fatality shooting, huh? I take it you guys wrote the coverage for the police department."

"Right," Gordon said. "We had the police professional liability on the insured. Their SWAT team took down the perpetrator, whose family filed a wrongful death action, and—"

"Hold it," Castleback interrupted. "There's the story on Jack Linet you were talking about at Luther's place."

Gordon glanced at the article, a small sidebar story lower down on the page. "You're right," he said, "this is it. That was one of the names John mentioned, wasn't it?"

"Yes it was," Castleback said, but his eyes were on something else. He moved closer to the screen, bent over slightly. "This picture here," he said, and Gordon shifted his vision to it.

"Oh, those are our insured's cops," he said. "They were the defendants in the lawsuit."

"Can you make this bigger?" Castleback asked.

"Sure," Gordon said, and rolled the mouse, moving the cursor around. He tapped the control and dragged the mouse, and a thin yellow line appeared, expanding into a rectangle. Gordon adjusted it until it bracketed the photograph. He moved the cursor to the menu bar at the top of the screen and selected another command. Instantly the picture jumped half again as large.

"You can change the size even more with the plus/minus key here," Gordon said, demonstrating. The picture expanded smoothly.

"Hold it," Castleback said, "that's good." He studied the line of officers staring back at them. "Look familiar, Kev?" he said, touching his finger to the figure. "Last week, at the Arms Tech demo at Cincinnatti?"

Parsons leaned in further and took a few moments. "Could be," he said. "Put a mustache on him, and give him some hair."

Gordon stared at the officer's face. A black man, sans facial hair and with his head apparently shaved beneath his uniform hat, looked back. Grainy as the news photo was, it still had picked up the intensity behind the man's eyes. He read off the caption at the bottom. "Frank Morey," he said, "SWAT team sniper with the department." He turned his head toward Castleback. "You think you've seen him before?"

"I know I've seen him before. Last week for sure, and at least one other time before that," Castleback said. "It was, what . . . like back in '81 or '82. He was younger, of course, with a SWAT team out or Illinois or Indiana, I think. They came through Quantico on a training gig. I was working with the bureau's hostage rescue people at the academy for a time."

Castleback shook his head. "Funny how the eyes miss the obvious, huh? Never occurred to me I'd see the same guy more than once. Of course, he's changed his appearance a little bit. He had hair then, but same job: tac team long gunner. He was one hell of a shot, that I remember real well. Don't often see anyone quite that good." He looked up at Gordon. "Until last week. It's the same fellow, I'm sure of it."

Parsons was thinking back, too. "Didn't John say one of the first victims was in Illinois?"

Castleback nodded. "Right. A guy by the name of Perriman, I believe."

"And the year seems right, too, when you saw him," Parsons said. "Early '81 or '82 was when Perriman was killed, according to John. Makes you wonder a bit, doesn't it?"

"It makes sense," Castleback said. "The guy works as a cop, maybe even on a departmental tactical team as a sniper."

"A job like that would give him good cover during the day," Parsons picked up the thought. "He could afford to scope out the next target on his list, take his time before doing the job."

"Right," Castleback said, warming up to their mutual idea. "And being a cop he could keep an eye on the investigation after the hit, and make sure he's not in danger of being caught."

"Why not? After everything settles down, he pulls up stakes, leaves the department, and fades away."

Gordon had been following the conversation and picked up on it now. "So he changes his name, maybe his appearance too, and reapplies to a police department near his next victim." He looked at his two visitors. "I think you guys just found out something important here."

"Maybe," Parsons said. "Could be science fiction, too. But I'll pass it along to John. He can check into it, if he wants. Makes sense to me, though, the more I think about it."

"Me, too," Castleback said. He was caught up in the mystery of it.

"If this is who John is looking for, it may explain how the suspect has been getting around," Parsons said. "He shuffles from department to department, changing his ID each time."

"But no one picks up on that?" Castleback said. "I mean, the shooter is moving from location to location. You'd think sooner or later someone's going to call him out and check up on his background."

"Not necessarily," Gordon said, intrigued with his discovery. "We see this kind of thing all the time. Cops with bad reps often slide from place to place, taking their problems with them. But they don't get discovered because most municipalities are happy to pick up an experienced officer, especially one they don't have to spend money training."

"So what if he is challenged?" Castleback asked. "Sooner or later the odds will catch up. Someone's going to check him out."

"And if they do, so what?" Gordon replied. "He pulls up stakes and tries a new place. No big deal for him."

"I can see how it could work," Parsons said. "We'd better pass this on to John."

"If this is the guy the Feds are looking for then the system failed big-time," Castleback said. "Hell of a thing," he added, remembering the last time he had seen the face in the picture. "Hope they catch him."

October 26

Lincoln, Kansas

High-altitude cirrus clouds refracted the midmorning sunlight, picking out details clearly on distant objects. Still, the bright hazy light was almost painful, and Manos adjusted the sunglasses he wore. He watched out the side window as the countryside passed. He was seated behind Husta, who rode up front in Russell Lancola's big green GMC Suburban.

The lawyer motioned out the window as he drove down the narrow lane, guarded from the fields on either side by sagging barbed wire, strung between weathered posts.

"That's it, the Longbaugh place." He pointed toward a sprawling single-story brick-and-stone ranch house, slightly elevated from the road they were on. Half a dozen large cottonwood trees protected the house, while the acreage around it was covered by thick grass gone to seed. A gravel drive a hundred yards long split off the country lane they traveled on. It wound toward the house between a dozen large mulberry trees. The driveway terminated at the right wing of the home, which appeared to be the garage.

"Ralph Longbaugh had this place built in the late fifties," Lancola said, braking lightly, turning the nose of the GMC into the driveway. "He intended to retire here. Now it belongs to Aaron."

They rolled slowly toward the substantial structure. Lancola eased to a stop in front of the closed garage doors.

"Doesn't appear like anyone's been here in a while," Husta said. Some paper debris and other wind-driven flotsam lay blown against the foundation. The entire place was quiet, neglected, but not rundown. Lancola explained why.

"I have a caretaker come out twice a year to knock down the grass, check the house out far winter. The pipes, furnace, you know. But he isn't due out for another few weeks."

It brought up a question for Manos. "Would Aaron know the schedule?"

Lancola shut off the ignition and turned in his seat to look back at Manos. "Yes, he would."

"I'd guess he wouldn't want to run into the maintenance guy, then."

Lancola gazed back for a few moments, knowing what the CID man was thinking. "So let's go find out if your suspicions are correct," he said.

The three men exited the GMC, closing each door in a rippling thunk of sound that carried flatly across the rural quiet.

"This way, gentlemen," Lancola said, producing a key from his overcoat pocket. The court order granting permission to enter and search the house rested in the same pocket. He'd called the county district judge to get it, explaining the reasons why. Whatever they might find would be legal now. He wanted to make sure it stayed that way.

They crunched across the gravel and onto the long concrete porch that ran along the front of the house. As Manos and Husta stepped onto the porch both men unbuttoned their coats. Lancola caught the movement, then Manos's eye. An understanding passed between them.

"A precaution," Manos said by way of explanation. He was acutely aware of the Colt .45 pistol snugged into the holster over his right hip. Husta was similarly armed.

"He won't be here, you know that," Lancola said.

Manos nodded. "I know." He didn't have to say what might happen if Aaron was inside. But he'd made it clear to the lawyer that no chances were being taken.

Lancola turned back to the door, a large wooden one, thick and solid. An ornate brass handle and deadbolt testified to the security of the place. The lawyer inserted both keys, turned them in turn, and pushed down on the thumb latch. The door opened slightly and easily. Without waiting for the two CID men, he straight-armed the door all the way open. It swung back quickly, striking the floor stop behind it with a loud thump, and rebounded a few inches. No sound came from inside the house.

Lancola stepped back, and motioned inward. "After you," he said with a slight smile.

Manos stared back at him. "No problem," he said, and stepped inside. His left hand pressed the door back against the stop again and held it there. His other hand remained at his side. His senses were primed, on alert, feeding that peculiar subliminal part of the professional cop. He reached out into the large home, probing, feeling the vibrations. There was nothing there, no feedback of any kind. There was no danger; no one was waiting. He walked deeper into the house.

Lancola started turning on lights as they went and opening blinds and curtains. Bright Kansas daylight entered the silent place. It illuminated the dust that had settled onto polished surfaces and the floor. He stated the obvious. "No one's home."

Manos and Husta paused in the middle of the spacious living room, decorated in a style both southwestern yet early sixties. They felt they had stepped back a couple of decades in time.

"Looking for anything in particular?" Lancola asked. He was both reluctant and eager to start the search. Part of him had become convinced of Aaron's participation in the killings. The other part wanted to protect him. That was the side Lancola chose at the moment.

"We'll know it when we find it," Husta commented, ambling toward the hallway.

They found it in the basement an hour later, after checking the main floor and finding nothing.

* * *

Their first view of the basement provided nothing they didn't expect to see. They had descended the stairs into a finished room, as large as the living room above. It was paneled in a light-finished wood, with a multicolored shag carpet with brown and beige overtones. A suspended ceiling contained recessed light panels. The furniture was made of darkly oiled heavy pine, indicating the room had been used as a family room of sorts. A large console television took up space in a corner, while a hi-fi center stood nearby on a custom cabinet.

Across the room a set of bifold doors separated the finished section from the rest of the basement. Lancola pushed them back to reveal a utility room opposite what appeared to be the furnace room, containing the large oil-burning unit. A small workbench with an assortment of tools hanging on a pegboard on the wall behind it was just past the furnace room's open doorway. At the far end the basement ended with a blank concrete block wall.

Manos strolled down to it, then turned and looked back down the length of the room, and up at the exposed joists of the house. "Funny, I'd judge there's still twenty-five or thirty feet more on the other side." He began a closer inspection of the wall, checking seams along the blocks. He paused for a few moments, running his fingertips along the grout between several bricks.

"Tony? Take a look here," he said.

Husta walked over beside him and leaned down to look closer. "Yeah, I see it, I think," he said, then straightened up and took a few paces back. He nodded. "Yeah, you can see it better from here."

"See what?" Lancola asked, curious.

"The grout on this section of wall," Husta said, motioning with his hand. "It looks different from the rest of the wall. You can follow it around," he said, pointing to illustrate.

"It's like a section was torn down, then reset," Manos joined in. "The blocks look the same, but I'd bet this whole section here has been taken out and rebuilt."

He turned to Lancola. "Any idea what's on the other side? Did the major keep anything back here?"

Lancola began to check the grout line himself. "No," he said, touching the wall. "I really have no idea if there's anything behind this. I confess I haven't been down here all that much. I frankly have no idea what could be behind here. Maybe nothing. Why?"

Manos began looking around, busying himself. "Because I think there *is* something behind this, Russ," he said. "I have a feeling this bit has been torn down and resealed more than once."

"Well, the only way to find out is to knock it down," Lancola said, "and I'm not so sure . . ."

"Hola, mano," Husta said. He held up a fifteen-pound sledge-hammer he had found near the workbench. "This ought to do it."

"Hold on," Lancola said, taking a step forward. "I don't know that I can condone physical destruction to this residence."

"Does the warrant cover this?" Manos interrupted him.

"It does," Lancola agreed after a few moments. He was clearly uncomfortable with what was about to happen, but he couldn't interfere.

"Close enough," Manos said. "We'll have it repaired. But if I'm right . . ." he looked from the lawyer to Husta. "Tony?"

Husta hefted the sledge and took up a position in front of the wall. He checked his swing range and, satisfied, took the first stroke. The head of the sledge bit through the first block with a thump, and pieces flew, bigger chunks failing to the floor. He swung again, knocking clear through the block. He paused and waved the dust away from the ragged hole. He bent and peered in. "Appears hollow behind this, Jim," he said.

"Go for it," Manos said.

Husta squared off again and began swinging in earnest. In a remarkably short time he'd cleared a hole four feet high and three across. He set the sledge down and, using a crowbar Manos retrieved from the workbench, began pulling more blocks down, clearing the final courses down to floor level. It was noisy work, but over within a few minutes.

He stepped back, catching his breath, and motioned to Manos.

"You all right?" Manos asked.

"Sure," Husta said, breathing deeply. He cocked his head at the hole in the wall and the shattered bits of block scattered around the floor. "After you, mano," he said.

Manos ducked, stepping carefully around several large pieces of block, and entered the space beyond. "There's a room here," he called back through. "Wait a minute," and light flooded on suddenly. "Well, well," he said under his breath. Lancola stood beside him, taking in the sight.

"Got a real gunsmith here," Husta said, stepping through the hole behind them.

The room had been semifinished with an industrial dark green carpet on the floor and a suspended ceiling. Four dual-bulb fluorescent shoplight units shone down, flooding the room with a purposeful, shadow-free light. Exposed studs adorned the unfinished walls, to which were fastened a series of wooden shelves, varying in width depending on the items stored neatly on them.

"Got to wonder why he'd keep it secret," Manos said, not bothering to say the name. The why to his question suddenly appeared to present itself.

"There's your answer," Husta said, pointing across to the far wall. A small but heavy workbench stood beneath the shelves above it. Several vises had been attached along one side and the front edge. Power tools were racked above the bench. Standing a few paces away from the bench were a drill press, table saw, and two different lathes. The shelves above the bench held neatly stacked small square and rectangular brightly colored cardboard boxes.

Manos recognized some of the brand names. "Speer, Winchester, Hercules, IMR. He's been loading his own, I'd say."

"Right," Husta said. "Scales, Dillon press, powder measures, case trimmer, everything you'd expect to see." He was looking closely at some of the boxes on the shelves above the bench. "Powder, primers, case-cleaning stuff, and loaded rounds," he said, taking a box down to read off the typed label on the end of it. "One-hundred-seventy-three-grain boat-tail match-grade," he said, and added, "7.62 NATO. No wonder he kept it hidden."

"Gets better all the time," Manos said. "Damn." He hadn't wanted to see what they had found. Wishful thinking, he thought silently.

On the wall opposite the bench, held in what appeared to be a custom wooden rack designed for them, were rifle barrels and stocks, half a dozen of each. Husta reached over and pulled a replacement barrel assembly off the rack. "M-14," he said, looking at it. "Actually, a match-grade version. The barrel shaft's heavier from the breech to the gas port assembly here," he said. "Probably an M-21. These others are far a target-grade bolt action." He leaned over to look at the letters engraved on the surface of one. "Remington, 7.62 NATO," he said. It was enough for the two of them.

Manos said aloud what they were both thinking. "Obviously he has two rifles. He had the extra parts because he changed them out after each hit. He comes back here and fits a new barrel, bolt, firing pin, extractor, the whole nine yards. He's eliminating any forensic and ballistic evidence on the off-chance the rifle is discovered or seized. Even so, he's extremely careful not to leave anything behind at the scene. All the field reports we've seen remark in unison how sterile the shooting sites have been." He looked around in grudging admiration. "Man, that's a lot of work, tearing this wall down and rebuilding each time. Just to keep this room hidden."

"Meticulous," Husta concurred.

"Premeditated," Manos added.

"A professional," Lancola said behind them as he stepped forward. He looked down at the rifle parts, his eyes saddened. "But then, he was trained to be one, wasn't he?"

"Yes he was, and he still is," Manos said. "Best get hold of Jovenall and Paraletto," Husta said, "and tell them what we found."

"Sure," Manos said, pulling his cell phone out of his overcoat pocket. He paused before dialing the number. "This confirms he has the means, but there's nothing on the squad here. How has he been keeping track of them? What's he been doing between killings? We still don't have a clue on finding out what he's doing, or who he is right at this moment." His frustration showed. "We're closer to him, but not that close." He dialed the number from memory and raised the unit to his ear. His eyes swept the room carefully. "Damn it, Aaron," he swore under his breath. "Damn you," he added. The connection went through.

October 26

Office of the FBI, Cincinnati, Ohio

Both calls arrived within minutes of each other, Manos's from Kansas, and Kevin Parson's from Arizona. Special Agent John Paraletto told Peter Jovenall the news. Jovenall had returned after checking on the security arrangements at Michael Madison's house.

"Looks like Manos and Husta have a positive ID on the shooter. It's Aaron Longbaugh, all right. They discovered a weapons cache in his home in Kansas. Seems he's been using two rifles, both 7.62 NATO caliber. He's apparently been changing the barrels and other crucial parts after each shooting."

"That's pretty telling," Jovenall said, "but circumstantial so far. Anything tying him in directly with the victims?"

"No, unfortunately," Paraletto said, "but Kevin may have something. One of Luther's people, Gordon Hatton, flashed on the name of one of the victims, Jack Linet. He remembered it from one of his claim files."

"And?" Jovenall asked.

"Anyway, Gordon pulled up the file. Linet was mentioned in a sidebar story on the same newspaper page as an article about the claim file. The claim concerned a police department Trans Patriot insured, down in Georgia. It was a wrongful death claim, against the department's SWAT team."

Jovenall listened patiently, wondering about the point of John's story.

John saw the look and grinned. "Hang on, Pete, here's the punch line. The paper printed pictures of the SWAT team. Both Kevin and Thom Castleback recognized one of the cops in the picture from a firearms exhibition a week ago. The cop in the picture was with a different department this time."

Now Jovenall made the connection, and his lips twisted into an ironic smile.

"Yeah, I thought you'd see it, at least the possibility. The Trans

Patriot Georgia case occurred about the same time as the Linet murder. But the clincher is Thom remembers the same guy from an even earlier training gig he did at Quantico, back in 1981 or '82. And again, the guy was with a different PD. Thom is pretty sure he came from Illinois or Indiana."

Jovenall was thinking, running the facts down in his head. "Wait a minute, the early eighties, that was Max Perriman, wasn't it?" He sat back and turned his face up to the ceiling, letting the pieces fall into place. "Oh, this is too good. Don't tell me. The shooter who tagged Linet was working as a cop? Aaron Longbaugh's a cop? You gotta be kidding!"

"Appears that way," John confirmed. "It sure would explain a lot if it's true."

"Hold on," Jovenall said. "Where did Thom and Kevin see this guy last week?"

"Here," John said, "in Ohio. The Cincinnati office hosted a weapons demonstration of a new tactical rifle. They invited several tac teams from surrounding departments."

"Jesus, he's after William Landau!" Jovenall said, stating the obvious next target. "Which department was it?"

"Not sure," John said. "Neither Kevin nor Thom connected with him that day. But we know he's in the area. We'll pull the list of departments that were invited to the exhibition and start running them down. We have the photograph of Aaron Longbaugh from his DD214 military file that Manos and Husta left us. Should be able to match him to one of those departments fairly quickly. Manos and Husta are due back tonight from Kansas. They're bringing the Longbaughs' family lawyer with them, a Russell Lancola."

"Why's he coming along?" Jovenall asked.

"Looking out for Aaron, according to Manos. Says if it really is him, he'll be there to defend the boy."

"He understands the Army retains jurisdiction in this matter, doesn't he?" Jovenall asked.

"I asked Manos the same question. He says Lancola understands that. He just wants to be here. Says it's the least he can do. The boy's his client."

"All right then, no problem," Jovenall said. He looked across the desk at John. "Seems pretty easy, don't you think? Finding him this fast."

"Yeah," John said soberly. "The easy ones are usually the ones that go south in a hurry."

Jovenall nodded. He'd seen his share of sure things go bad, too. They couldn't take any chances on this one, either. "We'll get him, John. But we'll make sure he can't get anyone else, either. We'll pull in Madison, too, while we're at it. I'll leave now. It's a couple hours' drive to Connersville. The team's been sitting on him pretty close so far. I'll accompany them back here with Madison and his family. We'll bring him back here in the morning."

"Is he still denying anything concerning Major Longbaugh's supposed fragging?" John asked.

"Yeah, so far. Madison's a piece of work, I have to say."

John shook his head. "The war screwed up a lot of guys," he said, "some legitimate and some not. This kind of thing, though . . ." He stretched, hands behind his head. "This was the worst of what came out of fourteen years of fucked-up policy," he said. "Guys like Madison and his pals were an abomination, Pete. An absolute waste."

"Yeah, well, at least he's still alive, John. We did that much for him, if nothing else."

"It won't mean much if we don't find Bill Landau."

"Tell me about it," Jovenall said. "We've got a national APB out for him now. The man's dropped off the board."

Paraletto rocked back in his chair, pushing back and forth with the toes of his feet. "No," he said. "Landau's running, sure, but he's out of his depth. You can't predict what an amateur will do, but you can find him, for the same reason. He'll do something dumb, and it'll look as bright as a road flare. Either that, or we'll find someone who knows where he's gotten himself to."

"Maybe," Jovenall replied. "But we'd better do it quick. Longbaugh's not wasting any time either."

His phone rang at that moment. "Jovenall," he said, listened a moment, then said, "He's right here, just a second." He handed the receiver to Paraletto. "Quantico . . . Investigative Support Unit, for you. Al Nadder," he said.

Alex Nadder, head of the ISU, had been running the profile on the sniper for the last few days. Paraletto took the phone quickly.

"Hey, Al . . . John . . . yeah, thanks, man. What've you come up with?" He looked at Jovenall while Nadder ran down the teams' findings. The big agent nodded a few times as the description continued.

"Really," Paraletto said once, his eyes flickering back to Jovenall. "All right, Al, fax it over as soon as you can, hard copy to follow overnight." He nodded again, and grinned quickly. "No, I'll tell 'im. And thanks, Al. Nice job, as always."

He hung up the phone. "Fax is on the way, Pete," he said, "but the highlights are we're looking for a male, late thirties, probably thirty-seven or -eight, military background, infantry to be exact, almost certainly special-operations-trained."

"Like Ranger qualified, or Special Forces?" Jovenall asked.

"You got it," Paraletto said. "And here's the interesting part. The shooter is probably related to the victims through a common prior event. I guess we know what that is, huh? But Al says the shooter is also getting close to each victim through his job." He emphasized his last comment with a raised eyebrow.

Jovenall nodded. The profilers back at the Quantico academy had nailed it, again. "A cop, right? Al says the shooter's a cop."

Paraletto pointed a finger at him and raised his thumb, then dropped it. "Right on, Pete. Not only a cop, but a black cop."

Jovenall shook his head. "You know, if Manos hadn't just called to say the same thing I wouldn't have guessed it. We have a vigilante kid out there looking to balance the books on his old man."

"Well, calling him a kid is a bit off, but considering the rest, Longbaugh is definitely going to have a serious problem for the remaining two targets. He hasn't missed yet. And I'll bet you even money he already knows where Landau's gotten himself to."

Jovenall nodded. "No bet, John. I think you're right. We've got a big problem here."

Right at that moment neither agent had any notion how prophetic that last statement would turn out to be.

October 27

Predawn, Connersville, Indiana

Peter Jovenall arrived at the Madisons' home with two cars holding three additional HRT agents each, the Hostage/Rescue specialists of the FBI. The counter-sniper team drove in their own vehicle, a large, square Step Van. It matched the armored security van brought along to transport the Madison family. The inside of the special van was lined with ballistic plates and Kevlar panels, while the only windows were the bullet-resistant glass of the windshield and both front doors. A bulkhead behind the driver's position sealed off the passenger compartment from view. Short of an anti-tank rocket, those riding inside were safer than they would be in the typical bank armored car.

The agents dismounted, dressed in full black tactical gear with helmets, web gear, automatic weapons, and ballistic vests. The six of them were joined by the four agents in the house, now also clad in identical gear. The counter-sniper team huddled briefly over several topographical maps, discussing optional locations. Clothed in woodland camouflage uniforms, they presented a different appearance from the HRT group. The four men, each equipped with scope-sighted, heavy-barreled, bolt-action rifles, split into two-man teams. The leader was bothered by the situation. He motioned Agent Jovenall over to explain.

"It's like I said back at the shop, Pete," he said, gesturing at the maps spread out over the hood of the car. "The terrain here is tough. There's just too many good places for a shooter to set up." He looked up, scanning the distance. "We can cover some of this, but no guarantees." He looked back at Jovenall. "Ideally we should have more time for this. And more men."

Jovenall returned his pointed gaze. "We ran out of time. The shooter, this Aaron Longbaugh, is in the area, you know that. You also know how capable he is. If he's going to try for Madison it's going to be soon. We have no choice in the matter. If we don't move him now we won't be able to. You'll have to give it your best estimate."

The leader shook his head once. "Give this guy an estimate and Madison's a dead man."

Jovenall didn't reply. Instead he checked his watch. "How much time will you need?"

The leader looked eastward. "It'll be full light in forty minutes. I'll set us up by then. Give me another thirty to clear the area, and I'll give you a heads-up. When you get the call, get Madison out of the house and into the van ASAP. You know the drill."

Jovenall nodded.

"No dragging, Pete," the leader emphasized. "You'll have a few seconds at best to get him into cover. It's the best I can give you."

"It'll have to do," Jovenall replied. He signaled to the others. "Let's go." He led them into the house, while the counter-sniper leader led his small group off. He had the toughest job: trying to determine where Aaron Longbaugh might be, if he was there at all. The leader relied on real-world experience, and he was good.

He came close, actually, given the circumstances. But as he had warned Jovenall, there were just too many good places to cover. And he was up against the best.

Jovenall stood inside the kitchen an hour and a half later, out-lining the scene.

"Okay, then. We'll waltz the Madisons out of here once the perimeter is secure. We have Indiana DPS escort to the Ohio line, where Ohio Highway Patrol will pick us up and remain with us to Cincy." He looked around at his men. "This is straightforward, people. Let's take Madison first, then his wife, then the kids. Nice and quick, out the kitchen side door, into the van, no problems. Questions?" He looked around. There were none.

"Fine. Team leaders, let's get it done. Brady, when we get the call, give me the high sign and keep your people sharp."

"Roger that," Agent Brady replied, and pulled on his helmet. He checked the wireless mike, calling quickly around on the tactical radio net with each of his people. A fast series of positive responses squawked into his earpiece. He nodded to Jovenall and said, "Set. I'll call."

He motioned to his five men, who checked the condition of their individual MP-5A2 submachine guns. Magazines snapped home with practiced ease and a rapid cascade of clicks and snicks followed as bolts were cycled and safeties were set.

Dressed in black, the six men slid out of the kitchen door and moved quickly and quietly to secure the area around the house. It took under four minutes to establish a solid perimeter, covering every possible approach. Their eyes made quartering sweeps, methodically checking the area in fifty-yard sections, covering the expanding distance out to three hundred yards. Any potential threat within their vision's range would be instantly contained, or eliminated by the counter-sniper teams. The house was secure.

Three hundred yards was a fair distance, even a reasonable one. But the danger was farther out. Four hundred and forty-one yards farther out, to be precise.

* * *

Aaron lay prone, observing the scene through the eyepiece of the ART/MPC variable scope, run up to 9X, its highest setting. The suppressor-tipped Remington rested motionless on its bipod, pointing toward Madison's house. His right hand held the pistol grip firmly, index finger alongside the trigger guard.

It had taken him three hours to get into this new hide, necessarily different from the last time he'd readied the shoot. That position was blown, as far as he was concerned. He was closer to the house now, but still he felt comfortable with the setup. Aaron wore his Ghillie suit, with his face and hands fully camouflaged. A small hump in the ground, covered with low scrub growth, served to hide him from direct observation from the house. He was satisfied with his preparations. This time there would be no interruptions.

He studied the extra vehicles, taking special note of the security van, a slab-sided Step Van. He knew what it was and why it was there. They were going to move Madison, probably for safekeeping. It wouldn't do any good.

Briefly Aaron replayed the last couple of days. Since he'd discovered the presence of the federal agents, he had acted on his alternate plan, including the decision to leave the Westport PD. That matter had been resolved, a little more easily than he thought it would be. Now with that worry out of the way, he had spent considerable time analyzing his chances of finishing his mission. His identity was known, of that there was no doubt. But they would be looking for him in a different direction now. He had time, he figured, if he worked quickly. Two strikes, one right after the other, and it would be all over. And while they reacted to the threat, too late, he would be gone again, this time for good.

He observed the HRT members moving to secure the perimeter after the van had backed itself toward the side kitchen door. He knew it was only minutes away. He had been watching the counter-sniper teams working into position earlier. He knew who they were, of course, and the threat they presented to him. But they weren't in the right places. The closest to him was still over five hundred yards away. They were working on where they thought he might be. It wasn't their fault, really. There were just too many possibilities. And they'd guessed wrong.

Aaron was aware of the early morning light and how it would work to his advantage in this circumstance. The long shadows from the sun's low angle aided his natural-appearing camouflage. The report of the suppressed shot would be lost in the mild breeze, which blew toward his position at five to eight miles per hour. The breeze would lift his shot slightly. He'd compensate for it easily.

Carefully he bracketed an eighteen-inch measurement off the house, using a section of the kitchen door and window frame to do so. He rotated the camming ring until the measurement was between the stadia wires. He was dead on for the shot. He pushed the safety off and settled in. Now it was up to the Feds to give him his target.

He didn't have long to wait.

*　*　*

Mike Madison was not happy. In fact, he was quite vocal about the invasion of his house and the extraordinary intrusion of federal agents into his life. But more than the rage that fed his belligerence was the fear. Absolute, white-knuckled, stomach-churning fear. Worse than the pointed accusations from his wife, Alma. Worse than the whining questions and withering stares from his teenage kids. Worse than the gut-slamming jolt that his most carefully hidden secret had been dredged into the light. Worse than all of that was the certain knowledge, as clear as the brightest day, that *he* was out there. The shooter had come for him.

He didn't know what had become of Landau. The agents refused to talk about him. And given their presence in his house, Madison had to assume Landau had failed in his preparations, despite the warning he had sent him.

Bill's dead, too, he had thought, the grim realization coming to him in the quiet of the night, while he lay hidden in his own basement, out of sight, under the noses and guns of these damned Feds! I'm the last one, and the bastard's comin' for me now. So they've come to protect me from him. A little too late, wouldn't ya say, boys?

He almost laughed aloud, but nothing was funny anymore. There was no escaping the shooter. He looked at them, cursing them in their black military outfits, with their automatic weapons. They had given him and his family similar clothing, complete with vests and helmets to wear, as they had explained the drill.

"We'll move you out of the side door, straight into the back of the van," the one named Jovenall told him. "It's parked close by, twenty-five feet to the double doors in the back. You'll be shielded by agents on either side, and one in front. It'll only take a few seconds, and then we'll escort your wife, then your children."

Madison pulled on the one-piece black coverall, jamming his booted feet down the long pant legs. He saw the look in the man's eyes as Jovenall explained the routine, saw the distaste on his face.

"Can't stand to be in the same room with me, can ya?" he said. He straightened up, shrugging into the sleeves. "You don't believe anything I've said about the major, do you?" He saw it was no use, but his wife was staring at him again, and the accusation and ugliness was in her eyes. He wanted so much to whip his hand out at her and smash that look clean off her face. "What're you lookin' at?" he growled instead.

The tears welled up one more time. It hadn't been the first time since the Feds arrived. God-*damn*, would she ever stop?!

"Nothing, Mike," she said, her voice husky from crying. "I ain't

lookin' at anything," she repeated, lowering her head. "Not anymore," she added softly.

Madison turned away from her, instantly stifling the sneer on
his face when he saw Jovenall's eyes. Summoning up a craftier
look, he finished buttoning the front of the coverall.

"He's out there, y'know," he said, as if it were the surest thing in
the world. "This man don't mess around. You boys ought to know
that by now. He's taken all of us down, one by one. All except Hector and Burris, poor bastards. Probably Landau, too, I guess. So
I'm it, the last one." He shook his head. "It's all a lie," he said, more
for his own benefit now. "The whole thing's a lie. Army set us up
for the fall. It was Charlie that blew the major away, but we
couldn't ever convince them of that. Poor old Madrid must have
been whacked clear out of his head to come up with a story like he
told them two captains." He almost chuckled, in a sad fashion. It
was a nice touch, he thought.

"Old Carlos, he was facing life in Leavenworth for knifing that
FNG. I guess if I were in that boat I'd've done some quick talkin'
too. But to say what he said? Hang us all like that? Man, we went
through the shit together. We was *tight,* I'll tell you. We kept each
other alive through the worst of it." He shook his head again.
"Don't make much sense," he said, liking the effect of his denial,
thinking it was really working. He glanced at his wife to gauge her
reaction. The look she returned was part pity, part incredulity. He
wasn't sure what the rest of it was, but it made his stomach tighten
just a bit more.

"Mr. Madison," Agent Jovenall said, the sound of his voice getting Madison's attention. "We're here to keep you alive. All you
have to do is follow my instructions, and that's all. I've heard
enough from you the last few days to have heard all I need to. Just
. . . save it, all right?"

Madison started to reply, but the look in Jovenall's eyes stopped
him cold.

Jovenall ignored him and spoke into his wireless mike, clipped
inside his Kevlar helmet. "We're ready here," he said. He paused,
listening. "All right," he said. "Mr. Madison?" he said, gesturing
with his hand.

Madison paused as another agent checked the fitting of the heavy vest around his upper body.

"Helmet," the agent said, handing it to him. "Make sure the chin strap's fastened tight," he said.

Madison grabbed the helmet, surprised by its lightness. He'd expected it to be heavier, "I know something about these things, boy," he said, pulling it on. He checked the fit, and fastened the wide chinstrap around. He glanced at the agent beside him. "You go into combat, y'know, the real thing, with the chinstrap on," he said, "and concussion from an explosion will rip your head clean off."

"We won't have that problem today, Mr. Madison," Jovenall said. He looked at Madison's wife, who stood near the stairs leading to the basement. "We'll be back for you in a minute, Mrs. Madison." He dredged up a reassuring smile for her. "Don't worry."

She didn't say anything, but the roundness of her eyes revealed her fear. She nodded hesitantly instead. Then her hand came up. "Mike?" she began, but he didn't hear her.

He had been standing next to the door when Jovenall heard the terse command from the counter-sniper leader. Jovenall's hand pointed to the agents beside Madison, and they had suddenly pushed the door open, and then three of them were hustling him out and down the stairs.

* * *

Madison cleared the door, an agent on either arm, their hands gripping his upper arms tight, almost carrying him along. Another agent was in front of them, weapon at the ready in a high port position, his head sweeping back and forth. A fourth waited for them in the back of the open dark blue van. Madison had taken exactly three steps off the short stoop outside the door, moving fast. But he was still sixteen feet from the safety of the van. It was too far . . .

Aaron was psyched into the rifle, his concentration precisely tuned, his eye focused through the scope on the side door of the house. It suddenly opened outward, and the four figures in black exploded from it, moving quickly. The one in the middle was Madison, he knew, and the crosshairs settled on his head instantly, then dropped a shade to Madison's nose, a few inches under the rim of the helmet. The bobbing image of the helmeted face was almost luminescent in the bright circular view through the scope. The slightly surreal glow was an effect of the scope's magnifying lenses.

His concentration for the shot seemed to slow the undulating head. Already his breath was synchronizing, his finger squeezing minutely on the smooth surface of the trigger. The shot went off with a slight surprise, and the Remington recoiled sharply into his shoulder. Even before he checked the result, his shooting thumb had flicked quickly upward against the handle of the bolt, a practiced move. The handle moved up smartly, and the bolt flicked back while his open palm caught the expended shell casing ejected from the chamber. In almost the same motion he reversed the process, slamming the bolt home, locking a new round into the breech. The expended shell dropped beside the rifle as his hand returned to the stock. The crosshairs settled on target instantly, but the target was no longer standing . . .

*   *   *

The agents heard the impact, a solid thwack of sound, a millisecond before the supersonic crack of the bullet. They never did hear the faint pop from the distant rifle. The 173-grain bullet struck Madison a quarter-inch to the right of his nose, midway between the bridge and his upper lip. It transected his sinus cavity and the base of his brain, cutting cleanly through the cerebellum, and blew out the base of his skull and the back of the Kevlar helmet. The bullet, its tip deformed now, continued to bury itself six feet up in the wall at the outside corner of the house.

Madison's head jerked a little from neurological reaction, and his forward momentum carried him in a tumbling fall face-down onto the driveway, his legs vibrating spasmodically, tangling one of the agents, who fell with him.

"What . . .!" one shouted, diving out of the way.

"Christ!" the one who fell with the body shouted.

The lead man skidded to a halt and spun back around, narrowly missing the dead man who fell toward him.

The agent in the van saw the bullet strike and flinched instinctively. Then he jumped out, but it was already too late.

Jovenall saw it all from the kitchen. He leaped out of the doorway toward the scene a few steps away.

The agent on the ground disengaged himself from Madison's body, spinning away, going for his weapon. Madison lay completely inert, face full down in the gravel. His left leg jerked still, the dying nerves running down. The hole in the back of his helmet was barely an inch wide, with a large crack running in a jagged line upward.

The counter-sniper teams saw the hit and heard the high-pitched crack, which seemed to radiate generally from their left. They swung in that direction, calculating quickly, mental trajectories merging with visual references as they aimed their rifles and spotting scopes toward the line of the bullet's suspected flight. But no hostile target appeared in the circles of their scopes. Nothing moved in the mild breeze that wasn't naturally there. It only took seconds.

Jovenall and the agent pushed up off the ground and began to move for the body, intent on grabbing Madison under the arms and lifting him out of the way. They never completed the move. The second shot struck just then, straight into the crown of the lifeless head.

Jovenall's own shoulders hunched up instinctively from the thudding snap of the bullet's strike into the top of the helmet. Again the high-speed crack followed, echoing off the side of the house.

"Christ!" the other agent said, and dove out of the way.

Jovenall had taken cover behind the bulk of the van and immediately called to the HRT team members. "Madison's down!" he said, his voice tight, and his eyes flicked quickly to the prone form, noting the ugly exit hole in the helmet. He called their counter-sniper team leader. "Where's the shooter?"

"Don't see a damn thing," the team leader called back, and under his breath, "this guy is *good!*" Louder he added, "We can approximate the location. It was a suppressed shot . . . he could be anywhere."

Jovenall heard the frustration in the man's tone. He took a breath, slowing his pulse rate, adrenaline still pushing through him. Jesus, he was fast! he thought to himself. Then to the team leader he said, "The shooter'll be gone before we get a fix on him." He looked at the body, his jaw tight. "He's done what he came to do. I don't think there will be any more incoming. Call in the locals, let them start a search. We'll secure things here."

He realized the pitiful irony in his last line. Yeah, we secured things just great, he admonished himself. He kept his eyes on Madison. They'd blown it, and in a big way. Jovenall was responsible for his safety, and he'd failed. He heard the commotion from inside the house, and Alma Madison struggled to the door, fighting the restraining arms of the agent trying to hold her back.

"Oh, God, Michael," she wailed, seeing his body, and her eyes jolted up to meet Jovenall's. They said it all. She held the agent's for a moment, far too long for Jovenall ever to forget the way they looked, the way they questioned and burned at the same time. Then she was pulling away from her protector and coming down the step.

It was the opening act for a very long, very bad day. There would be one more death to be witnessed and accounted for before it was over.

* * *

Aaron slid his hand carefully over the ejected shell casing and palmed it. His heavy Ghillie suit masked the tiny movement. He slowly put his eye to the spotting scope and continued watching the counter-sniper teams look for him. From their actions he was certain they hadn't seen him.

"A little while longer," he cautioned himself in a quiet voice. "Wait for them to break it up first. Then ease on out of here." He knew they would have difficulty finding his hide. His two shots had been too close together, and the suppressor had effectively masked his direction of fire. He would be able to slip out of the area unseen.

Slowly he rotated the spotting scope in the direction of his victim. He watched the people moving around the fallen body.

"That's seven," he said. He felt nothing for the dead man. He thought of Bill Landau, his remaining target, and realization flooded over him. "One left to go," he whispered, not believing at first what he had just said. Finally, after all this time. He brought up the dream memory, seeing his father in his mind's eye striding toward him in full uniform, all of his medals and awards glittering in radiant colors on his chest. His hand reached out to him, closer now.

"One left, Dad," he said, confirming his promise. "The last one . . . for you."

The image of his father's face lingered even as Aaron returned his attention to the scope. There was something in his eyes, just before they faded. He'd seen it before . . . the minor thought was gone. Keep your mind on the mission, he told himself. No mistakes now. You're almost home . . .

He studied the activity of the agents milling around the distant house, satisfied he was all right. But that look from his father nagged at him still. Later, he promised himself.

Think about it later.

October 27

Morning, Trans Patriot Insurance, Hamilton, Ohio

Vanessa Tau was confused. She asked her question again. "Are you sure there's no record?" she asked. "Lieutenant Dean Barlot. He was supposed to have checked in to your department on some sort of transfer/promotion." She waited for the person on the other end to reply, and the answer kept the fine lines on her brow furrowed. "Well, that's the information I was given," she said. "He accepted a promotional position with the Chehalis PD. Now you tell me not only did he not arrive, but that you have no such position open." She paused as she listened to the reply, and sighed.

"Well, obviously one of us received the wrong information. Yes, I will call back his department here. No, thank you anyway for your time. I'm sorry for the mixup." She smiled quickly. "Yes, you too. G'bye."

She replaced the receiver slowly, her mind working on the conversation. She'd had a few answers left to complete on the interrogatories for defense counsel Arthur Gabel, which concerned Dean Barlot. One of Gabel's associates had called, asking her if she could check on the answers. It should have been a simple matter to complete, and she'd placed a call to the City of Chehalis, south of Tacoma, Washington, to which Charles Kedrick had told her Barlot had gone.

The city clerk who had taken her call seemed confused at first, as she had never heard of anyone by that name. At Vanessa's insistence the clerk had checked with their personnel department. The job position Barlot was supposed to have assumed had never been posted. No one by that name had arrived, or was expected to.

She picked up the receiver again and dialed Kedrick's number at Westport. His secretary transferred her to him after a few moments.

"Charles? Vanessa Tau. Fine, thanks, and you?" She glanced at the brief notes she had taken while speaking with the Chehalis city clerk. "Listen, there's seems to be a problem with Lieutenant Barlot's transfer."

Kedrick on the other end seemed surprised, and said so.

Vanessa leaned back in her chair. "Well, the problem in a nutshell is the Chehalis PD never heard of him. Are you sure that's where he was going?"

Kedrick's reply came quickly, but she sensed there was something bothering him. "Certainly, Vanessa," he said. "That's what Dean advised us. I'm confused myself, given what you've just said. Exactly why were trying to reach him?"

She explained, adding she didn't think it was going to be a big deal, since Barlot had left assurances he was available to help out on the legal discovery involving the Bennet lawsuit. Apparently now it was a big deal, since Barlot was clearly among the missing, for real.

"I'm sorry," Kedrick said. "None of this makes any sense, but I'm sure it can be straightened out. Can you come by my office today? There's a few things I might be able to do to clear this up for you."

Vanessa checked her planner and saw she had the time if she left the office now. "As it happens I can do it right now," she said. "I've got a call I can put off, but I can be there in forty-five minutes. Is that all right?"

"Perfect," Kedrick replied, and again she detected something there, almost a sense of relief on his part. "I'll see you soon. And Vanessa," he added, "I'm sure this isn't a big deal. We'll take care of it."

"That's all I ask, Charles," she said, and rang off. This entire case is getting stranger by the day, she thought. Then she thought of Nathan. Maybe she would get a chance to see him at the station. The idea brightened her up, and temporarily replaced the problem of the whereabouts of Dean Barlot.

October 27

Morning, FBI Regional Office, Cincinnati, Ohio

John Paraletto's tight visage reflected the tension in the room. Michael Madison had been killed right under their noses and they had been powerless to stop it. He passed the telephone receiver over to Jim Manos. This was Peter Jovenall's third call, but he was able to give them little that was new. The on-site investigation was in full swing. Neither agent believed, however, that Aaron Longbaugh was still in the immediate area.

Manos, running on only two hours' sleep he had managed on the entire flight from Kansas, took the status report, his face grim as he asked pointed questions. The answers were what he didn't want to hear. "I knew he was good," he said, his face grim. "I didn't think we'd get a graphic demonstration."

Tony Husta watched him on the phone, his stomach chilled from the news. Madison's security had obviously slipped up. They should have had a better appreciation of Longbaugh's capabilities. This was one hell of a way to learn, but he wisely kept his criticism to himself.

Russell Lancola sat at the borrowed desk, his chin on his gnarled and weathered hands. He couldn't believe what he had heard. The attorney's fragile hope that Aaron wasn't the man they were pursuing had been effectively shattered now. His concern now centered on hoping Aaron was found before he got to the last intended victim, William Landau.

"Well, keep on it," Manos said, and added, "yeah, I thought as much. We're all a step behind Longbaugh." He hung up the phone.

"Nothing so far," he said, confirming what Jovenall had told him. An extensive search by the Indiana State Police had failed to find anything but the empty position where the sniper had been. No shell casings or any other evidence was discovered. The site was empty save for the depression where the shooting mat had been laid.

"Same scenario," Manos said. "Two rounds, both head shots. And fast, too, Pete said. They'd barely cleared the house when the first one hit."

"He was waiting for them to bring him out," Husta said. "What does that tell you?"

"It tells me he wanted Madison next, no matter what. He obviously scoped out the area and the routine at Madison's home. He must have guessed they were going to move him for security's sake." He looked around the office and added what they all surmised now. "He's saving Landau for the finale."

Lancola shook his close cropped head. "You know, even after you discovered the rifle evidence back at the house, I didn't believe it was true . . . didn't *want* to believe it. Now . . ." His face mirrored the pain he felt inside. "Can we still get him?"

Manos sighed and turned to John Paraletto. "What about it, John? Are we any closer to finding the department he's been at?"

Paraletto scrubbed his knuckles into his eyes in a futile effort to rub away the hours of fatigue. "Almost," he said. "We've cleared the departments with computerized personnel records. The remaining five had to be done by hand. We've had teams at each of them since late last night." He looked up at the wall clock. It was almost eight o'clock in the morning. "We ought to hear something before too long."

The others glanced at the clock, all of them sensitized to the importance of time now. Aaron Longbaugh had escaped them one more time, but had also left them with a deadly firsthand notice of his expertise, as if they had needed any further convincing.

Manos got up and rummaged for a cigarette, then remembered where he was. There was no smoking inside the Bureau's building. "I'm going outside for a moment," he said.

Lancola stood up quickly. "Mind if I join you? I could use the exercise."

"Sure, Russ," Manos replied. "Why not? Nothing to do but wait it out, right? We got a shooter and his last victim out there somewhere, and we have no idea where either one of 'em are. So I guess all we do is wait for the next call." His frustration had come out as sarcasm, but they all felt the same. He waited for Lancola to shrug into his rumpled suit jacket, and the two of them left the office.

Paraletto started to say something to Husta when the telephone rang.

"Special Agent Paraletto," he said, and waited, then said, "really? No question? A good ID, huh?"

The person on the other end spoke again, this time longer. Paraletto jotted a few notes down on the pad next to the phone. "Got it. No, that's fine. Yeah, call in the support. We're on the way."

He replaced the receiver quickly, his face excited. "Go find Jim," he said to Husta. "They've found Longbaugh."

Husta was up and moving instantly. "Where?" he asked, reaching for the door.

"City of Westport," Paraletto said. "He's been on their tactical team."

"No question about it?" Husta asked.

"None. Positive identification off their personnel file. It's Aaron Longbaugh."

Husta's face tightened. "Okay, then. Let's go get the man."

Paraletto picked up the phone again. "I'll get the troops lined up while you're looking for Jim."

"And Landau?" Husta asked.

"He's out of the way for now. We'll keep one of the bastards alive, at least."

"Let's hope so," Husta said. He paused again. "Name," he said to Paraletto. "What name has he been going under?"

Paraletto glanced at his hurried notes. "Samm," he replied. "Sergeant Nathan Samm."

October 27

Morning, Somerville, Ohio

William Landau shook another Camel out of the half-empty pack and tapped it against his thumbnail. He reversed it, lit it with his Zippo, and checked the view out of the apartment window again. It was only midmorning and already he'd smoked a third of a pack. He exhaled the smoke nervously against the partially opened blinds and said aloud, "You're getting real paranoid, troop."

He satisfied himself that there was nothing unusual on the street below and returned to his chair in the small living room. Somerville was a quiet, small place, a backwater farming town that had never quite reached that status. Its evolution stopped somewhere around the size of a decent community, three dozen or so homes constituting the extent of it. There was no town hall, no fire department, and the local constable lived in his own two-story house. It was the perfect place to hide.

No one in the small town paid him any attention. It was as private a place as he knew, but it wouldn't keep him safe for long. He needed a plan.

He had told Madison they'd work it out somehow, figure a way to stop the man hunting them. Now he wasn't so sure. The Feds were in on it, too, which suggested they knew who the shooter was. The other possibility that Landau had reluctantly come to was that there was no shooter in fact. Instead it was the Army itself, working through those two CID investigators, Manos and Husta, who had been tracking down him and the other members of the squad. Maybe someone in Washington was closing the books on an embarrassing event. The conspiracy idea fed his lingering distrust of the government in general. He knew all about conspiracies and covers. Hell, he'd been part of a conspiracy of sorts his whole life. He crushed the half-finished cigarette into the ashtray.

Landau snorted at the thought. "Oh, yeah," he chided himself. "Big conspirators we were. Lied to the CID, lied to JAG lawyers, lied to ourselves . . ." he stopped, staring at the floor. "Yes indeed," he whispered. "We lied to ourselves."

He saw their faces. Linet, Roselli, Aceto, Perriman, all of them. Once they all had been closer to him than his own family. It was the bond and the chemistry of combat that tied them to each other. Was it the same bond that had warped what he thought loyalty was? Did that explain why he had gone along with murder, because of some twisted sense of loyalty to his mates? What had happened to them? What in the name of God had *happened* to them? He remembered the special pride he had felt and shared with them, but that memory was gone for him. That pride died when they had become blood brothers in a different type of killing. They had shared that, too. That single act had eradicated all the justifiable honor they could have claimed.

He shuddered with the weight of the loss that descended upon him. The good memories gone, the legitimate feeling of accomplishing something worthwhile ruined, a place in history defiled.

Why now? he anguished. Hadn't he paid enough, suffered enough? He had tried to atone for it, he argued against the silent, remorseless voice inside him. Teach your children well, he remembered the old song lyric. That's what he had chosen to do, to make the generation that came after him see with new eyes what he relived every waking day. The students he instructed could never appreciate the ghosts that came to him in the dark, when he was most vulnerable.

But as terrible as those night visions were at times, he'd shunned the professional help so readily available to him now. That too was part of the penance. Landau had accepted his masochistic decision to gut it out on his own, cloaking himself with his guilt like a hardened and scaly skin.

He offered up his daily suffering to the spirit of the man he had helped kill. It was a small offering just the same. Nothing he did would ever serve as an appropriate sentence. And that was the bitch of it all, in the end. He hadn't the nerve, or the inner strength, to do the right thing. He was too much the coward, too ashamed, and finally, too afraid to make it official. The double standard was not lost on him.

No statute on murder one, he remembered. And now it was time to pay, so it seemed. Could he run this time? Was there anywhere to go, really? What might be out there after him was no worse than what was inside him, what had been trailing him half his life. He could try, he argued. It would buy him some time, and wasn't that what it was all about? Just a little longer?

Time's run out, the voice echoed back. No more running, William. The rest of them aren't running anymore. Time you stopped, too.

He stared at the Browning that lay on the table before him. He tried not to second-guess himself. This wasn't a game. It never had been. He had to get it right, and once given the opportunity, he had to go through with it. Maybe there was a way, a redemption of sorts. If he had the nerve, for once in his life. If he could make the decision. No Jack Linet oiling up to him, no pointed gazing from squad mates, no arguments over the plan. This time, God forgive him, this time he was alone. His choice.

There was no other way.

Landau ignored the other warning voices whispering incessantly to him. One was primal, offering the easier way out. Run, far and fast. Leave it behind for someone else to figure out. Just run away. You've done it before, been doing it for years. It's easy.

He shut it out. He had taken it down to choices, one more time. No herd mentality, no joint resolution to fall back on as an excuse. He was alone with his choice, and the only one he had left to argue against was himself. He was tired of the argument. So damn tired.

October 27

Morning, Westport, Ohio

Aaron Longbaugh's address was a fairly new one, but the intended raid was anticlimatic. The manager of the twelve-unit complex, a thin man in his early sixties, pulled the pin before anything got started.

"He moved out," he announced to the two FBI agents who had contacted him in his office. "That was two days ago," he said to John Paraletto. The manager scratched the side of his thinning hair and went back to his file drawer. He found the file he was searching for and handed it over to them. "I had this out this morning, clearing up the last details of the unit's inspection. I really hate to lose Sergeant Samm," he said. "Been one of my best tenants. Heck of a nice guy, always there for help, things like that. Of course, having a police officer in the quad didn't hurt, either."

John skimmed through the lease agreement, noting the information on prior addresses. He handed the file to Peter Jovenall.

"I don't suppose Sergeant Samm gave any indication where he was moving to?"

The manager sat down in his desk chair and shook his head. "Just what I told you earlier. He said he was being transferred to a new job, in the Southwest, he said. He seemed like he had quite a lot on his mind, and apologized for the short notice. Said he wished he'd had more advance notice, but the transfer came up suddenly, and that was that."

He pointed out the window at the long row of parking slots that ran down the center of the quadrangle. "Yep, he packed up that big silver Dodge pickup of his with his personal stuff, paid off his lease, and left. Too bad," he said again. "He'll be missed around here."

Both agents exchanged knowing glances. The manager was closer to the truth than he knew.

"What is it exactly you needed to see him about?" he asked.

"It's a police matter," Jovenall replied blithely. He reached into his inside coat breast pocket and pulled out a business card. "If Sergeant Samm should call you, for any reason, would you let me know? I appreciate all your help."

"Sure," the manager said, taking the card. "You can return that file any time," he said. "Regular mail's fine."

Both agents shook hands with the old man quickly. They had a new priority now, and more. Two dozen tactical agents, armed to the teeth, waited just a short distance away from the main gate to the complex. Jovenall had obtained the no-knock warrant and entry order on the way over. Now it was all over.

"Let's get over to the department, John," he said. "Maybe Chief Tusca can enlighten us on where we can look next."

"Considering his reaction when your people told him who Aaron Longbaugh was, I'd say that might be a little difficult," John said.

"You have a point," Jovenall said, fishing out his car keys. "I guess I'd be a bit out of shape if I'd found out one of my people was a rogue killer, too."

"Which still leaves the problem of William Landau," John added. "We better find the man, and soon."

"Yeah," Jovenall said, unlocking the car door. "I have a bad feeling about this."

"Never say that," John said, sliding his big frame into the passenger side. "Even when it's true, never say it."

Jovenall started the engine and looked over. "You have one too, don't you?"

John gazed back steadily. "In spades, brother, in spades. Let's go."

Jovenall backed the four-door Caprice out smartly and reversed direction, gunning out of the parking lot. But his feeling didn't go away.

October 27

Midday, City Hall, Westport, Ohio

Chief Daniel Tusca looked over the men seated in the crowded office. He knew why they were here, of course. He was behind the curve on this one, a position he hated being in. Peter Jovenall's initial call had rocked the chief back on his feet. He couldn't believe what the agent had told him. He had ordered the meeting to get all the facts.

Present were Manos, Husta, Agents Paraletto and Peter Jovenall, and Russell Lancola. Perfunctory introductions had already been made. Before saying anything further Tusca had called Charles Kedrick to join him. Kedrick's secretary informed him the city attorney was on his way.

Peter Jovenall, his face strained, began. "Dan, I understand your situation here."

"You do, huh?" Tusca snapped. His eyes swept from one man to the next, and returned to Jovenall. "Pete, we've known each other a long time. You want to tell me what's going on here? With all due respect," and he inclined his head to the others, "what you've told me about Nathan Samm is pretty damn unbelievable. I'd like to see everything you have on this before we go any further."

Jim Manos leaned forward slightly. "Pete, if I may?"

Jovenall started to speak, then motioned his acknowledgment to Manos. "Go ahead, Jim," he said. "It might actually be better coming from you."

Manos bent down beside him and extracted a thick file from a legal-size briefcase. Rolling off the rubber band holding it all together, he began to spread the contents on the desktop. Several eight-by-ten photos were among the documents.

"Chief Tusca," he began, "what Peter told you on the phone is correct. Nathan Samm's real name is Aaron Longbaugh. He's the son of an Army officer murdered in a fragging episode in Vietnam. The Army couldn't prosecute those men at the time. I'll give you the details later. The important fact here is Aaron found out about the men, and what they did to his father." He glanced at Tony Husta before continuing. "And he's been hunting them down and killing them, one by one."

"How did this happen?" Tusca asked. "If all this is true, how did Nate . . . this Aaron Longbaugh find out about the murder in the first place?"

Manos answered directly. "I told him," he said. "He's out there taking these guys down because of me."

Tusca acted as if he hadn't heard the reply. He picked up a photo, looked at it, then frowned, his eyes suddenly intense. "This is one of the finest officers I've ever had, certainly one of the best this department's ever had. Are you seriously telling me he's been living under an alias, using this department as a cover while he premeditates a murder?"

"There's no longer any question about that," Manos said. "This is his pattern, and your department isn't the first to be used this way. We have hard evidence of his involvement in five sniping murders, all the way back to 1982. Believe me, we wouldn't be here if we didn't have the case made, and we wouldn't insult you, or your department, with such accusations, unless we were absolutely certain."

Russell Lancola had listened silently and finally spoke up. "If I may, gentlemen?" he said. "I won't address the allegations expressed by Colonel Manos just now. That will be better served in a court of law. Presuming we can get that far." He addressed Tusca.

"The priority right now is twofold, Chief. Find Professor William Landau, the last man on Aaron's supposed list, and safeguard him. Second, find Aaron, or Nathan Samm to you, and stop him from completing his apparent mission. Unfortunately both men have disappeared. Your help in locating Aaron is critical. Without finding him, we can't begin to help him."

Tusca looked at him, surprised. "Help him? I get the feeling you people would rather take him out first."

Manos leaned in. "The truth is, Chief, that it might just be better all the way around if he just . . . stopped. Believe me, the last thing I want to do is see Aaron injured or killed." He acknowledged Lancola's position in the matter with a nod. "After this is all over the debate will drag on for a long time concerning what's right and wrong here. I have my own ideas about that." He held Tusca with his dark eyes. "But as sure as I am that it is Aaron Longbaugh who's been hunting these men down, I'm just as sure that if we can't find him, we'll never be able to stop him. Can you help us?"

Tusca reached between them and picked up the photograph again. The evidence on the table before him seemed very strong, but he was loath to take down one of his own. Aaron Longbaugh had burrowed his way into the department and used it as a cover to kill. He had abused the faith and trust Tusca had placed in him. The feeling of being betrayed bit deep in the chief. How could he have been so tragically wrong about the man?

"Goddamn it!" he swore suddenly. He looked off for several long moments, while the others seated at the table could only imagine the decisions that tumbled through his mind. He gently laid the photo down and pushed back from his desk. "All right," he said. "I'll do what I can. But it may not be enough. You said he moved out of his place two days ago?"

Tony Husta nodded. "No clue where he might have gone, either. Obviously he hadn't left such word with the department. We were hoping there might be something in his personnel file."

"Wait one," Tusca said. He picked up his telephone receiver and punched one button on the console. "Melanie? I need a personnel file ASAP." He gave her the name. "Nathan Samm. The file should have been reviewed on the Bureau request from last night."

His secretary knocked a few minutes later and handed him a manila file folder. She left quickly, quietly pulling the office door shut behind her.

Tusca handed the folder over to Husta. "My officers are at your disposal. They'll do whatever they can. It may be a little rough, though."

"I figured it would be, Chief," Husta said. He opened the folder and began reading it.

A knock sounded on the chief's closed door just then, and Charles Kedrick stuck his head in. "Dan? Something's come up with Barlot . . ." he paused, seeing the gathering of men in Tusca's office. He recognized Pete Jovenall, but the others were strangers. He started to apologize when Tusca waved to him.

"Charlie, come in. We have a problem of our own here. I think you should hear this. You're not going to believe it," Tusca said. He waited for Kedrick to pull out a chair near his desk and told him the entire story in condensed form, taking just a few minutes.

Kedrick was stunned by the news. Something like this wasn't possible, was it? But there was no mistaking the urgency of the situation. They needed to find Nathan, or Aaron, right now. An odd look came over his face. "I'm not sure what this may have to do with anything," he said slowly. "But there may be someone who can help on this. The Trans Patriot adjuster, Vanessa Tau," he said.

"What about her?" Tusca asked, not seeing any connection.

"I just found this out myself. I thought it was just an office rumor, but Ms. Tau confirmed it when I asked her, the last time we spoke. She's been seeing Nathan Samm. I guess you'd have to call it an affair." He paused. "But she was worried about Nathan, too. There was something going on with him, she said, and wanted to know from me if he was in trouble of some kind." He looked around the room. "I guess he is."

Manos was unclear what the connection to Vanessa was. "Who is this girl, and Trans Patriot Insurance?"

Kedrick told him quickly, explaining the litigation pending against the city and the department.

Manos looked at his partner and the agents. "Maybe we'd best talk to Ms. Tau."

Kedrick fished a small binder out of his inside suit coat pocket and withdrew a business card. "She works out of the company's Hamilton office," he said. "Would you like me to call?"

Tusca nodded, and Kedrick dialed the number. He had a brief conversation with the person on the other end and hung up.

"She's not in the office today. She took the day off to study at home for some heavy exams." He wrote on a yellow Post-it note and peeled it off the pad, handing it to Manos. "This is her address in Oxford."

Manos accepted the note and stood up. "It's worth a try," he said. He motioned to Husta and the two agents. "Tony and I will interview her. You guys want to see what you may turn up here? I'll call you from Oxford with whatever we get."

Tusca nodded for the rest of them. "Good luck. I'll set up interviews with the officers Nathan works with here."

"Chief," Manos said, offering his hand. "I wish this had been different. I hope you know that."

Tusca stood up to accept the man's hand. They shook firmly. "I wish it had been different, too. It's still taking some getting used to, I can't deny it." He held on for a moment. "Let's try to end this as best we can, all right?"

Manos nodded. "We'll try, Chief. We'll try." He dropped his hand, but inside he had a bad feeling. Inside he wasn't near as optimistic as he would like to be. Not at all.

* * *

Vanessa glanced up at the knock on her apartment door after replacing the cap on her highlighter.

Dani, preparing to leave for her next class, finished slipping on her nylon windbreaker. "I'll get it, Van," she said, and crossed the living room quickly. She opened the door to find two swarthy men in dark suits.

"Is Vanessa Tau home?" one of the men asked.

"Who is it?" Vanessa asked, hearing her name mentioned. She joined Dani at the door. "Yes? I'm Vanessa Tau," she said.

Manos presented her with his credentials and motioned to his partner. "I'm Colonel James Manos, Army Criminal Investigation Division, and this is Colonel Anthony Husta. We'd like to talk to you about Sergeant Nathan Samm."

Vanessa's heart skipped a beat, but she didn't know why.

"I'm sorry," she said. "You're with the Army? What would that have to do with Nathan? Is he all right?" she asked quickly. Both men looked very serious just standing there. She had a sudden ill feeling.

Manos's gaze softened a degree. "I think it might be best if we talked inside, Ms. Tau. Your help in this matter is very much appreciated."

"Van, I don't thi—"

Vanessa hushed her, and motioned to her it was all right. She backed into the room, holding the door for them. "Come in," she said, allowing them to enter. She detected a bad feeling as they passed by her, and her anxiety over Nathan deepened. She led the way into the living room and completed introductions with Dani.

Vanessa directed the two visitors to the easy chairs facing the couch. She sat down there, but Dani remained standing.

"Do you want me to stay, Vanessa?" she asked. She could afford to skip this class, and besides, she didn't want to leave Vanessa alone in this odd situation.

Vanessa nodded once. "Please, if you can . . ." and looked at Manos. "Is that all right with you?"

"There's no reason you shouldn't stay," Manos said, directing his reply to Dani.

She joined Vanessa on the couch, watching the two men warily. Something serious was up.

Beside her Vanessa shifted, drawing her legs up beneath her. Inside, below her stomach, a cold tightness appeared, spreading outward slowly. What she learned in the next intense minutes was worse than anything she could imagine. Much worse.

Throughout Manos's long explanation Vanessa sat quietly, her eyes bright, following his every word closely. Only a thinning of her gently curved lips betrayed her emotions.

Late-afternoon light shone through the large living-room picture window before Manos was done. Inwardly he was impressed by Vanessa. Though she had asked only a few questions during his lengthy story, she never once lost control, even though he could see the confusion and hurt in her eyes. It was clear to him and Husta that she was wrestling with the terrible news he'd told her, which made him realize just how serious she was about Aaron, or Nathan, as she knew him.

Vanessa sat in silence, head lowered, looking at her hands folded carefully in her lap. Manos and Husta seemed to be collectively holding their breaths. Without raising her head, she asked, "Are you certain about all of this?"

Manos heard the slight hitch in her voice. "I'm certain, Vanessa. There's no chance of a mistake."

He shook his head. "As I told you, we have evidence from his family's home in Kansas that implicates him in the shootings." He took a breath. "And then there's Michael Madison's killing this morning."

"It's all true then," she said, "all of it. The murder of Nathan's father," she corrected, her voice coming back a little stronger. She kept her head looking down.

"He told me he had a cousin who died in the war," she said, and Manos caught the first tear sliding down her perfect cheek. "He was in the Air Force, he said."

She raised her face slowly, her anguish apparent, and he saw the painful struggle she was going through to maintain control. Her hands tightened and relaxed, kneading each other until the fingers were white. Her dark eyes, glittering with her tears, fixed on Manos. "He lied to me . . ." she said, her voice so soft it barely carried. "He lied about . . . everything."

Dani edged closer to her and placed a protective hand on top of hers, trying to comfort her.

"Vanessa," Husta started to say, and she turned to him, a gracious movement of her head, ebony hair silky about her shoulders.

"No, that's all right. I appreciate your concern, but I'm fine." Her voice firmed. "This will just take some time to . . . to accept. And to deal with," she added. That was the outward self, the image that was so important to maintain in the face of terrible adversity. She did that for them, she knew, as her culture demanded. Above all else, one maintains control.

Inside, she was brokenhearted, close to hysteria over the terrible story Manos had told her. Oh, God, Nathan! she cried to herself. How can this be possible?! How can you be two people like this? Her heart offered up his face, his closeness, and his warmth, but his visage distorted before her inner eyes, warping into the face of someone . . . something . . . she could not focus on. She sensed it rather than saw it, the darkness emanating from the stoic, cold figure.

Small details suddenly came to her, words and looks, phrases spoken almost as throwaway lines, a glance from his eyes, simple things unnoticed but suddenly as bright as neon, and she realized what they were. Suddenly she understood his procrastination with the interrogatories into his background. He had been stalling her all along. His questions about it, how far they would look into him, all of it an obvious danger to him. Yet he had been so cool through it all. Signs of the real man beneath the one she thought she had known. She'd never guessed, never sensed the ugliness he had kept hidden so well.

She remembered their night together, and the initial reason for it, to talk about the legal discovery in his lawsuit Had he used her then? Had it all been a setup, just so that he could get his hands on the interrogatory questions? He had promised to return them later, but he never had. Was she just a part of his charade?

Stop it! her little voice all but shouted aloud. Look again! it said. Look at the real man, Vanessa. You know him . . . you *know* him. Did he lie? Did he lead you on, pretend the words he said, the moments you shared? Do you really think you mean nothing to him? Look again . . . look deep, as deep as you can, then deeper still.

She tried, forcing her heart and her soul into a place she thought she trusted once, afraid to ever go there again now, and saw . . . the truth. It surprised her, so clear it was, carrying more meaning than anything Colonel Manos had told her. And she knew it was true, and better than that, she knew it was right . . . that *she* was right. The knowledge brought a resolve, so sudden it almost hurt, driving away the numbing pain that lingered in the pit of her stomach, easing away the doubt.

She took a breath and settled herself for these men. "What do you want me to do?" she asked.

"Can you think of any place he could be now?" Manos asked.

She considered his question, and what her answer might mean to Nathan. Too many possibilities streamed through her anxious mind, battling the crushing news about him. They wanted to find him and stop him. Stop him, or worse. She didn't want to think about that.

Was it her place to help them? To save him she probably would, she knew it. But her mind was a blank. There was no place she could think of where he might have gone. She felt something briefly, but it skittered away. Her heart controlled her emotions, diverting her concentration.

She tried to recall things he had told her, raking her memory for the slightest clue, but there was nothing there. Other memories, warmer ones, safer ones, kept intruding, refusing to allow her to concentrate. She shook her head in frustration.

"No, there's nothing that I can think of," she said, and the first hint of the misery she held tightly inside touched her speech.

"You want to find them both," Dani said suddenly, her voice quiet. She was trying to deal with the terrible news she had heard.

"You said you want to find Nathan . . . Aaron," she struggled, "to stop him, you said." She looked from one man to the other. "But you also want to find Professor Landau."

"That's true," Manos said. He had a feeling about her.

"Maybe I can help," she said. "I think I know where Landau might be." She had their attention now, even Vanessa, who was watching her oddly.

"The professor had an affair last year," Dani began. "I know the girl. She told me about it, after it was all over. They broke up at the end of the term. But they were discreet about it. The professor rented a place for them, off-campus."

"Where is this place?" Husta asked.

"It's in a small town a few miles northeast of Oxford, off of Route 744," she said. "My friend took me by it once. The apartment's on the second floor of an old Victorian house. I can show you . . ."

"Can you describe it instead?" Manos said gently. "Maybe draw a map for us?" His inference was clear: He didn't want her coming along, either of them.

"What makes you think Landau would be there?" Husta asked.

"He held on to the place after they broke up," Dani said. "She had to go back once to pick up some things she'd left there. He still had the key, and he let her borrow it. But that was last summer. Maybe he doesn't have it anymore."

She walked over to the dining table where their books were piled. She tore off a sheet of notepaper and began drawing a map for them.

Manos turned to Vanessa. "I know how hard this is for you. I can imagine what's going through your mind now. We really do want to find him. There's been enough violence, Vanessa. It's time to end it. Do you have any ideas that might help us find him, before he gets to Landau?"

She took a deep breath and let it out slowly. She felt better, her emotions coming back into check. "No, nothing," she said.

"We'll look into this apartment idea, then," Manos said, getting up from his chair. He and Husta waited for Dani to finish.

"What if Nathan's there, too?" Vanessa asked. She couldn't bring herself to call him Aaron. That name belonged to someone she didn't know, could never have known. "You're not just going to check this out," she said, getting up now. "If this is your best lead you're going there with more men, and more guns, right? If Landau did what you said, you're going there to arrest him."

The two men exchanged looks. "That's right," Manos said. "A tactical team will be used, and we'd like to take Landau into protective custody, if we can. The idea is to contain the situation, Vanessa."

She heard the words, but another thought pushed into her head, bringing along a new fear. "And what if Nathan knows about the apartment somehow? What if he's already on his way there? He would go there if he knew, wouldn't he? You said the professor is the last man on his list. He'll try to kill him there, won't he?" she continued, stepping closer to them, aware her voice was climbing in pitch, her fear turning to anger.

"Vanessa," Dani said, alarmed for her friend.

Vanessa paused, fighting for control, her eyes softening suddenly, and she said, "Oh, God, if it's true, don't hurt him. Please don't hurt him . . ."

Dani dropped her pen and went to her, putting an arm around Vanessa's shoulders, hugging her tight.

Manos was uncomfortable. The passion the girl felt for Aaron was clear, and the depth of her commitment to him made him uneasy. Why had Aaron gotten involved with her? he asked himself. Surely he knew how dangerous a relationship like this was to him. What an incredible chance he's taken, and how much pain he's caused. I wonder if he knows how this girl feels about him?

Vanessa certainly wasn't what he had ever expected to appear in Aaron's life. A sudden resolve swept through him. If there was any way he could make it work for them . . .

"Look, Vanessa," he said to her, his voice gentle. "There's an outside chance at best that Landau is at this place." He tried to get it across to her as best he could. "It's an even less likely chance that Aaron will be there. If he *is* there, it's my intention to keep him from doing any more harm. Too many men have died for a mistake made too many years ago. It has to stop. *He* has to stop." He studied her carefully, wanting her to understand what he was saying to her.

"Aaron's spent too much of his life living like this. He's made too many changes, given up too much to pursue his hate. Until he met you. You changed him, Vanessa, just a little bit. But he can change some more. That's the key here," he said. "He can turn away from it. Leave it alone." He felt he had her, that she knew what he was saying. Was he sure himself? He spoke his own answer. "All he has to do is stop."

Vanessa saw it in his eyes, and knew. Was it false hope? She didn't think so. Manos seemed very intense, true, but at the same time he didn't seem insincere. She believed him, and his intention, and just then, the nagging thought she had about Nathan clarified itself, and she jumped on it.

"A simple wish, Colonel Manos," she replied. "So easy to say, but maybe so hard to do. Can you keep him alive? *Will* you keep him alive?"

Good girl, he thought. She understands. "If we find him in time," he said.

She nodded. "You'll call me when you've finished in Somerville?" she said. "No matter how it checks out?"

"Yes," Manos said. "No matter how. We'll be careful, but you understand, if Aaron, or Nathan, *is* there, it's not up to us."

"I understand," she said, and the truth was, she really did. There was a way, she thought. "Good luck," she said.

"And to you," Manos said. To Husta he said, "Ready?"

Husta held up the page of notepaper with the map on it. "Let's go," he said.

They left the apartment quickly, preparations on their minds for what was next on their list. Walking down the hallway Husta said, "I'll call Jovenall and see if he's got anything new at his end." He was silent a few moments. "You think Landau's at this place?"

"I'm not sure," Manos replied, "but I kind've got a feeling, you know?"

"Yeah, mano," Husta said. "I got the same one."

They went down the stairs to the first floor and stepped out, heading for their car in the back parking lot. As they neared the car, Husta said, "She knows where Aaron is, doesn't she?"

Manos smiled. "Either that, or how to reach him."

Husta said it for the two of them. "She'd better do it pretty damn quick, then."

* * *

Upstairs Vanessa was dialing the phone number off the business card in her hand.

Dani looked on, wondering what she was doing. "Who are you calling?" she asked.

Vanessa finished, feeling the tension rushing through her. "Nathan's pager number," she said. "His private number," she added as the connection went through. She tapped in her phone number in reply and hung up. She held on to the receiver a few moments, her forehead pressed against it. "Please answer," she prayed. "Please, Nathan, be there. Be there and answer."

She didn't want to think about what could happen . . . what

would happen, if he didn't, despite Colonel Manos's assurances. She understood too well how deadly serious the situation was.

"Be there for me," she said, and added, because she had to, "be there for us."

*   *   *

The silver Dodge Ram pickup was parked bedside the twenty-four-foot AirStream trailer. The trailer park itself was an old one, in the outskirts of Dayton, not far from the Carrollton Mall. Aaron had bought the AirStream five years before and had moved it around with him. It was his haven, his alternate place. No one knew he had it, since he always kept a primary residence somewhere else. But that was blown, and he had been forced to retreat to the AirStream. Still, he would be all right here for a little while. He wouldn't need that much time, anyway.

He knew Landau had effectively vanished. After his discovery of the FBI agents at Madison's place, Aaron had tried contacting Landau. He'd left messages with the history department but was told Landau was not available for a few days. He'd gone to his home on Route 73 and found more agents in place, but no Landau. He knew the professor had slipped away before the Feds got to him.

Working on a hunch, he had checked the Somerville apartment the day before. Not surprisingly, Aaron had confirmed the professor was at the apartment. A quick, quiet reconnaissance of the house in the middle of the small town had done the job. Watching from the tree line with the sixty-power spotting scope, Aaron had caught a glimpse of Landau's face in an upstairs window. It was all he needed. He felt sure the man would still be there for a while, at least.

Since the Madison shooting this morning Aaron had kept a low profile, returning to the AirStream to remain out of sight until dark. One last operation. In a couple of hours it would be time to go. He had chosen a good hide just three hundred yards outside of town, on a small slope that would put him roughly on the same elevation as the second-floor apartment. All he had to do was wait for the opportunity, and the shot.

He considered the possibility that the man had run again, and wouldn't be there. If so, then he'd track him. A man on the run did stupid things, and eventually he would find him. There was no way Bill Landau was going to get away.

Aaron lay back on the bed in the small trailer and closed his eyes. He needed to rest, to keep his edge. He relaxed, pushing the tension and fatigue out of his body. He'd worked under pressure before. All he needed was a little sleep. He sent the order to his subconscious, trusting to his internal clock to wake him. Just a few hours' sleep . . .

Vanessa's face appeared, just like that, and he groaned. Not from the pleasure of her memory, but from the bitter sense of loss. Guilt slammed him, guilt for what he had done, daring to get close to her even when all his alarms shouted at the folly of it. But he had ignored them, for the first time in his life. He had never done this before, never chanced a relationship. There had always been too many reasons not to.

So why now? he challenged himself. Why did you risk it now? This was a major mistake, getting involved with her. Forget the danger to himself. How could he justify what he was doing to her? The lies, the betrayal . . . using her. Was that it? Was that all she was, a quick physical thing, something to satisfy cravings that had been too long ignored, too long suppressed?

No! he shouted down. Vanessa was that one in a million, the luck shot, power ball, you name it. She had suddenly been there, and it all went click inside his head, and heart. There was no explanation for it, just the absolute, can't-be-denied certainty of it almost the second he saw her.

And that was all it took. But it was wrong, he told himself. You didn't have the right. You can't have her, ever again. You shouldn't have tried, because look at the cost. This was something for which the price paid would never be enough. It wasn't just him anymore. He'd involved another life with him, someone offering him a future.

And that was the irony. He had no future. Once this last one was done it was over . . . *he* was over. How could he be so bold as to assume he could have anything even close to a normal, decent life again? He would always be on the run, no matter how carefully he covered his tracks. That too had been a risk he had accepted. That was part of the duty.

But now there she was. What future could he have with a girl like her? The answer hurt, but couldn't be ignored. Cut her loose, he told himself through the ache. Let her go, man. It's the best thing you can do.

Aaron dropped his arm over his eyes, trying to push her face from his mind. But she remained, beautiful and vulnerable, but untouchable for him . . . forever.

* * *

His father walked up the drive, class-A uniform crisp, looking sharp. Aaron heard the water rushing out of the hose as it lay on the driveway. He let the big sponge drop, heavy with sudsy water, and waited. He felt the bright sun on his head and shoulders, saw it glint off the brass insignia of his father's uniform. This time it was different. His father was coming farther up the drive this time, closer to him. Aaron watched him approach, knowing this was the same dream but aware that the sequence was altered from before. His father's face was somber, no smile of greeting. Only his eyes showed purpose behind them, and they were firm and steady, but they were off somehow . . . they were dark, much darker than he remembered, their shape different. They were familiar, but not, and an uneasiness touched Aaron. He waited for the dream to end as it always had in the past, but it went on . . .

His father came all the way up to him and looked down at him from his superior height. His back was straight, his bearing formal, all military, all business.

"Aaron," he said, and Aaron almost leaped from the sound of his (not his) voice. Not his! Hers! It was Vanessa's voice that he heard coming from his father's image.

"You have to stop," his father said in her melodic, soft voice, and Aaron's heart spasmed with the weight of the love he felt. "You have to stop," he repeated, holding his eyes firmly, and Aaron re-membered then and realized with no surprise now, they're her eyes, too. Vanessa's eyes, only they were his father's too, giving him that no-nonsense, you'd-better-be-paying-attention-boy look. "You have to stop killing them . . ."

* * *

Aaron shot awake, crying out, disoriented. His chest shuddered, and he dragged in his next breath, shaken by the dream, by the image of his father, and Vanessa's voice. Sweat had beaded on his temples, and the muscles of his face felt tightly drawn. He was hurt, perplexed, heartsick.

He knew it was a sign, but savagely pushed the idea away. Sometimes premonitions were real, he knew. Hadn't he looked on his military training in exactly that way? It had prepared him for his life's work, and the chance meeting with Major Manos . . . wasn't that more of the same? What were the odds of that?

But it had been right, too. It was right that he had learned the truth about his father's death, and right that he was the one person able to avenge him. This dream had been coming to him for years, always stopping right before his father spoke. Was his father reaching out to him for real? Sending him a message?

Aaron considered the idea, but only half-believed in it. Fate was one thing. Messages from beyond the grave were something else. His dreams of his father were driven by his love for him, nothing more. Yes, it hurt to know his father was never coming home again. He had carried that special loss a long time, and it never faded, never got any better.

That's all this was, too. An image created by the real-time events in his life. Vanessa had become part of him, entwining her presence in his soul. It didn't surprise him, now that he was awake and rational, that her presence would manifest itself to him in this way. It only underscored the sad truth of the situation. He had lost his father. And now he was about to lose her, too. He had no choice. The mission had to come first, and had to be completed. If he stopped now, quit it entirely, what would change? The answer was simple . . . nothing.

He had been a fool to think starting up with her could change that. And now it would cost him. He knew it would hurt her, too, but eventually she would get past it, and get over him. There was no other way. She deserved better. His life had a different agenda from hers. Better to cut it off now.

* * *

Aaron pushed himself off the bed and checked outside. It was almost dark. He needed to get started with his preparations. Before the night was out his job would be over at last. He would be on his way again, maybe for the last time. What would he do? He considered, not for the first time, the occupation he had chosen to cover his mission. And the truth of it was he had become a pretty good cop. He enjoyed it, with the knowledge of a professional comfortable with his capabilities. He could find another town that needed a good man . . .

Aaron paused. Was he? Was he a good man? The question begged for answers he didn't want to consider, at least not right now. He needed a new start, a fresh place, and time to forget.

"I'm sorry, Vanessa," he whispered aloud.

He took a slow, deep breath. It was time. Get your head into the mission, troop, he told himself. In seconds he was transformed, all business now. Clear night, no clouds, he thought, and lifted up the long, flat case from beside the bed. Unsnapping the latches, he revealed the M-21 nestled into the egg-carton foam lining inside. Good conditions for the Starlight scope, he thought, and took the weapon out. He began assembling his equipment for the final mission.

October 27

Evening, Somerville, Ohio

Full dark had arrived some three hours before, and the new moon made sure the darkness enveloped everything. A slight breeze ratcheted through the branches of the trees, scattering leaves along singly and in pairs.

Jim Manos was driving. In the black full-size Tahoe four-wheel-drive pickup with him were Husta and Chief Tusca. Following them were Pete Jovenall and John Paraletto, along with a dozen Ohio Highway Patrol cars, led by a Captain Miller. Somerville was in the captain's jurisdiction. The state troopers were there to quietly clear the houses for a block radius around Landau's position.

Taking the professor shouldn't be a problem, more important was whether Aaron Longbaugh was in the area. He had already given Peter Jovenall's agents a deadly demonstration of his precision and expertise. No chances with civilian lives were going to be taken.

A six-man Westport tactical team followed in a GMC Step Van. Jovenall had also arranged for a Bureau HRT unit, another six men, who followed in a similar van. Shadowing them from above was a Highway Patrol MD-500 helicopter. It was fitted with high-intensity Xenon searchlights and sophisticated passive light-intensity imaging and active infrared surveillance gear.

Manos was uneasy about the fast timetable, but he also knew that if Landau was really there, now was probably the best chance to grab him. He felt the strangeness of that possibility. It would be the first time he and Tony Husta would meet one of the squad members since 1970. It promised to be a peculiar reunion.

* * *

Bill Landau's nerves were tightening up. He reached across the table and hefted the 9 mm Browning. He held it up before his face, rotating it in his hand, looking at the weapon from several angles. In the last few hours he had become fixated on it.

"Big war hero," he said. "Yeah, that's what I am, all right." It had all been such a tragic, insane waste. Killing Major Longbaugh hadn't stopped the operations in the valley. Landau felt the bitter futility of the abhorrent act, underscored by the weapon in his hand. He and the others had used their guns to kill a man, in order to stop the madness. But they had failed, and in their failure had earned the title of murderers instead. And now . . .

Has it come down to this? he thought. He felt the power of the weapon, but there was something else offered him.

"Freedom," he whispered, looking at the menacing pistol. He understood it now, surprised it had taken him this long to admit it was possible, that he could actually do it. Put the muzzle in the right place, and a few pounds of pressure would stop it all, finally.

Would it? he challenged himself. Was this the only way left to him? Suicide, after all he had been through, all the years he had suffered with the guilt and the remorse, and the self-loathing. Did it all come down to this, a final act of cowardice? Being a coward had trapped him into murder in the first place. Was his life the only way to atone for that now?

Landau thought of the dead men in the squad, men who used to be his friends, his brothers. Someone had decided their lives should be forfeit, that's for sure. Someone had been rather insistent on that. Why should he miss out on all that fun?

Landau laughed aloud at the madness of the idea, the sound harsh and slightly mad itself. "You're losing it, William," he said, and immediately sobered up. The initial sense of having found an answer was gone. The gun held nothing for him. He suddenly loathed the feel of it, and what it represented.

He jammed the pistol back into the belt holster lying on the table, snapping the strap down between the cocked hammer and the frame.

A profound sense of gloom settled over him, draining him physically. "God, I'm tired of it," he said aloud. "So damn tired of running from this."

But there was no one in the room to hear him, save the ghosts in his memory.

* * *

Tusca rolled to a stop three blocks away from the address Dani had given him, near a stand of trees. There were only a few street lights, but none close enough to their convoy to cause them any problems. The large contingent of police and agents emptied out of their vehicles, each group falling to their specific tasks quickly. State troopers paired up and set off to the silent houses surrounding Landau's place.

Husta and Manos stood beside the HRG's large van. The back double doors were open, while Chief Tusca sat beside a technician inside at a console, talking quietly to the crew in the MD-500 overhead. On one of three monitor screens before him the technician was watching a multicolored display of the IR, the infrared pictures transmitted by the chopper. The IR scanner was sensitive enough to pick up human body heat in the predominately wood-framed homes. The helicopter's crew scanned each home as the state troopers roused its occupants and escorted them to safety. One by one the structures around Landau's house showed themselves to be empty of any endangered life. It didn't take long, despite some of the confused reactions from the townspeople involved.

Tusca nodded as the operation progressed. "Tell them to check Landau now," he told the tech, who passed the order on to the airborne crew. They heard the pitch change in the droning hum of the helo as the pilot set up on a course to cover the target house.

Manos and Husta watched the controlled confusion, then turned their attention up the street to the target house.

"That's it, on the corner there," Husta said.

Several hours before they had run down the listing of the owners of the old house and found the retired couple in Hamilton. A quick visit by a couple of Westport PD officers had secured the couple's cooperation, and the keys to the house. Once the troopers had cleared the area, it would make entry into the place by the HRG much easier. They had also confirmed that Professor Landau did indeed still carry the lease on the apartment.

That information had prompted a driveby of the house shortly thereafter. The officers had spotted a car parked behind the house on the grass beneath a big oak tree. A DMV check established it was a rental car from Cincinnati. The renter had made the mistake of putting it on his MC card. It was William Landau.

Chief Tusca had kept an unmarked unit in town since then, keeping the house under surveillance until the tactical teams and other reinforcements could arrive. Those two officers now assisted in the briefing of the situation for the Westport HRG team and the Bureau's people.

"The big two-story house," one of the officers said. "The apartment's on the second floor. His car's still around the back. He hasn't moved all day. We've seen glimpses of him through the windows, though. Landau's definitely in there."

Tusca nodded. "All right. We'll have IR pictures in a moment or two. How about entrances?"

"Covered, Chief," Jerry Lanier answered. He had asked for this assignment. The revelations about Nathan Samm had stunned him. He felt an obligation to be involved. Tusca hadn't denied him that.

"There are two. One comes off the corner on the outside, here," he said, pointing at a diagram spread out. "It has a storm door and main door, wood core. But the owner says the locks are stiff and would make too much noise if we came in that way." He indicated the center of the floor plan. "There's a main entrance round the porch, and right here the original staircase in the middle of the house goes up to the second floor. There are two doors, again wood core, securing the stairwell that connects to the apartment. There are deadbolt locks only on each door. We'll go in that way. The HRT guys will take the outside corner entrance."

Tusca looked around slowly. "No lights inside on the first floor, and that one porch light showing outside beside the main entrance," he said. "Upstairs, where the suspect is, there's a light in the front room showing. Keep in mind Landau is under protective custody," he said. "No opposition is expected, but we've reduced the risk factors as much as we can. Still, these old frame houses won't backstop an overpenetration round. If you have to, bag him."

He referred to the large-barreled single-shot weapon one of his men carried. It fired a thirty-seven-millimeter shell loaded with a heavy bag of plastic pellets that expanded rapidly when fired, designed to knock the wind out of the intended target.

Corporal Lanier and his men were outfitted in standard black tactical gear. Besides the beanbag piece, another carried a Remington 870 twelve-gauge shotgun. Lanier and the rest carried suppressed CAR-15s, short-barreled M-16s, or the almost obligatory H&K MP-5s. The Bureau HRT team was similarly armed. The state patrol boys would be perimeter security. They were along in a purely administrative capacity. Their captain looked on, listening to the plan. He already knew how this would go down. He nodded at his men, who drew back to set up blocking positions on the two roadways out of town.

Overhead a thousand feet up the pilot in the MD-500 began a gentle orbit. His copilot directed the infrared scanners at the target house. The information came back quickly.

"First floor appears clear," Chief Tusca heard over the command radio speaker above the technician. "There's a single body signature on the second floor, front/east room, nearly centered. Check the placement."

On the monitor screen showing the outline of the house a

heated image, a seeming blob of red with yellow and green highlights appeared.

"Ten-four, we see him," Tusca replied. "He's in the front room, all right."

They all heard the noise of the helo fade as the pilot took it around in a wide arc. Tusca was about to speak to Lanier when the copilot came back on.

"Wait one. We've got another body signature out here."

"Where?" Tusca asked, automatically looking up at the night sky.

"North of your position, approximately 430 meters out. Figure's definitely human, lying prone, under a group of trees. We've got him on the IR."

Manos exchanged a rapid glance with Husta, and they both turned to Tusca. "What do you think, Chief?"

Tusca shifted to stare out at the darkness, unable to see what he suddenly knew was out there. "Could be Nathan . . ." he shook his head. "Sorry, Aaron," he corrected. "There's one way to be sure."

He keyed his radio, talking to the chopper crew. "Stay away from him, but pull him up on the screen. I don't want him to know we've picked him up." The Hughes infrared scanner was equipped with a variable-power television lens.

"Wait one," came back the reply.

On the screen appeared the magnified image, showing the prone figure of a man in the same layered colors as Landau. There was no mistaking his positioning.

"Got to be him, Chief," Lanier said, a hint of regret in his voice. If it was his longtime friend out there, things were going to get tougher in a short while. "We can set up on him," Lanier said, referring to a topographical map of the area, matching Aaron's position to the terrain.

Manos spoke up then. "No, wait a minute. He's already in position, and he's got the elevation advantage. If you try to move people around him now, someone's going to get hurt . . . or killed."

Tusca looked at him. "If it is Longbaugh then from what you've told me so far he hasn't killed anyone but the people on that damn squad. Madison's shooting underscores just how good he really is. He hit him surrounded by Jovenall's people. And none of them were hurt." He nodded at the monitor screen. "I don't think he'll fire on any cops."

Manos returned his stare. "Hell of a thing to ask your guys to do, Chief," he said. "Aaron wasn't in danger before. If he finds himself cornered, I guarantee you that there will be a lot of dead people before this is over."

Tusca's anger flushed his face suddenly, but he controlled his voice with an effort. "Look, Colonel Manos. With all due respect to you Army people, the objective of this mission is to get Professor Landau into protective custody before Longbaugh kills him. And coincidentally, if Longbaugh himself happens to be on the scene, we're supposed to apprehend him before he manages to do just that. Now you're telling me it's too risky? Just what the hell are we doing out here, then?" He glared from Manos to Husta and back again.

Manos understood what the chief was going through. But he also knew that trying to take Aaron down was not the answer. He had thought it would work before, but now he saw there way another way to go. One that would serve their collective purposes in the long run.

"What we're trying to do is stop this vendetta from going further, Chief. Now . . . tonight. If you'll send your people in and take Landau out, I think this will all work itself out."

"You want my men to go in under Longbaugh's gun?"

"He won't fire once he sees us going in," Manos replied, hoping he was right. He had a feeling about it, though, and he wanted to push it.

"He took out Madison," Lanier reminded him. "It didn't seem to matter how many agents were around him, either."

"I understand that," Manos said. "But you have to understand him, too. He saved Landau for the end, the last one. Why? There's something special about the professor, a reason why Aaron would want him to be the last one."

"What reason?" Tusca asked, irritated. He didn't like the idea Manos was proposing. It was too risky, and dangerous for his men.

"I'm not sure, Chief," Manos said truthfully. "Maybe it has something to do with Landau's education. He was the only one on the squad with any college behind him. Maybe it's the way he's tried to live his life, as if he were trying to make amends for what he did to Aaron's father. He's the only one of the nine men who wasn't a loser, either before Vietnam or after."

"That's not a reason," Tusca said, getting ready to dismiss Manos and Husta. "That's speculation, and I won't have my guys waltzing into that house with Longbaugh's crosshairs on them, based on speculation."

"There's another reason," Husta said.

Tusca and Lanier looked at him.

Husta caught his partner's eye and nodded briefly. "I don't think he'll shoot because he wants us to take Landau down. I think he wants to quit, Chief."

"That's crazy," Tusca snorted. "Why would he think that?"

"It's the system," Husta said. "The system failed to prosecute these men a long time ago. Aaron's been rectifying that error all this time, but he's been doing it from within the system itself. Don't you see? He became a cop to find them, but he dealt only with them. No one but the guilty parties have paid the price. He's gone out of his way to make sure of that. But this is the end, tonight. And the system's here. Jim and I are it, we're the system. I think he wants us to take Landau for him. He wants to prove the system was right, after all of this."

Manos kept silent. Husta had said it for the two of them. But there was something more, too, and he and Tony needed the freedom to do it. It had to end with them.

Tusca considered what Husta had said for a long moment. He clearly wasn't convinced, and it showed. His reply surprised them as a result.

"All right. We'll do it your way. But I'm keeping the chopper crew on him all the time. And if he so much as twitches I'll order them to drop him right where he's at. Understood?"

"Understood, Chief," Manos replied. He would have felt better about the chief's decision under other circumstances, but all he needed to know was that they had effectively removed Aaron from the equation. And from what was about to happen. He was sure more than ever that Aaron was not going to make a try for Landau now, not after he saw them go in for him. Manos was sure he was watching them all through a spotting scope right now. "Thanks," he added.

Tusca didn't say anything for a few seconds, then sighed. "Right," he said. He turned to Lanier. "Nice and easy, Jerry. Let's take him down quiet. I don't want his feathers ruffled too badly. The CID will take him off our hands." He motioned to Manos and Husta standing with them.

"Got it, Chief," Lanier said. He wasn't entirely convinced either in the decision to leave Longbaugh alone, but part of him was thankful. At least he wouldn't have to go after his friend now. To his men he added, "Let's do it, boys." They checked their equipment and radios and faded into the night.

"Hope you're right, Jim" Pete Jovenall said. He had stayed out of the conversation. Manos had seemed convinced in his position. Now he hoped he was right. "Maybe it'll go down with no problem."

Tusca didn't say anything. They all knew appearances were the last thing to trust on a forced entry. The tension was palpable as the minutes ticked by. Overhead the hum of the orbiting helo reminded them of the deadly threat watching in silence out there in the dark.

Chief Tusca touched his finger to his earpiece, lowering his head. He was silent, and nodded a couple of times. "They're in," he said quietly, and raised his head to watch the old house. The FBI team was lost in the shadows, but he knew from their radio report they were waiting on Lanier's team to breach the upstairs door before they went in. He saw the flicker of powerful flashlights move quickly from one room to another on the first floor. Then they went out. Suddenly they heard the commotion of the outside door being forced with a dull thud, and the sound of boots thudding up the staircase, muffled by the distance. Half a minute later another message came from Lanier.

"They got him," Tusca said. "We can go in now."

* * *

Aaron watched with continued interest as the convoy of vehicles prowled into town. He was prone on a depression of the gentle slope of a small hill, under the cover of a group of maple trees. The hill was part of a farmer's pasture, but it overlooked the small town from across the highway. Aaron's position was 441 yards away from the house he knew Landau was in.

He watched as the sizable contingent of vehicles passed slightly below him, then slowed, turning away from him as they exited the state highway, bouncing slightly as they crossed over the rail tracks, and headed into town. He had already recognized both officers earlier. Their car, parked a few blocks away from Landau's place, was the giveaway. He knew the car, too.

It hadn't surprised him, seeing his own people watching Landau. After the scene at Madison's place he expected a similar scenario tonight. It wouldn't make any difference. He was confident he could still take out the target, no matter how many people they put around him. The arrival of both the HRG and the Bureau's HRT teams complicated the problem, but didn't substantially alter his plan.

He also knew what the helicopter overhead was all about. It was there to support the operation against Landau, for sure. But it was also possible it might come looking for him. If it had the right equipment it could find him. He had his escape plan well thought out. If they came for him he would see it long before they could get close. He wasn't about to get caught in a trap now. He readied himself just to be sure. But the presence of the officers and troopers down below held his attention. He continued to watch.

The activity increased, and it became clear to Aaron that they were preparing to enter the house to take Landau by force. Could this be a response to his having killed Madison out from under them this morning? Apparently they weren't going to take any more chances. If they were fast enough, they could conceivably remove Landau in such a manner as to thwart any clear shot he might have at the man. He couldn't allow that to happen. If Landau went into deep protective custody it would force Aaron to remain in the area far too long, waiting for another opportunity. It had to be now.

He moved the tripod-mounted spotting scope aside and settled in behind the M-21. Reaching up, he flicked up the small toggle switch on the AN-PVS4 Starlight scope, initiating its light intensifying circuits. Pressing his eye to the rubber eyepiece he studied the lime-green-tinted image, magnified four times. He steadied the rifle, following the tactical team's figures as they approached the house.

They set up quickly, then went in the main entrance, apparently with the help of a key. He lifted the inverted T dotted crosshairs to one of the living-room windows on the second floor, covered by a thin white curtain. He had no clear target, but waited patiently. Sooner or later they would have to leave with Landau. There were only two exits, and he had them both covered.

The seconds crawled into minutes, and Aaron glimpsed a jumble of shadows suddenly flashed across the opaque curtain. He could guess what had just happened.

"Any time," he muttered under his breath, and pushed the safety forward from inside the front bow of the trigger guard. He was synched into the weapon now, settling his breathing into a steady rate, waiting.

And waiting. The minutes dragged on, and still no appearance of the tac team leaving the house with Landau amidst them. Instead, a group of men separated themselves from the vehicles and walked toward the house. They entered from the corner doorway and disappeared from sight.

Aaron was confused, wondering why the break in what he presumed the routine would be. They should have taken Landau out by know. Hadn't that been the point, to get him under protective guard? And who were the men in suits who had just gone in? He had an uneasy feeling.

Reluctantly he reset the safety. Whatever was going on, he would wait. His hide was still secure, and he still had the advantage. He continued to watch through the night vision scope.

* * *

Bill Landau had gotten up from the small dining table set in the center of what passed for the living room in the apartment. His back was to the door that opened onto the small landing, and the long staircase connecting the apartment with the first floor. He barely heard the lock click as the officer behind it turned the key and kicked it in quickly.

When the door flew back with a crash Landau instinctively

flinched and started to whirl toward the sound when rough hands hit him from behind, his legs buckled, and he was slammed in a controlled crash face-down into the thin carpet.

"Don't move," he heard a voice right next to his ear, so close the breath lifted hairs on his temple. His hands were forced behind him and handcuffs were quickly cinched around his wrists.

"Got a gun here," he heard another voice a few steps away.

"Call it," a third said.

Still face-down, Landau heard them moving now, going from room to room, several of them, and he realized they were cops. It took little imagination for him to figure out why. Still, he felt he had to go through the motions.

"What's going on?" he said, and turned his head to the left, trying to see. All he saw were boots and black-covered legs.

"Wait for it," a voice said.

Landau heard someone descending the corner staircase, his boots thudding on the bare wooden risers. The door opened and several voices began talking all at once. The brief conversation ended, and more steps ascended the stairs.

"Get him up," he heard a voice say, with a slight Hispanic accent.

Hands lifted him and walked him backward to a chair pulled out from the table. Landau glanced back to make sure he didn't fall as he was roughly guided into the seat. He winced from the constriction of the cuffs when his hands hit the seat back.

"Hey!" he said, and turned back, scanning the small crowd of people crammed into the apartment, all staring at him. Most of them were in tactical gear, weapons hovering. A couple were in suits, and he almost went right past two of them, but he froze, and looked again. Sometimes old memories remain sharp and clear, despite the years. This was one of them. His heart thudded at once, the skin of his head tingling in sudden recognition. They were older, sure. Faces lined, and gray hair evident, but there was no mistaking them even so.

"Captain Manos," he said, surprise and fear mixed. "And Husta," he added.

Manos smiled, but his eyes held Landau steady, pinning him in a way that was far too familiar. "It's Colonel Manos now," he said. "'Been a long time, Bill."

"You don't look so good, William," Husta added with the same humorless grin. "Let's talk awhile, eh?" he said.

Landau stifled the cry that almost erupted from deep inside. "I should have known," he groaned instead. "I should have known it was you two. When Madison called and told me someone had been killing us off . . ." His voice trailed away.

Manos exchanged a look with Husta. "Madison's dead," he said, his hands in his overcoat pocket. "But it wasn't us who did it."

Landau froze. "What?! When?"

"This morning," Manos said. "We were trying to move him to safety." He took a step closer to a chair and sat down, hooking one leg over the other knee, almost relaxed. Husta remained standing, and the rest of the force opened up around them, silently watching.

"We tried to tell him he was in danger," Manos said, "but Madison wouldn't believe it. Couldn't buy into the truth, even when his life was on the line. He kept denying what we all know is the real truth, don't we, Bill?" He remained relaxed, but his eyes were intense again, resurrecting the ancient fear once again.

"We thought you and the others might be talking to each other, despite what we warned you about. Considering how this has turned out, it appears you should have started sooner. Maybe more of you might be alive now."

To Landau Manos and Husta looked like men who had all the answers. The bitch of it was, they probably did. What did he have? He didn't want to know just then.

"You're not going to be that stupid, are you, Billy?" Husta drawled, his tone underscoring Landau's thought. They knew, all right. They always had. "It's time to set it right, man. There's someone out there who intends to collect on all of you heroes, and you're the last name on the list."

"Who is it, if not you two?" Landau asked suddenly, desperate to know. Who had been doing this?

Manos shook his head and glanced at Husta. "He really thinks it was us behind this. I told you he would. These boys never thought far enough ahead, never considered . . ." and he turned back to Landau, "that there might be other people affected by their murderous plot. You never stopped to think what you were doing. You didn't end anything out there, when you and Linet and the others sprung that ambush. It didn't matter that we couldn't prosecute you. You'd already signed your own death warrants."

"What are you talking about?" Landau said, recovering slowly from his fright. "What didn't we consider? Who's doing this?"

It was time, Manos thought, seeing it coming together in his mind. The way Landau had come to ground in the sorry hideaway, the Browning pistol the tactical team had discovered, and the fact that Aaron was here, but still silent. So far. The picture was formed, clear to him now. If Landau played his part. If he had the nerve. But he had to say it, first. He had to put it on the record, once and for all. Close the circle, for everyone's sake.

"Major Longbaugh's son," he said, "Aaron Longbaugh. He was just a boy when you killed his father. But he grew up, and he learned to soldier, just like his father. Aaron learned about you, and the truth, Bill. He already knew how to kill by then. The Army taught him that. He was a scout-sniper, don't you see? Then he learned the last part, the final ingredient. He learned to hate."

Landau shivered. Now he understood what had happened. Now he knew what they had really started. Their bullets might have killed the major, but their guns were aimed at themselves. He never saw it coming. He, the educated one, had not once considered the possibility something like this could happen. There was no future then. They lived for the day . . . to survive just one more day. They thought of going home, sure, but few actually believed they'd make it.

So they killed the major, to get the edge, to buy insurance. They went home, all right, with no immediate retribution for their actions. But they became virtual prisoners to a lifetime of guilt and doubts, disgraced, less than the men they had gone to war to become.

"Oh, Christ, what did we do?" he said, lowering his head.

Manos motioned to Chief Tusca and Peter Jovenall, and spoke in low tones for a few minutes.

When he was through Jovenall looked over at Landau and said, "You're sure this is how you want to handle this?"

"Yes," Manos said. "It's been heading this way for a long time."

"Watch yourself," Tusca cautioned, and lifted his eyes, seeming to look out beyond the walls. He paused a moment, then to Lanier he said, "Take off the cuffs."

Lanier had caught enough of the conversation to understand. It still seemed a big risk, but it wasn't his call.

Landau hadn't heard the exchange clearly himself. He'd been too immersed in his own self-pity and anguish to pay any attention. Suddenly the cuffs were being removed, and people started drifting away, thumping down the stairs.

"What's going on?" he asked, but no one answered as the room slowly emptied around him. The two Bureau agents paused at the top of the stairs, and Peter Jovenall handed something to Manos. Landau saw it was his Browning, still strapped into its holster. Then they too trooped down the stairs, leaving Landau alone with Manos and Husta.

Landau rubbed his wrists nervously, watching the two silent men. "What's this about?" he asked again, feeling a tiny bit of confidence. Maybe they were going to let him go. Maybe it wasn't that bad after all.

Tony Husta motioned to the dining table behind him. "Why don't you have a seat over there, Bill?" he said, and stepped forward to take his own seat at the table's edge.

Manos joined him, taking another chair, leaving a space for Landau. The professor stood, turned his chair around, and sat down.

Manos kept the Browning in his lap, still holstered. "You're in a hell of a bind, troop," he began. "It doesn't really matter what we do to you now. Back in Vietnam you and the others should have been court-martialed, you know that."

Landau remained silent.

Manos continued. "I'll give you credit for one thing, though. You've kept to the party line for twenty-five years. Deniability, all the way, even when we had you guys cold."

"Not so cold," Landau remembered, feeling another shade better. Talking was good. Talking meant there might be a way out of this yet. "If you'd had us then we wouldn't be sitting here now, would we?"

"Feeling confident again, Bill?" Husta interjected. "I'm surprised at you. You're the educated one. Worked your way into a teaching degree, and a full university professorship." He leaned forward on his elbows, fingers laced together. "What was that, some attempt to make amends, to atone for what you did by doing something positive with your miserable excuse of a life? All that education and you still don't see it." His dark eyes bore into Landau's.

Landau started to reply, stung by Husta's words. The man had described his life to a tee just now. "How did you—"

Husta cut him off. "There's a man out there waiting to *kill* you, Professor! A real shooter, too. Look at his track record, man. They're all *dead,* every one of them. You should have seen Madison this morning. Hit him twice in something under five seconds, with a full FBI SWAT team surrounding him. He's dead, Bill . . . they're all dead. Except for you. You're the last name on his list. He's been saving you for the end. And now it's here."

"My partner's always been pretty direct," Manos said, his voice calm, soft, persuasive. He felt the pressure mounting inside, as if the air in the room was becoming explosive.

"What it means is," he said, holding Landau's attention, "whatever we do with you from here on won't make the slightest difference. You're a dead man. No matter where we might lock you up, no matter where we might try to hide you, you're a dead man. Aaron Longbaugh is on a life's mission. You people murdered his father, and he's not going to forget, or forgive. He has an entirely different solution to the problem."

Landau suddenly caught on. "What are you saying? There's no way to stop this guy?"

"You're catching on. Protection like that doesn't exist, for anyone. The Secret Service can't even protect the president. Not if someone wants him bad enough. That's what this is about. Aaron wants you bad enough. Believe me."

He watched Landau for a reaction, watched his eyes. It was critical now. Let him figure it out, he thought, watching the doomed man. He's already considered it, he knew. He couldn't avoid thinking about it. His education would almost force him to the idea. Just push the right buttons and . . .

"There is a way," he said, his voice in that same soft tone. "It's time to clear the slate, for the record. Tell us the truth, for one last time. There may not be another chance for you. Right here in this room, between us. Right now," his finger tapped on the tabletop. "You did it, didn't you? You and the rest of the squad murdered Major Ralph Longbaugh."

Landau looked from one man to the next. He had a premonition now. It *had* reached the end. And he knew how it would be. For a moment he'd actually thought he could walk on this, but that was the ultimate lie, wasn't it? Nothing comes without a price. Everyone paid, eventually. Interest may accrue, but sooner or later the purchase price had to be met.

Could he do it? A hell of a question, considering. It wasn't the violence of it. That part seemed fitting. It was the *will*. He had gone along on the murder, letting the others carry him, make the decision for him. This time he made his own decision. And once made, there was no turning back.

"The future," he said sadly, ironically. "Once I thought there really was one. That's why we did it, you know, why we decided to kill the major. We thought we were making a future for us. That's all we wanted to do." His admission had slipped out almost unnoticed. He raised his head and looked from one man to the other. "Yeah, we killed him. We just wanted to live," he said, the finality of his loss deepening the shadows around his eyes, making his face appear older than it was. "We wanted the ride," he said. "We wanted to take the Freedom Bird back to the World . . . as heroes." His voice trailed off.

Manos brought the Browning out from under the table and slid it out from its holster. The weapon had been unloaded by the officer who had found it. Now Manos slipped the heavy magazine back into the butt and racked the slide, chambering the round, the noise loud and metallic in the small living room. Hammer back, he set the safety, and ejected the magazine, leaving the single cartridge locked and loaded.

He set the pistol down on the tabletop before Landau. He held the man's eyes with his own. "Welcome home, Professor Landau."

Beside him Husta had inconspicuously opened his overcoat and drawn the Colt .45 from his hip holster. He covered Landau with it from beneath the table.

Manos noticed the movement and did the same, watching Landau all the while for any overt move.

But Landau failed to see either man's precautionary moves. His attention was drawn to the Browning. The time had come, and a faint chant started in the back of his mind, coming out of the depths, getting louder and louder, drowning out any opposition to what he was about to do.

He reached forward slowly and rotated the pistol so he could pick it up. Husta shifted just a bit, his finger on the trigger of the .45. There was a chance . . .

Manos sat back a little, giving Landau room, wanting him to know no one would interfere with him. This was his choice, his decision, and the only way out.

Landau had the gun now, and felt his breathing deepening. Adrenaline flooded through him, and a tremor rattled down his nerves. The chant was louder in his head, beating in time to his pounding heart, suffusing his entire being with its power, pushing him in one direction. His hand tightened on the gun, and his thumb moved enough to pull the safety off.

With a sudden moan he reversed the pistol and pushed the muzzle into his chest, right hand bent awkwardly, left hand gripping the slide and frame, his fingers white with the effort. He pulled back, both hands forcing the Browning's muzzle hard over the center of his heart, heartbeats booming louder . . . louder . . . until his finger jerked the trigger back . . .

Pain blotted out the loud crack of the shot, pain that hammered into him, searing his entire body, a red-purple bolt that rocked him, and he felt himself bounce off the back of the chair and tip sideways, floating as the red haze deepened over his vision and his head hit the floor, but he didn't feel it, and even the crushing pain in his chest was dulling out, blackness edging in on him, and the last thing he saw was the flowered pattern of the worn carpet, until it faded, too, faded quietly into the darkness . . .

* * *

Jovenall watched the two men exit the house a few minutes later. They had seen the sudden flash of light that accompanied the flattened report of the shot. It was over.

Manos came up to him, but included them all as he spoke. "He's gone," he said without emotion.

"Jesus," Lanier said. He hadn't believed Landau would actually do it. The idea seemed bizarre to him, despite his own experience with violence. He felt revulsion at Manos and tried to shake it off.

"Well," he said, but his voice trailed off. There was nothing more to be said. He turned away, signaling to his men.

Chief Tusca walked up to them, stopped, but didn't say anything at first. He turned to look over his shoulder, not at the house, but off into the distant darkness, in Aaron's direction. "Chopper crew says he's up and moving. Away from here. I told them to let him go." He turned back around. "Seemed like the best thing to do."

Manos and Husta remained silent. "We'll lose him, you know that? He'll just fade away now." He looked at both men. "But that's kind of the point, isn't it? It's over."

"Yeah, it's over," Husta replied.

"Hell of a thing," Tusca said. "Hope you two can live with this. Me? It's going to take a long time." He looked down at his feet, then back up. "A damn long time." He turned on his heel and walked away.

The two CID men suddenly found themselves partially deserted as the others all seemed to find other business to do just then. Husta watched them and said, "Can't blame them, or the chief either. I feel sort of the same way about it."

"I know," Manos said. "But if we didn't feel it, I'd begin to worry about us."

Husta turned to look back at the house as Lanier and his men returned to it in the dark.

"I think I'll call her," Manos said.

"You read my mind," Husta replied without turning around.

Manos took his cell phone out of his inside pocket and pulled up the antenna. Then he dialed her number.

"Vanessa?" he said when she answered. "It's Colonel Manos. We're in Somerville." He paused while he listened to her a few moments. "No, he wasn't here," he lied. It didn't matter now. Aaron would have seen. And he'd be gone now.

He waited, her relief apparent. When she slowed down, he said it, straight out. "Vanessa, listen. It's over. Landau's dead."

She spoke again, briefly, a question only.

"Suicide," he said, and caught Husta's eye. "He killed himself . . . no I don't know." He listened to her a few more moments. "- We're taking care of things here, but I wanted you to know, that's all. It's over. All of it," he added. "You understand?"

Her final answer was also brief.

"Yes, thank you," he said, and punched the disconnect.

"Will she call him?" Husta asked.

Manos turned slowly to look back at the now-silent house. "I hope so," he replied. "I really do."

* * *

Aaron's warning system was on full alert. The flash of light from the single gunshot inside the silent house had been unmistakable.

That had followed the emergence of the uniformed police, as Aaron watched the tactical team leave the house and return to the vehicles. He made a quick head count and determined that all but two of the men he had watched enter the place were now out. What were the other two doing? And where was Landau?

Several more anxious minutes passed with nothing else happening. There had been a little movement at first, judging from the shifting shadows across the curtain, then things seemed to settle down. The shot came out of left field.

"What the hell?!" he had said, instinctively flicking the safety off for the second time. He remained steady behind the M-21, intently watching now. Something drastic had happened in that house.

A minute or two later the corner door opened. Aaron swung the weapon that way, bracketing the first figure to appear. It was one of the suits. He waited, finger alongside the trigger, and saw a second man appear. At this distance at only four power he couldn't make out facial features, but he was positive. Neither man was Bill Landau.

He watched the men walk back slowly toward the others, all

waiting around the cars and trucks. Still no one else came out of the house. The conclusion was obvious. For whatever reason Landau was dead. Maybe he had tried to make a break, maybe he had attacked the two men in suits. Again the possibilities were many, but all came back to the same thing. The man was dead. His final target was gone.

A strong feeling of frustration came over him. All these years, all this effort, the work and dedication, to come down to this. Someone else takes care of the last man on his list. The most important one of all, as far as Aaron was concerned.

"Damn!" he cursed under his breath. There didn't seem any doubt about it now. He watched as the group split up, and several walked back to the house. None of them seemed to be in any great hurry.

It's over, he told himself again, not yet ready to resign himself to it. But what the hell happened down there? What happened?

He broke down the hide quickly. In the dark, camouflaged in his heavy Ghillie suit, he was invisible to the men in the town below, beginning to clean up the scene just ended. Without another backward glance, Aaron moved quietly and efficiently back to his parked pickup.

In the shadows of the trees that hid it he secured the rifle and equipment in the camper shell, then stripped off the Ghillie suit. He shivered from the cool air that struck the sweat generated from the heavy outfit. He took out a hand towel from his equipment bag and dried his face and hands. He hadn't worn any camouflage stick on his exposed features. The suit had taken care of that.

Aaron walked up to the cab, unlocked the door, and reached in, removing a light jacket from the seat. Landau's apparent death still bothered him. He badly wanted to know what had occurred behind the walls of that house just now. But the operation was still on. He had to get moving. They would be looking for him.

He pulled the jacket on and felt something bump against his side. He reached in absently to shift it and felt his cell phone pager. Almost from habit he pulled it out to look at it. He'd switched the tone off, as he often did when he was going to be away from the unit.

Now he looked at the top of it and noted a call had come in. He recognized the number immediately. Vanessa! He took a few breaths, calming himself. He remembered the dream and shivered.

He climbed into the cab and pulled the door shut, his emotions tumbling around. He had inserted the key in the ignition but paused, and his eyes moved to the cell phone clipped to the dash.

Don't! a warning voice shouted in his head. Don't do it . . . don't call her. Let it go, man.

He almost did. He knew he should, but something else was urging him on. Maybe it would be his last chance to speak to her. Did he owe her that much at least? Does it matter? another voice offered up. Talk to her, he told himself. Whatever happens, get it done, here and now. Don't run from this. There's been enough running.

His hand closed on the cell phone and he dialed her number.

She picked up after the second ring.

"Vanessa—" he started to say.

"Nathan! Thank God you're all right!" she cut him off, her voice excited, breathless, the same as in his dream, but her next words floored him. "I've been so worried. I called before. I know about them," she said in a rush. "Perriman, Roselli, Linet . . ." she paused, and he felt himself go cold all over. "Michael Madison . . . and Professor Landau," she continued, slowing down. "He's dead, too," she said. "Landau's dead."

It was true! he shouted inside. But how did she . . .

"Wait," he said, interrupting her. "How do you know? Who told you?"

"Colonel Manos," she replied. "He told me all of it, Nathan. I know about all of them. I know the whole story, and who you are."

Her damning words ripped through his mind, and he almost lost it right there, not believing what she had just said.

"Manos was here a few hours ago, with his partner, Colonel Husta. Nathan, they told me your real name, and what happened to your father . . . and what you've been doing." Now she did stop, wanting him to say something, but he was frozen in place, in time, even his breathing, immobilized by her revelation.

Vanessa continued, carefully. The last thing she wanted him to do was hang up. "They knew about Landau and his place in So-merville, Nathan. They said they wanted to pick him up. To put him in protective custody."

"Colonel Manos," he said, as if the name was alien to him. "How did he . . . how did you . . .?"

She had too much to tell him, and she needed more time. She had to warn him, make him understand what Manos had been telling her.

"Not now, Nathan, all right? I know it all, but we can talk about it later. What you need to know is you can't go to Somerville," she said instead. "It's over, don't you see. But they'll be there, the au-thorities, with men and guns, and if you're there, too . . ."

She didn't have to tell him. He had watched them prepare, not just for Landau, but for him, too. Aaron knew only too well what would have happened.

"It won't make any difference," he said. "Manos must have told you why. They won't let me walk away, either. They'll make sure of that. If not tonight, then sometime later, some other place, but they'll find me, don't you see? They won't stop looking."

"I understand," she said, "and so do Colonel Manos and Colonel Husta. That's the point, Nathan. They know they proba-bly couldn't have stopped you. I think that's why they came to see me, to tell me."

"What? To give up?" he said, anger tinting his reply.

"No," she said, cutting him off. "Not give up, not that. Manos wants you to stop."

"He wants me to stop?" Aaron replied, almost mockingly. "Just like that? And what'll he do then? Let me go?"

Before he could say anything further she said, "I think that's ex-actly what Manos will do. Listen to me, Nathan. He said it's over. No arrest, no trial, no one looking for you for the rest of your life, trying to catch you, or worse." She paused, and he felt her desire twist deep into him again.

"He said all of that?"

"Not in those exacts words, but I *know* what he meant. Please, you must believe me. There's nothing more for you to do. It's up to you. Nathan. Only you."

"Why?" he asked her. "If you know who I am, and what I've

done, why did you call?" He didn't want to hear her answer, but had no choice.

She was quiet a few moments, and when she did answer he heard the tightness in her voice, and it cut him sharper than any blade could.

"Oh, Nathan, don't you know?"

And he knew, finally. Knew that she loved him, knew how much, and how far she was willing to go to protect him, and the irony slammed him. Because he felt exactly the same way about her.

"I know, Vanessa," he said, his throat thick. "God, how I know."

He heard her intake of breath over the line, and thought he heard a hitch in her voice as she said, "I needed to hear you say that."

He heard hope in her words and was confused by that. She knew about him, and what he had done to those men. Even so, she was willing to take a chance on him. She offered him hope, and that was the last thing he expected from her. But she was still on the phone, and still talking to him . . .

"Meet me. Let me see you, talk to you. Please, Nathan."

He considered what she was asking, and all the risks involved between them. He also understood all too clearly what she was asking him to do. Suddenly he had the strongest feeling that the weight of it, smothering him all these years, was gone. Landau was dead, the last of the nine men. The record was complete. There was no more unfinished business, if Manos was to be believed.

That was a new prospect to be considered. And Vanessa. Instead of an ending, he sensed the beginning of something, something much better than he had ever imagined could be his.

"Where?" he said finally, just when she thought he was going to hang up.

"The phone may not be safe," she said suddenly, her sense of caution reminding him how precarious a position he really was in. "By the movie theater," she said. "Remember? Meet me there in an hour."

He was humbled before this girl, in a way that still felt right. Why did he feel this way? he asked himself. Why should someone this good care at all, especially now? Go and find out, the voice answered him.

"I'll be there," he said, noting suddenly that she hadn't called him by his true name. Time for that later, he thought. But there was something that needed to be said, something he should have said long before now.

"Vanessa," he began, "I've done damn little in my life to deserve someone like you." He had to keep talking. If he stopped he'd never get it out. "I once told you that you didn't know me. I guess you do now." His emotions were running away with him again, and he had to pause and take a breath. "I don't want to lose you. Not now." He took another breath, and let it go with the words he needed to say. "I love you, Vanessa."

He could feel her on the other end of the line, but he was afraid to say anything more.

"I hoped so hard that you would say that," she said finally. "I think I've always known it, even from the beginning."

He felt his heart swelling, felt it tugging the corners of his mouth.

"I love you, too, Nathan," she said back to him. "I'll look for you."

"I'll be there," he promised, and meant it.

She hung up quietly. Nathan stared at the cell phone. Was it possible? He felt the elation rampant inside him before a sobering thought returned. Colonel James Manos. The same man who had given him cause to begin his life's mission now had apparently offered him an end to it.

October 27

Carrollton Hills Mall, Ohio

Vanessa had been waiting fifteen minutes on the second level, standing nervously in front of the movie theater complex. Her back was to him when she heard his voice.

"Vanessa."

She whirled into him, and he caught her, holding her tightly against him for a few moments.

She clutched him back, face pressed against his chest, not daring to believe he was really there.

"I wasn't sure you would come," she said.

"I wasn't sure, either," he replied.

She pushed back from him and looked up into his eyes. His arms remained around her. She took a calming breath.

"I came alone," she said.

"I know," he said. "I've been watching."

She nodded, not taking her eyes from his. "I knew you would," she said. "Are we safe?"

"Yes, no one followed you. We're alone," he said, and motioned with his hand. "Let's walk a bit."

She turned with him, and they began strolling along the storefronts, just another couple doing late-evening shopping.

"What should I call you?" she asked. "Nathan or Aaron?"

He looked down at her. "What do you feel comfortable with?"

"Nathan," she said quickly. "I don't know who Aaron Longbaugh is."

"Let's talk about him anyway," he said. "He's not someone I can just forget about."

She slowed a step but kept walking. "He doesn't seem like you."

Now he stopped completely and turned to her. "And who am I supposed to be?" he asked. "You said Colonel Manos told you the whole story. Then you know what those men did to my father. And what I did to them."

"You say it like it was some sort of simple quid pro quo," Vanessa replied. "And I know it wasn't like that at all. I know how hard it must have been for you."

"Don't patronize me, Vanessa, please. What I've done all these years, the way I've lived my life . . . I used to think I had a choice about that. But it wasn't just about choice. It was about obligations. It was about blood. He was my *father!*" he hissed between clenched teeth. "And those bastards murdered him!"

She looked back at him, and a strength appeared he hadn't seen before. "Yes," she said. "They murdered him. The war did that. And you killed them for it. *Your* war did that. And now it's over. All of it. Wars come to an end, Nathan. There's no more blood left to spill. It's time to come home."

He smiled at that, but there was no humor in it. Instead she saw only pain.

"Time to come home," he said. "How I'd like to do just that. But where would I go? And to whom would I return?"

She studied him carefully. "Isn't that why you came here tonight? To find out?"

He looked away suddenly. She was so good at reading him, and it was so hard to want her this bad, yet to think that he could . . .

"What I've done," he said slowly, trying to get it right the first time. He wasn't sure he could say it a second time. ". . . is something I feel I had a right to do. But there's a price for that, Vanessa. There's always a price. Events and life have to be balanced in the end." He looked at her for several long moments.

"I know what you're offering. And I want it . . . want *you* so bad. I can't describe the depth of it." His hands went to her arms, holding her in place. "But I can't involve you in it, either. I don't have that right, don't you see? You deserve more than I can offer. I can't ask you to come with me."

Vanessa touched his face, her fingers soft. "You're right, Nathan," she said. "You can't ask me. Isn't it *my* choice to make?"

He shook his head. "You don't understa—"

She put her fingertips on his lips, silencing him. "I understand too well. This all comes from the war. I know that, too. I grew up with it, saw what it did. This is no different. You have strong feelings for your father. He obviously taught you well what life means, and the way you live it."

She spoke to his heart, her voice gentle but persuasive. "What you've been through, and your reasons for doing what you did, that was about you. Now it's finished, and the reasons are gone. What you do from here, from this moment right here, is about us. You can't make that decision alone. I won't let you. If you're asking me to give you up, then I respectfully decline. I could no more let you go than stop breathing."

Vanessa traced his jaw, and let her hand rest against his chest. "You're too much a part of me now, Nathan Samm. That's the man I know. That's the man I'm in love with. That's the man I want to be with."

He shook his head slowly, repeatedly, as much for his incredible fortune as for his misdirected gallantry. He wanted to say he accepted what she said, but there was an ugly reality that threatened to ruin whatever future she could have with him.

"All right," he said. "Tell me this, then. And be sure, Vanessa, be completely sure, because your life may depend on your answer. You know the truth now, all of it. Can you still live with that?"

She shook her head. "The question is, can *you* handle it? Can you deal with it, and all the ramifications that might come with it? All I can say to that is I will be there to help you, as much as I can, because I have to."

She held him with the depth of her eyes now. "I can't go on without you, not now. Especially not now. And I don't think you can go on without me, either. This is how it is, Nathan. This is how it was meant to be with us. Tell me you see it the same way."

He looked back at her a long time, oblivious to the people that walked past them.

"Yes," he said. "I see it the same way. The price for staying with me is that it's for a lifetime. Is that too much to ask?"

She smiled at him now and pulled him gently forward, her lips meeting his. She spoke to him softly then. "That is a price I willingly pay. I love you, Nathan Samm."

"I love you, too," he said, satisfied with his name, and kissed her a second time. He was satisfied with a lot of things at that moment. With a determined push he silenced the warnings that echoed way back in his mind. She was worth the risk, he knew. Whatever might lie ahead for them was worth the risk.

April 29

Seaside Heights, New Jersey

Jim Manos stood scraping paint off the side of the garage wall, not bothering to curse the life of a civilian again. He was still settling into the mode. He had retired his commission from the Army three months before. The end of the Longbaugh case had seemed the opportune time to end it, anyway. The most troublesome case of his thirty-plus-year career had been resolved. At least to his satisfaction, it had been.

He had lost any further interest in chasing wrongdoers. To be honest with himself, to continue seemed a bit hypocritical, considering his part in ending the Longbaugh affair.

He and Tony Husta had spent more than a few long hours over some serious alcohol, coming to terms with what had happened. The end result had been a simple acknowledgment to themselves that the record had been made right. Justice had prevailed, and all that. They both chose to ignore the bitter aftertaste left by their pact.

Curiously, or maybe not so curiously, Husta had also put in his papers. Now he and has family were living the good life out in Reno, Nevada. Husta thought he might write a book about the CID. Manos had wished him luck. Still, the things he and Husta had talked about would remain with him a long, long time.

He turned back to the scraper when his wife called from around the corner.

"Jim, call for you, hon."

He waved at her and dropped the scraper. "There's got to be an easier way," he said, wiping his hands as he returned to the beach-front house.

Inside he accepted a cup of coffee from his wife and picked up the phone. "Manos here," he said, and took a sip.

"Colonel Manos," the familiar voice replied. "How's retirement treating you?"

"Well, Russell," he said to the Longbaugh family lawyer, "as they say, it takes some getting used to. What can I do for you, sir?"

They had talked infrequently since the events in Ohio had been resolved. Neither had mentioned anything about Aaron Longbaugh, nor his whereabouts. Manos had been true to his word, though. No further action had been taken to try to locate the man. The case was over.

"Just passing some news along," Lancola replied. "The Longbaugh place is up for sale. Don't suppose you'd be interested in moving to Kansas, would you?"

"Bit far away for us," Manos said, eyeing his wife.

"I thought as much," Lancola said. "It's interesting, though. The owner called me. Said to put it on the market. If it sells he'll tell me where to send the money."

Aaron! Manos thought instantly. He knew better than to ask, though. He didn't want to know.

"How is he?" he asked finally.

"Doing fine," Lancola said, and Manos could almost see the bemused smile on the old lawyer's weathered face.

"Is she still with him?" Manos asked. It would make a difference in how he thought of him, he knew.

"Still, yes," Lancola said. "And for a long time to come."

Manos winked at his wife, catching her eye. "Good, that's good, Russ. Tell him for me, if you should hear from him again."

"I'd be glad to," Lancola said. The silence ran on for a few long seconds.

"What ever happened to that lawsuit against Westport?" Manos asked finally.

"Dismissed by motion," Lancola said. "Seems the U.S. District Court judge wasn't so taken by the plaintiffs' case. Dismissed on its merits, with prejudice. Funny thing is, the plaintiffs didn't appeal it."

"Maybe their lawyer talked them out of it," Manos said, making small talk. "It was a righteous shoot, after all."

"Indeed," Lancola agreed. "It certainly was that." He paused a moment. "There was something else, Jim. He asked me to tell you."

"What's that?"

"He said to say thanks," Lancola said. "Thanks for the beginning."

Manos smiled into the phone. Maybe . . . just maybe, it works out, he thought.

"Tell him for me it wasn't a hard thing to do, OK? Tell him he was due a bit of a break."

"He knows," Lancola said. "As do I, Jim. But I'll pass it along."

"You do that," Manos said, feeling better. He was still smiling when he hung up the phone.